Michael Walsh, music critic of *Time* magazine for sixteen years, is currently a visiting professor of journalism at Boston University. *As Time Goes By* is his second novel.

Also by Michael Walsh:

FICTION

Exchange Alley

NON-FICTION

Who's Afraid of Opera
Who's Afraid of Classical Music
Andrew Lloyd Webber: His Life and Works
The First One Hundred Years of Carnegie Hall

AS TIME GOES BY

A Novel of *Casablanca*

MICHAEL WALSH

A *Warner* Book

Published by arrangement with Warner Books, Inc.,
New York, NY, USA

First published in Great Britain in 1998
by Little, Brown and Company
This edition published by Warner Books in 1999

A CIP catalogue record for this book
is available from the British Library.

ISBN 0 7515 2653 3

Typeset in Stempel Garamond by M Rules
Printed and bound in Great Britain by
Clays Ltd, St Ives plc

Warner Books
A Division of
Little, Brown and Company (UK)
Brettenham House
Lancaster Place
London WC2E 7EN

For Kathleen, Alexandra,
and Clare

PREFACE

MOVIETONE NEWS FOR DECEMBER 7, 1941

(cue martial music)

EUROPE REELS BEFORE THE HUN!

BRITONS HUNKER IN BUNKERS AS BOMBS FALL!

HITLER MASTER OF ALL HE SURVEYS:

CAN ANYONE STOP HIM?

(cue voice-over)

War! From the Sahara to the steppes of central Asia, Europe is on fire. Directed from Berlin, Adolf Hitler's legions have overrun Poland, Denmark, Norway, the Low Countries, and France; driven deep into the Soviet Union; and carved off the top of North Africa. Wehrmacht troops shell Moscow and strut down the Champs-Élysées, while nightly the Luftwaffe sets the docks of London ablaze and deadly Nazi U-boats turn the shipping lanes of the North Atlantic into a watery graveyard.

Suffering Europe casts its eyes to heaven, with one question on its lips: Can anyone stop the Germans?

Brave men and women are trying. Across occupied Europe resistance movements have sprung up. From his headquarters in Brazzaville, General Charles De Gaulle is leading a rearguard action against the Nazi beast in *la belle France*. In the teeth of Goering's bombers, Czech and Norwegian patriots have regrouped in London and plot acts of violence and retribution against the usurpers of their homelands. Whether by political action, or outright sabotage and terror, resistance is growing daily.

But the Wehrmacht's seemingly inexorable march across the European continent has meant dislocation for millions. A Refugee Trail has sprung up: Paris to Marseille – across the Mediterranean to Oran – then by train – or auto – or foot – across the rim of Africa to French Morocco, and finally here, to Casablanca.

Casablanca! Its very name evokes magic and mystery. A windswept place, trapped between ocean and desert, where anything can happen – and does, every day. Where human beings sell one another like cattle or sheep. Where gold is cheap, jewelry is worthless, and the only thing of value is an exit visa. Where the plane to Lisbon is a minor deity and the Clipper to America is God Himself. A place where desperation rules, uncertainty is king, and the cast of a die – or the turn of a card, or the spin of a roulette wheel – can mean the difference between life and death. A place where Spaniard huddles with Frenchman, where Russian drinks with Englishman, where expatriate American matches wits with German. Casablanca, which holds your life in the palm of its hand, and asks only: What is it worth to you?

Safe behind its two wide oceans, neutral America looks on. How much longer?

THIS IS CASEY ROBINSON REPORTING FROM CASABLANCA

(bursts of static)

(sounds of French police radio being tuned in)

8:00 P.M. *Attention, attention! All units: Czech resistance leader Victor Laszlo, wanted by the Gestapo for crimes against the Third Reich, has escaped on the Lisbon plane. He is using the letters of transit stolen from German couriers murdered on the train from Oran three days ago.*

8:10 P.M. *Attention, attention! Major Heinrich Strasser of the Gestapo has been shot at the Casablanca airport! Round up the usual suspects, on orders of Captain Louis Renault, Prefect of Police.*

8:25 P.M. *All units: Major Strasser has died of his wounds en route to the hospital. Captain Renault, come in, please. Calling Captain Renault. Where are you?*

8:35 P.M. *Attention, all units: Louis Renault has disappeared. Last seen in the company of M. Richard Blaine, owner of Rick's Café Americain. Has possibly met with foul play. Arrest M. Blaine at once. He is armed and extremely dangerous. Beware!*

8:45 P.M. *Attention, all units: Captain Renault spotted walking with Rick Blaine on the outskirts of the airport. They are to be apprehended at once. Possibly heading for the Free French garrison in Brazzaville. Block all roads to the south immediately.*

8:46 P.M. *Attention, attention: The German Consul, Herr Heinze, reports that Gestapo headquarters has dispatched agents to intercept the fugitives. Matters are now in the hands of the Germans. That is all.*

(radio off)

FADE IN:

CASABLANCA AIRPORT.

NIGHT

CHAPTER ONE

The Lisbon plane soared away from the dense, swirling fog of Casablanca, up and into the night. Below, the airport was plunged deep into the North African darkness, its only illumination the revolving beacon that perched atop the conning tower. The sirens of the French colonial police cars had faded into the night. Everything was quiet but the wind.

Almost lost in the mist, two men were walking together, away from the airport, away from the city, and into an uncertain future.

'. . . of a beautiful friendship,' said Richard Blaine, tugging on a cigarette as he walked. His hat was pulled down low on his forehead, and his trench coat was cinched tightly against the damp. Rick felt calmer than he had in years. In fact, he tried to remember when he had felt this certain of what he had just done, and what he was about to do.

The shorter man walking beside him nodded. 'Well, my friend, Victor Laszlo and Ilsa Lund are on their way to Lisbon,' said Louis Renault. 'I might have known you'd mix your newfound patriotism with a little larceny.' He fished in his pocket and came up with ten thousand francs.

'That must have been very difficult for you, Ricky,' he said. 'Miss Lund is an extremely beautiful woman. I don't know that I should have been so gallant, even with money at stake.'

'I guess that's the difference between me and you, Louie,' Rick replied.

Ilsa Lund! Had it been only two days ago that she had walked back into his life? It seemed like a year. How could a woman change a man's fate so much so fast? Now his duty was to follow that fate, no matter where it might lead him.

'Anyway, you were gallant enough not to have me arrested, even though I'd just given the letters of transit to the most wanted man in the Third Reich and shot a Gestapo officer. By rights I ought to be in your hoosegow, getting ready to face a firing squad. Why the sudden change of heart? I never let you win that much at roulette.'

The little man, smart and well turned out in his black colonial policeman's uniform, trod so softly beside Rick Blaine that even in the stillness his footfalls were inaudible. Over the years, Louis Renault had found it preferable to leave as little a mark on his surroundings as possible.

'I don't know,' Renault replied. 'Maybe it's because I like you. Maybe it's because I didn't like the late Heinrich Strasser. Maybe it's because you've cheated me out of the favors of two lovely ladies who were in dire need of my services in obtaining exit visas, and I insist on proper retribution. Maybe it's because you won our bet, and I'd like a chance to get my money back.'

'And maybe it's because you're cheap,' said Rick. 'What difference does it make? You lost, fair and square.' He finished his cigarette and sent the glowing butt sparking across the tarmac. He searched the sky, but her plane was long gone. 'So did I.'

Abruptly, Renault halted and grabbed Rick by the arm. 'I was right: you are a rank sentimentalist,' he exclaimed. 'You're still in love with her, aren't you?'

'Why don't you mind your own business?' retorted Rick.

'This *is* my business – indeed, my two favorite businesses: money and women,' answered Renault. 'A less charitable man than I might claim he'd been cheated. You knew all along that you were going to give those letters of transit to Victor Laszlo and his wife. I wouldn't be at all surprised if the lady knew it, too.'

'It's hard to know what women know, isn't it?' Rick replied, starting to walk again and picking up the pace. 'It's even harder to know how they know it before we do.'

Their path was taking them deeper into the darkness. 'Where are we going, if you don't mind my asking?' asked Renault. His complicity in the death of Major Strasser was so spontaneous that he had little more than the clothes on his back and the francs in his wallet. He hoped his friend knew what he was doing. 'If we really want to go to the Free French garrison at Brazzaville, we'd better think about commandeering a transport flight out before the Germans wake up. It's a long way to the Congo – three thousand miles, at least.'

Rick scuffed the ground with his shoe. 'Forget Brazzaville. I've got a better use for your money.' His eyes stabbed the darkness. There it was! In the distance, he could make out the dimly defined shape of a large automobile parked at the far end of the airfield. Sacha and Sam, right in place and right on time.

Louis nodded appreciatively as Rick's Buick 81C convertible came more clearly into view. He tugged at his kepi and smoothed down his dark uniform. In Renault's opinion, to look anything other than one's best ill suited a Frenchman. Especially a newly Free Frenchman. Especially a really free Frenchman. 'You leave nothing to chance, do you? Tell me, did you plan to kill Major Strasser all along, or was that just inspired improvisation?'

'Let's just say I got lucky when he drew first,' replied Rick, opening the automobile's back door and climbing in.

'Where did you learn to handle a gun like that, if you don't mind my asking? One might think you had some wartime experience.'

'I was in a lot of little wars around New York,' said Rick.

'You weren't really going to shoot me back there, were you, Ricky?'

'Not if you didn't make me,' replied Rick. 'I try not to make a habit of killing my friends. I don't always succeed.'

'Everything okay, Mister Rick?' Sam inquired anxiously from the driver's seat.

'Everything's just ducky,' said Rick. 'Now step on it. We've got to make Port Lyautey before daybreak.'

'Right, boss,' said Sam, and floored it.

Port Lyautey, north of Rabat, was about two hundred miles away. Founded by the French in 1912 when they established the protectorate, the city on the Sebou River was a major transportation hub, with a seaport at Mehdia, a railroad, and, best of all, an airfield. Come hell or high water, they were going to follow Victor Laszlo and Ilsa Lund to Lisbon.

Unfortunately, each and every one of those two hundred miles was bad road. Well, that's why God built Buicks and charged so much for them, thought Rick: shipped over from the States and smuggled into Casablanca, his had cost more than $2,000.

Sam Waters hit the accelerator so hard, Rick and Louis were thrust back into the leather rear seats as if they were in an airplane. In the front passenger seat, Sacha Yurchenko laughed and fondled the .38 Smith & Wesson that Rick had given him as a bonus the year before.

'You want I should shoot him, boss?' shouted Sacha, the big Russian bartender at Rick's place. Except for Yvonne, the girlfriend he had inherited from Rick, Sacha didn't much like the French. In truth, Sacha didn't much like anybody, and the feeling was mutual.

'Not yet,' said Rick. 'Maybe later. Maybe never. It all depends.'

'Awww,' said Sacha, disappointed.

Renault let out a long breath. Time to exhibit some of that famous French savoir faire.

'A beautiful car is like a beautiful woman, don't you think, Ricky?' he said. 'The lines, the curves, the hidden power under the hood.' Renault admired American cars, which was a good thing, since the European automakers had long since switched to war production. 'So many exit visas, so little time.' He gave a little shake of his head in regret.

'Speaking of which,' said Rick, 'we're going to need a few of those ourselves. Think you can help out?'

'I believe I still carry some authority in these parts,' said Renault, reaching into the breast pocket of his uniform. Long ago he had learned that one should never travel without a valid ticket to safety secreted somewhere upon one's person. 'Here they are: two exit visas.'

'Make it three.'

'Three?'

'One for me, one for you, and one for Sam.'

'I see,' said Renault. He counted them out as if they were legal tender, except more valuable. 'All they require is an authorized signature, which fortunately – for the time being, at least – is mine.' He scratched his name with a flourish, three times.

From his pocket Rick produced a flask of bourbon, took a tug on it, and offered it to Renault. The little Frenchman savored the liquor appreciatively. Rick didn't offer one to Sam. He knew better. Sam didn't drink with the customers, and Sam didn't drink with Rick. Sam didn't even drink with himself very often.

'Let's hope your John Hancock's good until tomorrow morning,' said Rick.

Inside the Buick it was warm and dry. Renault could feel the night's chill starting to disperse. He had never liked Morocco all that much anyway. He wouldn't be sorry to leave it. 'Things are becoming clearer to me now. You and Laszlo knew the end of the script before either of you said a line back there.' He wished he had something to smoke. 'When did you hatch this plan?'

'When you had Laszlo in the holding pen, of course.' Rick lit another cigarette and offered the captain one as well. 'After you'd arrested him for being at the Underground meeting. I told you that you couldn't hold him very long on that petty charge.'

'And you promised that you'd entrap him for me by handing over the letters of transit,' interrupted Renault.

'The setup was perfect for you,' Rick continued. 'When you saw Laszlo and Ilsa walk into my café, you must have thought you were in seventh heaven, because they were in the one place in the world where you had the power of life and death over them. I gave you the chance to nab Laszlo and make yourself a hero with Strasser, and you fell for it like a ton of bricks.'

'I did indeed,' admitted Renault. 'There's one thing I don't understand, though. Why did you give the letters of transit to Laszlo and his wife? Why did you change your mind about helping him escape Casablanca for Lisbon and America? You, who always prided yourself on sticking your neck out for no man. Surely there must have been more in it for you than the relatively trifling sum of ten thousand francs.'

Rick looked out the window, at nothing. 'You might say I liked the potential payday. Or you might say I was tired of looking for the waters in Casablanca and coming up with nothing but sand.' He took a deep drag on his Chesterfield and exhaled. 'Or you just might say that destiny finally caught up with me.'

Her letter was in his breast pocket. Sam had given it to him in the café, before he had left for the airport and his fatal encounter with Major Strasser. It had been hidden in Sam's piano, the same place Rick himself had hidden the stolen letters of transit that enabled Laszlo and Ilsa to get away.

My dearest Richard,

If you are reading this letter, it means that I have escaped with Victor.

I thought that after Paris I should never have to part from you this way again. Yet here we are, having to say good-bye twice, once with our lips and once more with our hearts.

You must believe me when I tell you that when we met I thought Victor was dead. We said no questions, and I never questioned the fact that I was free to love you. Some women search all their lives for a man to love. I have found two.

As I write these words, I don't know what will happen tonight at the airport. Like the last time we parted, I cannot be sure that we shall meet again. But unlike the last time, I can hope.

In Lisbon, we shall stay at the Hotel Aviz. After that, only God knows. Please come if you can. If not for my sake, then for Victor's. We both need you.

Ilsa –

The big car sailed through the damp night like an ocean liner on a calm sea, picking up speed despite the poor roadway. Sam piloted the vehicle expertly, the way he played the piano. He sensed rather than saw the turnoffs, reading them the way a blind man read Braille. They were well away from the city now.

'Turn on the radio, will you, Sacha?' asked Rick. He was tired of talking, and before they lost the signal he wanted to hear some music. Maybe something from Benny Goodman and his band. He was also wondering whether the news of Major Strasser's death had been broadcast yet.

'Sure, boss,' said Sacha. He shot out one oversize hand and

began worrying the radio dial until he managed to find a station. 'Blah blah blah is all that's on.'

'Then turn the blah blah blah up so we can at least hear it,' Rick ordered. After all his time in Casablanca and in Paris, his French was still only passable, and sometimes he had trouble understanding on the telephone or over the radio. If anything important was going on, Louis would tell him soon enough. Or Sam, who learned languages the way he learned the piano, by ear.

Renault was about to say something when something caught his attention. 'Quiet!' he shouted in a tone that shocked everybody into silence.

Sacha fiddled with the volume, and an excited voice suddenly filled the car. Even Rick knew what the announcer was saying. He just didn't want to believe it.

In far-off Hawaii, the Japanese had just bombed Pearl Harbor.

'Boss, we got trouble,' Sam said from the front seat.

'I know that,' snapped Rick, trying to listen to the radio. He caught Sam's gaze in the rearview mirror.

'I mean we got company,' Sam explained calmly, slamming the car into high gear.

Rick twisted in his seat. A pair of yellow headlamps was gaining on them.

The silence was broken by the unmistakable sound of automatic weapons. A bullet *ping*ed off the trunk of the Buick.

'Gimme a clip, Sacha,' Rick said.

'Right here, boss,' said the Russian, happy at last.

Rick slammed it into his Colt .45. He had always wanted to see if a phaeton with a 141-horsepower engine could outrun a Mercedes-Benz, and now he was about to find out.

CHAPTER TWO

Ilsa Lund turned to face her husband as their plane ascended into the night sky. They flew directly over the city at first, then banked steeply out toward the sea. Her last view of Casablanca was of Rick's place. Illuminated only by the street lamps, it looked silent and forlorn.

Traces of her tears remained on her cheeks. She didn't want to wipe them away. They were all she had left. 'Everything's happened so fast,' she murmured. Too fast. The surprise, the shock, the excitement, the danger, and now the relief – relief so tinged with sadness and regret.

'I didn't know he would be in Casablanca!' she whispered, more to herself than to Victor. 'How could I have? What fate led us to him – to him, who had the letters of transit! I know you're upset about what happened in Paris between Rick and me, but please try not to be. Didn't everything work out for the best? Where would we be without those letters? What would we have done?'

She clutched his arm and imagined that the beating of her

heart could be heard over the drone of the airplane's engines. 'Oh, Victor,' she said, 'don't you see? I thought you were dead, and I thought my life was over, too. I was lonely. I had nothing, not even hope. Oh, I don't know. I don't know anything anymore!' She started to cry again, but she was not sure why or for whom. She dabbed at her eyes with her handkerchief as the plane bumped its way through the clouds.

'Then I learned that you were alive, and how much you needed me to help you in your struggle,' she said, regaining control. 'You could have abandoned me a dozen times in the past eighteen months – in Lille, when I was having trouble with the authorities, in Marseille, when I was sick for two weeks and you nursed me back to health – and in Casablanca, when you might have purchased one of those letters and fled. But you didn't. Now I understand why you have kept our marriage a secret even from our friends, so that the Gestapo would never suspect that I was your wife.'

She managed to look over at Victor, but he was staring straight ahead again, as if lost in thought. She wondered, not for the first time, if he had heard a single word she had said. He had so much on his mind. 'Tell me . . . tell me you're not too angry with me,' she concluded.

He reached over and patted her arm affectionately and a little distractedly. 'Anger and jealousy are two emotions I choose to live without,' he said. 'Besides, how could I ever be angry with you when there is so much important work ahead?'

'Yes, Victor,' replied Ilsa. Did he not understand what she was trying to say, or was it impossible for him? 'How could you?'

For a while they sat together in silence. If the other passengers on the plane had noticed anything out of the ordinary about the handsome couple, they did not let their curiosity show. In wartime Europe, keeping one's curiosity private was always wise.

Victor leaned his head close to Ilsa's. 'When we get to Lisbon, my dear, I want you to do exactly as I tell you.'

'When have I ever not?' asked Ilsa, but Victor was still talking.

'The slightest hesitation could be fatal for both of us. Until now, I've been unable to tell you very much about my mission.' His voice softened a bit. 'I couldn't breathe a word of it to anyone back in Casablanca – not even you. I'm sure you understand.'

'I'm sure I do,' replied Ilsa.

The plane climbed above the Atlantic, buffeted by the winds. Once or twice Ilsa felt her stomach lurch, but Victor remained imperturbable. He had faced far worse dangers than a simple airplane trip, she knew, and she envied him his calm certitude. She wondered if that was an emotion she would ever experience for herself.

'Even at this moment, I cannot confide in you the full details of our plan,' Victor went on. 'Indeed, I myself do not know them fully yet.'

Ilsa interrupted him by placing her hand on his forearm. He winced, and then she remembered the wound he had suffered back in Casablanca, when the police broke up the Underground meeting just before his arrest. 'It's very dangerous, isn't it?' she asked.

'More dangerous than anything I've ever done,' said Victor. 'But don't worry, everything will work out. Our cause is just and theirs is not, and in the end we shall win. When even a man as blind to the fate of nations as Richard Blaine can see the difference between us and the Germans, the virtue of our cause must be clear to everyone.'

'What do you mean, Victor?'

Laszlo gave his wife a small smile. 'I mean simply that his action in giving us the transit letters was the mark of a man who has stopped running from himself. Who has finally realized, as you and I did long ago, that there are far more important things in this life than oneself or one's own happiness. Why do you suppose he did what he did back there? Why did he give us the letters of transit, when he might have kept them for himself?'

'I'm sure I don't know,' replied Ilsa. Her mind flashed back to the last time she had seen Rick alone, in his apartment above the café last night. She had been ready to sleep with him or shoot him, whatever it took to get the letters of transit that were her husband's passport to freedom. She had not shot him.

'When he might have turned me over to Major Strasser as casually as swatting a fly,' continued Victor. 'When' – his face darkened a bit – 'he might have tried to take you away with him.'

'Why, Victor?' breathed Ilsa.

'Because your saloon keeper has finally become a man, and declared his willingness to join us in our fight,' said her husband. 'He knew that I must escape Casablanca, and he knew I needed you to come with me. Whatever his true feelings for you might be, they were of no moment. Because the cause is all.'

Their plane landed in Lisbon without incident. Victor and

Ilsa passed through the border formalities easily. They took their rooms in the Hotel Aviz without question. They slept together that night without passion.

The next morning Ilsa was startled to wakefulness by a soft knock at the door. Two years ago she never would have noticed it, not so softly and not so far away. Since 1939 no one in occupied Europe had slept well or soundly. Instinctively she reached for her husband, but he was not there. Up and dressed, he was just closing the bedroom door behind him.

Outside she could hear voices. They were raised from time to time, but not in anger. In her nightgown she padded across the bed chamber and tried the door, but it was locked. Victor had locked it from the outside. For her safety? Or for his?

She bent down to the keyhole. The room beyond was still plunged in the darkness of the coming winter solstice. Listening intently, she could just make out some of the words. To judge from the differing voices, there were two other men in the front room with her husband.

'. . . changes everything . . .,' Victor was saying.

'. . . British Intelligence . . .,' said someone else.

'. . . danger . . . no chance . . . alive . . .,' said the second stranger.

'. . . *der Henker* . . .'

'. . . Prague . . .'

'As soon as possible!' Victor said, putting an end to the discussion.

She heard the front door shut softly. She jumped back into bed when she heard the turn of the key in the bedroom door.

'Is that you, Victor?' She feigned sleepiness.

'Yes, my dear,' he said.

She wiped some imaginary sand out of her eyes. 'Are you up so soon?'

'I went for an early morning stroll,' said Laszlo. 'You can't believe how good it feels to breathe free air once more. After Mauthausen, I never thought I'd have the chance again.'

Ilsa propped herself up slowly, yawned, and stretched. 'I can only imagine how it must feel,' she said.

'Of course you can.' He stroked her hair lightly, absent-mindedly. 'There has been some extraordinary news, my dear. The Japanese have attacked the Americans at Pearl Harbor in Hawaii.'

Ilsa sat bolt upright; no need to feign sleepiness now. 'What?' she exclaimed.

'It happened yesterday, a surprise attack on the U.S. Navy at Pearl Harbor near Honolulu. Most of the ships were destroyed in the harbor, and many men were killed. President Roosevelt has asked Congress for a declaration of war on Japan.' Victor seemed almost joyful. 'Now the Americans will have to join in our struggle.'

He got up and walked around the room excitedly. 'Don't you see, Ilsa? This is what we have hoped for. This is what I hoped for during all those long months in the camps, when it seemed that no one would come to our aid. The English look beaten. The Russians are reeling on three fronts. But this changes everything! Everything!'

Impulsively he swept his wife up in his arms.

'With the Americans on our side, we cannot lose! Oh, we won't be victorious right away; it will take years to roll back the Germans, destroy their armies, and free Europe once more. But the die is cast now, and there is no turning back. There are no Rick Blaines in America anymore, men who hide behind their cowardice and call it neutrality. It will take time, but from this moment on, Germany is finished.'

As abruptly as he had embraced her, he released her. 'We must make haste – more haste than ever. Quickly!' He found her suitcase and threw it on the bed. 'The taxi is downstairs, and the plane leaves in less than an hour.'

Ilsa rose quickly and began to pack. 'I have always wanted to see New York,' she said. 'Now that the Americans are on our side—'

'There is no longer any point in going to America,' Victor said. His bags were already packed, and he stood in the doorway impatiently. He was barely able to contain his excitement. 'The time for speech making and fund-raising is over, thank God. Now the time for action is at hand!'

'Then where are we going?' asked Ilsa.

'To the headquarters of the Czech government-in-exile since the fall of France,' he said as he closed the door behind them. 'To London.'

'London!' exclaimed Ilsa. That was where King Haakon lived now, along with the Norwegian government-in-exile, ever since Vidkun Quisling and his Nasjonal Samling, aided by some traitorous army officers, helped the Germans to occupy their homeland.

That was where her mother was.

Her thoughts raced back to Rick as Victor settled their account. She had asked him to follow, and now she must tell him where. Impulsively she scribbled unobserved a private note for Mr. Richard Blaine and left it with the chief reservations clerk, the one who had looked at her so appreciatively when they'd checked in the night before. The note was brief and to the point. 'To London.' 'British Intelligence.' '*Der*

Henker(?).' 'Danger.' 'Prague.' And 'Come quickly.' It was signed simply, 'I.'

That was all. She hoped Rick would understand what it meant, because she didn't.

She smiled at the clerk as she handed him the note. He looked back at her with the same mixture of awe, admiration, and desire that she had seen in the faces of men since she was fourteen years old.

'For Mr. Blaine only,' she said, gazing into his eyes to make sure he wouldn't forget. 'You understand?'

'You have my word on it, madam,' said the clerk, impressed.

Then she heard her husband's voice in her ear, felt his hand on her arm – 'Hurry, Ilsa, hurry' – and she was whisked away.

The waiting taxi sped them to their destination. They boarded the London-bound plane and took their seats. A pair of young, tough men, Slavs by the look of them, got on with them. They said nothing to Victor, but Ilsa knew they were watching them.

As the plane took off, she brought her mouth to her husband's ear. 'Victor,' she said, 'let me help you this time. Please.' Laszlo, however, stared straight ahead, his mind not on the present, but on the future.

CHAPTER THREE

Rick reached across the seat and shoved Renault hard. 'Get down, Louie,' he barked. 'I've seen a man get his head blown off, and believe me, it isn't a pretty sight.'

Renault ducked. 'I happily defer to your obviously greater experience in these matters,' he said.

From the backseat, Rick could see that the two cars were about three hundred yards apart. As the Buick roared along, the Mercedes no longer seemed to be closing on them, but neither was it receding.

'What have they got, Sam? Tommies?' asked Rick as their pursuers' bullets whizzed by.

'Prob'ly some new Krupp thing,' demurred Sam, two hands on the wheel. 'Tommies is old now, boss, or ain't you noticed?'

'Yeah, well, I wish we had one.'

'You and me both,' said Sam, eyes straight ahead.

'What've we got?'

'Your forty-five, Sacha's thirty-eight, my twenty-two . . . what you got, Mr. Louis?'

Renault unholstered his sidearm and looked at it, as if for the first time. 'A thirty-eight,' he said. 'Not that I've ever had to use it.'

'Except to impress the girls,' said Rick.

Sacha leaned out the window and squeezed off a couple of shots.

'Cut it out, you idiot!' yelled Rick. 'Never let 'em know what you've got until you have to. If they know all we have is pistols, they'll cut us to pieces.'

'Sorry, boss,' Sacha said.

The road to Rabat was pitch dark. The coastal fog made the moon irrelevant. The only problem was that the Buick was in the Mercedes' headlights and not the other way around.

'Gimme a little distance, will ya, Sam?' ordered Rick. 'I'd like to see if I'm getting the horsepower I paid for.'

'You got it, boss.'

Under Sam's urging, slowly but inexorably the Buick pulled away. Three hundred and fifty yards, four hundred yards . . . Rick decided it was safe to stick his head out the window.

'Is there a turnoff anyplace soon?' he shouted over the roar of the slipstream. They might be able to outrun the Mercedes, but then again they might not: a flat, an accident . . . better to get the drop on the Germans if they could and get it over with.

'There's always a turnoff, if you don't mind jungle,' said Sam.

'Then turn off, damn it.'

Sam spun the car so hard to the left that Renault thought he would fly out the window. He was amazed to see Rick sitting bolt upright and leaning out of the car as calmly as if he were at the track on a Sunday afternoon, studying a racing form. Except that he had a gun in his hand instead of a pencil.

'Gimme a count, Sam,' said Rick as the car began to rotate.

'One Mississippi, two Mississippi . . .'

Steered and braked expertly by Sam, the Buick revolved a full 360 degrees in a controlled skid, returning to its original direction at the exact moment the Mercedes caught up with them.

'. . . three!'

The Mercedes was right beside them. Rick caught a glimpse of the amazed face of the driver.

'*Laissez le bon temps rouler*,' said Sam.

'Now, Sach',' shouted Rick.

The Russian and the American opened up on the Germans. Sacha's shot put out the window on the driver's side. Rick's shot put out the driver's left eye.

Rick caught a glimpse of the gunman in the backseat as the crippled Mercedes veered sharply to the right and headed for the trees. The Nazi managed to get off a couple of wild shots before they smashed into a grove of mangoes.

The explosion sent an orange ball of flame into the sky, scorching the fronds as it billowed. Sam slammed on the brakes so they could survey their handiwork.

'Piece of cake, boss,' he said as he backed up the Buick.

The fireball was consuming most of the big Mercedes by the time they got there. Over each headlight was a small flag bearing the emblem of the swastika, now burning merrily. Rick could see that the car had three occupants, but it was too late to help any of them.

'Nice shooting, boss,' complimented Sacha.

'Fish in a barrel,' said Rick.

'I never see fish in a barrel, boss.' Sacha threw his arms around Rick's neck. 'Can I kiss you?'

'Get away from me, you crazy Russian,' said Rick.

The fire burned for what seemed like an eternity. Privately Renault wondered why they didn't drive on, but Rick seemed disinclined to leave. He sat, head bowed, lips moving, but no sound emerging. Was he praying? Rick Blaine was full of surprises this evening.

'Come on, let's go,' Rick said abruptly. 'We've got a plane to catch.'

The Buick pulled back onto the road.

The glare from the burning Mercedes receded rapidly in Sam's rearview mirror, which made him happy. Sam disliked violence, even when it was necessary. He'd seen enough of it.

'Very impressive, Ricky,' said Renault. 'And here all this time I thought you were a simple saloon keeper. Still waters indeed.'

'That's just what I plan to be again someday,' said Rick, popping open his flask and taking another drink. 'As soon as this war is over.'

'Somehow, my friend,' said Renault, 'I don't think fate is going to let you. You are destined for greater things.'

'Don't count on it,' said Rick.

Renault settled back into his seat. Now that the excitement was over, his mind was free to concentrate on more important things. America attacked! He knew that Rick was stunned. He had long suspected that Rick's *c'est la vie* attitude was only a pose, a carapace that covered a soft heart. Rick might have left his country years before – why, he still had no idea – and seemed loath to return, but he remembered the way Rick had stared down the boastful Major Strasser and the fawning consul Heinze when he'd advised them not to try to invade certain sections of New York. As one whose country had already fallen to the Nazis, Renault sympathized, and his heart went out to his friend.

What did this mean for him? Since his first trip to the gaming tables in Deauville – which, as luck would have it, coincided with his discovery of *la différence* at age twelve – Louis Renault had believed that gambling was a profession, not a pastime, and he regarded his police duties as the unfortunately necessary surety that enabled him to pursue a higher calling. Still, he much preferred a fixed roulette wheel to actual games of honest chance. He had spent most of his adult life calculating odds and acting on them, and up until a few hours ago he'd been quite happy leaving his chips on the Nazis' number and watching his winnings add up. Now, though, he wasn't so sure. Which, he supposed, was one of the reasons he was in this car instead of back in Casablanca, enjoying the favors of some delectable young lady whose lust for freedom coincided with his lust for her body. A fair exchange, Renault had always thought, and he'd made the pursuit of it his life.

On the outskirts of Rabat, Sam swung around the city. It would not do for them to be stopped by an officious cop. Not in an American car with a Russian in the front seat, a Vichy police official in the back, alongside the soon-to-be persona non grata Rick Blaine. But the capital city of wartime French Morocco was shrouded in darkness, and if anyone noticed their passing, he wisely kept it to himself.

From Rabat to Port Lyautey was only about fifty miles, and they made it in just over an hour.

They found Jean-Claude Chausson waiting for them at daybreak at the tiny airfield a few miles outside the city. He was standing beside a Fokker 500, which could carry several passengers, one pilot, and any sort of contraband a smuggler's heart could wish for – and had, many times.

'*Allo, Monsieur Rick*,' said Chausson.

'How are you, Jean-Claude?' said Rick, shaking the pilot's hand.

'Bored,' came the reply.

'Let's see if we can do something about that,' said Rick.

Chausson was a Free Frenchman of decidedly anti-Nazi sympathies. Rick had first met him in Spain, when Jean-Claude was running arms to the Loyalists. Since that defeat he had made a far more lucrative living running unstamped liquor into French Morocco, much of it destined for Rick's café, and guns wherever they were most profitably needed. In Africa that was nearly everywhere.

'Give Sacha the keys to the car, Sam,' ordered Rick as they boarded the plane. 'Take good care of her, Sacha.'

'You mean the Buick or Yvonne, boss?' asked Sacha with a leer.

'Take your pick,' said Rick, as the plane's door closed. 'They're both expensive.'

The flight to Lisbon was uneventful. Portugal had learned early in the conflict that not being interested in the comings and goings of the people passing through was far more remunerative than worrying about either their pasts or their futures. Some place had to be a port of exit from Europe, and Lisbon was only too happy to oblige. With Franco's neutral Spain as its buffer zone, business was very good.

They headed straight for the Aviz, where Rick inquired

first about Mr. and Mrs. Victor Laszlo. Away from the Nazis, he thought, they might finally be traveling together as husband and wife.

He was wrong. The head clerk, who bore a nametag that proclaimed his surname to be Medeiros, shook his head sadly. 'I am sorry to say we have no record of them,' he told Rick.

'Are you sure?' Rick asked as politely as he could.

'Very sure,' replied Medeiros. He was not about to betray a lady's confidence so easily. 'It is my job, after all, to know who comes and who goes here.'

Well, there was a Ferrari in every crowd, thought Rick. 'Try under a different name, Miss Ilsa Lund. Try to remember the most beautiful woman you have—'

Medeiros didn't let Rick get any farther. 'Oh yes, Miss Lund,' he exclaimed with delight, and Rick could see the memory of Ilsa in his eyes. A man didn't forget a face or a figure like hers. 'You are Mr. Richard Blaine?' asked the clerk.

'The only one who'll admit to it,' replied Rick.

'Then this is for you.' Medeiros proudly handed him Ilsa's note. 'She left it for you not two hours ago.'

Rick scanned it rapidly, then stuffed it in his pocket. Following her trail, he was beginning to feel like one of the children in 'Hansel and Gretel.' He just hoped the Wicked Witch wouldn't be waiting for them both, somewhere in the dark German woods.

CHAPTER FOUR

Victor Laszlo arrived in London to a hero's welcome, albeit a secret one. He and Ilsa were met on the tarmac at Luton airfield on December 8, 1941, not by a committee, but by a single man, military in mien and brusque of manner, who introduced himself as Major Sir Harold Miles and shook hands in a brisk, businesslike fashion. After a brief conversation with Laszlo, the major bundled them into a waiting Lancia and sped them into town. An hour later the car pulled up in front of a large but nondescript house in a residential neighborhood, and they were hustled up the front steps and inside. Ilsa was told to wear her coat collar turned up and her hat pulled down low.

Once inside, however, everything was different. Ilsa had not been sure what to expect, but it wasn't this.

The parlor floor was warm and cozy. Elegant William Morris wallpaper adorned the walls, and the hearty over-stuffed furniture was covered in bright prints. The curtains were brocade and the ceilings ornamented with plaster. A coal fire burned in the hearth, casting off a welcoming warmth, and two chairs nestled invitingly on either side of it. It looked like home, certainly more of a home than she had had in the past year and a half.

A kindly woman, verging on elderly but still evidently with all her wits and strength about her, took her things and handed her a glass of tea. 'I'm Mrs. Bunton,' she said by way of introduction. 'I should expect you've had a long and difficult journey. This will take some of the chill off.'

At the other end of the room, Ilsa watched her husband conferring with Major Miles and another man, who was dressed in the formal morning coat of a diplomat. They were too far away, and speaking too softly, for her to hear their words.

She took her tea from Mrs. Bunton gratefully, and as she drank it she felt some warmth come back into her bones. After a few minutes Victor broke away from his conversation and walked over to her. 'You must be very tired, my dear,' he said. 'Why don't you go upstairs and rest for a while? I'll join you shortly.'

'Oh, Victor,' she said, 'couldn't I stay here, for just a few more minutes?'

Victor glanced back at the two other men in the room. 'I'm afraid I must insist.'

There was no point in struggling. 'Very well,' she said. Mrs. Bunton led her up the stairs and into a beautifully appointed double room. 'I'm sure you'll be quite comfortable here,' she said, shutting the door.

Although she was very tired, for a long time Ilsa lay in bed, unable to fall asleep. She knew the real reason that underlay Victor's solicitude: the conversation he was having had nothing to do with her. She had played out this scene dozens of times before. The meetings in the middle of the night. The strange men in the parlor, some with the faces muffled against recognition. Always it ended the same way, with Victor asking her to leave and closing a door on her. She didn't want it to be that way any longer.

For the first time in months she felt safe – safe and yet very, very alone. That, she thought, was the story of her married life with Victor Laszlo. His wife, but only when he felt it safe to acknowledge her. At his side when she could be, but never really *with* him. Part of his cause, but not, in the end, his cause. More than a helpmeet, less than a mate.

Yet as she'd watched him these past few days, she couldn't help once more being impressed with him. This was the man she had fallen in love with as an impressionable girl; this was the man to whom she was now wedded as a mature woman. Victor was tall and well proportioned, with a noble head and kind eyes that had seen suffering she could not begin to fathom. He stood and moved with great dignity, as if responsibility for the fate of the world were resting on his shoulders. Who was to say that, at this moment in history, it wasn't? How she admired him!

She knew as well how much she meant to him. Hadn't he risked his life for her, time and again? Even if he didn't let her be a part of it, didn't he always tell her how important she was to his work? Didn't he, from time to time, tell her how much he loved her? Her heart swelled with pride as she watched him, so stately and dignified, yet so intent and so commanding.

Then she thought about Rick Blaine.

Had she done the right thing by leaving him notes, first in Casablanca and then in Lisbon? Had he even received them?

Had he followed her and Victor, as she hoped? Was he here? What would Victor say if he found out? How would he react? What was she hoping for? That Rick had followed – or that he hadn't?

She felt herself becoming upset and tried to calm down. She started to let herself believe that Rick had never received her note in Lisbon. That he was still back in Casablanca or, better yet, somewhere far away. That the accident of meeting him again and Rick's giving them the letters of transit was just that – an accident, proof of the rightness of Victor's cause, proof that her place was by Victor's side, now and forever, that . . . There, that was better, wasn't it?

No, it wasn't. Rick had given her something she had never felt before. It wasn't just the physical joy she felt when she was with him. Rather, it was a closeness, a tenderness, a passion, an excitement far beyond the capacity of other men to give.

With sudden insight she realized the truth: The way she felt about Rick was exactly the way Victor felt about the cause. It was one thing to love a cause, however; it was another to love a man. But which man did she really love? She struggled to sort out her feelings. Her head told her that while her heart might be conflicted, her duty was clear. Though she might love Rick, her place was with her husband. She had to show Victor that she was worthy of him and, even more important, worthy of his cause. Besides, she would never see Rick again, would she?

Therefore, Ilsa decided, she would play a greater role in that cause. She was tired of being a pawn in a game played by men: this was not just a man's war, but everybody's. Were the Nazis sparing women in their assault on civilization? She knew from firsthand experience they were not. From now on this was Ilsa Lund's war, too.

Just then the door opened and someone came in. She expected that it would be Mrs. Bunton, but it was not. It was Victor. 'Are you all right, my dear?' he asked, sitting lightly on the bed beside her.

'Yes, Victor,' replied Ilsa. 'I'm fine. In fact, I'm feeling quite myself again.'

'Good,' Victor said. 'I was worried about you. You looked so pale on the flight, so tired, that I feared you might be ill. The stress—'

'Victor,' said Ilsa, 'there's something I need to say to you.' She sat up and faced her husband. He smoothed the covers while he listened.

'I don't know why we are here, or what you are planning,' she began.

'That is for your own safety,' he interjected.

She stopped by placing her right hand on his arm. 'But that's just it!' she exclaimed. 'I don't want it to be that way anymore! I am no longer the schoolgirl you fell in love with. I'm your wife. All over Europe, girls half my age are dying for what they believe in. How can I do any less?'

'I don't know what you mean, Ilsa,' Victor said.

'I mean that I want to be a part of what you are a part of,' she said, her words pouring forth. 'If there is danger, I want to share it with you. If there is glory, I want to seek it with you.'

Victor shook his head. 'That is impossible.'

'It is not,' replied Ilsa, gripping her husband's arm. 'You say you are grateful for all the things I have done for you, but I've only done what you've let me. I want to do more. You say you love me. Then prove it, by treating me like a woman and not like a child, by treating me like your wife instead of your daughter.'

For the first time since she had met him, Victor seemed confused and unsure of himself. 'I can't,' he said at last. 'I cannot put you in such peril.'

Ilsa looked her husband in the eye. 'You already have,' she said. 'What else have we shared but peril for the past year and a half? If I have already endured the danger, then let me share in the glory.'

Victor withdrew from her grasp and stood up. 'You are certain this is what you want?'

'I want the same thing that you want,' she replied. 'Nothing more, nothing less.'

Victor's self-control had re-established itself. 'Very well, then,' he said. 'Let us go downstairs together and meet the others.'

As they returned to the parlor, Ilsa noticed that the two men who had been on the plane with them had joined the group.

'Gentlemen,' Victor announced loudly, 'I have the honor of introducing my wife, Miss Ilsa Lund. Ilsa, this is Sir Ernest Spencer, the British Secretary of War. Major Miles you already know. And these two brave men are Jan Kubiš and Josef Gabčík, free citizens of Czechoslovakia and comrades-in-arms.'

Ilsa shook hands with them all. Sir Ernest was a tall, ascetic-looking man with an aristocratically refined face and a small pencil mustache. Major Miles was a powerfully built military man. By contrast, Kubiš and Gabčík seemed hardly more than boys. 'Very pleased to meet you all,' she said.

'Before we go on,' said Victor, 'my wife has something to say.'

Ilsa gave him a slight bow. 'Gentlemen, the past two years have been especially trying for both my husband and me. There were times when, frankly, I despaired. For a while I thought Victor was dead. Later, I myself was seriously ill. But, as you can see, we have both survived.'

How radiant she looks, thought Laszlo as he watched her performance with growing admiration. He was very proud to call her his wife – and now, in the safety of London, he could.

'And because we have both survived,' Ilsa went on, 'it is now time for us to fully consummate our partnership.' She smiled at her husband, the smile that had first caught his eye and then won his heart. 'Therefore, from this moment on I have the honor and pleasure to inform you that I shall be a fully active partner in this operation – anything that you can say in front of Victor you can say in front of me.'

Sir Ernest cleared his throat. 'Well said, Mrs. Laszlo,' he remarked. 'But surely you realize the extraordinary danger . . .'

'My husband and I have already discussed that. Any danger we encounter we wish to share.'

Major Miles looked at Victor. 'Mr. Laszlo, I congratulate you. With a brave and gallant wife like this, you hardly have need of our assistance.'

Inside, Victor was beaming. He knew that Ilsa was magnificent, but never before had he suspected just how splendid she really was.

'Gentlemen,' he said, picking up the skein, 'you can see how devoted my wife and I are to the cause. We are, both of us, prepared to die for our beliefs – as are our colleagues from Czechoslovakia in this noble endeavor.' The nod of his head indicated Jan and Josef. 'We do not ask the same sacrifice from you. Only that, when the time comes, you will be there for us – just as surely as we are here for you at this moment.'

Ilsa rose to go. 'I hope you gentlemen will please excuse me. There is someone very important whom I must see. Someone I have not seen in a very long time.'

There was a moment of silence, broken by Major Miles. 'I hope you will forgive me, madam, for asking who this someone might be.'

'What's the matter, Sir Harold?' she replied. 'Don't you trust me?'

'Nothing of the sort. But in an operation like this, one must maintain the highest level of security. Therefore, it is with the greatest regret that I must ask you who—'

'I am going to see my mother,' Ilsa said candidly. 'I hope that is all right with you gentlemen. I have not seen or spoken to her in two years. I'm sure you will all agree that it is high time that I visit her.'

Three of the men knew who Ilsa's mother was and what she had suffered at the hands of their enemy. 'Please allow me the honor of escorting you personally to that great lady,' said Major Miles, visibly chastened.

'That is most kind of you, Sir Harold,' Ilsa said. 'But I'm quite sure I can find my own way.'

She took her coat from Mrs. Bunton and went outside. A taxi came right along. She hailed it, gave the driver an address, and stepped into the cab.

CHAPTER FIVE

Ilsa Lund sat in the taxi, accompanied only by her thoughts. Involuntarily she let out a deep breath and felt a sense of relaxation sweep over her. This was the first time she had been both safe and alone in many months. Yet it seemed either a lifetime ago or only yesterday that she was bidding good-bye to her parents on the steps of their Oslo home, off to Paris for language study at the Sorbonne in the fall of 1938. Who could have imagined that the world she was leaving would so soon disappear? Or that the shy, naive student who was about to embark for France would also vanish, to be replaced by the determined, experienced woman now riding across London? No one, least of all her.

Instinctively she reached across the backseat of the taxi to take Victor's hand and was momentarily surprised when it wasn't there.

A natural linguist, she had been studying Slavic languages, with a concentration in Russian. Her father had encouraged her. 'We Scandinavians cannot expect the people of Europe to learn our languages, Ilsa, so we must learn theirs,' he told her. She threw herself into her studies, forsaking the nightlife of St. Michel for the hard work of Russian grammar and the rewards of being able to read Tolstoy in the original. She would have time later for celebration, she reasoned. Plenty of time.

Then, on the first of May 1939, she met Victor Laszlo.

'Get dressed, Ilsa!' said Angelique Casselle, her best friend, diving into Ilsa's closet, coming up with her best dress, and tossing it at her as she pored over a textbook. 'You can't stay in your room studying forever. Do you want to die an old maid?'

'But, the examination,' protested Ilsa.

Angelique put her lips together and blew, a typically French gesture of disparagement. 'Bah!' she said. 'You already speak Russian better than Stalin. What more do you want? Come on! There's somebody I want you to meet.'

Ilsa would never forget the address: 150, boulevard St.-Germain. She had stopped at the open-air market that lined both sides of the rue du Seine and bought some fresh cheese and a bottle of Bordeaux to bring as presents. When she pressed the buzzer of the flat, the door was opened by the handsomest man she had ever seen, a man who greeted her with continental elegance in perfect French.

'Miss Ilsa Lund, I believe,' he said, kissing her hand. 'My name is Victor Laszlo.' His eyes met hers. 'Miss Casselle told me you were the most beautiful girl in Paris. She lied. You are the most beautiful woman in all Europe.'

Ilsa was astonished. Everybody in Paris knew Victor Laszlo, the Czech patriot who, before the Munich Pact of 1938, had so resolutely opposed any accommodation with the Nazis in his daily newspaper, *Pravo*. Laszlo had fearlessly exposed the Nazis' record of brutality, redoubling his efforts after the Sudetenland was handed over to Germany. When Hitler annexed Bohemia and Moravia on March 15, 1939, Laszlo became a wanted man. He went underground for a time, continuing to publish. Finally, when the situation became too dangerous, he fled to Paris, where he joined the Czech government-in-exile and continued his opposition.

From that moment on, they were nearly inseparable. Victor fell in love not only with Ilsa's beauty, but with her intelligence and strength; he saw in her a partner in his grand crusade. For Ilsa, Laszlo opened up a whole world of knowledge and thoughts and ideals, and she looked up to him and worshiped him with a feeling she supposed was love. They worked together feverishly, not for themselves, but on behalf of all the captive peoples of Europe.

Swept away by his selfless dedication, Ilsa Lund secretly married Victor Laszlo in June 1939. Not even their closest friends knew of their wedding.

Despite her protestations, Victor returned to his homeland in July to carry the fight to the enemy. She told him it was too dangerous, but he wouldn't be dissuaded. 'Ilsa, I must go,' he had told her. 'How can I ask others to do what I myself will not?'

The Gestapo, however, was waiting for him; a few days after arriving in Prague, Victor was arrested and sent to the concentration camp at Mauthausen in German-occupied Austria. A short while later he was reported dead, shot while trying to escape.

Ilsa was despondent. For a time, she considered returning home to Oslo but quickly decided against it. Victor would have wanted her to stay and carry on their work. Besides, her brief experience with the Underground had given her a taste of the game the men were playing, and she liked it. Even when the rumors of war grew too loud to ignore, even when Hitler's saber rattling started to shake foundations from Warsaw to Paris, she stayed in France. When, in September 1939 the Wehrmacht attacked Poland, she knew she had made the right decision.

She did not worry about her family. Scandinavia was small and unthreatening. Aside from Swedish iron ore, it had nothing the Germans either needed or wanted. Letters from home gave no cause for alarm. Then in April 1940 the Germans attacked and conquered Norway. The King fled to London, and the letters from home suddenly stopped. When next she heard from her mother it was a month later, and the news was terrible indeed: her father was dead.

Ilsa watched the city flash by her window as the taxi maneuvered northeast through the rainswept, twisting streets. To her eye, London's gray, imposing buildings were clumped along the carriageways like descendants of Stonehenge, silent, magisterial, and more than a little forbidding. On this day they matched her mood.

London was nothing like either Oslo or Paris, she reflected. Her hometown was small and hilly, perched on the water's edge as if getting ready to cast its fishing nets into the sea at any moment. Oslo's houses were smaller than London's, less regimented, more neighborly. They were narrow, gabled, and made of wood. In the brief summer, they were ringed with greenery and bright flowers made all the more cheerful by their impermanence; sealed tight against the elements during the long, dark winter, the homes were warm and inviting. Paris straddled the Seine serenely, incorporating the river into its very conception of self, as if man, not God, had put the water there for the pleasure of the Parisians. Oslo was happy to let nature dominate; Paris was pleased to allow nature to participate.

The Thames was London's lifeline to the sea, but unless you were a dockworker or an MP, you could go for days without encountering the river. The buildings were at once grander and less elegant than their French counterparts, and the city's inhabitants moved more purposefully. The rainy weather and the sooty fog often erased the sun, but London preferred to ignore the elements rather than accommodate or kowtow to them. The business of London was not business but power, and it was to the keeping of that power that the country had rededicated itself in this war. Did Hitler know what a formidable opponent he had in the British? She doubted he did.

'Here, driver, here!' she cried as they turned into Myddleton Square in Islington. She threw a handful of coins at the cabby, leaped out, and rushed up the steps to her mother's flat, her heart beating furiously.

Inghild Lund rose to answer the doorbell. She opened the heavy door and beheld the daughter she thought she might never see again.

Before she could say anything, Ilsa threw her arms around her and the two women stood on the doorstep, hugging fiercely.

'I can't believe it's you,' whispered Inghild through her tears of joy.

'I'm here, Mama,' cried Ilsa, 'I'm here.'

They stayed locked together for longer than either of them

knew, not caring about the passersby or the rain, until Inghild at last released her daughter. 'Come inside and tell me what miracle has finally brought you back to me.'

The little flat was homey and comfortable; though it was far from Norway, to Ilsa it sang of home. A picture of King Haakon VII hung on one of the walls, and on a small side table stood a photograph of Edvard and Inghild Lund, taken on their wedding day in 1912. How handsome her father was in his dress suit, his left arm around his new wife and a cigarette in his right hand. Ilsa half expected him to walk in the door any minute, fresh from a meeting with the King; it was impossible to believe that she would never see him again.

Ilsa Lund had been born in Oslo on August 29, 1915, just ten years after Norway won independence from Sweden; Oslo was still called Christiania then. Ilsa's father, Edvard Lund, had been a member of parliament, the Storting, which had rejected the Swedish monarch, Oscar II, and established the modern Norwegian state. 'To those who question the depth of our desire,' he had said in a fiery speech, 'I reply: We are ready to prove it with the sacrifice of our lives and our homes – but never of our honor.' Ilsa's father was quickly elevated to the cabinet and there he remained until April 1940, when the Nazis appropriated Norway in the name of the Greater German Reich.

Inghild had been able to take along only a few belongings when she was spirited to London along with the King and the government-in-exile. Ilsa recognized them at once. A lace tablecloth that used to cover a heavy wooden table with thick carved legs, under which she liked to hide as a child. Some silverware. A few Persian rugs, one of which still bore the stains of a glass of milk she had thrown so long ago in a childish tantrum. A small wall clock that had been in her mother's family for generations. It ticked softly in a corner, every passing second a bitter reminder of the calamity that had befallen their homeland.

No, that was no way to think, Ilsa told herself. Every tick was one moment closer to liberation and freedom for them all. Whatever role she could play in that liberation, she was ready.

Inghild had been preparing some tea for herself, but now she added more water and left it to steep in the pot, to serve later. She produced some cookies, as mothers always will, and some schnapps, which mothers sometimes will.

'I've been beside myself with worry about you,' Inghild told her daughter, her voice alive with relief and delight. 'After the fall of France your letters suddenly stopped. The Underground were able to tell me you were alive, but little else. Over the next year or so, I got a few of your letters, smuggled in. From our agents, I knew you were in occupied France, but I didn't know where. When I learned that you were headed to Casablanca, I could not ask why, but at least I could do something about it.' She laughed. 'And now here you are! How I wish your father could see you.'

'So it was you who suggested I contact Berger!' exclaimed Ilsa. In this moment of exultation, she didn't want to think about her father; they would mourn him together later – after she had avenged him. 'I might have known my mother would still be watching over me.'

'Yes, my dear,' said Inghild. 'I may be only one lone woman, but I can still fight for my country – and for my child. Each week I receive briefings from the King's new minister of defense. The government, it seems, values my advice, although for the life of me I don't know why.'

Ilsa took her mother's still-youthful hand, the hand she remembered so well from her childhood. 'You know why, Mother,' she said. 'You and Father were always equal partners. He called you his other self, and he trusted you like none other. Everything he knew you knew, and our country was immeasurably the better for it.'

Inghild's eyes clouded at the memory of Edvard Lund, but she shook it off, unwilling to let it intrude on her happiness. 'The Defense Minister told me that Berger might possibly be able to produce a *laissez-passer* or letter of transit to get you out of Morocco, so I sent word for you to meet him in a café. I forget what it was called.'

'Rick's Café Americain,' said Ilsa. 'In Casablanca, sooner or later, everybody comes to Rick's.'

'Yes,' said her mother. 'I am so happy that Berger was able to get you safely out of Casablanca. Ole was a good boy, but always so skittish. Who would have suspected he had such courage in him? You cannot always tell a hero by his looks.'

Talk of home made Ilsa reminisce. If she closed her eyes, hearkened to the sound of her mother's voice, and inhaled the smells of her mother's kitchen, she could almost imagine herself back in Oslo.

'Tell me of home, Mother,' Ilsa requested.

Inghild smoothed her dress. 'Some of us are here in London, of course,' she began. 'Liv Olsen, who lived down the street, is with her husband, and Birgit Aasen – you remember Birgit, you used to play together when you were little – is living in America now. Bay Ridge, I think they call it.'

'I remember her,' said Ilsa. 'We used to walk down to the

Parliament building and pretend we were the King's most important councilors.'

'Someday you may be,' said Inghild. 'We arrived in June of 1940, after the King saw that resistance to the Nazis would be futile, and that the government could fight on more effectively from London. Many more stayed behind, though, and even now are working day and night against the Germans. Do you remember Arne Bjørnov?'

'Little Arne, who asked if he could take me to the picture show?' said Ilsa. 'He was so nervous. He must have thought Father was going to bite his head off. I would have gone with him, too, if he hadn't run off like that, as though a ghost were chasing him. And all because Father asked him, "Young man, what are your intentions?" He was only thirteen!'

'That frightened little boy has grown up to be a very brave man, Ilsa,' said Inghild. 'Thanks to Arne, the people have refused to cooperate with the edicts of the German commissioner Josef Terboven, and they simply ignore the proclamations of the Nasjonal Samling, which is the only legal political party. The traitor Quisling's establishment of martial law last September has only increased their will to resist, and the ranks of patriotic saboteurs and spies grow every day. The Germans are frustrated and furious, but what can they do? They can't kill us all – and to really conquer Norway, they would have to.'

Ilsa was thrilled to hear about her friends; now it was time to tell her mother about her own activities. 'Berger wasn't the one who helped us get the letters of transit, Mama. Another man got me – got us – out of Casablanca.'

Inghild caught the change of mood in her daughter's voice. 'Us?'

'Yes, us,' admitted Ilsa. 'For two years, I have been married to Victor Laszlo.'

'Married!' exclaimed her mother, all other thoughts driven from her mind. 'And to Victor Laszlo! All Europe knows and honors his name. This is wonderful news!' Inghild kissed her daughter, her heart bursting with pride; if only Edvard were here.

'I could not tell you of our wedding in my letters,' continued Ilsa. 'For his safety, and for mine, we have told no one. It was too dangerous – for both of us. But it was not Victor who got us out of Casablanca, either. Someone else did. Someone I need to talk to you about.'

Ilsa paused, unsure how to begin. 'Mother,' she began, 'is it possible to love two men at once? Really love them, each of them, with your whole heart and your whole soul, as if your own life depended on their very existence? If it is, how do you choose? Must you choose?'

Ilsa clasped her hands together tightly. She was sitting very close to her mother and felt even closer. 'Is it possible when one is so very different from the other?' she went on. 'When one appeals to the best side of your nature, and the other appeals to the very core of your nature itself?'

She sat expectantly, dreading and desiring the answer; not knowing what she wanted to hear.

Inghild considered her words carefully. If she was surprised to learn of her daughter's marriage and then, hard on its heels, of her dilemma, she did not let on. 'Why don't you tell me about him, Ilsa?' she said.

This was the speech she had been rehearsing in the taxi, only she hadn't known it then. 'His name is Richard,' she replied. 'Richard Blaine. He is an American from New York.'

She went on to tell Inghild everything, starting with how she had met Victor. About their brief life together in Paris. About the report of his death. About how she met Rick.

'I was in the Deux Magots one spring day, reading the newspapers. Talk of war was in the air. My newspaper got caught in a gust of wind. A man at the next table retrieved it for me before it blew into the street. "I believe this belongs to you, miss," he said in English. I thought he might be an American. He sat down at my table. I didn't invite him, but he did anyway. Then I knew he was an American. "The view is much better from here," he said, and ordered us both coffee in the worst French I ever heard. It made me laugh to hear him speak. "Which is funnier," he asked me, "my accent or my face?" After that, how could I ask him to leave?'

'When a man makes a woman laugh,' Inghild said, 'it is the first step to winning her heart.'

'My heart!' exclaimed Ilsa. 'I thought it was gone, dead, along with Victor. I was alone, and very lonely. I didn't know what to do or where to go. I couldn't go home to Oslo, not after . . .'

'Not after Quisling handed our country over to the Germans,' supplied her mother.

'Not after you had left,' Ilsa corrected her. 'Not after Father died.' Her voice trembled with barely suppressed grief. 'He suggested dinner that night, at La Tour d'Argent. I said yes. It seemed safe. We dined. The next day we danced. We went for a drive in his motorcar, and sailed along the Seine. We visited his nightclub, *La Belle Aurore*. We watched the dawn come up together, and it was very beautiful.'

'You fell in love,' said Inghild.

'I fell in love,' Ilsa concurred. 'Not with an idea this time, but with a man. Richard opened up for me a world I never knew existed, a world of romance and passion, and . . .'

'The physical love between a man and a woman,' said Inghild.

Ilsa nodded. 'Rick brought me back to life. And then Victor came back from the dead.'

'How?'

Ilsa felt herself growing agitated and steeled herself. When an exhausted and emaciated Victor suddenly reappeared on that rainy, wrenching day in Paris in June 1940, their life together became little more than desperate camouflage and unending flight as the Gestapo hunted them the length and breadth of France. If it hadn't been for that brave Algerian fisherman, who had smuggled them in his sloop across the Mediterranean from Marseille to Algiers, hidden under a load of stinking fish . . . She shuddered at the memory.

'The Germans were approaching,' she said. 'Everybody knew it was only a matter of time before they took Paris. The Czech government-in-exile had removed itself to London. Richard didn't want to leave, although I begged him to. I knew he was not the unfeeling cynic he pretended to be. I knew he had fought against Mussolini in Ethiopia and against Franco in Spain. The Germans knew his record, too; if he stayed, he would certainly be arrested. I couldn't let that happen to another man in my life. He wouldn't go without me, though. We decided to flee, together.'

'But you didn't.'

'I couldn't,' said Ilsa, casting her eyes down. 'The day before we were to leave for Marseille, I got word that Victor was still alive, hiding in a boxcar on the outskirts of Paris. He was ill and needed me. Oh, Mother, how could I not go to him? He was my husband.'

Ilsa was crying now, the tears she had so long suppressed flowing freely. 'I knew Victor had returned when I saw Rick for the last time. We were in his club, drinking the last of his champagne so the Germans wouldn't get it. I made some excuse to leave and promised to meet him that evening at the Gare de Lyon. I never showed up. Richard boarded the train for Marseille with only a note from me, telling him I could never see him again. I couldn't tell him why. I couldn't tell him anything. It was the hardest decision of my life. But what else could I do? Our work was more important than my feelings. Even my feelings for Richard Blaine. What did the happiness of two people matter when the lives of millions were at stake?'

A look of ineffable sadness crossed her mother's face. 'You are speaking not of your husband,' she observed, 'but of his work. They are not the same thing.'

Ilsa had never made that distinction before. 'Yes,' she admitted, 'his work. I fell in love with his work long before I met him. When we did meet, I could not believe that a great man like him could possibly love an inexperienced girl like me. He was doing heroic deeds for his country, and what was I doing? Studying languages.'

Inghild considered her next words carefully. 'I have not had the honor of meeting either of these two gentlemen, Ilsa. What is it that you love about each of them?'

Ilsa told her. That Victor had taught her what love was: love of country, love of principle, love of freedom, love of one's fellow human beings. That everything she ever was or had become had been because of him. That he was an easy man to love, and Ilsa had thought she loved him.

'What about the other man? Richard Blaine?'

Ilsa told her mother that Rick was everything Victor was not. That he was cynical where Victor was earnest; misanthropic where Victor was selfless. That he spoke crisply, and when necessary, he acted brutally. That he mocked where Victor praised, scoffed where Victor extolled. That even in his dinner jacket he carried with him an aura of violence. That he was a hard man to love, but that she knew she loved him.

Rick had also taught her what love was, another kind of love: a carnal, physical, all-embracing love that made her cry out with desire and joy. With Victor she was one of a multitude; with Rick the multitude vanished and she was the only woman in the world.

'Which man do you love more?'

Wasn't it obvious? Ilsa threw herself into her mother's arms, sobbing on her breast. Inghild stroked her daughter's hair fondly and whispered to her in the same soothing tones she had used when Ilsa was a child.

'I love Victor, Mother. Whatever he and his work demand, I am ready to give, including myself. What greater love can a woman have?'

'And Rick?'

'I love Rick, too. He makes me feel like a woman. When we are together, his kisses overwhelm my senses, drive all other thoughts from my mind, make me want to be with him forever. What greater love can there be?'

Inghild clutched her daughter tightly. 'I haven't seen you in two years, and I can only begin to imagine what you have been going through. But I know my daughter. I know that she is strong and honest, and that she would never do anything but what was right. Besides, I think you have already made your choice.'

'I thought I had, too.' Ilsa raised her head, and with her free hand, Inghild brushed away her daughter's tears. 'Until Casablanca, when I saw Rick again. Rick was the one who got the letters of transit for me and Victor. He saved our lives.' She told Inghild the story of their three days in Morocco, of meeting Rick again, of his bitterness, of the renewal of their love, and of his sacrifice at the airport.

'You want me to tell you what you should do,' said Inghild, and Ilsa nodded. 'I won't.'

Ilsa's face fell. 'Why not, Mother?' she pleaded.

'Because I can't. This is your life, Ilsa, not mine. Whatever you decide, my blessing goes with you. All I can say is this: Look in your heart. The answer lies there.'

It did. To love Rick would be to betray both her marriage vows and the Resistance itself. Rick said he stuck his neck out for nobody. She would show him: she would stick her neck out for everybody – for Victor, for Europe. Even for Rick Blaine, whether he liked it or not.

CHAPTER SIX

New York, June 1931

Yitzik Baline, whom everybody called Rick, met Lois Horowitz on his way downtown to buy a knish for his mother. He met Solomon Horowitz on his way back uptown to deliver Lois to her father.

He was riding the Second Avenue el down from his mother's apartment on East 116th Street, having walked over to visit her from his dump up in Washington Heights. He liked walking around New York and didn't mind the hike. Besides, he didn't own a car. He couldn't afford a car. He didn't mind visiting his mother from time to time either, even if that meant having to sit in her dining room and listen to her *kvell* about his good looks and *yiddische kopf* and kvetch about his lack of a job.

Strictly speaking, she was incorrect, for he had a job – or, rather, he had several. It was just that none of them was either very respectable or very good. Most of his time was spent trying to figure out how a guy as smart as him could be so poor.

Some small-time crap games here, a little bootlegging there, even running a team of newspaper *shtarkers* in Harlem to make sure the vendors were selling Pulitzer's *World* and not Hearst's *Journal.* The *shtarkers* were a fixture of the newspaper business in those days. Their function was to encourage newsstand vendors to carry their paper instead of its rivals, and their means of persuasion were generally baseball bats and suspicious fires. He wasn't proud about this line of work, but it paid reasonably well – even after kicking back part of his money to the cops so they might continue to look the other way until they got a better offer – well enough to keep him from looking like a bum, even if he often felt like one.

What he really wanted to do was run a speakeasy. Everything about nightlife attracted him, starting with the hours; he was a night owl living in an early bird world. Although he didn't play an instrument, an ear for music ran in the family, as his mother never tired of reminding him. The clink of glasses, the sound of fresh liquor being poured from a bottle, the satisfying *whoosh* of a beer keg being tapped – these were his instruments.

And the money! At his age, other fellows who ran speaks were riding around town in Duesenbergs, with a doll on each arm. Him, he was lucky to scare up car fare. He wanted to blame it on the Depression but knew he couldn't. He couldn't blame it on anybody but himself.

His destination, Ruby's Appetizing and Delicatessen, sat on the corner of Hester and Allen Streets in their old neighborhood, handy to the local el stop. This was his weekly *mitzvah*, going downtown to buy his mother a knish when there were perfectly fine knishes up and down Second Avenue. Miriam insisted that the best knishes – and the best latkes and the best gefilte fish and the best everything – were still to be found on the Lower East Side.

He liked to think of himself as a tough guy, and here he was, riding the el to buy an old lady a knish.

The Lower East Side was where he spent most of his childhood. The 'old neighborhood,' the old folks called it, using the same tone – nostalgia mixed with audible relief at not having to live there anymore – that they used when they talked about the old country. Which, for the Balines, as for most of the other Jewish families in East Harlem, was Russia, the Ukraine, or Poland. Ninety thousand Jews lived in East Harlem and eighty thousand more in Harlem proper, which made the area north of Central Park the second-largest Jewish neighborhood in the country, after the old neighborhood.

New York had plenty of German Jews, the *Deutscher Yehudim*, but many of them were established, rapidly assimilating snobs who took one look at their embarrassingly unwashed brethren pouring in from Eastern Europe and promptly changed their names. Take that fancy pants August Belmont, the big *macher* at the Metropolitan Opera: he had been born Schönberg. Rick swore to himself that he would never change his name. 'Yitzik' to 'Rick,' maybe; but Baline he was born and Baline he would stay.

That was his mother's influence. His father might have had an influence, too, but Rick had never known his father; Morris Baline had died before Rick was born. Miriam wanted better for her boy, but she also wanted him to remember where he had come from. She kept up with the news in the Yiddish-language *Daily Vorwärts*, one of the city's biggest and most important newspapers, and she never lost the opportunity to remind him about the importance of social justice. Miriam was an expert on social justice, since, coming from the old country, she had experienced so little of it, and she had a sense of *noblesse oblige* that was positively Belmontian; if the Jews could not be a lamp unto the feet of the gentiles, then who could? If there was one thing she taught her son, she was proud to say, it was tolerance; for Miriam, tolerance was a cardinal virtue because if you were tolerant of others, they would surely be tolerant of you. It was a kind of insurance policy against pogroms, and that was why she was proud to be an American, living here in the *goldeneh medina*, even though she spoke almost no English, read not a word of it, and, at her age, didn't intend to start.

It was the el and its younger sibling, the subway, that had made it possible for the immigrants jammed into Manhattan's most crowded precincts to escape the Lower East Side. Miriam Baline worried about losing her fatherless boy to the streets, and the streets of the Lower East Side were worse than any – prime recruiting territory for some of the toughest gangs in the city. Like mothers all over New York, she prayed that her son would not fall into gangland's clutches, not take up with a group of like-minded youngsters who would rather knock over a pushcart peddler or rob a stuss game than put in an honest day's work, not gawk at the gangsters like Dopey Benny and Gyp the Blood in their fancy suits and their shiny shoes, with a girl on their arm, a gun in their pocket, and a look on their face that dared you to crack wise about it.

Like many mothers all over New York, though, Miriam had been doomed to disappointment. Her son was heading south, not north.

The long ride downtown gave him ample time for reflection on his depressing trajectory. He had been born, he decided, under an unlucky star. He was too young to have been able to fight in the Great War; too poor to have gone to anywhere except City College, where he had been an indifferent student and finally had dropped out; too disinterested in knowledge for its own sake to pay very close attention to his lessons; and too easily distracted by girls to do much of anything. He had no motivation and, aside from a growing fondness for the bottle, no interests. Except for the speed of the elevated train, he was going nowhere slowly. He needed a cause.

It was hot that summer, the way it was always hot in New York, only hotter. All the men wore suits and ties, and underneath them the sweat ran down their arms like tiny rivers. Rick often wondered whether it would puddle high enough in your shoes to splash onto the floor and embarrass you in front of the ladies. With everyone packed into the el, cheek to jowl with their equally sweaty neighbors at rush hour, it was never a pleasant ride, but it was cheap and a lot faster than walking. With luck, Rick could get downtown and back again in less than an hour with a cloth sack filled with goodies from old man Ruby's display cases.

On this particular afternoon, however, the el was nearly empty. As he looked down into the city, Rick thought the only New Yorkers who were not stoop sitting or fire escape napping or standing with their heads in the icebox were himself and the sole other occupant of the car, an exceptionally pretty young woman who was sitting across from him.

To say she was the most beautiful creature he had ever seen would be an understatement. Her hair was jet black, her skin translucent white. Her figure was only partly concealed by her clothing, and the part that wasn't concealed had had his full attention for several stops. Although her skirts were long, her ankles were revealed, and as any young man would, Rick had instantly done the sum, extrapolating from the width of her ankle to the precise angle of the curve of her calf, to the length of her thigh, and so on right up to the top of her head. Before he even got there, he knew he liked what he saw.

The girl, who appeared to be about eighteen, kept her hands folded in her lap, as she was probably taught by her mother, and her eyes on the floor, as no doubt she had already learned from experience. No matter how well brought up, however, any woman could succumb to the heat when it was hot enough or when she wanted to. Rick was hardly surprised when the young lady suddenly slumped to the floor with the daintiest of sighs: a puff of breath, and then she keeled over like one of the tugboats in the harbor that had just been holed below the waterline by a rock.

Rick's stop was coming right up, but he forgot all about it as he leaped to her assistance. The el rattled past another ten blocks or so of third-floor windows before she opened her eyes, which were the purest blue Rick Baline had ever seen. Slowly he helped her to her feet, but she was still a little woozy from the inhalation of so much of Manhattan's dubious air, so he sat her down again, this time beside him. 'Are you okay, miss?' he asked.

For a long moment she didn't answer. Then she turned her head to the right and looked him in the face. 'Thanks, mister,' she said. 'That sure was swell of you, helpin' me up like that.'

She had a shy, almost apologetic little smile that seemed out of place on such a gorgeous face. He was trying to think of something to say when she grasped him by the arm and tugged hard.

'We've missed it! We've missed it!' she said with agitation.

'Missed what?' asked Rick.

'My stop,' she said. 'It was for my father.' As if that explained everything.

'What is?' said Rick, mystified, not for the first time, by the female mind.

'The gefilte fish,' she said. 'At Ruby's.' She smiled. 'It's the best.'

Here he had thought she was an Irish girl from Morrisania. 'Don't worry,' he said soothingly. 'We'll go right back. The conductor's a personal friend of mine.'

That made her laugh. 'My name's Lois,' she said, extending her hand.

'Mine's Yitzik,' he said, 'but my friends call me Rick.' He gave her what he thought might be a flirtatious wink. 'You can call me Rick.'

'That's swell,' said Lois. 'Only my father says I'm not allowed to have boyfriends until he says so.'

They got off at the next stop and walked back to Ruby's. 'What do you do, Rick?' asked Lois.

'This and that,' he replied evasively.

'Oh, unemployed, huh?' said Lois, and his heart fell. He didn't want her to think he was the bum he thought he was. 'Nothing wrong with that. Lots of fellas are. Maybe you ought to come home with me and meet Daddy. He gives away jobs like they was candy.'

'Yeah, sure,' said Rick. In his mind's eye he envisioned a

wild-haired Einstein, like the teachers at City College, or a sweatshop drudge with a bullwhip and a chip on his shoulder. 'What's his name?'

'Solomon Horowitz,' she said. 'Ever heard of him?'

Rick stopped talking, and then he stopped walking. Heard of him? Solomon Horowitz, the Mad Russian. Solomon Horowitz, the rackets king of upper Manhattan and the Bronx. From the uptown numbers games in Harlem, Washington Heights, and Inwood to loan-sharking in Riverdale, from arson-for-hire in East Tremont, right down to a couple of neighborhood crap games in Marble Hill, Solly had the territory covered. Heard of him? Hell, Rick wanted to *be* him someday.

Lois brought him home to meet her parents and to deliver the gefilte fish, more or less in that order. Rick felt a stab of disappointment when she stopped in front of a new law tenement on 127th Street just west of Lenox Avenue and said, 'Well, here we are. The Horowitz family mansion!' She laughed derisively. 'You were expecting maybe the Vanderbilt estate?'

Some of the apartment houses on the West Side had names. This one didn't. The anonymous building was no better or worse than any of its neighbors, and it certainly put on no airs. There was a violin shop on the ground floor and four levels of flats above it. Next door was a kosher wine shop – still legal, despite Prohibition. Around the corner was a movie theater and a grocery store.

'It's nice,' said Rick. That was not entirely a lie; it was nicer than his place.

They stood on the sidewalk for a moment together, sharing the same thoughts. The daughter of Solomon Horowitz deserves better than this, thought Rick, surprised; the daughter of Solomon Horowitz is going to get better than this, thought Lois, determined.

They walked up two flights of stairs to the third floor. Rick later learned that Solomon Horowitz had an aversion to living either on a low floor, where someone unwelcome could climb through his window, or on the top floor, where someone equally unwelcome might descend from the roof. In business he liked to play things right down the middle, and that was the way he lived as well.

Lois rapped on a door near the head of the stairs. 'It's me!' she said. 'I'm home.'

Rick could sense that he was being observed from the peephole, just for a moment, and then the door was opened and Lois stepped across the threshold. 'This is Mr. Baline,' she said. 'I fainted on the el. He helped me up. Be nice to him.'

The next thing he knew he was face-to-face with Solomon Horowitz, the Beer Baron of the Bronx.

A short, stout man with the iron grip of a steelworker looked at him as if he were eyeballing a dray horse. Horowitz was about five feet five inches tall and must have weighed close to two hundred pounds, very little of it fat. He wore a rumpled blue serge suit, a white shirt unbuttoned at the collar, and a loud floral tie. His shoes were off, and as Rick couldn't help noticing, his socks had been darned once or twice. To look at him, you'd never know he was one of the most successful gangsters in New York.

'A man who does mine a good turn has done me a good turn,' he said. 'And him I reward. You married?'

'No.'

'Like music?'

'If it's good.'

'Drink?'

'As much as the next guy.'

'You a lush?'

'Not yet.'

'Got a head for business?'

'Depends on what it is.'

'Can you handle yourself in a fight?'

'Sure.'

'Ever use a gun?'

'No, but I'm willing to learn.'

'Are you a coward or a *fegeleh*?'

'No.'

'You want to *shtup* my daughter?'

'*Daddy!*' cried Lois.

Rick looked at her. Her eyes told him not to, so he looked back at Mr. Horowitz. 'No,' he lied.

'Good; that you can forget about. I'm reserving her for a rich *shaygets*.' Horowitz resumed his interrogation: 'What's your father do?'

'Never met the man.'

'Dead?'

'That's what they tell me.'

'Mother?'

'Only one.'

'You afraid of anything besides her?'

'Just being a loser.'

'You get along with the *shvartzers*?'

'Well enough,' he said.

'You looking for a job?'

'You could talk me into it,' said Rick.

'Nightclub work okay?'

'You bet.'

Solomon Horowitz looked Yitzik Baline up, down, and sideways.

'The cut of this one's jib I like,' he finally announced. 'Unemployed I can always use. See me tomorrow, this address.' With that he began to close the door in Rick's face.

From behind her father's back, Lois blew him a kiss. 'Good night, Ricky,' she said. 'See you again someday.'

As he waved good-bye to her, he realized that he had forgotten all about his mother's knish. Right then and there, he knew he was in love.

CHAPTER SEVEN

New York, July 1931

The milk trucks came over the rise in Bedford Hills at dawn, just as Tick-Tock had said they would.

'Here you go, kid,' Solly said to Rick, handing him the revolver. It was a blue steel Smith & Wesson .38, primed and ready, with all six chambers loaded, and the way the daylight glinted off it, you could practically shave with it.

Rick nodded confidently. 'Thanks, Solly,' he said. This was his first armed action, and he was ready for it.

It was six-fifteen on the morning of July 4, 1931, and already it was hot and humid and stifling. The milk trucks belonged to Dion O'Hanlon, except they weren't carrying milk. They were carrying whiskey down from Canada to a thirsty midtown Manhattan. It was Solly's intention to make sure thirsts were quenched uptown and in the Bronx first.

This part of Westchester was supposed to be their cordon sanitaire, a place they could drive through without fear of molestation or hijacking. That's what O'Hanlon paid his protection money to the Westchester cops for, and that's what he expected to get in return. The boys driving his trucks had gotten lazy, though. Today, they were as unwary as the romping schoolkids at P.S. 31 in the Bronx. Today, O'Hanlon's money was no good here. Solomon Horowitz had outbid him. He felt it was his patriotic duty.

Not to mention he'd had to. He needed the liquor for his clubs, and O'Hanlon had recently euchred him out of a sweet deal up in Montreal that Horowitz had thought he'd locked up.

'*Zei gesunt*, Ricky,' said Solly. 'Remember, never pull your piece unless you plan to shoot somebody. Never shoot unless you plan to hit somebody. Otherwise maybe they get mad and hit you back.'

Rick watched the boss move away briskly. For a stout man, Solly was a nimble fellow.

Rick began to take aim as the first truck cab came into his sights. Tick-Tock Schapiro, Solly's right-hand man and his third cousin, in that order, slapped his hand down hard. 'Watch it, punk,' he growled. 'You might hurt somebody with that thing.'

Tick-Tock got no quarrel from Rick. Schapiro was six feet four if he was an inch, and every inch of him was mean. His given name was Emmanuel, but nobody ever used it. He had acquired his nickname when he was thirteen: the ticking of the grandfather clock in the tiny hallway of the Schapiro family apartment on Little Water Street was driving him nuts, so he went out and acquired his first piece from a Five Pointer over on Anthony Street, brought it home just as pleased as punch, and shot the bejesus out of the clock's face, taking special pleasure in watching the glass front shatter, the hands of the clock spin off, and the inner mechanism explode into a thousand pieces that no Swiss clockmaker could ever put back together again.

When his *oma* complained about what he had done to her clock, which she had brought over from Germany, he threw her down a flight of stairs. Tick-Tock told the cops she'd slipped. His mother, who'd seen the whole thing, gave them the same story. Tick-Tock had that effect on people.

Tick-Tock was also Solomon Horowitz's most valuable asset in his newly escalating battle with O'Hanlon. Schapiro was big, but he wasn't dumb, and he had developed the best inside information on the Irishman's booze shipments. How he did it was anybody's guess. Tick-Tock didn't talk much.

'Lemme show ya,' he said. Coolly Tick-Tock aimed his pistol at the lead truck and shot out the front tires. The vehicle swerved precipitously as its wheels were transformed into a shower of rubber shards. Schapiro was a hell of a shot, as even Kinsella, the driver of this particular truck, would have had to admit. But with no control over his truck he was helpless as it swerved off the road, grazed a tree, and rolled onto its side. Sweat, cordite, and burning rubber mingled in the air like some obscene perfume that wouldn't be offered for sale at the big new Bloomingdale's store on 59th Street any time soon.

That's why the gang carried fire extinguishers. Pinky Tannenbaum, Abie Cohen, and Laz Lowenstein sprinted toward the burning truck, spraying gunfire and foam more or less simultaneously. Meanwhile the rest of the boys enfiladed the convoy, riddling the cabs of the other three trucks like they were the metal turkeys at Luna Park, the ones you could pop to impress your girl, win a stuffed animal, and maybe get lucky, too.

In the teeth of the ambush, the Irishers jumped out of their trucks like Aran fishermen abandoning their curraghs in a storm. They fired as they dropped from steering wheels and shotgun positions, blasting back as they scuttled for safety, but they didn't have a chance. Horowitz's men were tough and disciplined, like their leader, and they wasted no lead. In less than a minute the battle of Bedford Hills was over, as even the dimmest of O'Hanlon's gangsters realized it was not worth dying to save a few thousand gallons of Canadian Club. They threw their pieces to the ground in surrender.

Tick-Tock wanted to shoot them all where they stood, but Solly refused. 'We're bootleggers, not red Indians,' he said. 'We take no scalps.' He turned to O'Hanlon's men, waving his pistol in the air and yelling, 'Get outta here, you sons of bitches bastards.'

O'Hanlon's boys didn't need to be told twice. They turned and ran. How they would get back to New York was their problem.

Although he knew O'Hanlon wouldn't see it like this, the way Solly Horowitz had things figured, this booze was his. He used to have a straight pipeline from the Michaelson family's distilleries in Quebec; he'd been doing business with them for years, ever since Congress had handed him a gift called the Volstead Act. Lately, though, O'Hanlon was bending, if not outright breaking, their understanding about who got what and from which suppliers, and he'd been chiseling him with Michaelson, bidding up the price and increasing the volume. That was no way to do business, unless Dion was trying to put Solly out of business.

Ordinarily the road through Bedford Hills was an O'Hanlon highway, while Solly generally brought his booze down the other side of the Hudson, through the Catskills via Newburgh and the river. In Solly's opinion he was only getting back what should have been his in the first place. Solomon Horowitz did not appreciate another man's taking what belonged to him.

O'Hanlon would be furious, Solly knew, but that was tough. He wasn't about to start letting himself get muscled by the Irishman and his new allies, Salucci and Weinberg. Why, Solomon Horowitz had been running gangs in New York when that little *pisher* Irving Weinberg was still wetting his short pants. And if the day ever came that a fresh-off-the-boat wop like Salucci could start pushing him around with impunity . . . well, that day would never come.

This would get their attention.

Horowitz strolled over to the now abandoned caravan. Rick was about to holster his gat when, out of the corner of his eye, he caught an arm, a hand, a finger, a trigger, all moving. Without thinking he knocked Solly to his knees and came up firing.

He'd raised his gun just as O'Hanlon's man had raised his. Rick was faster. His .38-caliber bullet slammed into the man's wrist and shattered it on the spot. He'd fired reflexively, just the way Solly had taught him in all those hours of practice in the Harlem backyards. Yitzik Baline was a natural with a heater.

Solly turned to look at Rick admiringly. 'Nice shooting,' he said. If his close brush with death bothered him, he wouldn't let it show. Solomon Horowitz never let anybody see him sweat.

'Yeah, Lois is gonna be real proud of you, hero,' sneered Tick-Tock, who had come back from the fray mad because he hadn't gotten to kill anybody. He walked over to the wounded man and shot him in the head. There: he felt much better now. 'You know,' he said, turning his attention back to Rick, 'I think she's kind of sweet on you.'

Solly didn't answer but instead glowered at his cousin. As far as Lois Horowitz was concerned, her father had big plans for her, and they didn't include any of the mugs and yeggs in the gang. In his presence, you didn't joke about Lois's being sweet on anybody. In fact, you didn't even mention her. Not if you wanted to live a long, prosperous, and healthy life. That went for everybody, and that went for Tick-Tock double, because after all, Tick-Tock was family. Sort of.

CHAPTER EIGHT

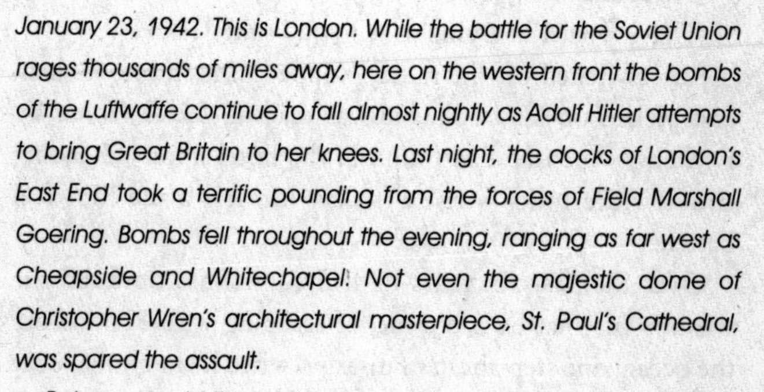

January 23, 1942. This is London. While the battle for the Soviet Union rages thousands of miles away, here on the western front the bombs of the Luftwaffe continue to fall almost nightly as Adolf Hitler attempts to bring Great Britain to her knees. Last night, the docks of London's East End took a terrific pounding from the forces of Field Marshall Goering. Bombs fell throughout the evening, ranging as far west as Cheapside and Whitechapel. Not even the majestic dome of Christopher Wren's architectural masterpiece, St. Paul's Cathedral, was spared the assault.

But even amid the rubble, there yet springs hope. For London is home to every anti-Nazi resistance movement in Europe, and their numbers are growing daily. Led by the exiled general Charles De Gaulle, the Free French are waging a fierce rearguard campaign against the Germans across North Africa and in the Middle East, striking first, unsuccessfully, at Dakar and then in Syria. The Norwegian government-in-exile is also here, working day and night to overthrow Vidkun Quisling's collaborationist government. Czech partisans are now calling the city home as well. Having seen their country first partitioned by the German annexation of the Sudetenland in 1938, and then destroyed by the establishment of the Protectorate of Bohemia and Moravia in 1939, they have sworn to overthrow both the Protectorate and the Nazi satellite state of Slovakia.

'Let the puppetmasters in Berlin be advised,' exiled President Eduard Beneš has declared. 'We shall not rest until our beloved Czech homeland is fully restored.'

'Shut it off, Sam.'

'Don't you want to hear the news?' asked Sam.

'Not unless it's good,' said Rick.

'There ain't no good news these days,' Sam objected.

'That's what I'm trying to tell you,' said Rick.

Sam switched off the radio, plopped himself into a chair, and picked up his book. He was reading *Bleak House* by Dickens, which he had found in the hotel library. Reading about white folks worse off than himself made him feel better.

Over the past six years he had sometimes doubted the wisdom of what he had done, of escaping with Rick across the ocean, one step ahead of disaster, when he might have sat the whole mess out in New York and waited for the smoke to clear; there was always a market in Manhattan for a good singing pianist . . . not to mention a first-class driver. How he longed for his favorite lake in the Catskills or, if he allowed his mind to drift back that far, his boyhood in the Missouri Ozarks, where the fish were always jumping, or his young manhood in New Orleans, where Lake Pontchartrain always beckoned.

Then he remembered Paris and all those French girls with

their small bosoms and their big noses, and their insatiable curiosity about all things *nègres*, and that was the end of that particular reverie. Who was to say that if he had stayed in New York he wouldn't have ended up like Horowitz and Meredith and the rest of them? All things considered, he hadn't made out so bad. Except that he didn't care for London very much. The buildings were monochrome, the skies were slate gray, and there was hardly a black face in sight. He went back to his book.

Rick, too, relaxed in reverie. With the money from the sale of the café to Ferrari, he had taken a suite of rooms at Brown's Hotel. Rick was posing as a theatrical agent, part of the fiction being that Sam was his manservant. The funds would not last indefinitely, but they would last long enough, or so Rick hoped, for them to find Victor and Ilsa. More than a month had already passed, however; despite their best efforts, neither Rick nor Renault had succeeded in locating Victor Laszlo.

What if Laszlo had played him for a fool? He'd like to think he'd learned a few lessons in treachery over the years, but it wouldn't be the first time he'd been had. What if Laszlo knew that Rick would be able to resist neither his appeals to Rick's patriotism nor his love for Ilsa and so had conned him out of the exit visas? Laszlo was just pigheaded enough to think he could take on the entire Third Reich all by himself.

What if that note in Lisbon had been meant to throw him off the scent, written by Ilsa under duress from her husband, who suspected that Rick's magnanimity was not entirely altruistic, and who had gone to New York – where Rick could not follow? What if the Laszlos weren't really in London at all? What if they really had gone to America?

Then that was that; he couldn't go back, unless he wanted a one-way ticket to Old Sparky at Sing Sing. But where could he go? He was beginning to run out of places.

'How long we gonna stay here, boss?' interjected Sam, reading his thoughts, as usual.

'Until we find Victor Laszlo.'

'*If* we find Mr. Laszlo,' corrected Sam.

'We will,' Rick answered, smoking a cigarette and looking down onto Dover Street. 'We have to.'

'If you say so,' said Sam. 'This sure ain't like Paris. Or New York. I mean, a fella can't hardly get something decent to eat.'

Rick turned to look at his friend. 'You know those are two places I told you not to talk about,' he growled.

'Aw shucks, boss, you can't go holdin' on to the bad memories forever. What's done is done: you can't change what happened back home.' Sam bit his lower lip. 'Anyway, it wasn't your fault, how things turned out.'

'Of course it was my fault,' snapped Rick. 'Who else's could it be?'

Sam was getting as agitated as Rick. 'If that's the way you want to be about it, fine,' he said. 'If you want to drag this thing around with you for the rest of your life, you go right ahead. But as for me, every time I bite into one of those awful steak-and-kidney pies, I'm gonna remember me the leg of lamb at the Tootsie-Wootsie –'

'Shut up, will you?'

'– and the steak *frites* at La Belle Aurore, and—'

'I said shut up!' A knock at the door interrupted the argument. 'Get that, will you?'

Sam padded over to the door and opened it.

'Hello, Sam,' said the visitor, entering. It was Renault. 'Ah, Ricky, still living the life of a man of leisure, I see.' The dapper little Frenchman had traded in his Vichy uniform for a Savile Row suit, atop which he wore an elegant homburg. He looked like a minor diplomat, which was how he was happy to pass himself off, especially to the English ladies. 'Whereas I have been working hard, procuring useful information.'

'The day will never come when you have to work hard for a living, Louie,' said Rick. 'Not without a fight.'

'Work is in the eye of the beholder,' Renault responded. 'Should I choose not to behold it, that is entirely my business.' With a flourish he produced a silver cigarette case and flipped it open. 'A gift from one of my new admirers.'

'What exactly was she admiring?'

Renault puffed out his chest. 'Resourcefulness is the hallmark of the true gentleman,' he said.

'I'll bet.' Rick took one of the offered cigarettes. 'What gives?'

Renault lit up, took a puff, and collected his thoughts. He smoked like a bird pecking for worms, darting at the cigarette rather than embracing it, whereas Rick preferred long, slow drags. Sam didn't smoke at all. It was another of the white man's vices he had learned to live without.

'Well, among other things, I think I may have found a way to discover the whereabouts of our friend Victor Laszlo – and, of course, of your friend Miss Lund as well.' Renault paused to savor the effect of this particular bit of intelligence on his listeners.

Rick, however, only nodded, a barely perceptible tilt of his head. 'Go on,' he said.

Renault smiled. 'Not even Victor Laszlo, whose consideration of the comfort and feelings of his fellow man is second only to his way with the fair sex, can expect us to wait here forever. Furthermore, my sense of duty as a Frenchman and a patriot has compelled me to contact De Gaulle's headquarters and offer my services in the struggle against Hitler.'

That had been part of their plan all along.

'It's about time,' said Rick.

Renault relaxed into a chair. One of the qualities he found most lacking in the Americans was a sense of style, of presentation, of savoir-faire. He made a little noise in his throat by way of preamble. 'Seriously, Ricky, it seems that a gentleman answering the description of Monsieur Laszlo has recently been sighted by one or two of my, er, new colleagues coming and going in the district of South Kensington.'

That got Rick's attention. 'You got an address?'

'Not yet,' Renault lied. He wasn't quite sure why he lied. Maybe it was just out of habit. Maybe he wanted to check the place out first, to make sure he had the right information. Another day or two wouldn't hurt.

'Well, get one, pronto,' said Rick. 'By the way, just who are these new "colleagues" of yours?'

'Now, Ricky, we ought to be able to have a few little secrets from each other.' Nervously Louis snapped another cigarette out of the case and lit it. 'Our countries may be allies, but that doesn't mean we have to share every bit of intelligence. Give me some time.'

'What do you mean, "our" countries? You know I haven't got a country, and probably never will.' Rick looked at Sam, who shrugged wordlessly. 'And as for you, the last time I looked, France was cut in two like a day-old baguette. Half of it is being run directly from Berlin, and the other half only pretends not to be. In other words,' he concluded, 'neither of us has a country, at least until we get the Germans out of Paris.'

'*Vive la France*,' said Renault.

'Get on with it. Time is one thing we don't have.'

'This is the way things seem to stand,' began Renault, wondering how much of the story to tell. It was not a question of lying, exactly, but rather of editing judiciously and hoping the excised bits didn't come back to haunt him. 'It should come as no surprise to you that the *Résistance* does not entirely trust the British. Part of that distrust is habitual, of course, but part of it has to do with our different war aims. For Britain, victory will have been achieved by defeating Hitler. What happens to France makes no difference to the English. Indeed, we suspect the restoration of *la gloire de la France* to be very low on Mr. Churchill's agenda.'

'You're probably right about that,' agreed Rick.

Renault nodded appreciatively. '*Monsieur le General*, though, sees things a bit differently,' he continued. 'For him the restoration of French honor and French glory is paramount. When Germany is defeated, France must and shall be the strongest Continental power. No other outcome would be acceptable.'

'It's no skin off my nose,' said Rick. 'In fact, Sam and I were just reminiscing about Paris in the good old days before you walked in, weren't we, Sam?'

'If that's what you call it,' said Sam.

'So what's the problem?' Rick asked.

'The problem,' replied Renault, 'is that any operations being run under the auspices of British Intelligence in central Europe are very much in the French interest as well. Which is why agents of the *Résistance* have been shadowing all known MI-six operatives in London.'

Rick laughed. 'In other words, your side is spying on the very men who are trying to boot the Germans off the Champs-Élysées and back to Unter den Linden.'

'You could put it that way,' Renault admitted.

'Sounds like the old days in New York,' muttered Sam.

'What do you Frenchies say, Louie: *plus ça change?*'

'Ricky, I'm disappointed in you,' said Renault. 'After all your time in France and in Casablanca, your French accent leaves much to be desired.'

'*Merci*, I'm sure,' said Rick.

Despite the banter, Renault began to fidget. Divided loyalties were certainly something to which he was no stranger, but he preferred his loyalties to be truly divided and not bumping up against each other like this. 'My, look at the time,' he exclaimed, rising. 'I'm afraid I've been indiscreet enough to have made a small assignation for this afternoon. The Savoy, for tea.'

Rick smiled, more a grimace than an expression of pleasure. 'And scones, no doubt.'

'If they should present themselves,' Renault replied with a slight leer. 'One never knows.'

'More information, Louie. We need more information,' said Rick as he walked away.

Outside on the street, Renault hailed a taxi and reflected on events. His friend was showing an alarming tendency toward moral scruples in the aftermath of his reunion with Ilsa Lund in Casablanca. But women made men do strange things, and besides, nobody was perfect.

He was making progress, however. Although some members of the Resistance understandably were skeptical of his recent conversion to the cause of liberation, his complicity in the death of Major Strasser and his dramatic exit from Casablanca had convinced them of his bona fides. You couldn't get much better than murdering a Gestapo officer and destroying a car full of his henchmen, and while Renault could not truthfully be said to have done either, the mere association with the deed was enough.

News of Victor Laszlo's arrival in London had not escaped the Resistance, and when they discovered that Renault had known Laszlo in Casablanca – indeed, had helped the freedom fighter escape – a mission had presented itself.

'Monsieur Renault, you are more than welcome to join us,' the Underground leader, who went by the *nom de guerre* of Raoul, had said. 'With your knowledge of the activities of the Vichy criminals in North Africa, you have already brought us valuable information. You will no doubt be pleased to know that several of the traitors have already paid with their lives; our reach is long, and our vengeance is terrible.'

Raoul sucked deeply on an expiring Gauloises. He wore his hair long, in the fashion of Rive Gauche intellectuals, and Renault could easily picture him sitting in Le Procope, chain-smoking and arguing with Jean-Paul Sartre. Then he remembered that Raoul was an expert shot and a master bomb maker; he doubted if the same could be said of Sartre.

'Victor Laszlo is a mystery to us,' said Raoul. 'We know of him and his work, of course. Laszlo's treatment at the hands of the Germans in Mauthausen, and his daring escape, have made him even more admired – and more feared by the Nazis. It is imperative that we make contact with him before the Germans find him.'

'For his sake or for ours?' asked Renault.

'What do you think?' Raoul replied. 'There are rumors that the Czechs, with the active cooperation of British Intelligence, are planning a major operation – a spectacular act of terrorism or sabotage or murder that will make the world sit up and take notice of them. Of course, such a *coup de théâtre* would have the most serious repercussions for all the Underground movements.' He stopped long enough to catch his breath. 'The problem is, we don't know what it is.'

With a sweeping, violent gesture, he struck a match against the wall. It burst into flame, and he lit up. 'Naturally, we wish our brothers in the conflict against Hitler well. But there must be limits even to a concept as dear to French hearts as *fraternité*.'

Raoul began to pace around the room, which was the second floor of a Victorian-era warehouse down by the docks. Night after night the area was being heavily bombed by the Luftwaffe, but Raoul hardly seemed to notice, much less care.

'What do you mean?' asked Renault.

Raoul snorted. 'The world is a compassionate place, but even compassion has limits. One beggar draws the empathy of the people; a dozen beggars inspire only revulsion and contempt. In Europe today we have more than our share of beggars – each of the countries conquered and occupied by the Germans. Who knows, soon the Soviet Union and perhaps even England will join their ranks.' From his demeanor, Raoul did not appear to think that England under the Nazi boot would be especially tragic.

'But there can be only one Underground in Europe. Only one movement upon which all free eyes and ears are fixed. One movement toward which the sympathy of the world naturally flows. And that one must and shall be French. *Vive la Résistance!*'

'*Vive la Résistance!*' echoed Renault.

Raoul stopped long enough to take a sip from a small glass of Bordeaux. 'Thus it is imperative that we find out what the Czechs are planning. It may be that what they are considering will not affect us in the slightest. On the other hand, it may be something that could seriously compromise operations of our own.'

'I thought we had a common enemy,' Renault objected.

'A common enemy, yes,' said Raoul. 'But not common goals. The shape of Europe after Hitler is something that concerns all of us – but not all of us see it in exactly the same way.' Raoul stubbed out his Gauloises and immediately lit another. 'What may happen to Poland or Czechoslovakia or even England is of no concern to us. The important thing is to ensure the future of France. I need not remind you that the needs and the glory of France come before all others, *n'est-ce pas?*'

'Of course,' Renault agreed.

'Very well, then,' said Raoul. 'You have your task. Find out about this Laszlo. What is he up to? What are the Czechs planning? If you know the man as well as you claim, this should not present a problem. We would even expect you to be able to infiltrate the operation to a certain extent. Such information, of course, would be invaluable, and your services would be greatly rewarded by France in the person of the General himself.'

Abruptly Raoul embraced Renault and kissed him twice on both cheeks. Then he stepped back and stared at him. 'On the other hand, if you should fail in this task, it would say to us that your profession of faith in the mission of the General is a fraud, and that perhaps you are in fact still an agent of Vichy, sent to penetrate us.' Raoul's eyes were little black lumps of cold, hard coal. 'And in that event, your usefulness to our cause would perforce be at an end. Do I make myself clear?'

Renault swallowed hard. 'Perfectly,' he said.

'Good,' said Raoul. 'Here is the number of the house in South Kensington where a man answering Victor Laszlo's description was sighted yesterday.' He wrote it on a piece of paper and handed it to Renault.

'Or perhaps I should say a woman answering Mlle. Lund's description. It seems our man was far more taken with the lady.'

'I would expect nothing less from a Frenchman,' said Renault.

'Unless that Frenchman's penchant for women supersedes his duty to his country.' With that, Raoul dismissed him.

Louis Renault intended to learn exactly where Victor Laszlo was, and what he was planning, as soon as possible. Renault had always believed that staying alive ought to be one's first priority, so that one might enjoy life's second and third priorities. For the moment, it seemed that, like Raoul, he had his priorities backward.

'Where did you say that was again, gov'nor?' asked the driver.

'Number Forty-two Clareville Street,' said Renault.

CHAPTER NINE

For a long time after Renault left, Rick remained sunk in his chair and deep in thought.

'What's the matter, boss?' asked Sam, as if he didn't know. He'd seen these reveries before. 'I thought you didn't like thinkin' about old times.'

'Sometimes the old times think about you,' said Rick. He started to pick up the newspaper, then remembered that for some strange reason, the British newspapers resolutely refused to cover baseball.

He longed for something to do, some activity that would help bring him closer to his goal of finding Ilsa. This inactivity was driving him crazy. He plucked her note from his pocket and read it for the thousandth time: 'To London.' 'British Intelligence.' '*Der Henker(?).*' 'Danger.' 'Prague.' 'Come quickly.'

He had spent the last month puzzling over it. The London part he understood well enough; here they were. 'British Intelligence' was self-evident, as were 'Danger' and 'Come quickly.' But who was *der Henker*? The word, he knew, meant 'executioner,' but what else? And what did Prague have to do with anything? Although, as he well knew, Victor Laszlo was Czech. . . .

'Sam,' he said, 'who's *der Henker*?'

'You got me, boss.'

Rick was disappointed. He had relied on Sam for so long that he was caught up short whenever Sam didn't know something. He expected Sam to know everything.

He rose from his chair. Passivity had always galled him. A walk around London, even a London still reeling from the almost nightly bombing runs of the Luftwaffe, was better than sitting here. It would be safe enough: thanks to the pioneering British work with radar, the Germans flew only at night.

'Where we goin'?' asked Sam, pulling on his coat.

'Someplace I haven't been in years,' replied Rick. 'The library.'

They taxied across London – down Dover Street to Piccadilly, across Piccadilly Circus to Leicester Square, up Charing Cross Road and into Great Russell Street – dodging the debris of the latest bombing. Although the Germans' main target was the East End docks, the heart of the English shipping industry, their bombers were either too inexperienced or too scared to drop their payloads with any particular accuracy. The witheringly accurate British anti-aircraft fire, as well as the bravery and professionalism of the Royal Air Force pilots, inflicted such heavy losses on the Nazi bombers that the German boys were only too happy to sight London, release their bombs, and get the hell out of there as fast as they could.

As they passed through Leicester Square, Rick and Sam observed that London's pleasure district was undaunted; the dance halls were full and the cinemas were running. Rick noticed that the Astor was playing *High Sierra*. 'STARRING HUMPHREY BOGART AND IDA LUPINO. DIRECTED BY RAOUL WALSH,' proclaimed the marquee. Rick could take or leave the movies. He much preferred the theater, especially musicals.

The British Museum and British Library squatted astride Russell Square. 'You ever been to a museum, Sam?' Rick asked as they climbed the stairs.

'No, sir,' replied Sam. 'Never had no time. Wanted to, but something always got in the way.'

'Bergman's pool hall?' said Rick. Bergman's was a Harlem institution, where Rick himself had hustled some change in the old days.

'No, sir,' Sam corrected. 'Bergman's was in the white part of town then. Or did you forget?'

'Try not to remind me,' said Rick, pulling open the huge door.

Their footfalls echoed across the marble as they walked. Rick walked boldly up to a uniformed guard.

'Anybody speak foreign languages around here?' he inquired.

The guard didn't miss a beat. 'I'm quite sure many people do, sir,' he answered.

'Yeah, well then, name one,' said Rick. At times like this his lack of formal education embarrassed him.

'Mr. Robbins would be your man, sir,' said the guard. 'Shall I ring him for you?'

'That would be nice,' said Rick.

Five minutes later Rick and Sam were being ushered into

the cramped offices of Jonathan Robbins, assistant curator of ancient languages.

'Mr. Blaine,' said Robbins, pumping Rick's hand enthusiastically. 'What can I do for you?'

'I've got a question for you,' said Rick. 'How many languages do you speak?'

'How many would you like?' answered Robbins with gusto. The only time the British ever seemed to show any emotion, thought Rick, was when they were dealing with total strangers about something absolutely impersonal and irrelevant. 'I'm fluent in ancient Egyptian, ancient Greek, Sumerian, Sanskrit, and Akkadian. I'm still working on Etruscan, though.' He chuckled. 'Aren't we all?'

'Terrific,' said Rick. Somehow he was willing to bet Robbins's linguistic proficiency did not include Yiddish. 'Does this mean anything to you?' He thrust a piece of paper at Robbins, on which he had written the word 'Henker.'

Robbins glanced at it. 'How rude of me,' he remarked. 'Won't you both please sit down? I'm sorry this office is so cramped, but, money, you know . . .'

'Money I know,' agreed Rick. 'How much will I owe you?'

Robbins laughed. 'Oh, there's no bother about that,' he assured Rick. 'We are a public trust here, the national library of Great Britain, an institution devoted to the good of all. I'll give you the answer to your question for free.' He took a breath. '*Der Henker*, masculine, means "the hangman" in German. Or "executioner." Someone whose acquaintance one fondly hopes never to make.'

'I know that,' said Rick. 'But who might it refer to?'

Robbins shook his head. 'Can't think of anybody in particular,' he said. His mind raced back through the centuries.

Old German was not exactly his field, but he prided himself on being able to stand in with all but the best scholars in any discussion of Anglo-Norman poetry of the twelfth century. 'No,' he said after a time. 'I've mentally run down everyone from Charlemagne to Bismarck and can't come up with a thing. Sorry.'

Rick was ready to go, but Sam held him back. 'I think what Mr. Rick means is anything more or less today.'

Robbins seemed astonished by the very idea of contemporaneousness. 'You mean in our own time?'

'That's exactly what I mean,' said Rick.

'You mean besides Reinhard Heydrich?' Robbins asked.

'Reinhard *who*?' asked Rick.

'Heydrich. The new Protector of Bohemia and Moravia. They call him *der Henker*.'

That must be it! Rick tried to contain his excitement. 'Where can I find out more about this guy?' he asked.

Robbins seemed surprised. 'Why, right here, Mr. Blaine,' he replied. 'We are, after all, a library.'

'Point me,' said Rick, rising.

Robbins gave them his card, on the back of which he had scribbled some instructions. 'Just show this to the librarian,' he told Rick. 'He'll help you.' On the back of the card, Rick noted, Robbins had written the words 'Reinhard Heydrich – recent cuttings.'

In the reading room, Rick duly handed Robbins's card to a librarian named Fullerton, a fastidious, even prissy, man in a houndstooth jacket. Fullerton studied it for a moment, as if it were a scientific specimen from another part of the museum. 'Follow me, please. Oh, and ask your man to wait outside. The reading room is for those doing research only.'

Rick was about to say something when Sam put a hand on his arm. 'I'll be downstairs, boss,' he said. 'Maybe I can find a good book somewhere.'

Fullerton led Rick into a private chamber and left him there. Ten minutes later he was back with a pile of newspaper clippings. Rick picked up the first one, which was also the most recent.

HEYDRICH ANNOUNCES LIMITED RATIONING IN BOHEMIA, read the headline in *The Times*.

The gist of it was that Reinhard Tristan Eugen Heydrich, the recently appointed Protector of Bohemia and Moravia, had issued a series of new regulations regarding ration cards for food and clothing on a productivity basis. Work or starve: it was a typically German idea. The Czech people were responding; after an initial period of resistance, which Heydrich had put down brutally, they had grudgingly come to a truce with their Nazi overlords. Writing from London, the *Times* correspondent was of the opinion that the Czech resistance to Hitler was waning and that the order imposed by the Germans was, in the eyes of many Czechs, preferable to the relative anarchy they had experienced in their brief experiment with democracy under Masaryk and Beneš. For that they had to thank *der Henker*: Reinhard Heydrich, the Hangman of Prague.

Rick hated him already.

The story also contained a reference to a conference convened by Heydrich at a villa in Wannsee, a lakeside suburb of Berlin, on January 20. The reports were sketchy:

> While the full import of the conference at Wannsee, which was attended by a number of top Nazis including Heinrich

Himmler, remains unclear, Whitehall sources report that the so-called Jewish problem was in fact the principal topic of discussion, and that the German government plan to take further measures against the Jews of Germany and occupied Europe beyond the existing Nuremberg Laws.

The Secretary for War, Mr. Spencer, declined to comment on the conference, but issued a stern warning: 'His Majesty's government are second to none in our loathing for Herr Hitler,' he said. 'Nevertheless, we hope and expect the German government to act responsibly in the matter of its treatment of the civilian and non-combatant population. We need not remind them that the whole world is watching.'

A fat lot of good that will do, thought Rick. In his limited experience, the Nazis were not about to let a little thing like world opinion stop them from doing whatever they wished to do.

That was, he realized, the mistake Major Strasser had made with Laszlo: he had let Renault's opinion prevent him from doing what he should have done right away. A real Nazi would have shot Victor Laszlo on the spot, the minute he walked into Rick's café with Ilsa on his arm. Hadn't Strasser just seen what happened to Ugarte? The little man who had murdered the two German couriers and stolen the precious letters of transit had been arrested right there in the Café Americain on Renault's orders, taken outside, and shot. Why, his friend Louie was more ruthless than Strasser. The major had been, of all things, too much the gentleman. A real gangster never let his enemies walk away.

Rick read on. He learned that Heydrich had helped set up the series of concentration camps across Germany, Austria, and occupied Eastern Europe in which Hitler was imprisoning and often murdering his enemies – a list that seemed to be growing daily. He was surprised to learn that like many of the top Nazis, including Hitler, Heydrich feared he might be part Jewish. That his father, the founder of the Halle Conservatory of Music, might have been named Süss, which could have been a Jewish name – or at least the Nazi hierarchy saw it that way. That Heydrich, hoping to rise high in the party, had his grandmother's name chipped off her tombstone because it was Sarah.

He also learned that Heydrich had been trained as a violinist as a young man and then joined the army, from which he had been cashiered for an affair with a teenage girl. Today, Heydrich was the head of something called the *Reichsicherheitshauptant*, a typical ten-dollar German word that meant the Nazi Party's security service. In other words, the goon squad. Rick knew something about goon squads.

There was even a picture of him. He was an impressive specimen of German manhood: tall, lean, rangy. He had a thin face with a touch of the hawk about the features – a predator for sure. His nose was patrician, his eyes clear and cold, his hair sandy. His hands were large, with wide palms and long fingers that tapered to a set of elegant nails. His uniform was pressed, his shirt collar immaculate, his shoes spit-polished. Rick knew that face. He had seen it before, on another man, back home in New York: not so tall, perhaps, but just as elegant and just as lethal.

Heydrich was also a thug and slugger who had clawed his way to power the way sluggers always did, by braining people. He was smart and he was nasty, and some said Hitler was grooming Heydrich as his successor. If and until that day ever came to pass, he was in charge of Bohemia and Moravia, the Nazis' term for what was left of Czechoslovakia after they had gotten finished dismembering the place. Heydrich had made his presence felt by a months-long campaign of brutality against the Czechs that earned him the sobriquet *der Henker*, or the Hangman, as he pacified the populace. It had worked: in fine weather Heydrich could ride through the streets of Prague in an open convertible with absolute impunity. That was either supreme confidence or supreme stupidity.

The pieces were beginning to fall into place. Ilsa's question mark after *Henker* in her note probably meant she hadn't heard the word clearly or didn't understand the reference.

But there he was: the Hangman of Prague. The man who – indirectly, at least – had sent Victor Laszlo to a concentration camp and would be delighted to see him back in one again. Could he be the target of a daring and very dangerous British and Czech operation – an operation headed by Victor Laszlo? If there was ever a candidate for assassination, Heydrich looked to be the man.

It didn't seem that difficult. As Rick had already seen, the Germans were so cocksure of themselves that they failed to take precautions even the dumbest gangster back in New York observed in his sleep. If Heydrich was riding through the streets of Prague in an open car, he was practically daring some poor bereaved parent to avenge the death of a son with a pistol, rifle, or bomb. Hell, anybody on the Lower East Side or Hell's Kitchen could have told him he was crazy to take a chance like that.

Right now Heydrich and the rest of the Master Race considered themselves invulnerable and unbeatable, and everything they had done since 1939 seemed to prove them right. They had rolled through Poland, folded up the French like a cheap suitcase, and smashed deep into Russia. They hadn't had to tackle the United States up to now, though.

The Germans and the Italians had declared war on America four days after Pearl Harbor, three days after Roosevelt declared war on Japan. That was just fine with Rick Blaine. He had no use for either Germans or Italians. Sitting in the chilly library, he let his mind run back over the past, to the Italians whose paths had crossed his: Ferrari, of course, and, in Ethiopia, the forces of Mussolini. Back home there was Salucci. As for Germans, wasn't Major Strasser enough German to last a lifetime?

Looking down at the arrogant, aquiline face of Reinhard Tristan Eugen Heydrich, Rick decided that if he was the man Laszlo might want to kill, then Victor Laszlo had his blessing. 'Come quickly,' Ilsa had written. Help was on its way.

Rick caught Fullerton's attention. 'Say, I don't suppose you'd know something about this Spencer character, would you?' he asked.

'Sir Ernest Spencer is the Secretary for War.'

'I know that,' Rick said patiently. 'What I mean is, where can I find him?'

'The Secretary for War ordinarily does not speak with members of the general public, sir,' Fullerton replied.

'Well, then, who does?'

'I'm quite sure I don't know, sir,' answered Fullerton, turning his back on Rick.

Rick had lost patience with politesse. Time to take a more

direct route. 'I came in here to get some information, not the high hat.'

Something in Rick's tone warned Fullerton not to ignore him. 'Perhaps his private secretary, Mr. Reginald Lumley,' he suggested.

'That's more like it. Do you know where I can find him?'

'As it happens, I do,' said Fullerton. 'Mr. Lumley, being a man of the theater, is a clubman at the Garrick.'

'What's the Garrick Club?' asked Rick.

'The Garrick, sir. Never the Garrick Club. The Garrick is the foremost theatrical club in England. Really, you must try to see *The Importance of Being Earnest* while you are in town, sir. The leading lady, Polly Nevins, is quite a special friend of Mr. Lumley's.' He looked at Rick. 'I trust I have been helpful, sir?'

'Very.'

Sam was waiting for him outside the door as he emerged from the reading room.

'Did you get the dope, boss?'

'You might say that,' replied Rick.

CHAPTER TEN

Shortly after their arrival in London, Rick had had some business cards printed up. They read:

THE SOLOMON HOROWITZ THEATRICAL AGENCY
145 W. 43rd Street, second floor
New York, New York
Richard Blaine, producer

Rick took one from his wallet and looked it over proudly. It would pass, he thought, and handsomely. The inside joke he would keep to himself. Sam was right: time to stop brooding about the past and start doing something about the present.

'Don't you want to take a cab, boss?' Sam asked.

'It's not far,' said Rick. 'Besides, you need the exercise.'

Sam shot him a look. 'The only exercise you get is lighting them cigarettes,' he observed. 'Boss, them coffin nails goin' to kill you someday.'

'If the drink doesn't get me first,' said Rick.

The Garrick's doorman nodded his head in Rick's direction as he and Sam approached. Rick looked presentable, even if he was obviously an American. Gentlemen were becoming scarce in these parlous times; someday they might even have to be rationed.

'Meet me back at the hotel in two hours,' said Rick, 'and try to stay out of trouble.'

'I don't see much trouble for me to get into,' said Sam. 'I think maybe I'll go look for our kind of club. Somewhere nice and smoky for me to play the piano in. Think they got any of those joints around here?'

'If they do, I'm sure you'll find them. Try Soho.'

'Okay, boss,' said Sam. 'One of us better start makin' some money, and I guess it might as well be me.'

'Some things never change, Sam.'

Inside, the club was damp and cold, but Rick was already getting used to the peculiar English notions of central heating.

'Good afternoon, sir,' said the club steward. 'My name is Blackwell. How may I be of assistance?'

'The name is Blaine,' Rick said. 'Richard Blaine. To see Mr. Lumley, if he's in. Please tell him it's urgent.' He fumbled for one of his business cards, scribbled something on the back, and proffered it to Blackwell.

Blackwell studied the face of the card for a moment; whatever was written on the reverse was none of his business. 'Mr. Blaine of the Horowitz Agency in New York.' Like most Englishmen, Blackwell accented the 'New' and the 'York' equally – as if anyone were likely to confuse the greatest city in the world with old York. 'I shall see if the gentleman is in, sir,' he said. 'I shan't be a moment.'

The Garrick, named after the great actor, was a splendid old pile – not much to look at from the outside, but within well appointed and comfortable. The walls were adorned with portraits of great figures of the English stage. Rick's taste ran more to *Abie's Irish Rose* than Shakespeare, but he decided not to let on.

True to his word, Blackwell was back in a few minutes. 'Mr. Lumley is pleased to make your acquaintance, Mr. Blaine, and begs your indulgence for a few minutes while he attends to some pressing business.' Blackwell's mien was apologetic. 'This dreadful war, you know. Please follow me, sir.'

Rick followed Blackwell up a grand staircase and into one of the most magnificent club rooms he had ever seen. The walls were hung with oil portraits and medieval tapestries, the furniture was plush, the teakwood tables polished to a fare-thee-well. This wasn't a club as he understood the term; this was the Grand Central Station of clubs.

Blackwell indicated an empty wing chair near a roaring fireplace. A companion chair stood empty across the hearth. 'If you wouldn't mind, sir,' he said, and departed.

Rick sank into the chair and looked around. He'd never thought he would ever be in a place like this. When he was a kid, the notion of his even stepping across the threshold of the Players Club at Gramercy Park was inconceivable.

The honorable members were scattered throughout the big room in conversational groups of twos or threes. They were spaced far enough away from each other that no conversation could be overheard easily – not that any gentleman would ever knowingly eavesdrop on another. Most of the men were either middle-aged or, more likely, getting on in years.

Nobody looked to be under forty. Rick remembered why – they were all in the military.

He thumbed through a copy of *The Times*. The stories were almost uniformly depressing. German advances here and there. British ineffectuality everywhere. The Russians rolling back and, it seemed, rolling over. Meanwhile, in America, the attack at Pearl Harbor still rankled. How hard could it have been for the United States to have seen that one coming? Unfortunately, warning signs, as he knew from bitter experience, were not always heeded.

He decided to amuse himself with his surroundings instead. He studied the portraits on the walls carefully and at once realized that what he had assumed were pictures of men in eighteenth-century dress were, in fact, portraits of Garrick himself in his various theatrical roles. There was the great man as King Lear, striking a suitably worried pose; as a fearful, black-robed Hamlet; as a dagger-drawn Macbeth.

Rick was still educating himself in the history of English theater when he became aware of a man standing beside him. 'Damned if he ain't the spitting image of my mother-in-law!' exclaimed the man. 'Especially with that dagger in his hand.'

'Mr. Lumley, I presume,' Rick said, jumping to his feet. He had no clear idea what to call him. What if, in private life, he was Lord Somebody, as every third uppercrust Englishman seemed to be?

'No presumption at all, sir,' remarked the man. 'Reginald Lumley at your service, Mr. Blaine.'

They shook hands. Rick liked him immediately, and liked him even better when, moments later, his host waved his hand in the air and Blackwell materialized with two drinks.

'I do hope you have a taste for Scotch whiskey at this hour,' said Lumley, raising his glass.

'It's after noon, isn't it?' replied Rick, savoring the warmth of the amber liquid as it slid down his throat. It wasn't Kentucky bourbon, but it would do nicely. One thing you could say about the British weather: it always called for a stiff drink.

The pair drained their glasses more or less simultaneously. 'Damned fine stuff, that!' said Lumley. 'Blackwell, would you be so kind?'

'Very good, sir,' said Blackwell, and toddled off.

Rick sized up his companion. Lumley was a short, slight man with dark wavy hair that splashed across his forehead. He was wearing a well-cut blue suit, a starched white shirt, and a floral tie. He looked like a banker who was considering you for a loan and hadn't made up his mind yet.

'Mr. Horowitz sends his compliments . . .,' Rick began.

'Beastly business last night, what?' interjected Lumley. 'Pity I'm not over there this go-round. Show the damned Jerrys a thing or two, I daresay. Eh?' In one smooth motion he scooped up his drink at the same instant Blackwell laid it down. 'Ever catch a whiff of the grapeshot yourself, Blaine?' he asked.

'Can't say that I have,' replied Rick. 'Except from the critics.'

Lumley chuckled. 'Know what you mean, sir, know what you mean. Myself, I took a swing or two at brother Boche in France back in eighteen, and I daresay I sent more than a few of the damned *Kameraden* to hell.' He tossed back his drink and swallowed half of it. 'Wouldn't mind adding a few more to the tally. Wouldn't mind it at all.'

Lumley produced Rick's card and peered at it. 'Solomon

Horowitz, eh?' he said. 'Mr. Horowitz would be a Jewish fellow, I should expect. I gather half the people in New York are Jewish these days.'

'The trick is telling which half,' said Rick.

'Lucky for you they're not Irish,' said Lumley. 'Neutral, in a war like this one! Can you believe it?'

'After all you've done for them, too,' said Rick.

Lumley perked up. 'Who needs them?' he asked brightly. 'Not with you Yanks in the fray. Damned glad to have you aboard.'

'Mr. Horowitz . . .,' Rick prompted.

'Ah, yes, Horowitz. Never met the man. But that's not the name you want to talk about, is it, Mr. Blaine?'

On the back of his phony business card, Rick had written a series of names: Polly Nevins. Victor Laszlo. Ilsa Lund. Reinhard Heydrich. At least one of them seemed to have gotten results.

'I'm particularly interested in Miss Nevins – professionally speaking,' Rick ventured, continuing the game. 'I gather that her performance as Gwendolyn is the talk of the town. My employer would be greatly interested in having her star in one of his own productions – when the war is over, of course, and once it is safe to travel.'

'Yes, Miss Nevins,' Lumley said. 'A woman of whom one can truly say not so much that her beauty becomes her as that she elevates the very notion of beauty. Especially on the stage, where she is quite the loveliest creature one has ever had the pleasure to behold.' He took a reflective sip of his whiskey and studied the back of Rick's business card. 'We are all of us helpless prey in the face of beautiful women, are we not?' He shook his head. 'The things we do for them. . . .'

'The things we want to do for them,' Rick corrected softly. 'I hope I have the chance to make her acquaintance while I'm in London.'

'Just how long might that be, Mr. Blaine?' inquired Lumley.

'Indefinitely, for the time being.'

'I shall make certain the two of you meet at the earliest possible opportunity.' Lumley's next words took him by surprise. 'What about tomorrow evening? Are you free for dinner?'

'If you're buying, I'm eating.'

'It's settled, then,' said Lumley. 'Tomorrow at eight o'clock. I'll send my driver round for you. Where are you staying?'

'Brown's.'

'Splendid. I live in South Kensington. It's not far. We'll all have a splendid natter.'

Things were moving fast. 'If it's more convenient, I'll be happy to find my way to you,' Rick said.

'Oh, no bother at all,' exclaimed Lumley. 'Damn! Look at the time. I've completely forgot all about an appointment at Whitehall. That's what I get for having a beaker or two in the afternoon. I'm afraid you'll have to excuse me, Mr. Blaine. In the meantime, may I suggest that you enjoy the hospitality of the Garrick with my compliments.'

Lumley waved for Blackwell, who materialized immediately. 'I say, Blackwell, would you mind terribly bringing Mr. Blaine a selection of the club's papers, there's a good fellow. Mr. Blaine is free to remain here as long as he likes this afternoon as my guest.'

'Very good, sir,' replied Blackwell.

'Keep an eye on him, will you?' Lumley requested.

'I shall take very good care of Mr. Blaine, sir,' replied Blackwell. 'You may rest assured on that account.'

Blackwell turned to Rick. 'Would the gentleman like another glass of cordial?' he inquired.

'The gentleman would,' said Rick.

CHAPTER ELEVEN

Their rooms had been gone through very carefully; that much was evident when he opened the door. Rick had seen better, but still this was not an amateur job. Just enough had been disturbed to let him know he'd had visitors. Just enough was put neatly back into place to let him know they were gentlemen. Just enough had been destroyed to let him know they meant business.

'Boss, we been tossed,' said Sam, who'd been back for an hour and hadn't told a soul or touched a thing. He'd seen this before.

'Any guesses who?' asked Rick, surveying the wreckage.

'I think I might have a suspicion,' said a voice behind him. It was Renault, hard on his heels.

'Come on in and make yourself comfortable, Louie,' said Rick. 'Somebody else already has.'

Renault glanced around quickly. 'Seems like old times,' he remarked, snapping open his cigarette case and settling into an easy chair by the electric fire.

'Don't flatter yourself,' said Rick. 'Your boys weren't this good.' He started to poke through the debris.

Their closets had been emptied. Clothes lay on the floor, pockets turned inside out, except for Rick's dinner jacket and trousers, which their visitors had thoughtfully left hanging so as not to rumple.

Renault smoked while Rick and Sam took inventory. 'When your curiosity gets the better of you, do let me know,' he said, puffing away. The dapper little Frenchman was resplendent in a new suit, new shoes, and a fedora.

'I thought you just bought a new suit,' said Rick.

'One must watch one's appearance at all times,' said Renault.

'I prefer to watch my back,' said Rick, surveying the room. 'I guess I'm not doing a very good job of it.'

Their passports were gone. Whoever had paid them such assiduous attention had wanted to make sure they wouldn't be going anywhere any time soon.

'Ricky, how many times have I told you to always carry your identity papers with you?' asked Renault. 'We Europeans do.'

'Maybe that's why so many of you want to become Americans,' replied Rick. 'We live in a free country.' He couldn't tell Renault that New York City gangsters never carried anything identifying themselves on their persons, so they could be free to give the cops any phony name they wished. Old habits died hard. 'Okay, Sam, forget it. We're here for the duration, so we might as well make the best of it.' He checked the liquor cabinet. 'At least they didn't drink our stash.'

Sam halted his search for the passports and poured Rick and Renault each a stiff drink.

'It's my fault,' began Rick. 'I've just spent the past few hours getting suckered by a limey.'

'Boss, you slippin',' said Sam under his breath.

Rick ignored him. 'Sitting on my duff at the Garrick while British Intelligence paid us a visit, courtesy of Reginald Lumley.'

'Or perhaps courtesy of Victor Laszlo,' retorted Renault.

Rick and Sam both turned to look at him. 'What?' said Rick incredulously.

Renault smiled inwardly. He enjoyed having the undivided attention of Richard Blaine, a man who had always held himself to be superior to the likes of Louis Renault. True, they were now friends and, even when they hadn't been, had done a great deal of profitable business together in Casablanca. Rick had always kept himself aloof from Renault and the refugee horde; he was in Casablanca, but not of Casablanca, and he never let anybody forget it. Until she walked back into his life. That, Renault decided, was what had finally separated Rick Blaine from his rival club owner, Arrigo Ferrari: a woman named Ilsa Lund.

'I mean, here we are, having followed Victor Laszlo and his wife from Casablanca to Lisbon to London, and what do we really know about them?' Renault took a sip of his drink. It was an Armagnac, his favorite. 'I wasn't Prefect of Police in Casablanca all that time without learning a thing or two about the human animal. About what motivates him, about what drives him. About what obsesses him.'

'I can think of a few things,' said Rick.

'So can we both, my friend,' replied Renault. 'Money, of course. And power. And women.' He laughed to himself. 'You know, Ricky, there was a time back there in Casablanca when I worried about you and women. You didn't seem to have any interest in them at all, and, well, I . . .'

'You what?'

Renault didn't bat an eye. 'Now don't take that the wrong way,' he explained. 'I simply meant that a man who doesn't like women even half as much as I do makes me nervous. What I mean is, I don't understand such a man.'

'Meaning me,' said Rick.

'No, meaning Laszlo,' said Renault. 'This Laszlo is an odd duck. He responds to neither money nor power. Indeed, the only thing that seems to interest him is his glorious cause.'

'What's wrong with that?' asked Rick.

Renault snapped open a cigarette case and withdrew a Players. They weren't Gauloises, but they would have to do. 'Mind you, Ricky, I'm sure altruism and selflessness have their place in this world of ours, but I must confess that for the life of me I can't see where if they are not accompanied by some other, more tangible, rewards.'

'Maybe Victor Laszlo really believes in something, Louie,' said Rick. 'Maybe he's even willing to die for it.' He took a sip of bourbon. 'And maybe he's just a chump.'

'Perhaps he's something more,' suggested Renault.

'Now you're losing me,' said Rick. He was nearly reclining in his wing chair, his head thrown back.

'How to broach this subject?' Renault waved his cigarette in the air. 'Rick, has it ever occurred to you to question any aspect of Laszlo's story?'

'Many times,' answered Rick. 'Ilsa's, too.'

'Precisely. Both of them have so many loose ends, so many unexplained occurrences, so much – well, sheer coincidence, not to put too fine a point on it. Don't you think?'

'Doesn't everybody?'

Renault was barely able to sit still in his chair. 'I mean, so much doesn't add up,' he said. 'For example: How did he escape so conveniently from the concentration camp at Mauthausen? How has he managed to slip through the Germans' fingers three times? Why has he been reported killed five times, only to turn up very much alive, and looking quite dapper, as if he were going on a safari instead of fleeing the Nazis, in Casablanca? Aside from that little scar on his face, there wasn't a mark on him to show that he'd been enjoying the hospitality of the Third Reich, as he claimed.' Renault was gesticulating now. 'I'm telling you, Ricky,' he said, 'a man who could contemplate walking out on a beautiful woman like Miss Lund is capable of anything.'

Rick was following the argument but wasn't convinced. 'She's *Mrs.* Laszlo, Louie, even if he tried to hide it from the world for her safety.'

'So he says,' observed Renault. 'How do you think Miss Lund feels about that?'

Rick wasn't prepared to answer that question. 'It's not that I don't agree with you. But I think you were in Casablanca so long, playing so many angles, that you don't trust anybody anymore.'

'I made a very handsome living doing so, too,' said Renault. 'Seriously, Ricky, I think we have to examine the possibility that Victor Laszlo is not who, or what, he says he is. Even his name doesn't fit: Victor Laszlo. If he's Czech, what's he doing with a Hungarian name? It's more than a little fishy, if you ask me.'

Rick poured another drink for himself and Renault. Over

in the corner Sam was reading a book on contract bridge. Sam enjoyed playing cards, but never for money.

'I don't know much about names,' Rick replied, 'but I gather they've moved the borders around here so often that hardly anybody is a citizen of the country in which he was born.' Not for the first time, he was glad to be an American. 'Besides, lots of people change their names, for lots of reasons.

'You mentioned Mauthausen a moment ago,' Rick went on. 'I can't prove it yet, but I'm beginning to think that whatever Victor Laszlo is up to in London has something to do with the guy who set that camp up, a man named Reinhard Heydrich. The bully who's running Czechoslovakia now. The one who probably had something to do with Laszlo's getting thrown in the jug in the first place.' He took a drag on his cigarette. 'The way I see it, Victor Laszlo and his boys might be getting ready to clip Heydrich. From the looks of him, nobody deserves it more.'

'Assuming Laszlo is who he says he is,' objected Renault. 'This Heydrich may be a beast, but even if he is, it may well be none of our concern who the target of Laszlo's operation is. The real question is whether it suits our interests to make it happen.' He rubbed his hands together meaningfully. '*All* of our interests.'

'Well, then let's assume it does suit our interests for the moment,' said Rick. 'Why not? You may be suspicious of him, and God knows I certainly have no reason to like him, but aside from his fancy suits, he's never given us any real indication he's a phony. Major Strasser certainly thought he was real enough. Real enough to die trying to stop him from getting away.'

'Don't forget he had information Major Strasser wanted desperately,' said Renault.

'And now he has information we want desperately,' said Rick, jumping to his feet. 'Listen, Louie, stop waving red herrings about Victor Laszlo in my face.' He looked down at Renault, who was still sitting in his chair. 'However, I think you may be on to something about this mess being Laszlo's doing.'

'Really?' said Renault, rising. Sam looked up briefly from his book.

'But not for the reasons you think. Today at the Garrick I met this fellow I told you about, Reginald Lumley. He's the man Friday of the Secretary for War in Churchill's cabinet. He's our kind of guy, Louie: he likes his drink and he likes his women. I gave him one of these.'

Rick produced one of his bogus business cards and showed it to Renault. 'I wrote a few names on the back, to get his attention. One was the name of his mistress.'

'You have been busy.'

'The others were Ilsa Lund, Victor Laszlo, and Reinhard Heydrich.'

'Which one hit the bull's-eye?'

Rick drained his bourbon. 'That's just it. I don't know.'

'But you suspect?'

'At this point,' he said, 'I suspect everything and everybody. Except maybe Sam, and sometimes I'm not too sure about him.'

Sam ignored him.

'What do you intend to do about it?' asked Renault.

'I intend to dine out on his nickel,' Rick replied. 'Tomorrow night. I'm invited to a dinner party, *chez* Lumley.

In South Kensington.' He looked around the room. 'With an invitation like this, how can I refuse? I may need my passport again someday.'

'Better you than I, my friend,' said Renault. 'The state of English cooking leaves much to be desired.'

'I'm not going there for the food, Louie,' said Rick.

'Indeed you are not,' stated Renault with certainty. 'I know precisely why you think you're going there. You're going there to find out more about the whereabouts of our mysterious M. Laszlo. Before you get carried away with your prospects, though . . .' He finished his drink. 'South Kensington you say? What's the house number?'

'He didn't tell me,' replied Rick. 'He said he'd send a car.'

Renault looked at his friend gravely. 'I wouldn't be taking that ride if I were you. Not after this – although, luckily for us, I fear they may have overplayed their hand.'

'Why not?' asked Rick.

'Because, if we're talking about the same house, I've already been there,' replied Renault. He let the effect of his words sink in.

'I'm all ears,' said Rick.

Renault asked for another drink and lit another Players while he was waiting. 'Thank you, Sam,' he said, taking a sip. Leaving out any reference to Raoul, he narrated his discovery of the address of the house that Laszlo had been seen entering by members of the Resistance. How he had taken a cab across London, from the worst of the bomb damage in the East End to the relatively unscathed precincts of the Royal Borough of Kensington and Chelsea, to see the place for himself. How he had walked around the neighborhood, hoping to discover some way in which the house distinguished itself from those elsewhere on the street. How he had noticed lights on in the upper floors, but only darkness below, long after the feeble daylight had waned. How, about an hour after sundown, in a flurry of activity, a number of men in suits, several of them carrying briefcases, came and went through the front door – which, as far as he could tell, was the only entrance from the street – but still no lights were to be seen on the parlor floor. How, after spending all night and part of the morning running up a fortune in cab fees, he had finally caught a glimpse of what he had hoped all along to see.

'Laszlo?' asked Rick.

'No,' said Renault. 'Ilsa Lund. Leaving the house and getting into a taxi.'

Rick was up and out the door before Louis had a chance to stub out his cigarette. Renault caught up with him just as he jumped in the cab.

'Number forty-two, Clareville Street,' Renault told the driver. He looked over at Rick. 'I thought you might like to know where we're going before you get there.'

'You're full of surprises, Louie.'

Renault bowed. 'It's part of my charm.'

'I bet you say that to all the girls,' replied Rick.

CHAPTER TWELVE

In less than fifteen minutes they reached the house in Clareville Street, just off the Brompton Road. A big white row house of five stories, it huddled indistinguishable from its brethren in a row of what the British called mansions. A small sign that read 'Blandford' was its only distinguishing characteristic. On either side of it were dark houses that bore signs reading 'To Let.' In New York you generally knew where the rich people lived just by looking at their houses. Not here. Here, you didn't know anything. Rick had long believed you should never trust people, but he'd never before realized that you shouldn't trust houses, either.

Rick's heart was hammering as he and Renault alighted from the taxi. 'The direct approach has gotten us this far,' he said. He walked up the stairs and punched the doorbell.

To his surprise, it was answered almost immediately by a little old lady.

'Good evening,' said Rick, raising his hat.

'Good evening to you, sir,' replied the woman. Her white

hair was pulled back in a tight bun, and she wore an apron around her waist. She eyed the pair of them with just a hint of interest – or was it suspicion? 'Would it be rooms you two gentlemen might be wanting?' she asked politely.

A rooming house? That would explain the men coming and going, the activity upstairs, and, to a certain extent, the lack of same downstairs. Had Renault just fed him a bum steer? 'As a matter of fact, we were,' said Rick. 'The hotels around here are full up.'

The woman shook her head. 'I'm afraid we're fully booked at the moment as well,' she informed him regretfully. 'You might try Mrs. Blake down the road at number sixteen. She's often got a room or two to spare.'

She started to close the door. Rick had spent part of the conversation trying to see into the house beyond her, but she was standing in a small anteroom, beyond which a pair of very solid-looking wooden double doors shielded the rest of the place from view.

'Are you quite sure, madam?' Louis asked in his most ingratiating manner. 'We have traveled a great distance, and have heard that your establishment is without compare.' To complete the continental effect, he bowed deeply.

'Oh, my,' said the woman. 'It's terrible, the lack of space in London these days. With all the Yanks arriving, it's awfully difficult finding a proper place to lay one's head.'

Renault spoke up again. 'I wonder if we might come in and have a look around? Just in case you were to have an unexpected vacancy in the next few days.' He clicked his heels together. 'An ally from Free France would be most obliged.'

The woman's face brightened considerably. 'By all means,'

she said. 'Blandford is the finest bed and breakfast in this part of London, and I'm happy to show it off, especially to two fine gentlemen such as yourselves.'

She opened the front door wide, and they stepped inside.

They were in the parlor of a well-to-do home. The room boasted fresh flowers in the vases, bookshelves along the side walls, and a picture window whose prospect was of a lovely summer garden, now faded and wan in the winter darkness. In the center of the room stood a grand piano, its top down and covered by a lace cloth, on which stood various family photographs. Rick looked them over, but the faces didn't mean anything to him. Just more strangers, half of whom were probably dead.

'I was given this address by some friends who I think may be staying here, Mrs. uh . . .,' said Rick, fumbling for an opening. The house certainly looked like what it purported to be. Neat as a pin, in the British way, with a tea service laid out in the parlor and pictures of cats interspersed with idealized portraits of the royal family on the walls.

'Mrs. Bunton,' the woman replied. 'At your service. Widowed going on twenty-six years, and not a day goes by that I don't think about the second Somme, and my poor Bertie, killed at Amiens and victory so close. Won't you please sit down?' She indicated a sofa. 'May I offer you some tea?'

Rick would have preferred something more substantial than tea, but Renault was agreeable. 'That would be very nice, Mrs. Bunton,' he said.

Rick and Renault sat down as she poured the tea. 'Just who might these friends of yours be?' she inquired politely.

'Mr. and Mrs. Victor Laszlo,' Rick replied.

Mrs. Bunton occupied herself with thinking for a moment. 'Mr. Laszlo?' she repeated. 'That would be a foreign gentleman, I expect.'

'Yes,' said Rick. 'He's a Czech. His wife, who also goes by the name of Ilsa Lund, is Norwegian.'

'I'm quite sure there's no one by that name here,' she said, pursing her lips.

'Maybe they're registered under another name,' Rick suggested.

Mrs. Bunton seemed to take offense at the thought. 'I'm quite sure everyone who stays here is who he says he is,' she retorted. 'The management insists on it.'

'Just who might this management be?' Rick asked idly. Mrs. Bunton did not reply but instead tugged on an old Victorian bell pull. Practically in the same motion, she drew a small pistol from the folds of her apron and trained it on them expertly. Rick and Louis held their teacups in midair, feeling ridiculous.

'That would be Mr. Lumley,' she informed them. 'He'll be along shortly. Now, if you gentlemen wouldn't mind keeping both your hands where I can see them, it won't be a moment.' She gave another hard tug on the bell pull.

Sure enough, not two minutes later into the room strode Reginald Lumley. 'If it isn't the inquisitive Mr. Richard Blaine,' he said. 'Unless I'm very much mistaken, you're a day early.'

'I wanted to make sure the menu was to my liking,' said Rick. 'My stomach, you know. . . .'

'And this must be Louis Renault, former Prefect of Police in Casablanca,' continued Lumley.

Renault nodded slightly. 'At your service, sir,' he said.

'Well, then,' said Lumley, 'since all the guests of honor save one are here, I see no reason why we can't start the party. Won't you follow me, please, gentlemen?'

Rick and Renault accompanied Lumley up three flights of stairs. Rick noticed that the second and third floors looked like a rooming house, or a small private hotel, but as they climbed one story higher, appearances changed. The entire floor had been given over to a kind of situation room: men pored over maps, women talked on telephones and pounded typewriters. A few servants moved quietly about the room, bringing food and drink where and when needed.

Rick whistled softly as they stood in the doorway. 'Nice setup you got here,' he said. 'Reminds me of the kind of thing we used to have back home. Except not so fancy, of course.'

'Glad you like it, Mr. Blaine,' said Lumley. 'We do aim to make our guests comfortable. Even when we're not sure they're entirely welcome.' He knocked loudly to announce their presence, then ushered the two men inside.

'Of course you know Victor Laszlo,' he said, nodding to one of the room's occupants.

Rick and Laszlo looked at each other for the first time since the tarmac in Casablanca. 'Monsieur Blaine,' said Laszlo, extending his hand, 'it is a very great pleasure to see you again.'

'The pleasure is all mine,' said Rick, lighting a cigarette.

Laszlo took him by the arm and guided him into a corner. 'We had to make sure the time was right,' he said softly. 'We had to be absolutely certain that our plan could work. And we had to know, really know, that you could be trusted.'

Rick took a puff. 'I think that you're here in one piece is proof of that.'

'Precisely,' said Laszlo. 'That's what I have been telling them since we arrived. The British don't trust anybody. They had to make sure of your bona fides. I regret it took so long.'

'Which is why they paid my rooms a little visit,' said Rick. 'Look, Laszlo, I'm as good as my word. You know that. Any man who doesn't is not someone I want to work with. I told you back in Casablanca when Louis had you in the holding pen that I was in, and I meant it. Where I come from, a man's word is his bond. Sometimes it's all he has. Right now, it's all I've got left, and I don't intend to devalue it.'

Laszlo nodded his head. 'Agreed and accepted. Let's get to work.' He brought Rick over to meet a mustachioed military man. 'Major Sir Harold Miles, may I present Monsieur Richard Blaine.'

Major Miles held out his hand and shook Rick's formally. 'Welcome to London,' he said. 'Shall we sit down?'

They sat at a large conference table: Rick, Renault, Lumley, Laszlo, and Major Miles. An adjutant stood nearby. A stenographer took notes.

'Gentlemen, I think we all know each other, at least by reputation,' said Major Miles, who seemed to be in charge. 'I represent the Special Operations Executive, which, as you know, is charged with clandestine activity. Mr. Lumley is here in his capacity as private secretary to Sir Ernest Spencer, the Secretary for War, who has ultimate authority over the operation.' He threw a set of photographs on the table. 'I trust you will forgive me if I dispense with the formalities, but time is short. This, gentlemen, is our target.' The same cruel face that Rick had been looking at in the British Library stared up at them: the face of Reinhard Heydrich.

'. . . the commander of the RSHA and Protector of Bohemia and Moravia,' the major was saying. 'Nietzsche's "Blond Beast" in the flesh. Handsome, cultured, talented, a connoisseur of food, wine, and women. The sort of chap one wouldn't mind entertaining at one's club, if he weren't also a cold-blooded killer.'

Rick studied the face in the photo, whose quality was so much better than the picture in the newspapers. He had seen that face a thousand times before, back in New York. The face of an opportunist. The face of a profiteer. The face of a double-crosser who would betray his own mother for a small personal gain. Rick saw a hint of the bully, but whether he was also a coward, Rick could not tell. You had to see a man in the flesh before you could sense that.

'A real pretty boy, isn't he?' he remarked.

'Don't let his looks fool you,' said the major. 'Heydrich is perhaps the most dangerous Nazi official outside of Hitler himself. Goering is a posturing buffoon, whose Luftwaffe can make our lives miserable for a while but won't be able to defend Germany when the time comes. Goebbels is a partisan, but he's also just a propagandist who will be singing a different tune should circumstances change. Himmler is a nasty little bastard with a chip on his shoulder. Heydrich is smarter than all three of them, and because of that, ten times as dangerous.'

'Why not go for Hitler and be done with it?' asked Rick. 'If you want to kill the beast, you don't cut off its tail, you cut off its head.'

The major looked at Rick as if he were mad. 'I'm afraid we can't do that,' he explained. 'It has already been decided at the highest levels of government that under The Hague convention, the assassination of rival heads of state, even belligerents, will not be countenanced. This is war, not a street brawl.'

Rick thought of the debris outside in the London streets and wasn't so sure. 'Looks to me that that's what the Luftwaffe's trying to do. Knock off Churchill, I mean.'

The major waved away Rick's objection. 'Aerial bombing's one thing, assassination's another,' he said. 'If Bomber Harris's RAF blows the Führer to hell, I can assure you we none of us will shed a tear about it. In any case, clandestine operations in Berlin are out of the question. We have very few Intelligence assets there.' He slapped his swagger stick against his thigh.

'So why Heydrich?' asked Rick. 'How'd he draw the short stick?'

'Because we can,' Major Miles replied.

'Because we have to!' exclaimed Lumley. 'I mean, how do these bloody Czechs expect us to beat back the Hun when they won't even lift a finger to help?'

'Because we must,' said Laszlo beneath his breath.

'What are you talking about?' Rick asked Lumley.

'The Czechs aren't putting up much of a fight at all,' said Lumley. 'Ever since this chap Heydrich arrived and shot a few of their johnnies, there's been hardly a peep out of them. Why, even the bloody frogs are giving a better account of themselves.'

'Ahem,' said Renault.

'Anyway,' Lumley concluded, 'it's high time we lit a fire under the bastards. Something to get their Irish up, so to speak.'

'I'm sure they'll be very grateful,' Renault remarked.

'Frankly,' said the major, 'we've been worried about the loyalties of the Czechs for some time. Bohemia and Moravia have always been as much German as Czech, culturally speaking, and they appear to be wearing the Nazi yoke a little too lightly for comfort.'

'I thought your man Chamberlain was supposed to save Czechoslovakia for democracy,' Rick observed.

'That's water under the dam,' retorted Sir Harold. 'Winston's the PM now, and he is determined to rectify his predecessor's errors of judgment.'

'If he doesn't, we most certainly will,' said Laszlo.

Rick wasn't convinced. 'I don't see why Heydrich is any worse, or any more dangerous, than the other top Nazis – especially when Heydrich is in Prague, not Berlin, where the decisions are made.'

'You might feel very differently, Monsieur Blaine,' said Laszlo, 'if Heydrich were *Gauleiter* of New York.'

'I might.'

The major glanced at him. 'Mr. Laszlo has informed me of your willingness to support the cause of the Resistance throughout Europe, Mr. Blaine,' he said. 'He has also briefed me on your background and your skills, which information we have thoroughly investigated ourselves.'

'Which is why you tossed my room and stole my passport.'

'We had to make sure you were who you purported to be,' replied the major. 'We couldn't take the risk you were an impostor sent by the Germans to discover the whereabouts of Mr. Laszlo. . . .'

'What if I had been?'

'We would have killed you,' Sir Harold responded with no

particular emotion. 'Fortunately for all of us, Mr. Laszlo vouched for you upon presentation of your passport, as well as making a visual identification this evening while you were enjoying Mrs. Bunton's hospitality.'

'Which the hound and which the hare?' wondered Renault. 'And which the fox?'

Major Miles threw Rick's and Sam's passports on the table. 'At this moment, Mr. Blaine,' he said, 'I think I do not flatter myself when I say that I know more about you than your own mother.'

Rick thought back to his meeting with another major, Strasser, in Renault's office in Casablanca, and of his dossier in the Nazi's clammy hands. Surely the English couldn't have any more information on him than the Germans did. It was time to find out. 'My mother never did know me that well,' he remarked, wishing he had a drink.

'But we do,' continued Miles. 'We know you ran arms into Ethiopia for the emperor Haile Selassie in 1935 and 1936 in his futile resistance to Mussolini. Very brave of you – and extremely quixotic, if you don't mind my saying so.'

'I've always had a soft spot for the underdog,' observed Rick. 'It's the American way.'

'Extremely unusual, too. Tell me, Mr. Blaine' – now it was the major's turn to light up a cigarette – 'what made you leave New York City so suddenly in October of 1935?'

'I really don't think that's any of your business,' said Rick as calmly as he could.

'So suddenly and with such finality that it is said that you can never return to your native land.' The major tapped an ash into the wastebasket. 'What made you go to, of all places, Ethiopia?'

'I didn't,' Rick told him. 'I stopped in Paris first, and left Sam there to scout the place.' He tightened his lips. 'I guess it's no secret that I was in the saloon business back home, and I heard Paris might be a nice place to open another one. I heard right.'

'Why did you go to Addis Ababa, then?' the major wanted to know.

'Let's just say I don't like bullies and leave it at that,' replied Rick.

Major Miles shuffled some papers. 'We also know you fought in Spain with the Loyalists against Franco. Once again, very brave, very quixotic – and very dangerous. You saw a good deal of action – in between making quite a tidy little sum running arms to the Republicans.'

Rick took a deep drag on his cigarette. 'That's not a secret, either,' he said. 'Tell me something your crack Intelligence service has discovered that the rest of the world doesn't already know.'

Sir Harold ignored the insult. 'Then in May or June of 1939 you turn up in Paris and stay until the day the Germans march in.'

'I didn't have much choice about leaving,' Rick explained. 'With my record in Spain, I had to get out unless I wanted to end up like Laszlo, as a guest of the Reich. The fact is, Major, Nazis don't much like me, and frankly, I don't much like them, either.'

'I find it hard to reconcile this, shall we say, idealism with the persona of a passive neutral that you have obviously so carefully cultivated in Casablanca.'

'Suit yourself,' replied Rick. 'It's pretty tough for me sometimes, too.' He finished off his cigarette and ground it out in an ashtray. He'd had about enough of this. 'You know,' he said heatedly, 'I went over this with Major Strasser in Casablanca, and I'll be damned if I'm going to sit here and go over it again with you. A man's entitled to keep at least part of his private life private. Why I've done what I've done is my business and nobody else's. Now, if there are no further questions . . .' He got up as if to leave.

'Wait, Richard, please.' It was her voice. It was *her*. When she had entered the room, he did not know. But she was there.

He wanted to turn to look at her, but he didn't. He couldn't. Not right now. He sat down again.

Victor Laszlo spoke up. 'Please, Monsieur Blaine, my wife and I are quite serious about needing your help. You cannot blame us if Sir Harold has investigated you. In an operation of this importance and this sensitivity, we must make absolutely certain where each man's loyalties lie.

'Monsieur Renault we understand,' continued Laszlo, nodding in Louis's direction. 'He is a man for whom money and pleasure are paramount. This is the sort of man with whom we can do business. But you are another story. I do not insult you again by offering you money. . . .'

'You offered me a hundred thousand francs for those letters of transit, remember?' Rick said. 'Or was it two hundred thousand?'

'And you refused to accept my offer. Instead, you gave them to me – or perhaps I should say, you gave the letters to her.'

'That's true,' muttered Rick.

'I was prepared – *we* were prepared – to do anything to get out of Casablanca. Ilsa's feelings for you were immaterial to me, as long as she and I could escape, to continue our work here.' Laszlo poured himself a small glass of water from a carafe on the table. 'A world war is no time to let personal emotions interfere with a cause. Your decision to join us superseded in my mind any designs you may have had on my wife. Therefore, let us seal the bargain we made in Casablanca.'

Laszlo stood. 'I offer you my hand, not in friendship, for I know that we can never be friends. Instead, I give it to you in comradeship.'

Several seconds elapsed before Rick extended his hand. Victor took it. 'Laszlo, I'll do everything my conscience will allow me to do for both you and Ilsa. Just how much that is will be determined by me and me alone. Agreed?'

'Once again,' said Laszlo, 'welcome back to the fight.'

'There's just one more thing,' added Rick. 'I meant what I said to Ilsa at the airport. That what I've got to do she can have no part of. We agreed on that.'

He could hear her footsteps as she walked over to the table. Her voice was loud in his ear. He could smell her perfume. He turned and, suddenly, was lost in her eyes.

'Major,' she said, 'would you please explain how things stand to Mr. Blaine?'

CHAPTER THIRTEEN

Sir Harold stood. 'Mr. Blaine,' he began, clearing his throat. 'Since the entry of the United States of America into the war, the circumstances of the conflict have profoundly changed.'

Rick sat impassively, listening, his heart pounding.

'This war is no longer simply the struggle of one lone, free nation, England, against the Third Reich. This war is no longer a competition among empires – the British versus the German. This war is no longer simply an academic question of whether fascism or communism or democracy is the superior form of government.

'This war,' he said, striking the table with his fist, 'is a battle to the death.'

Ilsa winced at the noise. Laszlo didn't.

'To the death,' repeated Major Miles. 'I'm not sure how much experience you personally have had with such a struggle, Mr. Blaine.'

'Enough to know I like to win,' remarked Rick, 'but also enough to know that I don't count on it.'

'Just so. Now, Mr. Blaine, our struggle is also your struggle.' The major pointed to one of several wall maps. 'This,' he said, 'is what remains of Czechoslovakia.' He rapped the map with a pointer. 'Here is Prague. You will notice that it is two hundred miles northwest of Vienna, not terribly far from either Munich or Berlin. In other words, Prague is not some eastern backwater, remote and inaccessible, but a sophisticated city located deep in the Reich and at the very heart of the European continent. I cannot overemphasize the city's strategic and psychological importance.'

That part made sense to Rick. If you wanted to rub out the other guy, best to do it in one of his own joints. It didn't hurt to have the aid of an insider, either, someone to betray the victim when the time was just right. That was another lesson he had learned the hard way. He still remembered the way Giuseppe Guglielmo had looked as Tick-Tock stuck a knife between his ribs and Abie Cohen shot off the front of his face and the would-be *capo di tutti capi* died right there, on the Persian carpet he'd probably overpaid for, in his office above Grand Central Station back in the good old days.

Miles's voice commanded attention. 'We believe that a bomb is the best way to dispose of Herr Heydrich. Mr. Laszlo has made a convincing case for a bomb attack, effected during one of Heydrich's daily drives through the city.'

Major Miles, Rick decided, was all business and no heart. He was a good British officer. He would have made a good gangster.

Sir Harold indicated a large map of the city of Prague. 'One of the arguments in favor of such a plan is the very nature of the streets of Prague. The medieval city is essentially intact, which allows a potential assassin to get very close almost unnoticed. For that same reason, a sniper attack is less desirable. A rifle poking from an open window is too easily spotted.'

'You mean it's far too dangerous for a sniper, then?' asked Renault.

Major Miles's mouth twitched beneath his brush-cut mustache. His opinion of the French, always low to begin with, had been further lowered by their pitiful performance against the Germans in 1940. If he could have had his way, this operation would have no place for a frog. But wartime allies made strange bedfellows, and besides, the Free French had to be placated.

'No, Monsieur Renault,' he corrected. 'I mean it offers too much opportunity for failure. It could seriously compromise the success of the mission and therefore embarrass His Majesty's government.'

'We can't have that, can we?' Renault observed.

'No, we can't,' said the major, missing the sarcasm. 'Poison is also out of the question because it presupposes a certain intimacy between assassin and victim, which we could hope for, but not count on. So, of course, does stabbing. Thus, a bomb is the most efficient and effective way of disposing of him.' The major's lips made a gesture that, for him, passed as a smile. 'It also ensures our team of their best chance of escape. This is not, after all, a suicide mission.'

'I'm not so sure about that,' said Rick.

'Gentlemen,' interrupted Laszlo. 'The major is right. Everything must and will go perfectly. We cannot have any misunderstandings, however slight. Nor can we have any compromises in our own security.' He looked at Renault, who stared back blandly.

Major Miles spoke up. 'The government believe it to be in the best interests of the war effort to give full and unequivocal support to this operation,' he said. 'I might also add that this plan has been personally approved by President Eduard Beneš and ratified by the Czech government-in-exile.'

Rick waved his lighted cigarette in the air. 'So where do Louie and I fit in?'

Major Miles had a ready answer. 'In Mr. Laszlo we have an exemplar of the central European resistance to Hitler. In Captain Renault, we will have a newly committed representative of Free France. And in Mr. Blaine' – he nodded in Rick's direction – 'we have personified the industrial might and moral strength of the United States of America.'

Despite himself, Rick felt a surge of patriotic pride. He hadn't felt that in a long time. Since 1935 hardly a day had gone by that he hadn't thought about New York, but this was the first time he had felt like an American again.

'Herr Heydrich has a number of weaknesses,' said Laszlo. 'He drinks too much. Thanks to his overweening arrogance, he takes unnecessary chances. He is resolutely unfaithful to his wife, who spends as much time in Berlin as she can, and he is fond of the company of beautiful women to a degree one might consider excessive.'

Rick didn't have to wonder who that 'one' might be.

'Although he is the head of the Reich security service, we believe his own personal security can be compromised and breached.'

'That doesn't sound too hard to me,' Rick remarked. 'I've read about his driving around Prague in an open car.'

'Yes,' agreed Laszlo, 'but that knowledge is useless without also knowing his schedule and his movements. Heydrich lies well protected behind the walls of Hradčany Castle. We need someone who will be able to get close to him without arousing his suspicions.'

'In other words, you need a spy in his headquarters.'

'Precisely.'

'Who?'

'Me,' Ilsa said softly.

Rick started, sending his cigarette ashes flying. Might as well send her straight to hell and ask her to keep tabs on the devil.

'I am proud to say that my wife, Ilsa, has agreed to act as our agent-in-place in Heydrich's headquarters,' said Victor. 'That is to say, as our eyes and ears in the command headquarters of the *Reichsicherheitshauptant* itself.'

'You can't be serious,' said Rick.

'I am,' Laszlo replied. 'Perfectly. So is Ilsa.'

Rick looked at Ilsa, but her eyes betrayed nothing, and her lips said nothing. Now it was clear: as far as Victor was concerned, this wasn't an impersonal act of war, the way it was to Major Miles. This was a grudge match between Laszlo and Reinhard Heydrich, the worst kind of fight.

Laszlo rose and began walking around. Rick prepared himself for a sermon by lighting another cigarette.

'We have a chance to strike a blow for freedom that is given to few men of our time. If I could, I would destroy Hitler himself. We can't. Therefore, regrettably, we must settle for one of his lieutenants. Reinhard Heydrich is the man we wish to kill.'

'You mean the man *you* wish to kill,' said Rick, 'because he slapped you in a concentration camp for a while. This is starting to sound personal to me.'

'Very well,' said Laszlo unemotionally, 'the man I wish to kill.'

Rick was struck again by the man's imperturbability. 'Still, there's something here I don't like. No, it's not the plan, or the bomb, or how we deliver the bomb. That's your business, not mine. You're the experts. I said a moment ago that this was starting to sound personal to me, and I'll say it again. I don't like it. I've had to kill a few men in my time, and I'm not proud of it. It was war, and it had to be done, whether it was Ne –' He caught himself. 'Whether it was in Spain or Africa or I don't know where. But when you kill a man, you'd better do it quick and you'd better do it right, or he'll come back after you with everything he's got. Because now it's personal for him, too.'

Renault spoke up. 'I must say my friend Ricky is right,' he began. 'I do not for a moment doubt the sincerity of Monsieur Laszlo's animus, nor do I question its origins. A stretch in one of the late Major Strasser's concentration camps is enough to put anyone off his feed. But I wonder, if you will permit a citizen of France and a true son of Descartes to say so, if emotion is getting the better of reason here.'

Major Miles looked at Renault with a grudging respect. 'I cannot stress enough,' he said, 'the seriousness of this mission and the importance my government attaches to its success. You have all been selected for it because of your skills, not your emotions.'

'I wasn't aware I was auditioning,' said Rick.

'Oh, but you were, Mr. Blaine,' said the major. 'In Ethiopia, and in Spain, when you went up against insurmountable odds – and lost.' Sir Harold turned to Louis. 'I can't say that your bona fides haven't given us some sleepless nights, Monsieur Renault. Your abrupt departure from Casablanca hard on the heels of Major Strasser's murder and Mr. Blaine's disappearance, however, has given you a convincing alibi as a nonperson. I have no doubt that you will impressively impersonate a Vichy official with the new identity we will give you.'

'I believe your offer is the only one on the table, Major,' said Renault. 'That makes it good enough for me.'

'As for you, Mr. Laszlo, there can be no doubt about your sincerity, or your desire to see justice done to the defiler of your homeland.' Laszlo nodded. 'With you, though, there is something more at work.' The major thumbed through a dossier. '"Victor Laszlo,"' he quoted, reading. '"Born in Pressburg, now known as Bratislava, Czechoslovakia. Languages: Hungarian, Czech, German, French, and English. Nationality . . ."' He paused. '"None."'

'A situation I have dedicated my life to rectifying,' said Laszlo.

'There, there, Mr. Laszlo,' Sir Harold soothed. 'One of the distinguishing peculiarities of this war is how so many of those involved are not what they first appear. Herr Hitler is not German, but Austrian. Mr. Stalin is not a Russian, but a Georgian. Even our own Prime Minister, Mr. Churchill, is half American.' The major paused to sip from a glass of water.

'My father was from Vienna,' Laszlo responded. 'But I feel myself Czech. Czech was my mother tongue. I was raised with the stories of Czech heroes, of Šarka and of the great rock at Vyšehrad, and of Hradčany Castle, the ancient residence of the Kings of Bohemia. In Czechoslovakia, we have been struggling against the Germans for hundreds of years.

They tried to destroy our language, they tried to destroy our people. They colonized Bohemia and Moravia, they forbade our music to be played in our theaters. Although we are Slavs, they have dragooned our blondest, most blue-eyed women into their evil *Lebensborn* program, and the rest of us they would enslave, as they would enslave all the Slavs whom they do not kill. Where, in fact, does your English word "slave" come from, if not from "Slav"?'

He turned to Rick. 'Yes, Mr. Blaine, it is personal. It has always been personal. And you dare criticize me – you, who have never spent one minute enjoying the hospitality of Reinhard Heydrich and his ilk! You, who have never seen your loved ones killed – simply for being your loved ones. . . .'

'I wouldn't be too sure of that,' Rick said under his breath.

Laszlo, however, had not heard him. 'You, from a country which has never suffered in wartime, never seen the slaughter of its people, never been challenged upon the international stage. You, with your jazz music and your skyscrapers and your Negroes and your Chicago gangsters. You, safe and secure behind your Atlantic Ocean barrier. While we Czechs sit in the heart of Europe, surrounded by enemies and yearning for freedom!' Laszlo wrung his hands. 'You say this is personal with me? I say – it should also be personal with you!'

'Maybe it is,' said Rick.

Laszlo fell silent for a moment. Then he spoke: 'You mean my wife.' It was a statement, not a question.

'Gentlemen,' said Major Miles, 'if we could please return to the business at hand.'

'With pleasure,' Renault agreed. 'Business is something we French understand. But have we considered the question of retaliation?'

Everyone was still, even Major Miles.

'It seems to me,' said Renault, taking advantage of the silence, 'that the Germans are not going to take the assassination of Heydrich lying down. Indeed, they've never shown the slightest inclination to do so in the past. When Tito's partisans shoot a Nazi in the Balkans, a hundred innocent people die in response. Our plot to blow up his cabrio as he tools through the streets of Prague may well succeed. But what about the innocent lives that may be lost? What about reprisals?'

Silence all around. Laszlo looked uncomfortable. Major Miles looked annoyed. Renault looked on.

'Now who's the sentimentalist?' Rick asked Louis.

'Not sentimentalist,' Renault replied. 'Pragmatist. There's a difference.'

Sir Harold cleared his throat. 'Do you suppose,' he asked Renault in a tone that suggested he'd been insulted, 'that we have not considered that eventuality?'

'That, Major,' said Renault, 'is exactly what worries me.'

A knock at the door brought an adjutant with some papers for Miles to sign. When the major turned back to the group, Rick spoke up.

'Did you think this up all by yourselves, or did you get it from Rube Goldberg?' he said. 'I mean, this is the dumbest thing I ever heard of. It's too complicated, for one thing. Too many people are involved, which means there's going to be leaks. The element of surprise will be gone.'

Agitated, he lit another cigarette. 'It's also far too dangerous.

You're talking about infiltrating a team led by Laszlo here behind Nazi lines. If the slightest thing goes wrong, we'll be rolled up in a matter of hours. Worse, you've got Ilsa, Miss Lund, stuck in Prague, where they'll probably execute her as soon as the operation goes sour. If Laszlo were captured alive, even if he was somehow able to hold out in the face of the worst kind of torture, how long would it be before they figured out that they had his beloved wife as well? Laszlo may not want to sing to save his own hide, but he'll croon like Crosby to save hers.'

He wished he could get a drink. 'It just won't work,' he concluded. 'Major Miles, I've been involved in some crazy schemes in my time, but this one takes the cake.'

'Monsieur Blaine . . .,' Laszlo started to say, but Rick turned on him.

'And you – I should have left with Ilsa on that plane and left you to rot in Casablanca,' he said angrily. 'I thought we had a deal, and in my book you've just welshed on it.' He sat down. 'There, I've made my speech,' he said. 'As far as I'm concerned, it's that simple.'

'No, Richard,' Ilsa said softly. 'It isn't.'

All eyes turned to her as she spoke.

'Richard,' she said, 'I want you to listen to me. Really listen.' The intensity of her glance left him no alternative.

'Every time I do, I get a different story,' said Rick, trying to fight her allure, and failing.

'This is no time for games!' she exclaimed. 'I'm not doing this because Victor has asked me to, or because the British have asked me to. I'm doing this because I *want* to. For me, for my family. For my father.'

Her eyes were flashing, as they hadn't since Paris. Then,

they'd flashed with the passion of love. Now, they flashed with another kind of passion.

'Remember back in Paris, when you asked me where I was ten years ago?'

'Yeah,' said Rick. 'You said you were having braces put on your teeth.'

'So I was,' Ilsa replied. 'Braces paid for by my parents, whom I loved very much. I was just a silly girl, only fifteen, but already I knew what a great man my father was, about the important work he was doing for my King and for my country. During the next decade I only grew prouder of him, as he rose in the cabinet, all the way to Minister of Defense. To be Edvard Lund's daughter was the greatest honor I could imagine – until, in Paris, I became Mrs. Victor Laszlo.'

Laszlo picked up the thread. 'A few weeks after the Germans marched into Prague, I fled to France,' he said. 'I tried to keep the presses running as long as possible, but it was no use. The Underground begged me to leave, to tell the world what the Germans were really like, about what they were planning for the rest of Europe. I didn't want to go to England, because of Chamberlain and the Munich Pact. Sweden might have been safer. But France seemed as committed as I to the struggle against Hitler.'

Ilsa resumed her narrative. 'I never worried about my parents back home in Oslo. Who would have imagined that the Nazis would invade Norway? Then, in April of 1940, they did. Everyone was taken completely by surprise. Yes, the British had mined our harbors, but we thought that would discourage the Germans, not provoke them. That false sense of security lasted right up to the moment they kicked the door to my father's house down, roused him and Mother from their beds, and forced them downstairs at gunpoint.'

She shivered at the recollection. Rick wanted to put his arms around her. Laszlo sat immobile.

'"Are you Edvard Lund?"' one of the soldiers demanded. When my father answered yes, the officer drew a pistol and shot him dead on the spot. They left my mother there, on the floor of her house, weeping over his body.

'I do not make this decision lightly,' Ilsa informed the gathering, but looking directly at Rick. 'Richard, you think this is Victor's idea, because he wants revenge for what they did to him in Mauthausen, and you're right. But this is my revenge, too. Don't try to take it away from me.'

Rick Blaine was amazed by what he had just learned about Ilsa Lund. Back in Paris they had said no questions. Back in Paris he'd thought he was the one with the bad memories. Back in Paris he'd thought he was the only hard-luck case in the world.

'I still don't see why you have to risk your life by going to Prague,' he objected. 'Why don't you leave that to Victor and Louie and me?' He turned to Sir Harold. 'Major, why can't we send a man to infiltrate Heydrich's operation? Surely there must be a Czech in London who speaks the lingo and knows the territory and—'

Victor Laszlo waved away his protests. 'Monsieur Blaine,' he said, 'I'm sure you do not mean to insult me by implying that I would willingly place my wife in unnecessary danger if there were another way. Allow me to explain to you why Ilsa, and Ilsa alone, must go.'

'No, Victor!' commanded Ilsa. 'Let me.'

She looked at Rick the same way she had the last time they

were together in Paris – at his club, *La Belle Aurore*, dancing to the strains of 'Perfidia' with the sounds of the big guns thundering in the distance. With tenderness, and love, and worry, and distraction, and a secret knowledge of what she was about to do. Only this time she was sharing that knowledge with him in advance.

'Richard,' she began, speaking to him, the tough guy from New York, as if he were a child, 'you don't know these people as we do. If we were to send a German-speaking Czech from the Resistance here in London, the chances that he would be recognized, informed upon, denounced, and shot within the first week are more likely than not. No one knows me there. With a little help from British Intelligence, I can be whoever I say I am.

'Thanks to Victor' – she nodded at her husband – 'our marriage, indeed our whole relationship, has been kept a secret from everyone. This was to protect me. But now I can wield it like a weapon against them. They will never suspect that I am the wife of Victor Laszlo.' She let out a little laugh of nervous excitement. 'Besides, a man could never get as close to Heydrich as a woman could.'

'Why not?' asked Rick. In his experience, no gangster worth a damn ever let a dame get close enough to see the color of his folding money except when he was out on the town with her. Women and business didn't mix.

'Because they don't think about women, that's why not!' said Ilsa. 'Because to the Germans, a woman is all but invisible except in the kitchen and, from time to time, in the bedroom. They would never have a room full of male secretaries handling top-secret documents because eventually they would have to shoot every one of them, just to be on the safe side. Why do you think Hitler has six secretaries – and except for Martin Bormann every one of them is a woman?'

He hadn't thought of it that way.

'Also,' she went on, 'there is the obvious. Reinhard Heydrich is notorious for his, shall we say, fondness, for attractive women, and I—'

'And Ilsa is a very beautiful woman,' said Laszlo, finishing the sentence for her. 'As you have noticed yourself, Monsieur Blaine.'

'You just can't wait to make her a part of your war, can you?' Rick snapped.

'You still don't understand, do you, Richard?' cried Ilsa. 'I've always been a part of it! Why do you think we went to Casablanca? Certainly not for me to meet you again! You remember Berger, the jewel dealer who was often in your café? He was *my* contact – not Victor's. I was trying to get my husband out of danger, not the other way around.'

'What?' said Rick.

'Yes, my contact,' Ilsa repeated. 'Berger was working for the Norwegian resistance. He was trying to get exit visas for us, and when he heard about the murder of the two German couriers and the existence of the letters of transit, he was going to try to purchase them from Ugarte. And then . . .'

'And then I interfered,' admitted Renault, 'and had Ugarte arrested at Rick's place to provide a little amusement for Major Strasser.' He looked around the table. 'I am sorry.'

'That's where you came in, Richard,' said Ilsa. 'You got those letters from Ugarte, and you gave them to us. When you did, you became part of it, too. We're all in this together now.' She stopped and blushed. 'Aren't we, Richard? Please tell me we are.'

He wanted to kiss her, right there in front of her husband, in front of everybody, and wondered why he didn't.

'I'll think it over,' was all he said.

CHAPTER FOURTEEN

Sam got in late that night. He was returning from his new gig, playing the piano in a smoky Soho nightclub located in a Greek Street basement that featured watered-down mixed drinks and a show of seminude girls that, in Sam's opinion, would not bear very close inspection in the daylight. The joint was called Morton's Cabaret Club, and it was run by a couple of Cockney gangsters, twin brothers named Melvin and Earl Canfield. The British civilians seemed to find them terrifying, but Sam simply found them amusing. The way they swaggered around in their tight black suits, which could not have concealed a cigarette lighter, much less a pistol, barking orders and generally acting as if they were tough guys! The very idea of an unarmed gangster made Sam laugh; the only unarmed gangsters he knew back home were dead gangsters.

The other black people at Morton's were a couple of dishwashers, and Sam didn't think much of them, either. They were West Indians, but far from the kind of Caribbean-born intellectuals he had encountered in Harlem, where the islanders more or less ruled the roost, socially speaking. Instead they were gentle and soft-spoken and unassertive, as if they feared that at any moment the British would notice they were black and ship them off across the ocean. Again.

At Morton's, the song in demand was 'Shine,' a jazzy coon song by Ford Dabney that Sam had never minded playing, whether it was with Josephine Baker in Paris or by himself at Rick's Café Americain. The white folks thought the joke was on him, but Sam knew it was really on them. He couldn't imagine colored people sitting around and paying to hear a white man make fun of himself.

'What kept you?' Rick demanded. He was alone in the sitting room, playing chess against himself. From his demeanor Sam found it hard to tell whether he was winning or losing.

'Nothing much, Mr. Rick,' he answered, taking off his topcoat and hanging it on the rack in the hall. He eyeballed the board as he came in: Rick was playing one of his favorites, a Paul Morphy game that featured a dazzling sacrifice of the black queen and victory on the seventy-sixth move. Sam and Rick had played it through just the other day. Why Morphy had played P-QR5 on the sixteenth move seemed obvious to Sam, but Rick apparently still didn't get it. He thought about lending the boss his copy of Philidor's *L'analyse du jeu des Échecs*, then remembered that Rick didn't read French very well. 'Just a couple of policemen who wanted to know what a colored man was doing walking the streets of London in the middle of the night, and did I know there was a war on?'

'What'd you tell them?' asked Rick.

'I told them it wasn't my war.'

'Maybe it is now.' Rick knocked over the white king in

resignation. 'Come on, let's go downstairs. I'm tired of sitting here drinking alone and beating myself at chess. I'd like to hear some music. Maybe even some of the old songs.'

'Fine with me, boss,' said Sam.

They went down to the lounge at Brown's. There were no lights on and few customers, but Sam managed at the piano by candlelight. Rick's bourbon didn't need any light at all; it was just fine in the dark.

'You wanna talk about it, boss?' asked Sam, his fingers moving lightly over the keys. The song was 'You Must Have Been a Beautiful Baby,' one of Rick's favorites. The boss always calmed down when he played.

'About what?' asked Rick.

'You know,' said Sam. 'Her. Miss Ilsa.' The Morphy game was the giveaway; when Rick was feeling optimistic, he replayed old Jose Capablanca games.

'I thought I told you not to talk about her,' snapped Rick. 'I wasn't aware that order had been rescinded.'

'Never mind, Mr. Richard,' said Sam. 'I just was thinkin'—'

'Who asked you to think?' Rick said.

He smoked and drank for a time in silence. Sam continued to improvise at the keyboard. Unconsciously he let his fingers slide over 'As Time Goes By.'

'Knock it off,' objected Rick, but Sam interrupted him quickly.

'You remember the first time we heard this song, Mr. Rick?' he said. 'It was back at the Tootsie-Wootsie Club, thirty-one or thirty-two, I think it was.'

'That sounds about right,' Rick grunted. 'Just around the time I became the manager.'

'It sure was.' Sam waggled his head in recollection. 'Wasn't that a time.' He started playing pianissimo and turned to face Rick.

'I remember like it was yesterday,' he said. 'That white boy Mr. Herman come marchin' through the front door and said he got a song in him and it got to come out and Mr. Solomon says get out and take your damn song with you, this is a colored club, we don't want no Jews here, but you says I'm the manager now, and then you says to Mr. Herman play it and he plays it.' Sam took a sip of water from the glass on top of the piano, leaving out only one insignificant measure in the left hand. 'And I been playin' it ever since.'

'You sure have,' agreed Rick.

'Tell you the truth, I don't much care for it. But it was always one of your favorites.'

'And hers,' Rick said. 'So cut it out.'

'I hear you, Mr. Rick,' said Sam, continuing to play, 'but I ain't listening to you.'

'You're fired,' said Rick.

'I believe that when you give me that damn raise you been promisin' me,' said Sam.

'He'll never fire you, Sam,' said Ilsa. 'You play "As Time Goes By" too beautifully for him ever to do that.'

Once more she came to him out of the darkness, an angel in white, as she had done in his café in Casablanca. Back then he'd thought he knew why she had come, and he had been wrong. Tonight, though, it was different. Tonight, he knew.

'When are you going?' he asked.

'Tomorrow.'

'Champagne?' It was what they had been drinking at La Belle Aurore the last time they had parted. It seemed appropriate.

'Champagne would be fine,' she said.

'Get the lady some champers, will you, Sam?' requested Rick. 'And make sure it's cold. I don't care who you have to bribe to get it, just get it.'

'Okay, boss,' said Sam, rising.

She composed herself for a moment while Sam was fetching the champagne.

'Victor told me about the agreement you two made back in Casablanca, when Captain Renault had him in the holding pen. About how you pretended to me that we would be leaving on that plane, when all along you planned to make me go with him. I want you to know that I'm grateful.'

'I wonder if I made the right choice,' said Rick.

'Never mind that now,' Ilsa said. 'The important thing is that we're here, together. The important thing is not what's been done. The important thing is what we *will* do – together.'

'Sounds like you've got everything figured out,' observed Rick. 'So what do you need me for?'

'I don't,' she replied, lowering her eyes. 'Victor does.'

Rick downed the rest of his drink. 'I've had better offers,' he said.

That was the wrong thing to say. 'Richard, don't be so stupid! Don't be so selfish! Can't you see this is bigger than you and me, bigger than Victor, bigger than all of us? This is not about the problems of three little people. If you can't see that – if you *won't* see that – then you're not half the man I thought you were. You're not half the man I fell in love with in Paris.'

She was crying now. 'Not half the man I'm still in love with,' she concluded, her voice trailing away.

Rick put his arm around her for support, and she sank back toward him, her head resting comfortably on his shoulder.

He kissed her, hard. She didn't pull back, not even for a second.

'Richard, don't you see?' she sobbed after their lips had parted. 'He'll die. I know he will. This thing obsesses him. It's all he thinks about. What the Germans have done to his homeland – what they've done to him – he cannot allow to stand. He has devoted his life to driving them out of Prague, out of Czechoslovakia, out of central Europe entirely if he can. The year he spent in Mauthausen has only made him more determined, not less. No matter what happens, he will succeed. Even if it kills him.'

She dabbed at her eyes with Rick's breast pocket handkerchief. 'That's why I'm asking you to help,' she said. 'Not for him, but for me. For us. Do you understand now?'

Reluctantly she drew away from Rick and sat back to look at him. 'The British are going to smuggle me into Prague. The Underground can get me into the RSHA headquarters and, with luck, into Heydrich's office. There is an opening for a secretary there, and with my languages I can easily pass for a White Russian.'

'So that's your story,' said Rick. 'I was wondering what it was going to be.'

'Yes,' said Ilsa. 'My name is to be Tamara Toumanova, the daughter of a Russian nobleman who was shot by the Bolsheviks after the October Revolution. I was raised by my mother across Europe, living in Stockholm, Paris, Munich, and Rome. I am at home everywhere, and nowhere.'

'What makes you think they'll fall for it?' Rick asked.

'They'll believe me all right,' replied Ilsa, 'because they'll want to. As a White Russian, I want revenge on the Communists for what they did to me and my family. Anyone who hates the Communists is more than welcome in Nazi circles.'

She shook her head as Rick began to refill her glass. 'No, Richard,' she said. 'I must have my wits about me at all times from now on.' She smiled at him, that same heartbreaking smile he remembered so well. The last time he had seen it was in La Belle Aurore, when she wore blue. Tonight, the only blue she was wearing was the blue of her eyes.

'You as well,' she said with a little laugh, reaching to take the bourbon from his hand.

'Leave a fellow's drink alone, will you?' objected Rick.

She looked at him earnestly, longing and desire dancing in her eyes. 'Then make it the last one,' she pleaded. 'I need you completely sober from here on. We all do, if we are to have any chance of success. Whatever it is you're hiding from, please don't hide behind liquor anymore.'

Reluctantly he put down the drink. Booze had been his boon companion for so long that, besides Sam, it was his best friend. Getting off the sauce was not going to be easy. It was a lot to ask of a guy. He looked at Ilsa in the candlelight, and suddenly he knew just how easy it was going to be. 'At least let me finish this one. A kind of hail and farewell.'

She leaned over and kissed him lightly on the cheek. 'You can finish it upstairs.'

'Keep playing, Sam,' said Rick.

'I ain't going nowhere,' said Sam.

Hand in hand, Ilsa Lund and Richard Blaine rose and left the lounge.

Very early the next morning, Tamara Toumanova departed for Prague.

CHAPTER FIFTEEN

New York, January 1932

'Ricky, you shoulda seen this place in old times,' said Solly after they had finished the policy racket collections, the beer deliveries, and the obligatory target practice one winter's morning. Solly still liked to collect on policy himself from time to time, perhaps to keep in touch with the roots of his success, and he would drag Rick around Harlem, collecting his tribute.

They were sitting in Solly's favorite counting house, a storefront saloon at 129th Street and St. Nicholas Avenue. The joint itself wasn't much, but that was the point. A long bar was on the left as you came in the narrow front door, and Solly's regular table at the back commanded a sweeping view of the whole room. Getting the drop on him would be difficult here, especially when he was with two or three of his boys or all by himself with just Tick-Tock Schapiro to keep him company. Tick-Tock was worth two or three ordinary boys any day of the week and twice on Saturday.

'German and Irish, it was, and of course Jewish. Now,

different.' He gestured with both palms facing up, a typically Horowitzian hand movement that meant What can you do? 'Some folks don't like it. *Feh* on them! Ricky, let me tell you something those boys downtown don't know: Coloreds is people, too.' By 'downtown,' Rick knew, Solly was talking not only about City Hall, but about Tammany Hall. And O'Hanlon. And Salucci and Weinberg in their headquarters on Mott Street, and all the other gangsters looking to muscle in on Solly's uptown turf.

'What is more,' Horowitz continued, 'they got money to spend, especially on policy! Everybody love policy. And I let them all play.' He thumped himself on the chest. 'I got big heart!' he exclaimed. 'The goyim, what do they know? They treat their own kind like *bupkus*, and they treat the coloreds worse. But not me. I treat everybody equal until proven they deserve otherwise.'

The numbers game was one of the most lucrative, and probably the easiest, of Horowitz's rackets; you practically had to beat the suckers away with a stick. The gambler picked a number between 1 and 999 and put down a bet, usually fifty cents. The winning lottery number was the last three digits of the handle at a particular racetrack on that day, which was published in the newspaper, so everybody knew if he or she had won. A winning bet should have paid off at 999 to 1, but once the cost of doing business and markups had been figured in, the real payoff was only half that. Still, that didn't seem to stop anybody from getting a bet down.

Little black boys in Irish caps would call out in greeting to Solly as he made his stately procession uptown. Every once in a while Solly and Rick would spy a particularly well-dressed black man, turned out in spats and sometimes even a monocle, whom the boys followed with stars in their eyes. That would be one of Solly's collectors, a big man in the community who could afford the finest things available to a Negro. 'You see,' he told Rick, 'they know I'm honest. I pay off, 500 to 1.'

'But the odds are 999 to 1,' Rick objected one time.

'Is not my problem,' said Solly. 'The rules say you pay off at 500 to 1 and that's what I do. Not 350 to 1. Not 400 to 1. Not even 499 to 1. Five hundred to 1, and not a penny less. I don't cheat them like Salucci does; I don't fix the handle the way Weinberg does with his phonus-balonus racetracks in Timbuktu. I treat 'em square, and I got no problems.' He gestured up and down Lenox Avenue and watched gratefully as the men tipped their hats to him. 'See?' he cried. 'Everybody love Solly Horowitz! The Grand Rebbe of Harlem!'

When Solly had muscled into this part of Harlem, he had had to contend with the formidable figure of Lilly DeLaurentien, a Haitian voodoo lady much given to bangles and beads who had had the colored numbers racket all to herself. Solly and Lilly clashed early and often, but after more than a few of her boys had ended up in the North River with their feet encased in blocks of cement, an uneasy truce had been called, with Lilly ceding most of her territory but retaining her social standing. There were whispers that Lilly and Solly had sealed their bargain with a roll in the hay, but no one really knew.

Solomon Horowitz confided in God and, once in a very great while and then only under duress, in Mrs. Horowitz. The only things he really trusted were his gat, which he kept well oiled, and his aim, which he kept well honed. This accrued to Solly's continued welfare and, indeed, existence, but it also had the added benefit of keeping the neighborhood's rat population handsomely in check. Horowitz hated rats, whether of the two- or four-legged variety.

In half a year Rick Baline had risen from green newcomer to one of Horowitz's most trusted advisers. Only Tick-Tock seemed to resent his rapid rise in the gang; the rest of them were clever enough to realize that Rick was smarter and braver than all of them. Killers Solly had plenty of, Schapiro foremost among them. Tick-Tock could put a bullet through a rat's eye at two hundred feet, which was a skill that came in quite handy down around the Five Points, where Tick-Tock had grown up. As the boss's bodyguard, Tick-Tock once had high hopes for himself in the succession department. Solly, though, was still the boss, and after him the boss would be whoever Solly said he would be. Solly knew it wasn't going to be Tick-Tock. Deep down, Tick-Tock did, too, and he didn't like it.

From Solly, Rick learned that while drink itself might be bad – 'the booze I can take or I can leave, but you should leave it alone' – drinking, and the art of it, was something with which a young man could profitably busy himself, and busily profit himself as well. Therefore, in addition to his other remunerative rackets, Solly owned and operated a string of blind tigers, blind pigs, dives, taverns, saloons, and speakeasies across upper Manhattan. Horowitz also owned a string of laundries, mostly in the Bronx, where he could change dirty money for clean, get his bartenders' aprons pressed, and from time to time cause to disappear in one or another of the lye vats a particularly troublesome corpse.

About the only illicit activity that did not go on in the

Mad Russian's empire was girls. 'This pimping, pah! This I leave to the guineas!' he would exclaim when one or another of the younger boys in the gang would ask him why, unlike Salucci, he didn't run dames. That put an end to the subject as far as Solly was concerned, but not as far as the younger fellows were concerned; and then one of the older boys would have to take the kid aside and explain that once, years ago, when he was fresh off the boat and could find no other way to make a living, Solly had run a few choice girls – girls who would do anything after arriving in America and finding out that the promised land was an eighteen-hour-a-day sweatshop on Allen Street sewing alongside your mother, your father, and all your cousins.

Then Prohibition had come along, and that was the end of that, thank God.

Rick loved the nightclubs, which Horowitz had scattered across the city, glamorous places where you could hobnob with the swells, listen to jazz, and gaze at the most beautiful women in New York, all for the price of a drink. An inflated price, to be sure: despite Prohibition, speaks weren't a particularly risky business, which made the steep markup on booze all the more delightful and remunerative.

The Noble Experiment was in its twelfth year and, everyone said, on its last legs. Earlier than most gangsters, Solly Horowitz had gleaned the happily awful truth that the Eighteenth Amendment was going to be extremely unpopular with most of the city's citizens, and he determined to slake their thirsts, Volstead Act or no Volstead Act. This bit of prescience had made him a rich man many times over, but he still lived simply and unostentatiously above old Mr. Grunwald's violin shop on 127th Street with his wife, Irma. Mrs.

Horowitz's recollection on almost every matter pertaining to her husband was doubtful, especially since she spoke almost no English. She knew nothing, she saw nothing, and most important, she remembered nothing, which was the way Solomon intended to keep it. 'What for she gotta learn English?' her husband used to exclaim whenever the subject came up. 'Yiddish ain't good enough for her?'

Horowitz was not a big man, but then most top gangsters weren't. They didn't have to be. In appearance he was short and a little rotund, but not fat: behind his affable exterior was both a formidable intellect and a strong physique. Not to his face, the boys called Solly 'the Mad Russian,' in honor of his birthplace somewhere in what was, what had been, or what would eventually again be Russia. Even Solly was a little fuzzy on the exact site of his nativity, although most of the betting men in the organization – which was to say all of them – put their money on Odessa. In his speech, the boss had the authentic Russian disregard for articles, definite or otherwise. 'Daddy,' Lois would exclaim in exasperation after a particularly Horowitzian enormity, 'you gotta learn to talk right!'

Solly was not the fashion plate O'Hanlon was, favoring off-the-rack suits from Ginzberg's on 125th Street; the occasional presence of an egg stain on one of his ties rarely dissuaded him from wearing it. Nor, for that matter, did Horowitz drive a snazzy Murphy Duesenberg around town for every flatfooted copper to spot. If you had seen Solomon Horowitz on the subway or the el, you might have mistaken him for a businessman – an insurance salesman, perhaps, working the immigrant communities for all they were worth. Which in his own mind, he was.

It was worth your life, however, to underestimate him – or worse, cheat him. One time, Big Julie Slepak, president of the Restaurant Workers' Benevolent Association, which was a wholly owned subsidiary of S. Horowitz Inc., had tried to skim a few grand off the top of money that rightfully belonged to the boss. Confronted with the evidence of his malfeasance, Julie tried to bluster his way out of his pickle until Solly put an end to it by yanking out the pistol that he always carried in the waistband of his trousers, shoving it in Big Julie's mouth, and pulling the trigger, thus shutting him up for good. That he did this right in front of his lawyer was a measure of the security Solly felt when conducting his business.

'Boys,' he said over the fallen flunky, 'a lesson to you this should only be. Never try to take from me that what is mine!'

Today, Rick could tell the Mad Russian was in an expansive mood, because he was smoking a cigar, a small indulgence he occasionally permitted himself. Normally Solomon Horowitz did not smoke or drink, and while he did not keep glatt kosher at home, he usually came as close to it as his appetites would permit. His vest was unbuttoned, and he sat comfortably at his rear table.

As usual, Tick-Tock Schapiro sat not far away, watching Solly's back.

Rick wanted to talk about Lois, to at least broach the subject, because while he loved Solly like a father, he loved Lois not at all like a sister. Solly's proscription against his daughter's dating any of the boys, though, was still very much in effect.

Rick glanced over at Tick-Tock and wondered if the big ape could read minds. If anybody were to tell Solly that he and Lois had been getting a little friendlier than Horowitz allowed . . . Not for the first time, he thought about Big Julie.

If Solly harbored any suspicions about Rick's intentions toward Lois, he gave no evidence. Instead he was off on one of his favorite subjects, which was the honor roll of Manhattan's great Jewish gangsters and his place as the last of them. Like some French King, after himself Solly saw only a deluge.

There was Dopey Benny Fein, him with the droopy eye. And Big Jack Zelig, with the crazy straw hat he used to wear all the time. And Louis Kushner, who shot Kid Dropper right in the back of a police car! And the greatest of them all, Monk Eastman, with his pigeons and his cats, who even fought in the war! Jesus, there was Jewish gangsters back then!

They were all familiar names to Rick Baline. He had grown up hearing of their exploits, like the time when Monk's gang, dubbed in honor of the boss (who was born Edward Ostermann) the Eastmans, had clashed with the Five Points boys led by Paul Kelly (who was really an Italian named Vacarelli). They shot up the intersection of Rivington and Allen Streets so thoroughly that it took a couple of hundred coppers to restore the peace and sent the *shmattes* who ran the crooked stuss games in the perpetual shadows of the els scurrying for cover for maybe three whole hours before resuming business as usual.

The reminiscences always started with the stories about Dopey Benny, so-called because a nerve or something had gone kaput in his cheek, which therefore drooped, occasioning any number of beatings, clobberings, and shootings provoked by the indiscriminate use by relative strangers of the hated nickname. From there, Solly's memory would quickstep through the years between the turn of the century and more or less the present day, and would always end with the *Shma* over the declining number of authentic gangsters of the Jewish faith, the kinds of fellas who could go toe to toe with the Irishers and the Italians without blinking and never took guff from nobody.

Rick always listened, his ears opened even wider than his eyes. Every time he went home to his dingy, solitary flat on West 182nd Street, Solomon Horowitz rose in his estimation with each stair that he climbed. Each step up those dark stairs, reeking with the smell of frying fish and boiling cabbage, seemed to him a step farther away from the kind of life he wanted to live, a step back in the direction of Chrystie Street, beyond which lay the boat, the shtetl, and Galicia. His mother had told him enough about her girlhood there, a dreary region of coal mines and (in her telling, at least) Cossacks, to make him never want to go to central Europe. Paris, he had decided, would be more his kind of place.

'Do you ever think about going straight, Solly?' asked Rick.

'Go straight?' Horowitz laughed. 'You gotta be kidding.'

'Well, why not?' persisted Rick.

'I tell you why not, smart guy,' Solly shouted. 'I tell you what straight is. Straight is cops with their hands out, shaking down Mr. Moskowitz on Second Avenue. Straight is Tammany politicians who slap on a yarmulke when they sit shiva for somebody they don't even know, and then ask you for your vote. Straight is when they put up another blind tiger on the Bowery, but neither a church nor a shul.' He spat contemptuously. 'That's what straight is, it is.'

Horowitz leaned over toward his protégé. 'Straight,' said Solly, 'is *meshugge*.'

In the distance, Schapiro grunted.

'Ricky, sometimes I think maybe you're *meshugge*, too. This worries me. You know the rules.'

'The rules?' said Rick.

'The Lois rules,' Solly answered. 'I hear things. I see things. Dumb I'm not.' He buttoned the top button on his vest. 'And neither are you. You can like, but you don't touch. You touch, Tick-Tock has to shoot you.'

'With pleasure,' Tick-Tock said from the shadows.

'What a waste!' Solly seemed saddened by the very thought of Rick's untimely demise. 'Because her I got plans for.' Rick was smart enough not to ask what those plans were and smart enough to glean that those plans did not involve him.

'And you, Ricky,' he said. 'I got plans for you, too. Not the same plans. But plans. A boy like you with a head for business, why, there is gelt to be made in the speaks, and easy gelt at that. Which is what I want to speak to you about.'

With that, Solomon Horowitz informed Rick Baline that henceforth he would be the manager of Solly's newest night spot, the Tootsie-Wootsie Club, just opened on the site of a former black social club. 'Me, I'm getting too old for this kids' stuff. Staying up until four in the morning, shmoozing the clientele, breaking up fights, cleaning up messes, *oy*. I should be in bed. Besides, you mix better with them.'

'With who?' asked Rick.

'The *goyim*, that's who! Not just the micks and the wops, but high society. Why, I should expect John Jacob Astor himself to walk in here if he was still alive, with his three hundred and ninety-nine best friends.' Solly rubbed his hands together. 'What we got here is the uptown version of Mrs. Astor's ballroom!'

Solly grasped him by his shoulders, held him at arm's length, and stared him right in the eyes. 'Remember this: The *goyim*, they trade with us, they buy from us. Sometimes they sleep with our women. But they don't drink with us. And, if you're smart, you won't drink with them, either. You keep them like this, always.' Slowly he let his hands fall from Rick's shoulders. 'You understand?'

'Don't worry, Solly,' said Rick. He could hardly believe one of his two dreams had just come true. 'I'll make it a point never to drink with the customers.' He looked at his boss. 'No matter who they sleep with.'

Now, for the other dream.

CHAPTER SIXTEEN

New York, April 1932

'Guess what I've got?' Rick Baline asked Lois Horowitz one night. They were sitting on the stoop in front of her building. The air was pleasantly brisk but not cold; Rick loved the way it raised the color in Lois's pale cheeks.

Rick's hands were behind his back, concealing something.

'Two bottles of Moxie?' she asked.

'You're cold.'

'A treasure map for some pirate's island?'

'You're ice cold, and besides, they were fresh out of those at Blinsky's when I asked.'

Lois bit her lower lip for a moment. 'I know,' she said. 'A ticket on the *Twentieth Century* to California!'

That, he knew, was what she really wanted. 'No,' he said, 'but you're warmer now.'

'I give up,' she said, pouting prettily.

'Here.' He handed over a pair of duckets: two in the orchestra for that evening's *Show Stoppers*, starring Ruby Keeler and Al Jolson at Henry Miller's Theatre.

This was going to be tricky. From time to time Solomon Horowitz allowed Rick Baline to escort his daughter to minor social functions, in the manner of a chaperone, but even those occasions were rare. A Broadway show and dinner afterward, though, was a full-fledged date, and those were strictly *verboten*. More and more Rick found himself resenting the restrictions. He wanted to take his best girl out on the town. After all, what was the point of being a gangster if you couldn't act like one?

The way Solly saw it, that was not going to happen. He may have lived contentedly, if not happily, above the violin shop, but he wanted better for his daughter. He did not aspire to Fifth Avenue, but he wanted her to do so. He was not a vain man, and he never envied O'Hanlon his silk suits and slicked-back hair, or Salucci his dark Italian good looks. Money he had aplenty, but it was being put aside – the safe at the Tootsie-Wootsie Club was stuffed with it – where it would come in handy someday, maybe even do some good, if not for him, then for his only child. He thought of it as a kind of dowry, but one that was reserved for Lois and not for her husband – who in any case had better be both rich and successful before Solomon would ever consent to any union with his issue.

Rick, however, had been enamored of her from the beginning, smitten by her raven hair and her cerulean eyes and her alabaster skin. There was more to Lois than simply looks, though, as he soon discovered. Like him, she wanted things out of life, big things. Not just a fancy car and a big house, either, but education and social standing as well. Lois was working hard to improve the way she spoke, hunting down her 'ain'ts' and rooting out her dropped 'g's,' and she was spending her afternoons in the public library reading everything she could find. The small allowance she got from her father she spent on stylish new clothes. Lois had never looked very much like the other girls in the neighborhood, but now she was distancing herself from them as fast as she could.

'Rick Baline!' she exclaimed. 'You certainly don't give a girl much time to get ready to see the hottest show on Broadway!'

'The most beautiful girl in Harlem doesn't need much time,' he said.

She ran up the front steps. As she opened the door, she blew him a kiss. 'Meet me back here in an hour,' she said, 'and don't be late. I hear the opening number is a knockout.'

Rick wasn't so sure. Throughout the first act Ruby Keeler danced like an elephant and sang like a chimpanzee. 'Jeez, she's terrible,' he remarked as they stood outside at intermission. Lois was smoking a cigarette, something her father would never allow her to do at home. Smoking was something the smart set did.

'Everybody knows that,' said Lois.

'So how does she get to be in a show with Jolson?'

'She's his girlfriend, that's how,' said Lois. 'Guys like to do things for their girlfriends, you know.'

Rick wanted to pursue the subject, especially the part about girlfriends, but Lois wasn't interested. She was gazing around at the theater crowd, at the fancy cars lining the streets, and up at the midtown skyline. 'It sure is a lot nicer here than it is in Harlem,' she said half to herself. 'Say, did you get a load of some of those joints we passed on the way down? Wouldn't you just die to live in a place like those someday? I sure would.'

'Don't you worry, Lois,' said Rick. 'We both will, before you know it.'

She grabbed his arm. 'Do you really think so? I can't wait.'

'I promise.'

'That's what I like about you, Rick,' said Lois. 'You're going places, too. Why, I'll bet you see the whole world someday.'

'If you'll go with me.'

The buzzer announcing the start of the second act prevented her reply. 'Come on, let's see how it all turns out,' said Lois, taking Rick by the arm.

The big number in act two was a duet for Ruby and Al, set beside an obviously fake waterfall; her name was Wanda and his was Joe. As far as Rick could make out, the plot of the piece had something to do with young lovers thrown together, despite the wishes of their parents, at a resort hotel in the Catskills, or maybe it was Lake George. Joe was a poor Irish bellhop on the make, and Wanda was a rich girl trying to throw over her current beau, a bloodless Protestant named Lester Thurman whom she quite clearly didn't love, in favor of Joe. The moral of the story seemed to be that anybody can be anything or anyone he wanted to be as long as he had the chutzpah to get away with it.

'Hungry?' he asked as they exited.

'I thought you'd never ask,' she said.

He took her to Rector's, the swanky restaurant on the West Side renowned for its food and its status as a gangland hangout. The refined clientele got a thrill knowing that the hard boys and brassy dames at the tables were very often the same folks they would read about in the Broadway columns and police stories the next morning. Hits, however, were strictly off limits at Rector's – nothing was worse for business than a couple of out-of-town salesmen catching a stray slug as they munched their veal chops. Rector's was a kind of gangland no-man's-land, where rivalries, if not guns, had to be checked at the door.

Off in a corner, Rick spied Damon Runyon, drinking whiskey hand over fist and chatting up a couple of dolls. Runyon liked to hang around the fringes of gangland, romanticizing the tough guys as colorful characters with hearts of gold in his tales, when in fact the relatively good ones were family men like Horowitz and the bad ones were sadistic killers like Tick-Tock and Salucci. The only gold in gangland was fool's gold.

Lois was thrilled. Solomon would never have let her come here, and Rick was already mentally explaining their presence there to his boss should it come to that. But he could see the gleam in her eyes and knew he had done the right thing in bringing her. This was the kind of glamorous life she wanted; minus the gangsters, this was the kind of life her father wanted for her also. 'It looks a little crowded,' she said.

'The first rule of restaurants,' he told her, 'is that there's always an empty table if you really want one.' He waved to the maître d'. 'I mean, if the President of the United States walked in here just now, they'd find him a table, wouldn't they? Well, the President is here!' Smoothly he palmed a $20 bill and slipped it to the man as he greeted them.

'Andrew Jackson,' he whispered to Lois as they were led to their table. 'Works every time.'

Then he spied the great Dion O'Hanlon himself, holding court at his usual table against the back wall, not far from the kitchen.

They said that as a youth, O'Hanlon had been lured into an ambush in a restaurant and, before he got any of the three pistols he always carried with him out of the special pockets he had had sewn into his custom-made suits, had been shot eleven times. Dion, however, survived; the three guys who tried to clip him were dead within a week. O'Hanlon was never seen in public again without both backup muscle and a handy escape route. Dion O'Hanlon was the Houdini of gangsters.

Rick was mesmerized at the sight of him. He had seen O'Hanlon only in odd photographs in the newspaper – the Irishman wanted to stay out of the papers, and fearful reporters happily obliged – but Rick knew it was him. It was like coming face-to-face with Satan.

'Champagne,' Rick told the hovering waiter. Tonight was special.

'Champagne!' exclaimed Lois. 'What's the occasion?'

'I'll tell you after it gets here,' said Rick.

O'Hanlon was a short, dapper, well-dressed fellow who filled out a dinner jacket like a small ice chest. Since nobody in gangland outranked him, he kept his hat on, wearing his fedora cocked low over his left eye, but Rick knew he could see everything that mattered. Mentally Rick compared O'Hanlon's splendor with Solly's rumpled proletarianism and tried to decide which look he preferred. It didn't take long.

Walter Winchell was talking to him earnestly: 'I got the dirt, I mean, do I ever!' He was shouting loudly enough for everyone in the room to hear, but O'Hanlon was paying only half attention to the scribe, apparently preferring his conversation with a handsome blond man in evening clothes. A real

Joe College type, thought Rick, the kind of guy he loathed on sight.

Suddenly O'Hanlon rose. 'Good evening, Mae,' he said, tipping his hat. He turned to Winchell. 'Walter, would you mind leaving us alone for a while?'

While Winchell scrammed, Mae West herself sauntered over as only Mae West could. She plunked herself down next to the gangster and began to whisper what Rick assumed were sweet nothings in O'Hanlon's ear. Everybody in New York said they had been an item once upon a time.

'Look!' exclaimed Lois. 'There's Mae West!'

Rick was contemplating the wonder that was Mae West when he noticed O'Hanlon glance his way and then nod to someone behind him. It was a short, brisk downward motion of the head, almost imperceptible unless you were looking for it.

Two seconds later he felt a hand on his shoulder. Not a friendly hand, not a 'Hey, buddy' hand, but just a hand, leaning on him as if he were a lamppost. Rick twisted his head to the side and saw that the hand belonged to another little man, about the same size as O'Hanlon and even sleeker. Rick hadn't heard him approach, but here he was. The man glided like a dancer, smooth and silent.

Rick knew who he was: George Raft, the society tea-dancer whom O'Hanlon was making into a movie star out in Hollywood. Some gangster picture called *Scarface*.

'Mr. O'Hanlon sends his greetings and invites you to join us at his table,' said Raft.

'Who's Mr. O'Hanlon?' Lois asked innocently.

'He's the gentleman with Miss West,' answered Raft. Lois was up and out of her seat before Rick had a chance to say anything. 'Smart girl you got there,' Raft said to Rick privately as they followed Lois.

O'Hanlon was on his feet and bowing graciously. 'It is an honor and a singular pleasure to welcome the daughter of a treasured business partner to my table on this fine evening,' he said. Lois extended her hand, and O'Hanlon took it in his, pressed his lips against it, and kissed it.

'Do sit down, Miss Horowitz,' he suggested. Although his speech patterns were Irish, he had a faint English accent, a legacy of his youth in the mill towns of England, where his parents had sweated enough money for the passage to America. 'You, too, Mr. Baline. I've heard a lot about you, and I am very pleased to make your acquaintance.' He snapped a finger in the air, and the headwaiter materialized instantly. 'Champagne, please.'

'We've already ordered some,' said Lois.

'I refuse to let such a lovely young lady as yourself drink ordinary champagne, miss,' he told her. 'As someone who knows a bit about the liquor business, I keep my own private stock here, precisely for moments like these.' His lips widened in a mirthless smile that showed no teeth.

'Of course you know Miss Mae West and Mr. George Raft,' O'Hanlon said as if of course they would. 'May I present Miss Lois Horowitz and Mr. Yitzik Baline, daughter and protégé, respectively, of my esteemed associate Mr. Solomon Horowitz of Harlem and the Bronx.'

Rick could hear the contempt for Horowitz, Harlem, and the Bronx in the Irishman's voice and hoped it was lost on Lois. It was found not in his tone, but rather in his manner or pronunciation, the way he separated each word in order to draw attention to it, the way he implied that Harlem and the

Bronx were now alien places that no decent person would live in if given a choice. It was the contempt of the city for the boroughs, of the big-time for the small-time, of the winner for the loser.

'Now to complete the introductions,' continued O'Hanlon, addressing Lois. 'This good-looking lad who's been struck dumb in obvious admiration of your great beauty is none other than Robert Haas Meredith, whom you may have been reading about in all the New York newspapers recently, and by that designation I do indeed include the *Journal*, the *American*, and by God, even the *Times*.'

Now Rick recognized the man. Meredith was the scion of a rich Upper East Side family, a Park Avenue lawyer in private practice with big political ambitions, who charged his rich clients a fortune to win equal justice under the law. Meredith was too smart to defend gangsters like O'Hanlon in public, but there was no law against helping out on the side – and besides, it never hurt one's image to be seen in their company. Why, Mayor Walker had made a career of it.

'Good evening, Miss Horowitz,' said Meredith.

'Charmed, I'm sure,' replied Lois, who was.

'Mr. Baline,' O'Hanlon said, addressing the table, 'has quite a head for business. In the space of a few short weeks, he has transformed the Tootsie-Wootsie Club uptown into the foremost rival of my own dear Boll Weevil.' As everyone knew, the Boll Weevil was Harlem's leading jazz nightspot – although not for long, if Rick could help it.

'Love that name, the Tootsie-Wootsie,' said Mae West, as only she could. 'I hear you've got quite a piano player there, you know, what's-his-name.'

'Sam Waters,' replied Rick.

'I'll have to come up and see him sometime,' said Mae.

'What's your line there, Baline?' Meredith asked.

'I'm—'

Just then the champagne arrived. Everyone was poured a glass except the attorney and the host, and after a brief toast by O'Hanlon, the sparkling wine went down smoothly. Even Rick had to admit it was good stuff.

'I'm a drunkard,' he said jocularly as he drained his glass. 'Or at least I will be after much more of this.'

'Mr. Baline exaggerates his fondness for the bottle, I'm sure,' said O'Hanlon. 'For with Prohibition the roaring success that it is, surely there is not a true drunkard left in America at the moment – and more's the pity! They were my best customers.' He took a sip of ice water. 'Mr. Baline is the manager,' he told Meredith. 'And would you think it to look at a young fellow like him?'

'I'd think a lotta things to look at him,' said Mae West, tugging on her champagne.

Everybody laughed. O'Hanlon set both his impeccably manicured hands on the tabletop. 'Mr. Meredith,' he said, 'I wonder if you would be so kind as to escort Miss Horowitz and the rest of the group to that empty table over there so that I might be permitted a few private words with Mr. Baline.'

O'Hanlon turned to Lois. 'I most heartily apologize for depriving you of the company of your escort, but I hope you'll have no objection to dining with Miss West, Mr. Raft, and Mr. Meredith.'

'The pleasure would be all mine,' added Meredith, taking her by the arm and starting to lead her away. 'Goodbye, Mr. Baline,' he said.

'Is it okay, Rick?' asked Lois, already in Meredith's grip.

Rick tried to read her expression but couldn't. 'I'll be right over,' he said reassuringly.

'I'll make this as brief as I can,' O'Hanlon said as they departed, and Rick realized that this was now serious business. He was not frightened by O'Hanlon so much as respectful of him. Solly's contemptuous dismissals of the man now seemed to ring very, very hollow.

'Mr. Baline, you will please tell the charming Miss Horowitz's father that I harbor no hard feelings toward him for what he's been doing to my Canadian trucks. If his boys can take my liquor away from my boys, then that is my problem and I am just going to have to find me some better boys. That is the nature of our business, and a very good business it has been up to now for all of us.'

'Solly says you've been chiseling him in Montreal with Michaelson,' countered Rick. 'That you're trying to put him out of business.'

O'Hanlon waved off his objections. 'Solomon Horowitz and I go back to the days of Lefty Louie and Big Jack Zelig and – God help me, for doesn't this date me as an old-timer – the great Monk Eastman, his own dear departed self. And wasn't Monk, who treated me like a son, a Hebrew like your own good self, and didn't I love him like a father.' He took another sip of his drink.

'Unlike so regrettably many of my fellow Christians, I have nothing whatsoever against Jewboys or sheenies of any kind,' O'Hanlon continued. 'Under the misguided scourge of the Noble Experiment, those of us who serve the common weal have got to work together in a spirit of harmony and mutual understanding, and sure, isn't there plenty of turf for us here in the great and united city of New York. I have no interest in Solomon's policy rackets in darktown, and what he does north of a Hundred and Tenth Street and along the Grand Concourse is basically of no interest to me.

'However,' O'Hanlon continued *sotto voce*, 'anything he does to affect my shipments from our brothers in Quebec very definitely *is* my business. It is messy, and messiness of any kind disturbs me greatly. Now I am a kind and gentle man, as you know, and I don't want any further trouble between us. Therefore, I have a proposition for him. Please tell your boss that I want a truce between us, and to that end I am prepared to offer him a considerable consideration, one of my most valuable and prized political assets – a lad I have been grooming myself for quite some time – in return for his promise to lay off.'

Rick was listening, but not quite understanding. His blank look proclaimed as much.

'It's known far and wide that the one thing that Solomon Horowitz wants is respectability,' said O'Hanlon, 'and he'll get it if he has to kill for it. There isn't a soul in New York he hasn't told that he's reserving his little girl for a big man. Now that I have met the young lady, I can see why. She's extremely beautiful, and I am a man who has known and loved a great many beautiful women in my time. And I intend to love a great many more before the good Lord calls me home.'

O'Hanlon drained his water glass and wiped his lips daintily on his napkin. 'In the shape and form of Mr. Robert Meredith here, I think I have quite the candidate for the hand of Miss Horowitz. He is everything Solomon hopes for in a son-in-law. He is independently wealthy. He is a lawyer, which is always a handy thing in our line of work. And he is a gentile with a distinguished name and a pedigree that would put a prize pigeon to shame. I had been intending to effect the introduction soon, but fate, it seems, has lent a hand.'

O'Hanlon had been fiddling with the tableware as he spoke. Now he looked up and into Rick's eyes.

'Just as I thought,' he said. 'Lovesick. You have my deepest sympathy, but I advise you to put the very thought out of your mind. She's not for you, lad, and there's no gainsaying it.' He began polishing a perfectly clean knife. 'But just as in the days of old, when warring kingdoms could settle their differences in a rational and civilized manner in the furtherance of their common interests, so can we today ameliorate our differences by letting the young people bring us together. Good for Solomon. Good for me. Good for her. And good for you, too, if you're smart enough to see it that way.'

He put the knife down. 'There's a lot of very hungry men in this town, lad,' he said.

'Aren't you big boys ever going to join us?' drawled Mae West, who had sashayed over from the other table. 'You know how rude it is to leave me with only two gentlemen?'

O'Hanlon stood up. 'I was just remarking how hungry I was gettin',' he said to her. 'Shall we join the ladies, Mr. Baline?'

Rick glanced over at the adjacent table. Raft appeared to be in the middle of a funny story. Meredith had both arms on the table, chortling away.

Lois was leaning against him, laughing gaily, her left hand on his arm, her hair brushing his face.

'I think maybe I'm not wanted over there,' he said.

O'Hanlon shrugged jauntily. 'Suit yourself, lad,' he said. 'It's the wise man who knows where his place isn't.'

They shook hands, and O'Hanlon pulled Rick close. 'I heard about what you did, saving your boss from taking a hit from one of my boys. Very brave of you. But very stupid as well. Remember: Only a sucker is willing to take a bullet for another man, no matter who he is. Stick your neck out for no one, that's my motto, Mr. Baline. You'll find you live longer that way.'

Rick made to leave. He couldn't wait to get out of there.

'One more thing,' said O'Hanlon. 'Always go with the winner, whether it's in a horse race, at the gaming tables, or at the fights. The smart man always knows who the winner's going to be in advance.' He patted Rick avuncularly on the arm. 'Your boss has been warned. And so have you. The smart man hears and heeds a warning. You look like a smart lad to me. It's your chief I'm not so sure about.'

At that instant, Rick saw Meredith kiss Lois, a quick peck on the cheek. Her eyes were shining like the diamonds he would never be able to give her. And here he was going to propose to her this very night. He felt like a fool.

'Ain't love grand!' said Mae West, who ought to know.

'I'll see she gets home safely,' Dion O'Hanlon said. 'You can count on me.'

CHAPTER SEVENTEEN

'Don't you see, Ricky?' Renault was saying. 'It's crazy. Even if the bomb goes off, even if it actually kills Heydrich – and I have my doubts on that score – the consequences will be dire for everybody left standing. And I most certainly include myself in that number.'

Renault was pacing around Rick's rooms at Brown's. Sam was playing at Morton's. Rick was sitting in a wing chair.

'A bomb thrown into his car as he comes over the Charles Bridge from the Staré Město! It's preposterous! The chances of its actually working are one in a hundred, maybe one in a thousand. How is the assassin supposed to get away? How is he even going to get close to him? What if the device malfunctions?'

'That's what the rest of the team is for,' Rick reminded him. 'That's why they're carrying guns.' He laughed. 'That's why they may even get a chance to use them.'

Renault was unconvinced. 'As if they would have a chance against Heydrich's security men.'

Rick blew a smoke ring into the air. 'I really don't think Victor Laszlo cares much whether he gets out of Prague alive, as long as Heydrich doesn't.'

'Why are you going, then?'

'Because it amuses me. Because I like lost causes. Because I have nowhere else to go and nothing else to do. Because it's time to stand and fight instead of sitting this one out on the sidelines.'

'Fight for her, you mean,' said Renault. 'For Ilsa Lund. Or is it more than that?'

'It's a lot of things.'

Renault looked at his friend. 'Ricky, back in Casablanca I asked you why you couldn't return to America. You gave me a very evasive answer.'

'It was the truth, Louie.'

'If you don't want to tell me –'

'I can't.'

'– or if you can't tell me, very well. But let me ask you this: After you left New York, why did you spend all those years in Ethiopia and Spain, fighting for the losing side? Surely a man of your sophistication would have known that neither the overwhelmed Ethiopians nor the outgunned Republicans had a Chinaman's chance.'

'Maybe I liked the odds.'

'Why?'

'Do I have to draw you a picture?' Rick fought the impulse to get angry; it wasn't Renault's fault he was curious. Hell, he'd be curious himself if he didn't already know the answer. 'I was trying to get myself killed.' He shrugged. 'I failed.'

'That really doesn't explain anything,' said Renault.

'Okay,' said Rick. 'Let's just say that a long time ago I did something I wasn't proud of. I made a mistake – hell, I made a whole series of mistakes – and before I knew what hit me, a lot of people I loved were dead and it was my fault. It cost me everything I had. I'm still paying for it.'

Rick and Renault both fell silent for a time. Neither was very comfortable exchanging confidences.

'What else is bothering you?' Rick said suddenly. 'You're acting like a cat on a hot stove. Don't tell me you're losing your nerve.'

Renault sat down in the chair across from Rick's. 'I'm not quite sure how to say this,' he began.

Rick looked up. It was not like Renault to speak with anything but derision. 'Try English. You know how bad my French is.'

'I'm serious, Ricky,' replied Renault. 'We have a saying in France, "*Albion perfide.*" Perfidious Albion. Treacherous England.'

'Maybe you should have stayed in Casablanca,' Rick suggested.

Renault rose, drawing himself up to his full height. It wasn't much, but it would have to do. 'What I mean,' he said angrily, 'is that something about this whole operation stinks to high heaven. I know something about fixes –'

'So do I,' Rick reminded him.

'– and I smell one now. Why should the British care about Reinhard Heydrich? Why should they exert all this effort to kill one obscure Nazi, when there are others far more important, others whose deaths might bring an end to this war much faster? Why are they financing Victor Laszlo and his crew? Why don't they want their fingerprints on the knife?'

'I give up,' said Rick.

'Because there's something in it for them, something very important.' Renault lit a cigarette. 'When we first met Major Miles, I raised the issues of reprisals. He brushed my concerns aside. Consider this, though: What if that's what they're really after? The British don't give a damn about Reinhard Heydrich. You heard Lumley complaining about the lack of Czech backbone, didn't you?' Renault's voice fell very low. 'Well, what if this whole thing is simply a way to provoke an atrocity and get the Czechs fighting again? It wouldn't be the first time the English have done something like this. Remember Norway.'

'What about Norway?' asked Rick, his curiosity rising.

Louis was happy to explain. 'When the English mined the harbors at Narvik in April of 1940, they were not trying to *prevent* a German invasion of Norway. They were trying to *incite* one, because they wanted to occupy Norway themselves and cut the German iron ore supply coming along the Kiruna-Narvik rail line. The problem was, the Germans outsmarted them and landed while the British ships were sailing home, awaiting the German response. The English got caught with their pants down once; they won't want it to happen again.'

'That's hard to believe,' muttered Rick.

'Hard to believe because that's the way they want it. Propaganda, dear boy – it's the name of the game. The English are as crooked as your roulette table.'

'You never complained about my roulette table before. So why are *you* going, then?'

'To retrieve the honor I thought I had lost forever,' Renault said glumly, sitting down.

'Honor?' said Rick, surprised. 'Why, Louie, I don't think I've ever heard you use that word.'

'I did once,' replied Renault.

'I guess there's a second time for everything, then,' said Rick, lighting another cigarette. Blindly his left hand sought the drink that was habitually at his side, until he recalled why it wasn't there anymore. Because of her. 'You want to tell me about it?'

'No more than you wanted to tell me,' said Renault. 'Still, they say confession is good for the soul.'

'I wouldn't know about that,' said Rick. 'Don't let me stop you, though.'

'Very well, then,' replied Renault, and told his story.

In 1926 Louis Renault had left his home in Lille to come to Paris and seek his fortune. He was twenty-six years old, witty, educated, articulate, and far more elegant than his drab, grimy, industrial hometown. Renault rightly considered Lille too small for the proper exercise and display of his talents. He had no interest in following his father into the lace-manufacturing business but was only too pleased to accept his father's money to assist him on the short journey to Paris and the foundation of a small establishment there.

Renault had envisioned a life as the darling of café society and the sensation of the salons. He had foreseen evenings at the Opéra and nights in the company of breathtaking women. As she had for so many other young roués, though, Paris proved herself an inhospitable mistress. Much to his surprise and chagrin, Louis found himself living not in an elegant suite of rooms in the rue Scribe, but in an unaesthetic flat on the fourth floor of a grimy building across from the Cimetière Montmartre in the rue Joseph le Mâitre and spending his dwindling funds in the dubious company of the ladies of Pigalle.

One early evening in May he trudged back up the hill from the Abbesses stop on the Métro, discouraged. The money from his father was running out, he had no particular prospects for employment (not that he really desired any), his attempts to penetrate the salons of the Eighth Arondissement had so far failed, and his wits, which had always served him so well back in school, were being put to the test as never before.

To his surprise, he found a young woman sitting disconsolately by the curb in front of his house. His concierge, a formidable brute of a woman named Madame de Montpellier, whose suspicion of outsiders and interlopers still extended to him, although he had rented his room for more than four months, was screaming imprecations at her; but the girl took no notice. The rain had not yet washed away the smell of cigarette smoke from her clothes, and her hair was uncombed. Renault tapped her on the shoulder, to ask if he could be of assistance, but she ignored him and stared straight ahead.

He lit a cigarette, breathing in the tobacco smoke deeply. Madame de Montpellier (privately he doubted the validity of the nobiliary particle) finished her tirade with some choice words of invective and slammed down the window. Louis knew she was still there, watching, so he continued to smoke and gaze out over Paris – the view was spectacular, even if the accommodations were not – until a decent interval had elapsed. Once again he addressed the waif.

'Louis Renault, at your service, mademoiselle,' he said with what he hoped was an aristocratic flourish.

Finally she deigned to look at him. In the twilight he could not tell the color of her eyes, but they were big and round, and he knew they must be blue. Her light blonde hair fell unarranged to her shoulders. It had not been washed in several days, but – *tant pis!* 'Renaud,' she said. 'That's a funny name. Are you running from the hounds, like me?' She giggled, and for a moment he wondered if she was a bit mad.

It was not the first time someone had made a pun on his name, but he acted as if it were and let out a chuckle. 'Indeed, mademoiselle,' he said, 'the hounds are baying at my heels at this very moment.' Which was something very near the truth.

'Then perhaps we should go inside, where we will be safe,' she suggested, and stood up.

She took his breath away. Not that every woman didn't take his breath away, but as he was growing older he was also growing more sophisticated in his appraisal of the female sex. Dirty and unkempt as she was, she was also special. That he could tell, even in the Parisian dusk, which after all was so much more romantic than the dusk in every other city.

'What is your name, child?' he asked her as they mounted the steps to his room. *Madame la Concierge* had retreated to her matins and her meal; even so, they tread lightly upon the stair.

'*Isabel,*' she replied. '*Isabel ne rien.*'

He fed her from his small store of cheese and bread. He drew a bath for her in the tub at the end of the hall; against all odds, the hot water was still working. He bathed her gently and washed her hair lovingly, wrapping both head and body in his only two towels and leading her gently back to his room. They made love with a bottle of cheap red wine to keep them company. She cried out softly when he touched her.

In the morning they were both awakened by a loud, angry knock at his door. From a distance, Renault could hear Madame de Montpellier shouting, but it wasn't her knock, which he knew so well from rent day, but another, fiercer pounding. He staggered out of bed and threw open the door.

A very large and extremely irate man was standing before him. The fellow had red hair and a red beard and red eyes and was dressed like a common laborer. Worse, he reeked from every pore. Instinctively Louis Renault recoiled from the apparition, thinking fleetingly that the fellow should fire his valet.

That reaction saved his life. In his right hand the man held a knife, which he wielded with dexterity, slashing the air where Louis's throat had been just a second before. Renault fell back, confused; the girl jumped up, alarmed. She screamed. Madame de Montpellier bellowed as she charged up the stairs. Doors throughout the house flew open. It was 5:26 A.M., an hour and a minute Louis Renault would never forget.

'Stop,' he cried as the intruder advanced toward Isabel. He moved toward the man as menacingly as he could, but the stranger only laughed at him.

'Come, coward,' he taunted. 'Let's see how you dance with a man.'

Renault wanted to move, but his feet were nailed to the floor. He tried to fight, but his hands were tied. He tried to speak, but his voice was gone. No, that was not it: he was simply afraid.

'Bah!' sneered the man, knocking Louis aside. 'See, Isabel, how brave your new lover is!'

Isabel was kneeling on the bed, her eyes wide. The sheets

had dropped from her body, and Renault's mind registered a fleeting glimpse of her beautiful body, naked and exposed in the morning sunlight, dotted with ugly bruises. Then she was covered in blood, and the sheets were covered in blood, her blood, and she had fallen to the floor, taking the bedclothes with her, the blade of the knife protruding from her breast, the handle of the knife still in the man's hand, that hand drenched with her blood. '*Henri, non!*' were her last words.

Exhausted from his murderous rage, the man named Henri collapsed in one corner of the small room, his chest heaving. Louis Renault sat transfixed in the other, impotent. Through the doorway careened the concierge, followed closely by the police. The *flics* beat Henri senseless, and then for good measure they turned their wrath on Renault. They pounded on his head until he could no longer think and could no longer see and then could no longer feel anything.

He awoke five hours later in the police station. A gendarme was applying a cold compress to his aching head. He was lying on a small metal cot. Two other men were in the room, both wearing suits.

'. . . very brave of you, *citoyen*,' said one of the men. 'Madame de Montpellier has explained everything. We have been looking for this man Boucher for several weeks. He was a pimp who beat his girls and killed at least two of them. A very bad man.'

Renault wasn't interested in M. Boucher. 'Isabel?' he croaked. He hoped he'd remembered her name correctly.

'*Oui, Isabel*,' said the man. '*Est morte, hélas!* There was no hope. The wounds were too grievous.'

Renault fell back, silent.

'Your courage in attempting to defend the honor of this esteemed daughter of France shall not be forgotten,' said the other man.

Renault had no idea what he was talking about.

'Isabel de Bononcière,' said the man, and all at once Renault knew. The daughter of a minister of France, who had disappeared from her home in the Faubourg St.-Honoré, not far from Élysée Palace. The police had been searching for her, unsuccessfully, for six months. It was thought she had run away. Reported sightings of her came from as far away as Amiens, Lyons, and Pau.

'This animal Boucher seduced a simple girl and led her unwillingly into a life of shame,' said the man, who was taller than his colleague. As Renault's eyes cleared, he could see that the speaker was a man of substance; on his lapel he wore the Croix de Guerre. Then he recognized the cabinet minister Édouard Daladier.

Daladier leaned over and kissed Renault on both cheeks. 'For your bravery, you have the undying gratitude of the Fourth Republic.'

Louis tried to prop himself up on one arm but failed. His head sank to the pillow once more. Perhaps some good would come out of this horrible mess. Perhaps his family would never have to find out. Perhaps . . .

'For your continued discretion, I have the honor to present you with' – Daladier fumbled for something in his pocket, and Renault's spirits rose – 'a commission in the colonial Prefecture of Police.' Daladier smoothed the front of his suit jacket. 'Should you ever return to this country, or breathe a word of this incident to anyone, then you should become a party to this dreadful murder, a compatriot of this miserable *cochon* Boucher and thus an enemy of France. I trust I make myself clear.'

Daladier smiled paternally when Renault managed a nod. 'Excellent!' he exclaimed. 'A grateful nation salutes both your judgment and your discretion.'

With that, Daladier left. The other man, Renault now noticed, was a policeman.

The next day he was released from the hospital and put on a military transport plane. Louis Renault spent the next fourteen years in every godforsaken outpost of France, from Vientiane to Cayenne to the Middle Congo, until, finally, he had washed up in French Morocco. In each country he had taken advantage of every man – and, more, every woman whose man could not protect her. He had kept his mouth shut and his head down, until Rick came along. Until Victor Laszlo and Heinrich Strasser and Ilsa Lund came along. Ilsa Lund, who reminded him so much of his dead Isabel and of his lost Paris.

Damn them! Not remembering had been so easy, and for so long.

Rick lit a cigarette as Renault finished his tale. 'I guess things are tough all over,' was all he said.

CHAPTER EIGHTEEN

New York, April 1932

Rick got in his car. He cursed O'Hanlon and Meredith. He cursed Rector's. He cursed George Raft and Mae West. He even cursed Ruby Keeler.

He turned over the ignition and started to drive – he wasn't sure where.

His car, a new DeSoto model CF eight-cylinder roadster that had cost him more than a thousand dollars, was parked heading downtown from Rector's, so that's the way he went. He sped angrily down Seventh Avenue, letting his subconscious direct him to 14th Street, then east to Broadway. He followed Broadway down to Little Italy, made a left on Broome and then a right on Mott. Now he knew where he was going.

As he negotiated the Manhattan streets, he decided to put Lois out of his mind for the moment and instead dwelled on other things. His future, for example. He loved being the boss of the Tootsie-Wootsie Club, but how long would that last? Repeal was already in the air. The same coalition of do-gooding suffragettes and thin-lipped Bible Belt preachers that had given the nation Prohibition was now thumping the tubs to get rid of it.

Besides, what kind of a job was crime for a Jewish boy? For Miriam Blaine's son? Leave it to him to get into crime when most Jews his age were getting out and getting degrees instead, abandoning the hard end of the business to doomed garment district thugs like Lepke or Murder Inc. hitmen like Kid Twist Reles. The kids he'd grown up with in East Harlem – what were they now? City College grads, scholars, thinkers, even a professor or two. He'd had his chance, and he'd already blown it. He loved his new life, his expensive car and flashy clothes and the ability to whip out a roll and peel twenties off the top like they were candy, but he was ashamed of it, too. Aside from the vaguest generalities, he had never been able to bring himself to tell his mother what he really did for a living, which was why he hardly ever saw her anymore.

Plus, he knew it couldn't last. Nothing ever did.

Was it already time to think about quitting? The Irish, by and large, already had. Probably because he was an immigrant, Dion O'Hanlon was the last of them; the rest of the paddies were busy pursuing more profitable, and legal, forms of corruption, such as the police force, the law, and politics. Maybe he ought to start planning his exit, get out and leave the business to the Italians. They seemed to enjoy it. But not until Solly got out, too.

He found himself parked across the street from 46 Mott Street. Like all gangster hangouts, the building was as nondescript as clever men could make it. In Rick's experience, gangsters preferred to attract attention to their clothes, their cars, and their women, not to their businesses; Salucci was no exception. Even at this hour, the building's upper floors were illuminated by electric light, while half a dozen or so hard boys were stationed around the perimeter, keeping the watch by night.

Once more, Rick had an opportunity to compare his uptown world with this one, and the comparison was not flattering. From the looks of things, if Salucci were not already bigger than Solly, he soon would be. He was younger, meaner, and would, when the time came, hit harder. What O'Hanlon had given Rick tonight was a warning. Now all he had to do was deliver it.

If he had the guts. After all, he couldn't just walk up to Solomon Horowitz and admit that yes, he had been seeing Lois behind his back, in contradiction of a direct order. Yes, he had taken her to Rector's. Yes, he had met with Dion O'Hanlon, Solly's rival and enemy. Yes, O'Hanlon was offering a truce in exchange for the one thing that Horowitz was least likely ever to consider part of his business: his daughter. Sure, Solly wanted respectability for Lois, but not if it came with O'Hanlon's marker attached to it.

He didn't know what to do. He added his own name to the list of people he was cursing, and he cursed himself a fool and a coward.

He put the car in gear and slowly slid away from Mott Street, heading back uptown again. There was very little traffic, and within half an hour he was standing in front of Horowitz's home on 127th Street.

The street was deserted. Solly didn't believe in having gorillas hanging around in front of his house. The light in a third-floor parlor window, the one that looked down into the street, meant Lois was still out – having fun with Meredith.

Rick shut off his engine and waited.

He must have dozed off, because the next thing he knew he was hearing the sound of pealing feminine laughter in counterpoint to deeper male guffaws. That, he knew, was the liquor laughing.

He saw Lois get out of a car, Meredith's car – a Duesenberg Model J, he noticed with chagrin; those things cost twenty times what his jalopy did. How could he compete with that?

He saw Meredith take her by the hand, across the sidewalk and up the stoop. 'You're going to have to learn to let me open doors for you, darling,' he said to her.

'Sorry,' she said, giggling.

They embraced near the front door. Meredith kissed her on the lips, for a long time. Then he walked backward, down the stairs and across the sidewalk, never taking his eyes off her.

She didn't take her eyes off him, either, even when he got in the car, started the engine, and, after she blew him one last kiss, took off down the street. She just stood there, looking down the street after him, long after his car had disappeared around the corner and he had headed back to whatever fancy-pants enclave on Fifth Avenue he was from.

Rick rolled down the window and called her name softly.

She looked up, startled.

'It's me,' he said, getting out of his car.

'Oh, hi, Ricky,' she said, brushing back her hair.

'Did you have a good time tonight?'

'I had a wonderful time,' she replied. 'The play was swell. Thanks.'

'Yeah,' he said. 'I hope dinner was, too.'

She said nothing, just bowed her head slightly, waiting.

'I'm sorry I had to run out on you like that,' he said, trying to preserve what little dignity he had left. 'Business. You know.'

'That's okay,' she said. 'Look, Rick, I better be getting upstairs. It's late. I'm going to have a hard enough time explaining everything to Papa as it is.'

Rick scuffed his shoes on the pavement. 'How are you going to explain him?' he asked. He couldn't bear to utter his name.

'Robert said he'd like to see me again,' she said. 'With Daddy's permission, of course. He's going to call me tomorrow.'

'Ain't that swell?' was all he could think to say.

In one horrible evening, Rick Blaine was seeing his whole carefully planned fantasy go up in smoke. The way he had it figured, he was going to rise and rise in the organization until Solly had no choice but to bestow his only daughter upon him, the way the Protestants did in business downtown. Marry the boss's little girl: that was his goal – and not just because she was the boss's daughter, either. Because he was in love with her and had been since the day they'd met.

He had never considered the possibility that she might not be in love with him. They both had their eyes on a bigger prize – except her prize didn't include him. Nor did it include anything around here: didn't include the rackets, didn't include Harlem, and damn sure didn't include the Bronx. From the shtetl to the state house in one generation: that was Solomon Horowitz's goal. And Lois's as well.

He could see why. As he'd sat in his car, waiting for her, he had had a chance to look the neighborhood over. Many more black faces were appearing on the streets than before, making

Rick wonder how long the Horowitzes were going to stay. The Jews were clearing out, evicted or evicting themselves. Maybe his earlier ruminations were right. Maybe it was time to get out. Maybe it was time to grow up.

'Nice night, huh?' he said.

'I gotta go,' she said.

No. Not yet.

'Let's take a walk around the block. I'd like to have a smoke.'

'Rick.'

'For old times' sake,' he begged. 'I got something to say.'

'Okay.'

Rick lit a cigarette as they started down the long block. 'Lois,' he began, 'I was going to ask you something tonight. Before . . . before . . .'

'I know,' she said.

'You do?'

'Sure.' In the glow of the streetlights, she looked more beautiful than ever. Her black hair had melted into the ink of the night, her pale, almost ghostly white face framed in purest ebony. She was Rachel, she was Sarah, she was every beauty of the Torah. Perhaps she was even Lilith; he didn't care.

'You want to know what Daddy thinks of you,' she said confidently. 'Well, Rick, let me tell you: he's crazy about you. He talks about you all the time. About how far you're going to go. About how happy he is that you and I met that day, about what would he do without you. Is that what you wanted to know?'

They had stopped walking, and she had turned to him. Her face was looking up at his. It might not be what she was expecting, but it was now or never.

'No, Lois,' he began, 'that's not it. There's something else

I've wanted to say to you for a long time.' He tried to collect his thoughts, sort out his emotions, marshal his argument, and screw up his courage. He failed miserably.

'I'm in love with you,' he blurted. 'I've always been in love with you. From the first time I saw you on the el, even before you fainted.' Impulsively he swept her up in his arms. 'Marry me,' he said.

He kissed her, the way he had seen Meredith kiss her. That would tell; a woman could never disguise her feelings in her kisses.

She kissed him back, but perfunctorily. Then she broke away. 'Stop,' she said. 'Somebody might see us.'

'So what?' he said, his passion rising. 'Marry me.' He tried to kiss her again, but she deflected his pass.

'Please, Rick, please!'

'Marry me, Lois,' he asked, begging now.

'Rick, no,' she said. 'I can't.'

'Can't or won't?' he asked.

'Both,' she said, and he knew he was finished. 'Besides,' she said, 'I never knew you thought of me that way before. Not really.'

Never knew? How could a woman not know how a man felt about her, not read it in his eyes, not hear it in his voice every time he spoke to her? How could she fall instead for some phony like that putz Meredith, O'Hanlon's *nachshlepper*, a man without even a mind or will of his own?

He tried to put his arm around her, but she shrugged him off. It was no use: the moment had passed.

'Look, Rick,' she said, 'even if I wanted to, I couldn't marry you. You know that. We both know that.' She smiled at him, that killer smile that matched her old man's killer eyes, that smile that no man alive could possibly refuse, even if he wanted to, which he didn't. But he could not tell if it was a smile of affection or a smile of pity.

'Ricky,' she said. She leaned forward and gave him a little kiss, the kind you'd give a child. 'You're sweet. Very sweet. I think you're swell. But you're not for me. It's not that I don't like you – or even . . .' She hesitated for a moment, searching for the right word. 'Or even that I don't love you, a little. You're a stand-up guy, and my dad thinks the world of you, and so do I. You're going places.' She had stopped smiling. 'It's just that the places that you're going and the places that I'm going aren't the same places.'

'Where's Meredith going?' Rick asked bitterly. 'Can he take you to the right places?'

'I don't know,' she said honestly, 'but he's got a better chance than you do. Isn't that what life is all about? Chances? Opportunities?'

'Yeah,' he said. 'I guess that's what life's all about.'

'Well, I've got to grab my chances when they come along!' she said excitedly. 'Don't you think I know what I face if I don't? Do you really think I want to spend the rest of my life up here, living like an old maid in a third-floor walk-up, and not knowing whether my father is going to come home alive each night? Has it ever crossed your mind that that's no life for a girl? And that Daddy knows it? And that he's trying to do something about it? And that it's selfish for you to try to take that away from me, no matter how you feel?'

Rick knew he had lost the battle, utterly. 'I guess I never thought about it that way.' He hung his head.

Lois kissed him once, quickly, on the cheek. 'You don't have to look like your dog just died,' she said. 'Buck up.

Things are going great. In fact, you know what?'

They were walking again and were almost back to her front door.

'What?' he said dully.

'I think that tough guy O'Hanlon's kind of impressed with you. Oh, I gathered tonight that he and Daddy don't get along all that well, but they've been doing business together for years. You could be some kind of go-between for them. Heck!' she exclaimed. 'You could end up runnin' the whole show after the old geezers quit if you play your cards right.'

'I never thought of that,' Rick admitted.

'Of course you haven't, you silly boy,' said Lois as she walked up the front stoop. 'You need a woman to think things through for you.' She looked at him one more time in the glow of the city's lights. 'It's just that it can't be me, is all.'

She kissed him again, this time the way he had always wanted her to kiss him. He drank her kiss in deeply, because he knew it would have to last him a lifetime. At that moment, he didn't care if Solly came down with a hand cannon and blew him into the street; it would have all been worth it for this kiss, this one kiss.

She pulled away again, this time more slowly, her lips the last part of her body to separate from his.

'Come on, let me go upstairs, lover boy. It's chilly out here, it's late, and I've got to get my beauty sleep.'

He stood forlornly on the sidewalk, across from his one-thousand-dollar DeSoto, and watched her walk up the stairs and out of his life.

One thing bothered him, though: Which was her real kiss? The first one, or the last?

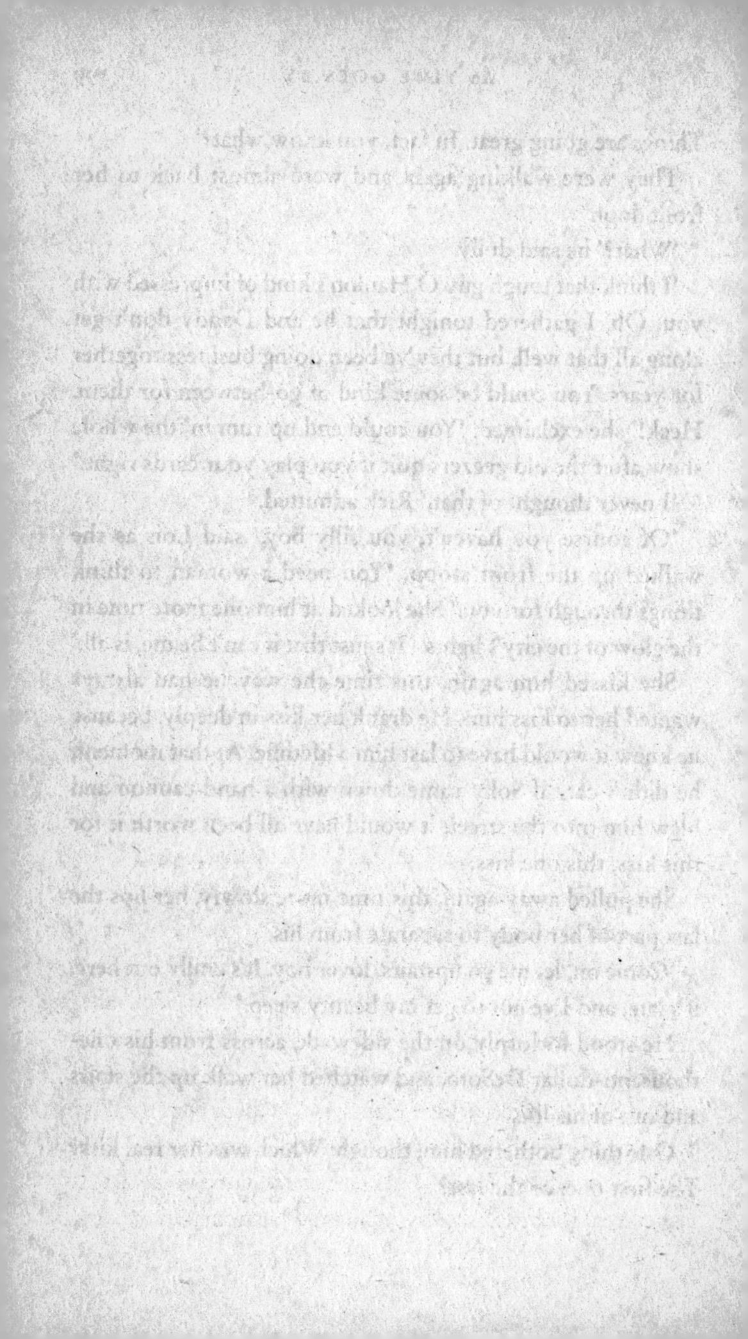

Things are going great. In fact, you know what?'

They were walking again and were almost back to her front door.

'What?' he said drily.

'I think that [illegible] got O'Hanlon kind of impressed with you. Oh, I gathered tonight that he and [illegible] don't get along all that well, but they've been doing business together for years. You could be some kind of go-between for them. Heck!' she exclaimed. 'You could end up running the whole show after the old geezer's quit if you play your cards right.'

'I'd never thought of that,' [illegible] admitted.

'Of course you haven't, you silly boy,' said Lois as she walked up the front steps. 'You need a woman to think things through for you.' She looked at him, [illegible] in the glow of the [illegible] lights. 'It's [illegible] that [illegible] me, [illegible].'

She kissed him again, this time the way he had always wanted her to kiss him. He didn't kiss [illegible] deeply, because he knew it would have to last him a lifetime. At that moment he didn't care if God came down with a hand-cannon and blew him onto the street; it would have all been worth it for one kiss, this one kiss.

She pulled away again, this time more slowly, her lips the last part of her body to separate from his.

'[illegible] on, [illegible] get [illegible] or [illegible]. It's only [illegible] of [illegible], and [illegible] at the beauty shop.'

He stood [illegible] on the sidewalk across from his [illegible] the [illegible], and watched her walk up the stairs and out of his life.

[illegible] thing [illegible] though. What was her real [illegible]

[illegible]?

CHAPTER NINETEEN

Major Sir Harold Miles reviewed their assignments one more time. They had already been over them on a dozen occasions, but once more wouldn't hurt. Who knew, it might even do some good. Maybe it would keep some good boys from getting killed unnecessarily. Still, Rick didn't hold out much hope. Good boys got killed because they didn't pay close enough attention, and no one could do anything about that.

Jan Kubiš and Josef Gabčík had joined them, and Laszlo introduced them to Rick as members of the Czech resistance movement in London whom he had hand-picked as his chief operatives. Together with Laszlo, Renault, and Rick, they would be parachuted into Czech territory by a Royal Air Force plane. The drop was to take place near Prague, at a small village called Lidice, where Kubiš and Gabčík were from. It was a small, tightly knit town of no more than a few hundred souls, all of whom, Laszlo had assured everyone, were deeply committed to the cause of repelling the Nazi invader.

For an operation of this magnitude, the equipment was surprisingly simple. The assassination device was a bomb of British manufacture that would be tossed into Heydrich's open car as he rode into town toward his office in Hradčany Castle. It had to be tossed in because Heydrich's car was an armor-plated Mercedes-Benz designed to roll over land mines and drive away unscathed.

'Don't they know how to make bombs in Czechoslovakia?' asked Rick. A bomb seemed to him a cowardly way to kill a man. 'I thought the Czechs were supposed to be good at things like bombs.'

'Not an explosive device like this,' interjected Major Miles. 'Even the Germans don't have a bomb like this one.' He seemed very pleased about it.

The major held a disarmed sample in his hands. At least Rick hoped it was disarmed, because Sir Harold proceeded to set the timer.

'Listen very closely, gentlemen,' he said. Rick glanced at Laszlo to see if he could detect any fear in the man's face, but his gaze was riveted on the bomb.

For ten agonizing seconds silence reigned in the room. At first, Rick wasn't quite sure what he was supposed to be listening for; then he figured it out: he was supposed to be listening for nothing, and nothing was exactly what he heard.

'Absolute quiet,' said Sir Harold, 'and absolutely reliable. Failure rate: zero. The Germans and the Czechs have hand-held bombs, of course, but they make the most frightful noise. As you have just heard, this bomb makes nothing of the kind. You could slip it into your wife's purse and she'd be none the wiser until the thing went off. Silent and deadly.' He permitted himself a small chuckle. 'Let's hope the Irish never get hold of one.'

Rick could think of one Irishman who probably already had: the same Irishman who had advised him, so long ago, to go with a winner, and whose advice he had studiously avoided taking ever since.

On the wall, Major Miles indicated a large map of Prague. 'We have considered a number of possible sites for the attack,' he began, 'but we are all now agreed that this is the best one.' He tapped with his pointer at the Karlův Most, the Charles Bridge, the most famous and beautiful bridge in the city, spanning the Vltava in a baroque orgy of statuary.

'Thanks to Miss Lund, whose progress in infiltrating Prague Castle has been extraordinary, we know that Heydrich rides in from his country villa to the castle by the same route every day. As you can see' – the major tapped the map with the tip of the pointer – 'as he approaches the bridge, he must pass by the Clementinum, then make a sharp left onto Křižovnická, and another sharp right onto the Charles Bridge. Even if his security men were able to clear the bridge of all civilian traffic – which so far they have shown no inclination to do – his Mercedes would still have to come almost to a complete stop to make this turn without throwing the Protector into the river.

'We have something else working in our favor. The Protector is extremely punctual. He hates lateness in others, and he absolutely detests it in himself. He crosses the bridge each morning at precisely seven-fifty, so he may drive through the gates of the castle at the stroke of eight o'clock.' The major seemed personally very pleased by his opponent's punctuality.

Armed with automatic pistols, Kubiš and Gabčík would man the posts on either side of the bridge while Laszlo stepped forward, as if he were about to cross the street once the Hangman's car had passed. When the car had achieved its lowest possible speed, when the driver's concentration was most focused on negotiating the curve, Renault would step out in front of the vehicle, forcing it to come to a stop. Laszlo would then move briskly behind the car, drop the bomb inside, and walk smartly away. The ten-second delay meant everybody would have to hurry.

A secondary diversion was to be provided by Rick, who, seconds after Laszlo had delivered his package, would lay down a smoke bomb just ahead of the car's path, on the bridge proper. As the car's occupants dealt with the perceived threat from the front, the bomb would go off in the backseat. That would give the conspirators the chance to disperse, and by the time the police were picking up the pieces they would be far away in different directions, later to reassemble in the sanctuary of the Church of St. Charles Borromeo.

'One last thing,' said Major Miles. 'Despite all our best efforts, there is always the chance something could go wrong. If it does, you will all be in the greatest danger.'

'So we need an abort signal,' Rick said.

'Mr. Blaine is right,' replied Sir Harold. 'Such a signal must be clear and easily understood, and invoked only in absolutely unexceptionable circumstances. In our planning we have relied absolutely upon Heydrich's German sense of punctuality. Through a prearranged signal, Miss Lund will confirm contact. The team will depart for the staging area in Lidice upon reception of her message, and the assassination will take place as soon as possible thereafter. Therefore, Mr.

Laszlo and I have agreed that if Heydrich is one second past five minutes late, the operation is to be considered compromised and everyone is to stand down at once. Any questions or objections?'

Rick's voice broke the somber stillness. 'Just a couple, Major,' he said. 'How can we be sure that we won't all be arrested the minute we hit the ground, and shot on the spot?'

Sir Harold looked only mildly discomfited at the thought. 'We have no reason to suppose anyone is talking out of school,' he said. 'A British gentleman's honor is paramount in these matters.' He waved his hand in the air as if to brush away the very notion.

'Another thing,' continued Rick. 'As Louis has already pointed out, how are we all going to live with ourselves – assuming we live at all – when after losing their beloved Heydrich, the Germans decide to get even by killing hundreds, maybe thousands, of innocent people in retaliation? They've done it before, and there's no reason to think they won't do it again.'

Now it was Laszlo's turn to reply. He rose to his feet.

'Monsieur Blaine,' he said, 'your concern for the welfare of others touches me deeply, especially insofar as it appears to be a recently acquired characteristic. You would obviously prefer to let this monster continue to walk the sacred earth of my homeland. Do you have any idea who this man is?'

Rick said that he had some idea.

'Not as I do. You were not at Mauthausen.'

'No, I wasn't,' Rick shot back. 'But I was at Addis Ababa and at the Ebro River. Do you think I haven't seen what you have? Do you think I haven't seen men suffer and die?' He smacked his fist on the table. 'Get the chip off your shoulder.

You're not the first guy who's ever had some tough luck, and you won't be the last. The way I see it,' he said, 'if I'm sticking my neck out, I have just as much right to an opinion as you do.'

Laszlo had never heard Richard Blaine speak with such passion. 'Let me tell you how the Nazis amuse themselves in Mauthausen,' he said. 'They take a man to the bottom of a deep stone quarry and then force him to walk to the top, carrying stones weighing twenty-seven kilos on his back. Every step of his journey is accompanied by blows. When he finally gets there he is sent back to the bottom again, and loaded down even more heavily for another ascent. When he stumbles, as eventually even the strongest man must, he is beaten with a bludgeon. So it goes until he is dead. One morning I counted twenty-one bodies lying on the side of the road. There were times when I almost wished myself among them.'

Laszlo sat down. 'I am grateful for your willingness to assist us in this matter. I do not flatter myself that it is I whom you think you are helping. Frankly, I don't care. Whatever occurred between you and my wife happened in the past. Understand this, however . . .'

His voice dropped low, as if he and Rick were the only two men in the room, perhaps in the world.

'I could not care less what happens after we kill Reinhard Heydrich. When I was in Mauthausen, the death of this man was my sole reason for living, and I swore to myself that should I escape, I should not rest, should not flee, until I saw him dead. Now I have him within my grasp. I will not let you or *anybody else* dissuade me from my task.

'If I die, so be it. If you die, or even if Ilsa dies, that is the price we must be willing to pay for the greater good of eliminating this man. And if it also means that others, innocents, must die in order that he does, too, then that is the price they must pay as well.'

'Sounds a little steep to me,' said Rick.

'Who are you to judge? What do you know of the enemy whom we face? What do you know of the suffering of the people of Europe? Do you know how long they have been waiting for this moment, waiting for a few brave souls to strike a blow against the oppressor and to give heart to everyone else? Within Germany itself there are those who are on our side – Hans and Sophie Scholl of the *Weisse Rose*, Bishop Galen, Professor Huber – but who outside Bavaria knows their names? And what, in any case, can they do?

'*We* can do something, however, and we shall. When we slay this monster Heydrich, we shall be offering the gift of hope to millions who thought hope had vanished from their lives forever. There are no noncombatants in this war, Monsieur Blaine, no neutrals. One is either for us or against us. Should you prove to be numbered among the latter instead of the former, then you shall be sacrificed with no more thought or regret than if you were a spring lamb.

'I have promised my wife that you will take part in this mission. She has assured me of your loyalty. She is my most trusted confidante. How and why she is so certain of you is of no import to me. Nor is what happens to any of us after we accomplish our mission. That I will leave to God. Should you try in any way to interfere with our chances for success, though, I will kill you myself. To do anything less would betray a sacred trust, and that is one thing, indeed the only thing, I am not prepared to do.'

Major Miles interposed himself. 'Very well, then, gentlemen, you have your orders. Upon receipt of Miss Lund's signal, you are all to report to the airfield at Luton at once. You will be issued your armaments at that time. I advise you all to set your affairs in order and to get plenty of rest. When the shooting starts you'll be glad you did.'

He put down his pointer. 'The mission upon which we are all embarking is fraught with danger. I won't deny that. His Majesty's government is as much a part of it as any of you, and it is in the highest interests of that government to make sure that Operation Hangman succeeds. It must, and it shall. That is all.'

If only that were true, thought Rick.

Rick and Renault shook hands with everyone in the room as they departed. When it came time to shake hands with Victor Laszlo, it was Rick this time who had to hold out his hand and wait several seconds before it was grasped.

'Good luck,' said Rick. 'It must be nice to always be right.'

'It is,' said Laszlo.

CHAPTER TWENTY

He knew what he promised Ilsa, and he cared. But not that much, and not right now.

Ilsa was in Prague. He was in London. A body of water and half of a bottle of Jack Daniel's lay between them, although not for long. She never had to know about it. Besides, he needed all the help he could get.

He drank straight from the bottle; this was no time to stand on ceremony. Demon rum had always helped him think before. After everything that had happened, after the worst that could happen had happened, it had still been his friend. It had protected him from the Italian bullets in Ethiopia, had shielded him from the gunfire of the Nationalists at the Ebro River, when victory had seemed so close and then evaporated so quickly, and had given him the courage to fight on, all the way to the end, when even the bottle could tell the difference between victory and defeat, if he still couldn't.

Rick the liberal. Rick the idealist. Rick the freedom fighter:

what a laugh. Couldn't they tell the difference between a man on a mission and a man on a suicide mission? In Ethiopia he had thought death would be simple. There was a war on; all you had to do was wander out on the killing ground and wait for the one with your name on it to show up. Selassie's battle against the Italians had seemed hopeless, which suited Rick just fine; but the Africans had surprised everybody by holding off Mussolini for almost eight months. From late November 1935, when he washed up in Addis Ababa because it was the most remote place he could think of on such short notice, until May 1936, when the new Roman legions had occupied the country, he had fought as best he could – not expecting to win, hoping somehow not to lose, but not caring much either way, and always ready to take a bullet. Just as long as he could take out a few Italians, especially the ones who reminded him of Salucci. They all reminded him of Salucci.

He got to Spain three months later, just in time for the civil war. He hadn't intended it that way, but his bad luck seemed to be following him around. The Spanish Civil War taught him a few things. The first thing it taught him was that he was glad he wasn't around for the American Civil War. Practically overnight, brother fought brother, father fought son, and everybody killed everybody in the most horribly imaginable way.

He didn't like to think about what he'd seen in Spain. Hemingway had written a whole novel about it, about the place where futility married brutality and their offspring was called the International Brigade. Hemingway had made the war sound heroic, but what did a writer know? Rick had seen the Internationals used for cannon fodder, chewed up and spat out by Hitler's Condor Legion and the Italian

Blackshirts, and there was nothing heroic about it. It was Ethiopia all over again, except with better food. He hated to see so many good boys fed to Franco's machine guns so cavalierly. Like him, they believed in the cause of fighting fascism; unlike him, they were willing to die for it. Not that he wasn't willing to die; it was just that he was trying to die for something else, and not succeeding.

Not like Luís, who wasn't trying to die at all. His death wasn't much in the grand scheme of things, just the exit of another kid who believed the slogans and the shouting, who trusted people he shouldn't have trusted and paid for it with the only coin he had: his life.

Luís Echeverria bought the farm at the Ebro River in September of 1938, which was near the end, just before Rick, like thousands of others on the losing side, had fled to France and the simulacrum of Maginot Line safety. Everybody said the Ebro River was the turning point of the war. That made it sound glamorous in retrospect, which it wasn't. Back home, the equivalent would have been the shot to the back of the head as you were strolling idly along the Fifth Avenue underpass at the new Rockefeller Center, or the pop between the eyes when your last vista was some Hackensack swamp, and here you thought you were just going out to get the papers with a bagel and a schmear on Second Avenue.

Luís was a handsome, black-haired boy of nineteen whose fondest wish was that he would get home alive to Marita, the girl he loved even more than he loved freedom, which was to say one hell of a lot. Luís had shown him the lone photograph of Marita he carried with him at all times, had shown him the letters he had received from her. Rick had not had the heart to tell him about the perfidy of women – hell, about the perfidy of people – because, after all, what difference would it have made? That was the sort of thing a young man had to find out for himself, the hard way, if he lived long enough to become an old man. Poor Luís, who wore his heart on his sleeve and the picture of Marita next to his heart and died in the fullness of his twentieth year.

'Rick,' asked Luís as they awaited the attack, 'are you scared?' He always asked Rick that question before a battle. It had become a kind of good-luck ritual between them. Luís was grinning his funny gap-toothed grin, the wind was in his hair, and he looked like a minor Greek god, disporting himself on the *Champs de Mars*.

'No,' he answered truthfully.

'Why not?'

'Because I don't care,' replied Rick. He knew Luís did care, that he cared too much for his own good, that he cared not only for himself and for Marita, but for Spain, which was far too much for one brave boy to care for.

The kid was right beside him as Franco's forces charged. The attack was only a feint, but nobody bothered to tell them that. The main offensive would take place somewhere else. Unfortunately the feint was in their direction, which made it the main offensive as far as Rick and Luís were concerned.

The Nationalists were coming at them, wave upon wave, and Rick was killing them as fast as he could. Something was wrong, though: it was too easy. Franco usually didn't fight like this, didn't give up this much so easily. The men were coming straight across the river, into the teeth of the entrenched Republican position. Well, that was their problem; with every shot he felt one step nearer to whatever vindication he could muster.

Rick kept firing as fast as he could. He loved being in these kinds of scrapes, so different from the wars in New York. Those had been conducted with brutal, practically corporate efficiency. In New York victory or defeat all depended on who got the drop on whom, and the fight was over in a matter of not minutes but seconds. Triumph was all in the planning. In Spain, in battle, you either bought it or you didn't, and there wasn't a damn thing you could do about either eventuality.

'Rick!' shouted Luís. 'Watch out!'

He whipped his head away from his smoking machine gun, but it was too late. A handful of Franco's men had crossed the river on horseback, sweeping around behind their platoon's position. Damn! he should have anticipated this: the old sucker punch. Frantically he struggled to turn the machine gun around. He was still struggling when the bullet entered Luís's head just above his left eyebrow. Rick saw the damage before its victim felt it. He knew Luís was dead before he did.

Luís died in his arms, his eyes still staring forward, in anticipation of the glorious victory that would never come.

Whispering softly, Rick laid him down to rest. He wished he knew some kind of Catholic requiem, but the Kaddish would have to do. It had done before.

He knew the end was near, of course. Right in the middle of the Ebro campaign had come word of the Munich Pact of September 29, 1938, signed by Hitler, Chamberlain, Daladier, and Mussolini. It cut the heart right out of the Loyalist cause. No help would be forthcoming from France, or Russia, or England – or, for that matter, from the United States. The good guys were alone; no cavalry would be charging over the hill to rescue them. Franco's German-trained air force pounded the Loyalists in the hills, Franco's troops slaughtered them in the streets of their cities. Somehow Rick managed to survive, staggering from defeat to defeat. Barcelona fell on January 26, Madrid on March 28. The civil war ended four days later, but Rick Blaine was already in Marseille, drunk and wondering what it took to kill yourself besides courage.

'Mr. Richard?' Sam's voice came out of the night and into his fog.

'What is it?' he asked. He tried to tidy up the sitting room, to make himself more presentable, but it was no use. Sam had seen him like this too many times to be fooled. He sank back into his chair, clutching his bottle like a baby.

Sam pretended not to notice. Instead he busied himself in Rick's bedroom, organizing his clothes, folding them neatly, and packing them into a duffel bag. The bag was all Rick was going to be allowed to take with him, but that didn't mean the clothes couldn't be neat.

'You all ready to go, boss?' Sam asked idly, knowing that Rick was looking for the answer in the bottle and, unlike most men, stood a pretty good chance of finding it there.

'As ready as I'm ever going to be,' replied Rick, trying to get up but unable to because the swallow or two left was still weighing him down.

Sam sat across from Rick. In his hand he held Rick's favorite Colt .45 automatic, the one he had brought with him from New York, the one he had used on Mussolini's men and on Franco's, the one he had shot Major Strasser with. He took the weapon apart lovingly, cleaned it, and oiled it. 'This one's always been your favorite,' he observed.

'Yup,' agreed Rick. 'I just wish I'd killed the right guy with it in the first place and saved us both a lot of trouble.'

Sam shook his head. 'Boss, you got to forget about that. It was all a long time ago. Besides, it wasn't your fault, everything that happened.'

Rick laughed bitterly. 'Whose was it, then? I didn't see anybody else standing in my shoes, wearing my clothes, driving my car.' He took another drink.

'I was driving your car. Or did you forget?'

'That was so long ago I don't remember.'

'Well, if I hadn't been driving your car, you wouldn't be here.'

'Next time, try not to do me any favors.'

'You was young, boss.'

'I was old enough to know better.'

'Whatever you say.' Sam laid out the pieces on the oilcloth and reassembled them carefully. 'Ain't it nice the way everything goes together,' he said. 'Each part fits in so well with the other. Don't you wish everything in life was like that?'

'Well, it isn't.' Rick had finished the bottle and was wondering what to do with it. 'You know, Sam,' he said, 'this may be it.'

Sam didn't even look at him. He knew what he was talking about, and he didn't like it any more than his boss did. 'Now don't you go talking that way, Mr. Richard,' he said. 'You done more dangerous things before, and you always come back. You know you do. So you just take this here gun and go do what you have to do, and then you come back here and you'n me'll light out for the territories, like we always plannin'.'

Rick snorted. 'Things are different now,' he said. 'In Africa, in Spain, I didn't care whether I came back or not. That's probably what kept me alive. Now I do.'

'Because of Miss Ilsa?' asked Sam.

'Mrs. Laszlo, you mean.'

'Miss Ilsa,' insisted Sam. 'She's the reason, ain't she?'

Some questions didn't require answers. Rick lit a cigarette. Sam snapped the last pieces of the gun back into place and handed it to Rick. 'Boss,' he said, 'why you got to go? This ain't your fight.'

'What makes you so sure?' Rick asked.

Sam muttered something to himself. Rick didn't even have to hear it to know what he was saying. He decided to ignore it.

'She's different, Sam. After Paris, I thought she might be Lois all over again, and when she showed up here with Laszlo, I was certain of it. Just another girl who married the wrong man, the kind of guy I could never compete with, and now wants me to save her from herself. But I was wrong. She's given me something to live for again. That's why I'm scared.'

He blew some smoke out of his lungs and crushed the cigarette viciously into the ashtray. 'So has Victor Laszlo, except he doesn't know it yet.'

'Boss, you never been scared of nothing,' said Sam.

'That's just the problem.' Rick threw the bourbon bottle into the fireplace, where it shattered with a resounding crash. He listened carefully until the last of the glass shards had stopped clattering to the floor.

CHAPTER TWENTY-ONE

New York, July 1932

If God had wanted to smile on those for whom He otherwise had very little time, Prohibition was surely a sign of divine favor. What had been meant as punishment for the most despised members of American society, the new immigrants from Ireland, Italy, Poland, Russia, and the Ukraine, had turned out instead to be a great gift to them. For Solomon Horowitz, who appreciated a present when it was offered and never turned one down, this turn of events only reinforced his notion that most laws achieved exactly the opposite of what they were intended for. He had learned this lesson as a young man, in the old country, and he had applied it, with great success, in the New World.

The summer sun was casting its first light over the Queens flatlands. The Tootsie-Wootsie's first customers would not begin arriving for hours, even the ones who couldn't control their thirst. Still, there were bills to be paid and proceeds to be counted, and the only people Solly trusted to do that were himself and Rick. Reclining slightly in an easy chair, his waistcoat mostly unbuttoned to give free rein to his expanding belly, Solly was puffing contemplatively on a cigar. He was the very picture of Central European ease and wisdom, transplanted to Manhattan.

'Ricky, you know what mistake that *shmendrick* Salucci makes?' inquired Solly.

Rick shook his head, even though he knew the answer. Solly liked his questions to go unanswered, except when he didn't: his boys had to tell the situations apart.

'He takes himself too serious!' Solly slapped his hand on the countertop, hard, and laughed heartily. 'And he takes business not serious enough. This is why I take him to laundry every day!' For a moment Rick wondered whether Solly was having a heart attack. His face habitually turned purple whenever he heard – or more likely told – a funny one, or at least one he thought was funny. 'He even drinks his own booze!'

'But you play the numbers,' objected Rick, who otherwise had no objection to gambling.

'I *run* the numbers,' Solly retorted.

'So you cheat yourself.'

'It ain't cheating when you cheat yourself!' Solly said heatedly.

'Sure it is,' replied Rick. 'It's the worst kind of cheating. Only a chump lets himself get cheated, and only an even bigger chump cheats himself. You told me that yourself.'

Solly looked over at his protégé. 'Maybe. Sometimes. Now and then.'

They were sitting in Rick's office at the back of the club, which was located on the second floor of an otherwise nondescript Harlem building near the intersection of 136th Street and Lenox Avenue. The only indication of the Tootsie-Wootsie's presence was a small awning, in front of which stood a uniformed colored doorman. A small grocery store occupied the ground floor, and three floors of flats topped the club. Solly owned the building and collected the rents. It was just one of the many buildings he owned in Harlem proper, which had turned mostly black, and East Harlem, which was holding the color line. 'East Harlem, you can't go wrong,' Solly would often say. 'You got the Polo Grounds and the new Yankee Stadium across the river in the Bronx. The white people will never let them go. It's baseball, for chrissakes!'

Solly belched loudly. 'Enough baseball,' he said. 'Let's talk business.' He glanced at his pocket watch, which he kept tucked in his vest. 'We gotta hurry.'

Rick Baline had the best head for business Solly had ever encountered outside of himself. Indeed, in Rick Solly saw much of himself, except with more advantages in life. Rick wasn't saddled with a thick shtetl accent; he talked real American. He wasn't like most other young fellows these days, chasing after the false gods of booze, broads, and Stutz bearcats when there was money to be made.

No, Rick was different. He had taken to the Tootsie-Wootsie Club as if he had been born in it. His sharp eye missed nothing. He knew which customers could pay and which couldn't and which of the latter it was important to let in anyway. He kept the staff from stealing, he kept the musicians from fighting over women, he kept the angry fathers whose young daughters were in the chorus line from getting too obstreperous, and he kept the band members away from the young daughters. He kept the songwriters paid and mostly sober. He made sure the pianists knew which songs were the most popular. Once in a while he even let a customer sing along, especially when that colored boy Sam Waters was at the keyboard playing 'Knock on Wood.' He kept his gat in his trousers or in the pocket of his dinner jacket just as smooth as silk and nobody the wiser, not even the cops who came there to drink and ogle.

From the day Solly had put Rick in charge, the Tootsie-Wootsie Club had become his most profitable business venture. Almost instinctively Rick knew where and how to get the best beer, and his connections with the whiskey manufacturers running product down from the French *Department* of St. Pierre, an island off the Canadian coast, had quickly become second to none. He played every angle and drove trucks through every loophole. For example, the law specifically exempted sacramental wine from its proscription, so Rick did a thriving trade with synagogue and church alike, using them as front organizations for his importation of fine French wines and kicking back a generous share of the profits to support charitable activities. He had gotten the notion one day down on Grand Street, when he saw a line of Irishmen outside a kosher wine store and suddenly realized just how attractive Judaism had become to a host of nominal anti-Semites.

Rick's taste in music was similarly well developed. Prior to the club's opening, the best place for jazz music in town had been O'Hanlon's Boll Weevil, a few blocks up the street, but Rick was not about to let his customers either drink second-rate liquor or listen to third-class music. He began aggressively to court the best songwriters and musicians, hiring Herman Hupfield as the house composer, bringing in bandleader Jimmie Lunceford from one of the Capone mob's Chicago clubs. Everyone agreed, however, that his greatest find was Sam Waters, a stride piano player from Cooper Street, north of the railroad tracks in Sedalia, Missouri. As a lad Sam had known Scott Joplin and, more important, had learned from him. Sam's ear for a tune was legendary, and his ability to pick up anything and play it had won him a large following.

Some members of the gang looked askance at Rick's friendship with Sam. They complained to Solly that it wasn't right for a white boy to be on such good terms with a *shvartzer*. Rick and Sam would sometimes disappear together on weekends, tooling up to the Catskills in Rick's DeSoto to go fishing. Tick-Tock said a Jew and a colored boy shouldn't be hanging out together, but Solly told him to shut up and mind his own business. 'If the rest of you bums could take care of your business the way Ricky takes care of his, why, we would all be rich instead of just me,' he told them.

Finally, Rick was always on good terms with the cops. Personally he had nothing against policemen, who by and large were working stiffs like himself, trying to get ahead. The way Rick saw it, the police were his friends. With the right amount of financial encouragement, they kept the booze trucks running smoothly (some off-duty cops even rode shotgun for him), kept the rival gangsters off each other's backs, and deflected the feds as much as they could. And when they couldn't, they warned him about it, so he could close the club down for 'renovations' until the feds ran out of expense money and went back to Washington, where they belonged.

It was a good life. The only person who didn't quite see it that way was his mother. The last time he'd seen her, which was months ago, she had asked him about the money and the clothes and most of all about the car, and he had been afraid to answer her. In fact, he hadn't even bothered to try, because he knew that she knew, and it was easier for both of them to pretend otherwise. He'd call her tonight, and if not tonight, soon, just as soon as he could. Really, he would. It was long past time for a mitzvah.

'Well, Solly,' said Rick, clearing his throat, 'there is some business I'd like to discuss. It's got to do with Lois.'

'*Nu?*' said Solly.

Rick had been putting off this conversation for three months, since the night he'd met O'Hanlon at Rector's. Since the night Lois gave him the brush-off. He had been fearful of telling the boss about meeting the Irishman and Meredith, and he still hadn't delivered O'Hanlon's message, afraid of Horowitz's unpredictable rage, afraid to reveal that he'd been taking his daughter to a gangland hangout when that was expressly against his orders.

So far, nothing untoward had happened. Solly and Dion continued their uneasy standoff, with Salucci and Weinberg lurking somewhere in the bushes south of 14th Street. Maybe O'Hanlon had forgotten all about it. Maybe enough time had elapsed that Solly wouldn't be tempted to put two and two together. Maybe Rick's proven ability to pour profits into the boss's pockets would make everybody forget about everything else.

Rick was still trying to figure out a way to broach the subject when Horowitz beat him to the punch. 'Isn't it great about her and that fancy lawyer!'

'Which fancy lawyer?' asked Rick.

'You keep this quiet now,' Solomon commanded him, tapping a finger alongside his nose, 'but she's thinking about maybe marrying. To a big man, too!' Solly rose from his chair and drew himself up to his full sixty-five-inch height. 'Make her papa proud!' He played with a cigar. 'Mrs. Robert Haas Meredith – it's got a good gong to it!'

'What?' exclaimed Rick.

He sat back with a particularly contented expression on his face. 'It's the American dream,' he said. 'Off the boat and aboard the ladder.'

He was bouncing both hands off his belly in delight when the first shot splintered the wood behind Solly's head. If he hadn't leaned back at just that moment, it would have hit him right between the eyes.

An instant later, the second shot skidded across the desktop, ricocheted off a cheap lamp, and crashed into the ceiling, sending down a shower of plaster.

The first two shots were nearly simultaneous. By the third shot both Rick and Solly were on the floor, guns drawn, and had come up firing. Rick marveled briefly at the boss's reflexes.

Neither he nor Horowitz had seen the gunmen – there must be at least two – nor could they see them now. But from prone positions on the floor they poured back return fire. Rick had a momentary impression of a splintering doorjamb and of a groan from just beyond it; of a shattering glass transom, of exploding light fixtures in the hallway.

Then he saw a foot in the doorway where someone had been standing. It was a lone foot, and it didn't seem to be moving much. The gunfire had also stopped. Maybe five seconds had elapsed since the attack, not even. They were both still alive.

'Goddamn sons of bitches bastards,' muttered Solly, snapping a new clip into his automatic. He was up on his feet in no time flat and charging out the door. Rick had youth on his side, but he was no match for the boss.

Solly paid no attention whatever to the foot in the door. As Rick rounded the corner he could see that the assailant to whom the foot belonged was still alive, but unarmed; Solly kicked his pistol away as he ran by him. 'Ricky, knife, alive!' he shouted before disappearing down the stairs. 'Goddamn sons of bitches bastards . . .'

Rick leaned over the wounded man. One of their slugs had caught him just above the heart, and he could plainly see the man wasn't going to make it. The guy on the floor was dark, with curly black hair, and as he leaned over him, Rick couldn't at first tell whether he was Italian or Jewish. Then he remembered his boss's warning about the knife.

The wounded hood whipped the stiletto past his face so close and so fast, Rick almost lost his nose.

Sicilian, for sure.

He could hear gunshots from below as he rendered the man harmless by socking him on the jaw. He left him there and hustled down the stairs.

Solomon Horowitz sat on the bottom step. The other Italian lay at his feet, quite dead, shot through the left ear at what must have been very close range. Had he tried to surrender? Rick didn't want to know.

'Salucci?' asked Rick, heading out the front door. They must have come uptown somehow. He looked up and down the street in vain for the getaway car. A few black passersby looked at him nervously; he didn't understand why until he realized he still had his pistol in his hand. He slipped it into the special pocket in his suit coat and stepped back inside.

Solly and the dead man had disappeared. He could hear a heavy tread on the stairway. He followed it up.

With the stiff slung around his shoulders, Solly had tramped up the stairs and back to the office. The accomplice was still alive. Solly dumped the corpse right next to him.

'Ricky, you speak some wop,' he said. 'Find out what's going on here before I get angry.'

Rick spoke to the dying man in Sicilian. Most of the Sicilian he had learned fighting the Italian kids in East Harlem had something to do with somebody's mother or sister, but it would have to do.

The dying man was croaking something unintelligible. Rick could understand that: if he had a bullet in his chest, he might not be easily understood, either. He bent his ear as close to the man's mouth as he dared; even in death some of these guys were known to bite off a nose, an ear, any body part they could get their teeth around.

'Son of a bitch bastard,' Solly said impatiently. 'With this *shtunk* we get nowhere.' All at once he snatched up the wounded Sicilian in his arms. Cradling him like a baby, Solly walked over to the elevator.

'Wait a second, Sol,' said Rick, but Horowitz wouldn't listen.

'Ricky,' he commanded, 'open the door.'

Rick started to ring for the operator, but Solly barked at him: 'I said open the door, not call the car.'

Rick pried open the safety doors.

With a grunt, Solly hurled the man down the elevator shaft. Then he went back, picked up the dead man, and threw him down the shaft as well.

For the first time Rick was able to get a good look at them:

The man with the knife lay on his back, his left leg splayed outward, his right arm bent at the elbow, his hand resting on his waistcoat. His left arm was raised as if in thought, its hand applied to the left side of his head, which was unmarked except for a bloodstain on his right cheek. His mouth stood slightly agape, as if he had been just about to say something. His dead companion's head was nestled in the first man's left armpit, as if they were brothers and still accustomed to sleeping together in the same bed. He lay spread-eagle and ungainly, both arms flung out to the sides as if in surrender, hands limp, toes pointing upward.

'Fresh off the boat Salucci no-goodniks, come to make mischief,' Solly said. 'Salucci thinks he can muscle in on Solomon Horowitz in Harlem? He sends these goombahs to whack me? Goddamn son of a bitch bastard!'

Rick wanted to hit back right away. He knew what this was all about, and a wave of guilt washed over him. He hadn't given the boss O'Hanlon's message because he didn't want him to find out about him and Lois – and this was the result.

Solomon would have none of it. 'Ricky,' he said, 'what for we got to go looking for Salucci? He should only come looking for us, and explain why he tries this *farpotshket* thing, and to beg my forgiveness before I come downtown and shoot him right in his whore's bed. So nothing is what we got to do. We sit tight, and mark my words, we get visitors. What we don't do is go looking for them, and what else we don't do is run away.'

He wasn't even breathing hard. 'Is old saying: "The rabbi whose congregation don't want to drive him out of town ain't much of a rabbi. And the rabbi they do drive out ain't much of a mensch." Right here is where I'm staying.'

Rick said he didn't understand why they didn't send Tick-Tock down to the Lower East Side to pay back Salucci several times over.

'Because we're not ready,' his boss replied. 'When you're not ready, and you do something anyway, why, you got nobody to blame but yourself when everything turns out a *farshtinkener* mess, is why.'

Why they weren't ready was a question that suddenly occurred to Rick. Where the hell was Tick-Tock Schapiro?

CHAPTER TWENTY-TWO

Two days later Rick and Solly were sitting in the freshly repaired back room of the Tootsie-Wootsie when Abie Cohen made a noise and the managers looked up to see, standing in the same doorway that the two Sicilians had so recently darkened, Dion O'Hanlon, Lorenzo Salucci, and Irving Weinberg. Behind them were Cohen and Tick-Tock. Nobody had a gun out.

Rick jumped to his feet, but Solly didn't move. 'Hello, boys,' he called out. 'I've been expecting you. Come in and make yourselves at home.' He acted as if nothing had happened.

O'Hanlon glided in on his tiny feet. Salucci, bigger, moved slowly and deliberately. At his side, Weinberg bobbed and nodded like one of those little birds that rides a rhinoceros.

'Good evening, Mr. Horowitz,' said the Irish gangster in his soft, lilting voice.

'Shall I pat him down?' Rick asked, but Solly wouldn't let him.

'Never insult an equal,' he said, sitting there like a Jewish Buddha. 'Otherwise he feels free to insult you back, and who knows where that all ends?'

'Solomon the Wise,' said O'Hanlon, making himself comfortable. 'And good evening to you, Mr., er . . .?'

The move was Rick's. 'Baline,' he replied as if he'd never seen O'Hanlon before. 'Rick Baline. I'm the manager here.'

O'Hanlon bowed. 'Baline,' he said, rolling the word around on his tongue as if trying to distinguish the taste. 'The name of course is familiar to me, and for a moment there I thought your face might be as well.' He pulled back both corners of his mouth to imitate a smile. 'It must be the light. My mistake.'

'Abie, some chairs for my guests,' said Solly.

Everybody sat, with their hats on and their hands in their laps. It was safer that way. For three top gangsters like these to come into Horowitz's stronghold with assassination in mind would be crazy, reflected Rick, and then he decided that was probably what Giuseppe Guglielmo had thought, too. He stayed cautious.

Solly opened the colloquy. 'Do I send my boys downtown to make trouble for you, Dion?' he asked, waving his hands in the air. He could not bring himself to address Salucci or Weinberg directly. 'Solomon Horowitz is a man of honor. He sticks to his agreements, and since Atlantic City in 1929 his agreement with O'Hanlon says that Harlem and East Harlem and the whole damn Bronx is his to do with as he pleases. Is this not still so?'

O'Hanlon smoothed an imaginary wrinkle off the front of his double-breasted suit, which he wore tightly buttoned up. 'That's what we're here to discuss,' he said, his voice cool.

'The two unfortunate lads who expired on your premises were blood relatives, cousins of some sort, I believe, of Mr. Salucci here, freshly arrived in this fair land of ours and sent north across a Hundred and Tenth Street by their distinguished relation in order to bring a certain business proposition to you. Mr. Salucci is very distressed to think of the discourtesy with which you greeted them, and by your impatience in not giving them a fair hearing.'

'The next time he has a business proposition for me, maybe he sends his boys unarmed, as always.' Solly busied himself with cutting and lighting a cigar. 'Then they get a fair hearing instead of ending up in a box.'

O'Hanlon looked distressed. 'The inexperience of poor immigrant foreigners,' he said, 'often has regrettable consequences.' He looked around the room. 'As no doubt all of us in this room, with the possible exception of Mr. Baline, can attest. These lads were armed for the simple reason that their own sad homeland of Sicily suffers from such a deplorable lack of law enforcement that honest citizens must perforce defend themselves.'

The Irish mob boss crossed his legs and sat back in his chair. 'But that is water past the Spuyten Duyvil now,' he said. 'The real reason for our visit is to put the memory of this unfortunate incident behind us. We cannot let even such a tragedy as this interfere with the larger purpose for which we have come here today.'

O'Hanlon rose and faced Solly like a priest about to pronounce a benediction. 'Lorenzo?' he invited, levitating his dainty hands. 'Solomon?'

Salucci rose sullenly and faced Solly across O'Hanlon's surprisingly wide shoulders. 'Please accept my most humble apologies for this sad misunderstanding,' said the Italian in a dull monotone.

Solomon just looked at him. 'This he calls an apology?' he said, immobile.

'Lorenzo's command of English leaves much to be desired, graciousness-wise,' O'Hanlon remarked affably. 'To translate, what he means is that it will not happen again, and you have my word on that.'

Solly got slowly to his feet, eyeing Salucci warily.

'Solomon, you and I go back a long way,' O'Hanlon reminded him. 'I am asking you as a friend to do this thing for me now.' He stepped back briskly, like a matador, as the two men came together, threw their arms around each other, and kissed each other on the cheeks.

'That is the end to it, then,' said O'Hanlon, satisfied, as they parted. Solly's face, Rick noticed, was flushed, Salucci's sallow. Everyone sat down again, except Rick, who had not budged.

'It seems to me such friendship should be celebrated with a suitable toast,' said O'Hanlon. 'Will the host please do the honors?'

Solly reached into the lower right-hand drawer of his desk. It was the same drawer, Rick knew, where he usually kept a small .22. He wondered if O'Hanlon knew that and decided he probably did. There didn't seem to be much that O'Hanlon didn't know.

Solly came up with a bottle of whiskey and three glasses. He poured small golden shots into each of them, kept one for himself, and handed the others to Salucci and O'Hanlon. 'A day like this demands the best.'

'To friendship,' offered O'Hanlon, and everybody drank. Then Solly rose.

'Today is a very special day,' he said. 'On two more counts. So I drink now a toast to my friend Yitzik Baline – the finest of my club managers, the straightest shot among my boys, and the man I love like a son. If God forbid anything should ever happen to me, he is my whattyacallit, my heir apparent.' Nobody snickered at the aspirated 'h,' Russian style. 'Everything I have shall be his. *L'chaim!*'

Everybody sipped politely. Tick-Tock frowned.

'Everything but one thing,' continued Solly. 'And now, Ricky, you should forgive me, another toast, this one even more important.' Solomon's face, Rick noticed, had taken on an uncharacteristically serious mien.

'To my daughter, my only daughter, Lois,' he began, and Rick felt his heart stop. 'Who today I proudly announce is betrothed to a very important man in this city of ours.'

Solly looked proud. Abie and Tick-Tock looked puzzled. O'Hanlon looked satisfied. Salucci looked mean. Weinberg just looked.

'Yes, and to none other than Robert Haas Meredith. Three months he has been courting her like a true gentleman, and now we got payoff. Always a bridesmaid and finally a mother!'

Rick clenched his jaw so tightly, he would have bitten off his tongue had it gotten caught in the mandibles.

'Solomon,' exclaimed O'Hanlon, rubbing his hands together. 'Sure, and I couldn't be more delighted. This happy event well and truly cements this peace treaty of ours, for haven't Mr. Meredith and I conducted some small business together most profitably in the past and look forward to doing so in the future? 'Tis truly a splendid day for all.'

O'Hanlon and Solly were laughing now, best of friends.

What was it the Irishman had said to him at Rector's about warring kingdoms? Now Rick understood.

A month later Lois Horowitz and Robert Meredith were married. The newspapers described the bride as Lois Harrow, the daughter of a successful property man from Darien. The ceremony at St. Stephen's Episcopal Church on Fifth Avenue was small and very private, and the few members of the public who happened to stumble upon it were ushered out by a phalanx of extremely large men in tight-fitting, bulging suits.

A teary-eyed Solomon Horowitz gave away the bride. Dion O'Hanlon was the best man. Rick Baline sat in a church for the first time in his life. Even he had to admit they made a handsome couple. He wondered if their lives would prove to be as uncomplicated as their looks.

When she emerged from the church, Lois threw her arms around Rick's neck. 'Isn't it swell, Ricky?' she breathed. 'I'm going places now!' Over her shoulder he could see Meredith shaking hands with his new father-in-law. 'We can still be friends, can't we?' Lois said as he trained his ears on the other conversation.

'Mr. Horowitz,' Meredith was saying, 'it is a pleasure doing business with you.'

He didn't see Lois again for three years.

CHAPTER TWENTY-THREE

'Fräulein Toumanova,' said the pursed-lipped Austrian secretary who sat in the outer office and surveyed the world with a gimlet eye, 'the *Herr Direktor* would like these reports typed up at once and delivered to him personally by four o'clock this afternoon.'

Irmgard Hentgen was the gatekeeper, Reinhard Heydrich's last line of defense against unwanted intrusions on his working day. She was not, strictly speaking, his private secretary: in the Nazi scheme of things, that job was reserved for a man. But she oversaw who came and who went, and she handled the details of Heydrich's schedule.

'*Sofort, Frau Hentgen*,' replied Ilsa Lund. She did not like Frau Hentgen and suspected that the woman had very little use for her.

'By *four o'clock*,' repeated Frau Hentgen, in case she hadn't been heard the first time. 'It is imperative that these . . .'

Ilsa ignored her. Life was too short to listen to Frau Hentgen repeating herself. Besides, she had work to do.

In the space of just four months she had risen from the anonymity of the typing pool to Heydrich's secretariat, where she was one of three women under the supervision of Frau Hentgen. Ilsa was not sure whether to attribute her rise to her intelligence, her skills, her looks, or some combination of the three, but she was not about to question it. She was close to Heydrich now, very close. All she had to do was get one step closer.

Her entrance into the headquarters of the *Reichsicherheitshauptant* had been surprisingly easy. White Russians were seen as natural, if inferior, allies in the war against Bolshevism and Marxism, and their bona fides were accepted with alacrity. Everybody thought the Germans were omniscient as well as omnipotent, which was what the Nazis wanted everyone to think. In many ways, though, they were surprisingly lax, shoddy even, so certain were they of the rightness of their cause and the inevitability of their victory.

'. . . and this must be done immediately!'

'Yes, thank you, Frau Hentgen,' said Ilsa, accepting another sheaf of papers with feigned good grace. Without even looking at them, she knew what they were. Reports on real or imagined activities against the Reich. She also knew in advance what the recommendation of the reporting agent, which was inscribed at the bottom just above the signature, would be: death. Death appeared to be the Nazi solution for everything.

Some, not many, she managed to lose. Even in the Reich, documents got misfiled or mislaid, and she had no reason to fear that Frau Hentgen or anyone else had the slightest idea of the double game she was playing. She had saved some lives, as surreptitiously as possible. Names were passed along, so that their owners might be warned, and some of them even managed to get away. But she couldn't save everybody without eventually directing suspicion back upon herself, so she had to choose, choose among perfect strangers, who should live and who must die.

A heart-stopping moment had come a week or so ago when, thumbing through the stack of death warrants, she had come across the name of one of their minor operatives, a laborer named Anton Novotny, who was involved in the construction of a new Gestapo prison. Novotny's arrest, however, turned out to have nothing to do with the Resistance at all; he had been denounced by a boy in his *Wohnquartier* for making a joke about Heydrich. A joke was all it took these days, and sentence had been both pronounced and carried out before what little laughter there had been had died away: a pair of RSHA men barged into a tavern where Anton was taking his leisure, frog-marched him outside, and shot him right there in the street.

Due to security considerations, she could have no direct contact with Victor, and she could only hope that her reports were filtering back to him and the rest of the team in London via the various cutouts and intermediaries along the network.

She couldn't tell whether she was having much success. The British, she learned, had been right: Czech resistance to Hitler was feeble. Unlike the citizens of Norway, Denmark, France, and Holland, the Czechs showed little inclination to throw the Germans out. Even Hitler's well-known contempt for the Slavs did not seem to offend them, and they continued their twin trades of arms making and beer brewing with the same aplomb they had shown before the war. Certain members of the Underground, she knew, were carrying on

Victor's work of pamphleteering, printing their broadsides in farmhouses and trucking them into the squares on donkey carts and the backs of old women. She even knew of a few partisans who were still waging a guerrilla war in the countryside, although their numbers were dwindling practically daily. Still, the uprising that everyone hoped for had not come; indeed, it seemed farther away than ever. Maybe Rick had been right. Maybe the whole thing was crazy. She went home each night feeling angrier and more discouraged.

They needed a bold stroke. What stroke bolder than to cut off the very head of the evil itself? Watching Heydrich's arrogant procession into and out of his office every day made her wish that she could kill him herself right at his desk, to avenge the torture of her husband, the rape of her country, and the death of her father at one blow.

British Intelligence had also been right about another thing: Reinhard Heydrich was a man of exceedingly fixed habits. Every morning he rose at precisely 6:30 A.M. in his bed at his villa. Breakfast was invariably preceded by a vigorous game of handball, after which he showered and shaved and put on a fresh uniform laid out by his valet the night before. At 7:25 A.M. his chauffeur appeared at the villa's front door with the car, its motor running, and Heydrich hopped aboard. The car arrived at his office in Hradčany Castle on the dot of eight. Although the staff officially went on duty at eight, everyone knew it was professional suicide to arrive after Heydrich did, so they generally got to work half an hour earlier. He worked straight through the day, stopping only for lunch at one P.M., which lasted until precisely two o'clock. He left the office at six P.M., took some exercise in the form of a brisk walk around the castle grounds no matter what the weather, boarded his limousine, and went off to dinner at seven-thirty P.M. He rarely dined alone, and he never slept alone. Heydrich had the reputation of tiring of his mistresses rather quickly, and word around the office was that his current partner was rapidly losing his interest.

Ilsa had encoded all this information and duly entrusted it to a rotating series of Underground couriers with whom she could meet without raising suspicion: postmen, waitresses, boarders in her rooming house on Skořepka Street, across the river from the castle. Whose eyes it may have found she did not know. Major Miles's? Victor's? Rick's?

She had heard nothing of Rick since she'd left London, and she had tried to put him out of her mind as best she could. How hard that was, with the memory of their last night together still so vivid.

Her hands trembled slightly as she leafed through the reports. She was just loading a piece of paper into her typewriter when a voice behind her startled her.

'How pleasant it is for me to see your glowing face each morning, Fräulein Toumanova.' It was Heydrich himself, reading the pages over her shoulder. He had never spoken to her before.

She put the papers down, folded her hands together on her desk, and waited. Now that the moment was here, she was not sure what to do next. 'Thank you, Herr Heydrich,' she managed to reply.

From his height of well over six feet, the Protector of Bohemia and Moravia stared down at the blonde secretary who had caught his eye. Truth to tell, he had spotted her some time ago, but the chief of the Reich security office could not be seen to have taken such quick notice of a girl in the typing pool. Better to wait to see if she had any brains – but not too many! – in that pretty head, to see if she could force her way past the other girls and into the secretariat, there to fall under the basilisk gaze of Frau Hentgen, who kept track of everything for him and whose instincts about people he had found to be unerring.

Frau Hentgen had been less than enthusiastic about Fräulein Toumanova, which was easily attributable to the young lady's Slavic ancestry: like a good Nazi and a better Austrian, Frau Hentgen thought the Slavs fit only for servitude. Or, perhaps, her antipathy was due to Miss Toumanova's uncommon skills; not only was she an excellent typist and fluent in several languages, but she even played the piano rather well. Not to mention that Miss Toumanova was beautiful and Frau Hentgen was ugly. One could never rule out jealousy when it came to women. It was one of the many ways in which he found them irrational. Just as the Germans were having to get used to all kinds of climates, however, so also would their rulers have to get used to all kinds of women. He was willing to experiment for the sake of the nation.

'Indeed,' said Heydrich, resting one hand lightly upon her shoulder, 'a beauty such as yours brings light to the darkness of a cursed and evil world. It reminds men like me of why we fight, why our struggle and ultimate victory is so important.'

She felt herself blushing, as if basking in his praise instead of flushing in rage. She kept her eyes lowered, toward the floor, until she realized she could see her own reflection staring back at her from the man's polished boots.

'Such very good work you have been doing, Fräulein Toumanova,' he continued. 'The Reich is pleased and proud to be able to employ a woman such as yourself in the ongoing struggle to the death against the Bolshevik usurpers of your homeland.' Almost imperceptibly, he began to caress her. 'Such initiative as well! Your tip about the reactionary cell in the Böhmenwald last week proved most accurate. Isn't that right, Frau Hentgen?' he concluded loudly.

'*Ja, Herr Heydrich*,' Frau Hentgen replied curtly. Cued by Frau Hentgen, the other women in the office took absolutely no notice of this conversation. They kept their heads down, bent over their work. No one dared type, and so create a disturbance, but each found plenty to do that needed the urgent attention of a fountain pen.

Heydrich's reference to the Böhmenwald made her shiver. From time to time the Underground would feed her information about a hideout for which it had no further use; very infrequently the Resistance would give up a comrade, one whose loyalties were suspect (so they assured her) and who had therefore been deemed a danger to the entire movement. She hated condemning those men to death, but she did not know what else to do.

'I have been meaning to congratulate you,' Heydrich continued. 'I hope you will allow me the honor to do so very soon.'

Ilsa finally dared look up. His manner was stiff and formal, but he was smiling. With his brushed-back blond hair, aquiline nose, and gleaming white teeth, he was at once handsome and repulsive.

'*Danke schön, Herr Heydrich*,' she said.

'Unfortunately, by the time my men got there, the rebellious scum had fled. How they knew we were coming is of course a mystery, but these Slavs are mysterious people. Isn't that right, Frau Hentgen?'

'*Jawohl, Herr Heydrich!*'

He leaned more heavily upon her, his grip tightening. Ilsa felt a chill dance up and down her spine.

'Oh, well,' said Heydrich, 'that sometimes cannot be helped. Even the most abject *Untermensch* has an animal's sensory apparatus, and if his nose twitches at just the right moment . . .' He sighed theatrically. 'I have time,' he concluded. 'A thousand years, at least.'

He withdrew his hand from her shoulder and stepped back smartly. 'However, we should speak of more pleasant things!' he exclaimed. 'I understand from Frau Hentgen that you are an accomplished pianist. I myself have some modest skill on the violin. It would be a great honor to have you accompany me. Tonight, perhaps?'

Ilsa took a deep breath. 'Herr Protector,' she began, 'such an honor . . .' She tried to fumble for words. 'Surely a poor Russian girl like me is not worthy . . .' She gave up and fluttered her hands.

'Nonsense!' shouted Heydrich, causing all the other women in the office, however briefly, to glance over at them. They had seen this unfolding tableau before, yet it remained fascinating, like watching a snake hypnotize its prey before swallowing it docile, uncomprehending, and whole.

The moment was here at last: Heydrich had made his approach. Mentally and emotionally she was ready. Now she had to play for time, had to get word back to London that contact had been made, that the opportunity for her to get close to the target was at hand, that the hunter was now the hunted.

She knew just what to do and what not to do. She could not plead a prior engagement, for Heydrich would simply ignore it or, worse, order the man she was to meet arrested and probably shot. She had to turn him down without making it look as though she were turning him down – and leaving the possibility open for another time. Rejecting him but luring him, onward, closer, into the trap – and trying not to get caught in it herself.

She blinked rapidly, then lowered her eyes. As she hoped, this gesture brought Heydrich's face down closer to hers. '*Mein Herr*,' she said, '*ich bitte Sie. Heute abend ist es nicht möglich wegen . . .*'

Tonight it is not possible because . . . Deliberately ambiguous, she waited to see how he would interpret her.

'*Ach, Frauen*,' he groaned. *Oh, women. . . .*

She laughed beguilingly. 'Oh no,' she said, feigning embarrassment. The look of brief confusion on Heydrich's face plainly indicated that he was thinking of sex, not music. 'It's just that I would not think of accompanying a man as distinguished as yourself without being able to practice first. Would a couple of days hence be all right?'

The Protector quickly regained his composure and looked at her with new respect. A gambit or a misunderstanding on his part? Perhaps this one was more clever than she looked. Good: he liked a challenge. 'I understand completely,' he said. 'Shall we say the day after tomorrow?' He gave her a leer that he habitually mistook for sophistication.

'The day after tomorrow,' she repeated loudly, for everyone in the room to hear. 'Two days is all it will take for me to get the complete reports on your desk, *mein Kommandant*.'

So they had a little conspiracy going. That pleased Heydrich. 'Excellent,' he said. 'Hail, victory. *Heil Hitler*.'

As one, the staff rose. '*Heil Hitler!*' they shouted in unison as the Protector entered his inner sanctum and flashed the old Roman salute the Nazis had appropriated.

That afternoon she stayed late, typing up some reports and forwarding them to the appropriate bureaus. When everyone had left but her, she wrote the number 22 on a small piece of paper and put it in her pocket. Twenty-two was Rick's lucky number; it was also today's date, May 22. The coincidence was a good omen.

On the way home, she stopped at Banaček's bakery and handed the clerk her number. To the casual observer, there was nothing untoward about this action; it was merely the number of an order made earlier in the day by telephone. The clerk, a small, inoffensive man named Helder, nodded as he read it and handed her half a dozen fresh rolls and a couple of pastries.

Number 22 was much more than that, however; it was the signal that contact had been made and the target would soon be ripe for the taking. It would be relayed at once by wireless to London. The plane carrying Victor, Rick, and the rest of the team would leave within the hour. Ilsa paid the clerk in coins and thanked him as she departed. Operation Hangman was under way.

That night she took extra precautions, for Heydrich's spies were everywhere. She practiced on the parlor piano for an hour, then complained loudly to her landlady that she was not feeling well. She requested a compress and a hot-water bottle and went upstairs to bed. She turned off all the lights in her room and sat by the window in the dark, searching for any sign of a watcher below. She could see none.

A soft tap at her door woke her from a doze. She crept over in her bare feet and opened it a crack. Helena was there, a new servant girl who had recently been engaged by the house. 'Pall Mall,' the girl said, which was the day's password. The test was not only to know the password, but to pronounce it properly, which she did. Ilsa opened the door just widely enough to admit Helena and then closed it tight.

Helena, she knew, would be bringing a message from the Underground in Prague. The Resistance used a constantly changing array of tradesmen and servants to convey messages, so there was nothing unusual about her sudden appearance. Indeed, Ilsa was expecting it.

'What news?' Ilsa whispered.

'Two messages,' said Helena, practically inaudibly. 'I don't understand them. They don't tell me what the words mean. I wrote them down to be sure I didn't forget.'

'That's for your own protection,' Ilsa explained. 'The less you understand, the safer you are.' She looked at the girl and saw that Helena couldn't be more than sixteen years old. They were enlisting children to fight a monster, except this was no Grimm's fairy tale. 'Just repeat exactly the words they told you. Don't worry about anything else. Do you think you can do that?'

Perhaps it was her nerves or maybe it was something in the girl's manner, but Ilsa began to suspect the worst. Had the operation been compromised? Had someone cracked or confessed? Had the drop zone been discovered? Had the Gestapo managed to infiltrate the Underground? Or, God forbid, had British Intelligence been penetrated by the Nazis back in London? The German spy network appeared to function best in central Europe and at the Russian front, but it was growing in sophistication each month and now was quite effective in France, where each week brought new reports of Resistance fighters rounded up and shot. Had she been discovered? Had something happened to Victor? To Rick? Were Heydrich's men outside the door, getting ready to burst in?

'Tell me,' she said, trying to stay calm, trying at least to sound calm, trying to keep the horrible urgency out of her voice.

Helena unfolded a little scrap of paper. 'The first message is from London. It says, "The blue parrot is out of his cage."'

Ilsa felt her heart leap. There was nothing to worry about at all! Her message had been received, and this was the reply. The 'blue parrot' was their code name for the team; 'out of his cage' meant they were on their way to Czechoslovakia. She almost laughed out loud.

'The second I received only a little while ago from the Underground,' continued Helena. She stared at her note, trying to make sense of the words. 'It says, "Operation Hangman. Tell London. Danger."' Helena looked up from her reading. 'They want to call it off. What does that mean?'

At first Ilsa thought she must have misheard her. Call off Operation Hangman? 'What?' she exclaimed, shaking Helena in her agitation. 'Why?'

'I don't know,' said the girl, clearly upset. 'I don't know!'

'Give me that,' Ilsa demanded, snatching the note and trying desperately to glean more. She tried to calm herself and failed. 'It's much too dangerous for you to have something like this in your possession.'

Her mind was working furiously. What had happened? Perhaps her fears that they had been betrayed were well founded after all. That damned Frau Hentgen: did she suspect something? Perhaps the Czechs really were cowards, afraid to go through with it. It was too late, though. The team was probably already on the ground. They couldn't stop now. They wouldn't stop now.

No, no, no, she told herself. *Not now. Not after what Victor has suffered. Not after what I have suffered. Not when we are this close. Not when I can make it happen.*

Not in a million years.

Not over my dead body.

CHAPTER TWENTY-FOUR

With Saxon punctuality, Reinhard Heydrich called for her two days later at the flat on Skořepka Street. Ilsa was expecting him. After work she had washed her dark blonde hair, perfumed herself, and put on a fresh dress.

'How lovely you look this evening, Fräulein Toumanova,' said Heydrich, bowing slightly from the waist. He stood outside the front door; behind him Ilsa could see his Mercedes, its motor idling, with a uniformed chauffeur in the front seat. 'If you will permit me to say so, I think we shall make a very handsome couple tonight.'

She had to admit he looked splendid in his impeccably tailored black-and-gray SS uniform, which had been cut to show off his trim fighting physique. As usual, his high black riding boots were shined to a mirror surface. His sandy hair, his well-fitting clothes, the way he stood at polite but rigid attention, even the way he held his hat in both hands, reminded her of someone. With a start, she suddenly remembered who.

God help her, he reminded her of Victor – except that Victor was pure and good, while Heydrich was the personification of evil.

'Good evening, Herr Heydrich,' she said noncommittally, allowing him to take her arm.

He held the door for her as she entered the car, a big, roomy sedan with walnut paneling and plush leather seats. She sank back and let her head rest as the driver put the car into first gear and stepped on the accelerator. Heydrich was sitting facing her, attentive and very close.

'For this evening, you may address me as Reinhard,' he said, taking her hand. 'But only in private. It would not do for others to think the Protector admits of familiarity so quickly.'

Ilsa glanced up quickly at the rearview mirror, but the chauffeur's eyes were on the road, professionally impassive.

With a purr the Mercedes moved away, the German driver expertly negotiating the narrow Czech streets. From a console on the back of the driver's seat, Heydrich produced a bottle of champagne and two glasses. He popped the cork and poured. Some of the froth spilled onto his immaculately manicured hands. He licked it off.

'You drink champagne, of course?' He handed Ilsa a glass.

'With pleasure,' she replied, accepting it.

As they glided through the streets of the city, Heydrich pointed out sight after sight, keeping up a running lecture on Prague, its history and important buildings. There wasn't much he didn't seem to know.

'Are you aware that Mozart's *Don Giovanni* was first performed here?' he asked her. 'This was his favorite city, and the good Germans of Prague made him feel especially welcome whenever he was here.' He poured more champagne for both of them. 'Prague has always been more German than Czech, and what we Germans are doing here today is simply restoring the city to its former glory as a member of the Greater German Reich. One of the ways we do it is by calling it by its proper German name, *Prag*, instead of *Praha*. In fact, we insist upon it.'

Ilsa had to admit Prague was beautiful – as beautiful in its own way as Paris was, but cold and remote where Paris was warm and welcoming. As if constructed by a bright, impudent child, the city was a medieval fantasy of steep spires and peaked red roofs. The many public squares were cobblestone, and the great Moldau River, called by the Czechs the Vltava, flowed majestically through the heart of the city. Prague was far more attractive than lumpen Vienna or bleak, windswept Berlin. No wonder the Nazis had occupied it, thought Ilsa; they would do anything to get out of their own ugly burgs.

They were in an unfamiliar quarter of the city now, ancient and crabbed. 'This is Josefov,' said Heydrich. Unlike most of the top Nazis, who were little more than peasants, he spoke elegant, very fashionable German. His speech possessed none of the ruralisms that still dotted the discourse of the Führer, and his crisp Saxon accent was far from Hitler's buffoonish Austrian intonation. 'Stop the car.'

They had been driving down a street called Pařižská, a broad boulevard that led from the Old Town Hall northward until it crossed the river. Now they were stopped in front of a large, spare, imposing edifice. The driver opened the car doors, first for Heydrich and then for her. 'Look around,' said the Protector.

To Ilsa's astonishment, they were standing in front of a

synagogue. On the streets, a few black-coated and bearded Orthodox Jews scurried away from the Mercedes as fast as they could. Heydrich let out a contemptuous laugh.

'Behold,' he said, 'the Jewish Quarter!'

Ilsa could hardly believe her eyes. Right here, under the Hangman's nose, was a settlement of Jews, apparently going about their business unmolested. She turned to Heydrich with obvious questions in her eyes.

'This is the *Alt-Neu* Synagogue,' he said, 'the oldest in Europe. It shall also be the last. Hebrew legend says that the foundation stones were flown over from the Holy Temple in Jerusalem, with the stipulation that they should be returned on the Last Day, the Day of Judgment. That day is coming much faster for the Jews than they ever could have imagined.'

'Why is it called the Old-New Synagogue?' Ilsa inquired.

Heydrich rubbed his hands together like a predator as he surveyed the building. 'The word for "stipulation" in Hebrew is *altnay*,' he said, 'but it sounds like the Yiddish pronunciation of *Alt-Neu*. I suppose it is a Jewish idea of a joke. Well, we are not laughing anymore, and neither are they.'

She shuddered in the light, fitful breeze. Since their arrival, Pařižská Street had become entirely deserted, but she could feel frightened eyes peering down at her from behind closed curtains.

Heydrich paid her no attention. He made a sweeping gesture that took in the surrounding blocks. 'Our Führer wishes Josefov preserved forever,' he said, 'as a kind of museum of Jewry, so that after our ultimate and inevitable victory, the Christian world may come and see the fate from which the great German people have so graciously spared it.'

'A noble service to mankind indeed,' said Ilsa. She shuddered once more. The operation could not be called off! It could not be! This monster and every other like him must be destroyed. Didn't the Czechs understand that? What could she do to make them understand?

Heydrich finally noticed her condition. 'You are shivering, child,' he said, taking her by the arm. 'I am sorry to subject you to such unpleasant sights, but both the Germans and the White Russians must know why we are fighting the Jewish Marxists in Russia.'

They rode together over the Čechův Most, across the river and through the big park called Letenské Sady – she silent, he garrulous. Strange, he seemed never to speak at all when he was in the RSHA office, even when he was within his own inner sanctum. He merely grunted orders in a low monotone, read infinite reports, and met, usually weekly, with high-placed Nazis from Vienna and Berlin. About once a month he would travel to Berlin, only a few hours away by car, stay for a night or two, and then return.

Now, in private, the Hangman revealed himself to be the soul of volubility. Indeed, his chatter had begun to take something of a personal turn, complaining about the stupidity of this or that official, praising Hitler, and even once letting slip a very mild criticism of his superior, Himmler.

So wrapped up in listening to Heydrich was she that she had not noticed they had left the city of Prague behind them and were now driving in the countryside.

'Is this a rural restaurant to which we are going, then, Herr Heydrich?' she inquired.

'Reinhard,' he reminded her, spitting out the hard 'd' sound at the end of his name. 'We are not going to a restaurant. My own chef is preparing our meal tonight at my villa.' He glanced over at her. 'Don't worry,' he said. 'Frau Heydrich is conveniently away in Berlin, so we shall be quite alone.'

Why was that piece of information not a surprise? Heydrich's intentions toward her could not have been clearer had he written them down and handed them to her. She would have to play him very carefully. 'This route we have taken is quite interesting,' she ventured.

Heydrich agreed. 'In a few days, when my security precautions are complete, I shall be taking it each morning. I could continue to cross the Charles Bridge, but I no longer wish to do so. Far better for me to pass over the Čechův Most, where my museum is taking shape before my very eyes. Oh, how I am collecting specimens now! Soon, all Europe will be one vast collection agency for my zoo. Each day I shall drive across the Čechův Most and let the animals see their master coming, to strike fear and wonder and awe into them. Those whom I, Reinhard Tristan Eugen Heydrich, have personally selected as being fit for my institution!'

'What about the others?' asked Ilsa.

'There will be no others,' said Heydrich. 'Wannsee has decided that, and our vengeance demands it.'

Her heart was pounding so hard she thought the whole country must surely hear it. So he would not be driving over the Karlův Most at all! But that had been their plan all along, to kill him on the Charles Bridge! Even if she could get word to Victor, it was too late to change now. Somehow she would have to get Heydrich to stay on the Charles Bridge.

Ilsa was so agitated that not until the door on her side opened and Heydrich was helping her out did she notice that the car had come to a stop outside a beautiful villa tucked away in a comely, sheltered valley. 'Welcome to my home,' he said graciously.

Still in a daze, Ilsa was escorted inside. An array of footmen and other servants stood in ranks near the door to greet the master of the house, each in turn nodding his or her head silently as the great man passed by. Ilsa saw fear and hatred in their eyes and knew he did not.

The formal dining room was prepared for dinner à deux. The table was bedecked with the finest silver and Meissen china. Heydrich guided her toward a love seat in the corner, in front of which stood a fresh bottle of champagne and two crystal glasses. The champagne had been freshly opened. Heydrich poured.

'*Prosit*,' he said, raising his glass. '*Sieg Heil!*' Hail, victory.

Although it was nearly nine o'clock, the late spring sun had only recently set. Heydrich set down his glass for a moment and drew the curtains together gently. 'This way,' he said, 'we can have some privacy.'

He kissed her far more quickly than she would have supposed or was prepared for. One minute he was drawing the curtains, the next she was in his arms, being forced upward so that her mouth might meet his. He devoured her hungrily but not rudely, and she finally broke away.

'Herr Heydrich,' she gasped, trying to force him back without angering him, '*bitte . . .*' Surprised, not angry: that was the way she had to play it.

He took a smart step back, as if he were going to salute her, but with a smirk on his lips, the lips that had so freshly tasted hers. 'You will forgive my impetuosity, Fräulein Toumanova,' he said unapologetically. 'I find it difficult to restrain my emotions when faced with incomparable beauty such as yours. The ability to judge beauty is the hallmark of the civilized man, wouldn't you agree?'

'Yes, Reinhard,' she said, softening her voice to disguise the loathing she felt. 'And the ability to restrain one's emotions is the mark of the true leader.'

At this moment she could not help but think of Victor, whose calm resolve contrasted so greatly with Heydrich's naked appetite. The mask had slipped away, and she could see the skull beneath the skin, just as clearly as the skull on the *Totenkopf* SS insignia he wore on his uniform.

The monster, she knew, had blinked. His lust was his weakness; that much they had known before. Now she also knew that he could be held off, at least for a time, by appeals to his honor. His desire could be intensified; the master manipulator could himself be manipulated. That was something she could exploit. But carefully, oh so carefully.

'We shall make some music now,' he said, recovering. 'You'll find the piano more than satisfactory, I am sure. It is a Bösendorfer made in Vienna to my specifications. Naturally, they are of the most demanding exactitude.'

He took his violin, an Amati, out of its case and began to tune it. 'Shall we try the *Kreutzer* Sonata?'

'With pleasure.' She had not played the piece since she was a teenager, but enough of it remained in her fingers that she could give a good account of herself.

'The greatest of the Beethoven violin sonatas,' he remarked just before they began. 'We don't even know which key it really is in. Is it the A major of the title? Or the A minor of the first movement?' He turned to her. 'What do you think, Tamara?'

'To me,' she said, 'it is simply in A.' She sounded the A for him to tune to. 'You see?'

He drew the bow over the strings expertly, painstakingly, until he was satisfied that they were perfectly in harmony.

'You are an empiricist, I see,' he said, nodding. 'It is the curse of your sex to take the world at face value, not to be able to perceive the depth and richness beneath. That is, I suppose, why all the greatest artists are men.'

'You are right, Reinhard,' she said.

'But the *Kreutzer* Sonata is so much more than simply "in A," my dear,' he said. 'It is also a Tolstoy story of surpassing power about a loveless marriage.' He looked down at her, seated at the keyboard. She wondered briefly if her décolletage were too deep. 'Can anything be more tragic than a marriage which joins two bodies but not two souls?'

She lowered her eyes and looked away. 'I'm sure I wouldn't know,' she replied, 'not being a married woman myself.'

He began to play the slow, unaccompanied opening of the sonata, leaning into its plaintive chords, voicing them perfectly. He was, she had to admit, quite good.

That the greatest of all Russian authors had written a short story about the *Kreutzer* Sonata was no wonder, thought Ilsa as she dug into her part. Together they played the music with great feeling and nuance, with only a few minor technical mishaps to mar what otherwise might have been a professional performance. For an all too brief twenty minutes Ilsa Lund forgot herself, forgot where she was and whom she was with. When the last run had dashed down the scale to culminate in the final chords, her exhilaration was overwhelming.

Heydrich finished with a flourish, his bow soaring skyward. Her hands bounced off the keys and into the air. They looked at each other.

'Magnificent,' he said. His face was flushed; even his coiffure was no longer perfect, for one lank strand of blond hair had fallen across his brow. 'I have long dreamed of such an accompanist. To find such a beautiful one into the bargain, well, a man could not ask for more.'

He gazed at her for what seemed like an eternity with those ice blue eyes.

'Shall we sit down?' he finally said. Out of nowhere, two servants appeared and escorted them to the table.

The meal was unexpectedly choice, a combination of German and Bohemian specialties whose centerpiece was a roast duck of surpassing tenderness. Her wineglass, she noticed, was kept filled throughout the dinner, the transition from a Moselle to a Beychevelle seamlessly accomplished. Her head was swimming as she rose from the table, and she resolved not to drink any more around him. Too dangerous.

'Reinhard,' she ventured, 'that was delicious.'

'My cook is the best in the Protectorate,' said Heydrich, taking her by the arm and guiding her out the dining room's French doors and into a starry, moonlit night.

'The lights of the city are not visible here,' he said. 'Which is as it should be. I do not need to always be reminded of my work.'

The night air was chilly. Heydrich put his arms protectively around her.

'I have enemies everywhere,' he said quietly, reflectively, as much to himself as to her. Or was this part of the seduction as well?

'Surely not,' she demurred. 'After all you have wrought here.'

He laughed bitterly. 'It is not enough. It will never be enough until I – until we – have achieved total victory. Until our enemies have been trampled underfoot, their villages razed and salt sown in the earth so that they may never rise again. Enemies like these Czech traitors in London who call themselves patriots while they plot my death like the cowards they really are.'

Her ears now achieved a kind of preternatural hearing: she fancied she could hear even the movement of his tongue as he formed his words.

'But we shall be ready for them. They think we do not know what they are planning, but they are wrong. Our spies are everywhere.'

He lit a cigarette, which he smoked attached to a long ebony filter. He did not offer her one. 'If perchance they should succeed in killing me, they should know that behind me are hundreds – no, thousands – more like me. We shall never rest until complete and total victory is ours.'

He drew her close with his free arm. 'I have had my eye on you for some time,' he said softly. Ilsa felt a chill pass over her.

'A long time,' he repeated, looking at the stars. 'Since you first arrived here, and offered your services to the glory of the Reich. Your intelligence, your beauty, your political instincts – so unusual in a woman – all served to bring you immediately to my attention. Despite the reservations of Frau Hentgen, I resolved to elevate you to the position you now hold once you had demonstrated your loyalty to my satisfaction.'

'Thank you, Reinhard,' she said. 'It is an honor.'

'That has all been a mere prelude,' he told her. 'I have always believed that a man does not really know a woman until he has made love with her. I would not, of course, presume to be so importunate as to suggest we do so immediately. With another woman, I might not be so forbearing. You, however, are deserving of respect.'

'Thank you,' she said softly.

'Nevertheless, I do hold out the hope and wish that someday soon we might consummate the meeting of souls that we have begun here tonight, that our exquisite music making might foretell a fuller, more complete union to come.' He bowed deeply, like an obscene cavalier.

'You will find your rooms more than satisfactory, I hope,' he said. 'I wish you good night, Fräulein Toumanova.'

Ilsa said nothing as his arms tightened around her, and he bent to kiss her lightly on the forehead. They stood there together, silent, in the moonlight, until at last he led her back into the house and shut the door, tightly, against the terrors of the night.

CHAPTER TWENTY-FIVE

They parachuted out of the RAF plane some time after midnight. The drop went as well as drops could go. Nobody shot at them.

As they stood in the hatchway, Renault patted Laszlo fraternally on the shoulder.

'Nervous?' he asked.

'No, why?' replied Laszlo.

'You ought to be,' said Louis. 'A man could get killed doing this.'

Rick jumped first, not really caring whether Laszlo followed or not.

His chute opened as planned, and he floated down into the Czechoslovakian night like an ungainly bird of prey searching for an evening's meal. With a war on, very few lights were visible in the countryside. The cities were another matter; there, the Germans were confident of the ability of the Luftwaffe, the English Channel, and the Baltic Sea to protect them from the Royal Air Force. But the Czech peasants seemed to be taking no chances.

Rick hit the ground hard, his chute billowing down over his head. He got out from underneath it quickly and cut away the cords. As near as he could tell, they were very close to the drop zone, which was a tribute to the skill of their pilot. They had had to take the long way, flying mostly over the Baltic, away from the well-defended German cities of Hamburg, Berlin, and Stettin. Now here he was, on the ground in one piece.

He heard Victor and the two Czechs moving somewhere nearby; at least he hoped it was them. Were he captured now, he would expect even less mercy than he would have in New York, which was to say none at all.

'Janaček,' he whispered, which was the password.

'Jenufa,' came the reply. Renault was walking gingerly, brushing debris from his camouflage: Always dapper, thought Rick admiringly.

'If you ask me, sky-jumping is very much overrated,' said Louis. 'I prefer indoor sports.'

'I'll bet you do,' said Rick.

A few moments later, Victor Laszlo stepped out of the shadows. Behind him came Kubiš and Gabčík, lugging the equipment with them. So far, so good.

They huddled together briefly, talking as softly as they could. Since Jan and Josef had been born nearby there was no need for a map.

'Where are we?' hissed Rick.

'Not far from Kladno,' said Gabčík, a young man grown prematurely old from his experiences over the past two years, 'near Lidice.'

The two Czechs led them through Bohemia's woods and fields. To Rick it looked like parts of Pennsylvania, only neater.

Presently they came to a small village and an even smaller house, snuggled up against its neighbors like cows in a rainstorm. Kubiš knocked twice softly, counted to seven in Czech, then knocked again. The door opened, to utter darkness.

Not for long. Someone found a shielded lantern, the dim light from which revealed the presence of an old woman, bent with age but clear of eye. She led them to a table in a back room, whereon a modest repast had been laid out; the men tucked into it as though it were dinner at the Ritz. They washed down the *nudeln* and the roast pork and the strudel with liter upon liter of cold Budvar beer.

Ten minutes later one never would have suspected anything had been consumed on the table; instead it was laden with rifles, pistols, and a bomb. Neat as a pin, thought Rick, just like the Germans. No wonder most of the Bohemians aren't putting up much of a fight: they're brothers under the skin.

Renault bid the company good night and went off to bed. Laszlo spread out a well-worn map of Prague and pored over it. Rick ignored him, preferring the company of his own thoughts. By now he could probably qualify as a taxi driver in the city, so many times had they gone over it. He knew every street in both the Staré Město and the Nové Město, and across the river to Hradčany. Hell, he could even name the statues of the saints on the Charles Bridge: Nepomuk, who was flung off the bridge and into the river and duly commemorated in 1683; the crucifix erected by a Jew thirteen years later in expiation of some blasphemy or other; and the lovely St. Luitgard, caught in 1710 in the middle of a wondrous vision of the Christ.

'Everything is clear, then?' Victor was saying.

Rick assured him that it was and rose from the table. 'I think I'll step outside and have a smoke,' he said. 'Jan, you want to join me? They're real Chesterfields.' Sam had given them to him as a present just before he left. Where he'd gotten them Rick had no idea, but Sam could always get things that no other human being could. Laszlo looked at the two of them suspiciously as they went out the door, but he said nothing.

He offered a cigarette to Kubiš and struck a match, cupping his hand around it so as not to let the wind blow it out. The young Czech leaned forward and inhaled; Rick followed his lead, then shook out the match and tossed it on the ground.

'Beautiful night,' he said.

Kubiš agreed. 'Our May nights,' he said, 'are the most beautiful on earth.'

Talk of beauty got Rick's mind around to what was really beautiful. 'You got a girl, Jan?' he asked.

The boy – he was about twenty-one but looked five years younger – nodded. 'Martina,' he said. The kid fished in his pocket for a photograph.

'That's a nice name,' Rick supplied. He supposed it was. Maybe it wasn't. It was all the same to him. He squinted at the picture in the moonlight. 'Pretty girl,' he said. He couldn't tell if she was or she wasn't.

Kubiš gazed soulfully at the picture. 'She was,' he said. 'She's dead.'

That got his attention. 'How?'

'How else?' Jan said softly. 'The Germans killed her. Right after Munich, when they marched into the Sudetenland. They were trying to expel her family from their home, she resisted, she died. It is a very short story.' He put the picture back in his jacket. 'She was only seventeen. She did not deserve it.'

Rick blew out a lungful of smoke. 'Nobody does,' he said, 'but everybody gets it anyway.'

They finished their cigarettes, then ground them underfoot in the green Czech grass.

'Very soon,' said Jan, 'she shall be avenged.'

Rick looked at him. '"Vengeance is mine, sayeth the Lord."'

'But He has abandoned us,' retorted Jan. 'It is up to us, by our actions, to bring Him back again.'

'Whatever you say,' said Rick. 'Tell me, though, have you thought about anyone else?'

By the look on his face, Jan plainly didn't know what Rick meant.

'I mean' – Rick lit another of his precious but dwindling supply of Chesterfields – 'have you given any thought at all to what might happen if we actually succeed?'

'Of course we will succeed,' said Kubiš. He seemed surprised there could be any question, any alternative to triumph.

'Let's suppose we do,' Rick argued. 'Let's suppose we blow Heydrich to hell and gone. Then what?' He tried to blow a smoke ring and failed; must be losing his touch.

'Then we will have succeeded and Martina will have been avenged. After that, I don't care.'

That was the way he used to talk. He found himself liking Jan. He hoped the boy wouldn't have to die.

'Maybe you should,' said Rick. 'Maybe you ought to give some thought to what might happen. Do you think the Germans are going to take this lying down? You've seen the way they are. Take out one of theirs and they kill a hundred, maybe a thousand of yours. Has Laszlo thought of that?'

'I doubt it.' Jan scuffed his shoe on the grass. 'Victor Laszlo is a hero to every true son of Czechoslovakia. There is not one of us who would not follow him to hell if he asked us to. Whatever happens after we kill Hangman Heydrich happens. There is nothing we can do about it.'

'Isn't there?' Rick wondered softly. 'Well, there's no sense standing out here debating it. Come on, let's go back inside.'

Gabčík had already retired for the night, if retired was the right word. The young soldier had fallen asleep in his clothes, his backpack slung over his shoulders and his loaded pistol on his lap. Kubiš bade both Rick and Laszlo a good night and departed to sleep in the barn.

'You still have your doubts, don't you?' said Laszlo.

'It's not kosher to have doubts about something after you've given your word,' said Rick. He wasn't in the mood for any of Victor's speeches. 'I'm just holding up my end of the bargain.'

Laszlo shook his head in disbelief. 'That is not what you said to me back in Casablanca. There you made a choice. A number of them, in fact. You chose to give us the letters of transit – excuse me, you chose to give *me* a letter of transit; my wife was going to obtain one no matter what. You chose to make your bargain with me after I was arrested. You chose to dupe Captain Renault, you chose to put us on that plane, and you chose to shoot Major Strasser when all you had to do was stand by and do nothing.'

'You weren't there,' Rick demurred. 'Major Strasser chose to draw on me first.'

Laszlo smiled. 'And like a good American cowboy you beat him to the draw and, as you say, gunned him down in cold blood.'

Rick let his hands rest on the tabletop. 'It was him or me.'

Laszlo trumped him. 'When it didn't have to be either. You could have walked away and let him try to stop our plane. You could have walked away in London as well. You might still be able to walk away now. You don't trust me, I know that. You think I am a fanatic.'

'That's where you're wrong,' Rick interrupted. 'I *know* you're a fanatic.'

'Very well, perhaps I am.' Laszlo poured himself a small glass of beer from one of the last remaining bottles. He didn't offer one to Rick. 'Sometimes one has to be. My question to you, though, remains: Why don't you just leave?'

'It's a little late for that now, don't you think?'

'Because of Ilsa?'

'Because of a lot of things,' Rick shot back. 'Look, Laszlo, we're both grown men. We don't need to beat around the bush here. I fell in love with your wife in Paris, before I knew she was your wife, and I'm still in love with her even though now I know she is your wife. If it wasn't for her, I wouldn't be here. But I am, and so are you, and we have to make the best of it.'

Laszlo took a deep breath. 'Monsieur Blaine,' he began, 'I told you in London that I would kill you myself if I suspected the slightest disloyalty to our cause. Let me reiterate that promise to you now. Like you, I am a man of my word;

it is the only thing the Nazis have permitted me to keep. It is my stock in trade. I do not expend it lightly or frivolously.'

He took a deep, satisfying breath of the smoke and exhaled elegantly. 'Perhaps I am naive, but I expect the same kind of behavior – the same ethics, as it were – from you. You have given me your word, and I have accepted it. Whatever occurred in the past between you and Mrs. Laszlo when I was *hors de combat* is of absolutely no import to me. However, what occurs in the days to come is very much my concern.'

Laszlo stopped talking for a moment and collected his thoughts. What he was about to say he had told no one.

'The reason goes beyond my personal feelings about Herr Heydrich,' he began. 'No, perhaps it doesn't.' Suddenly the smooth, self-confident Victor Laszlo seemed lost, vulnerable, confused.

'Monsieur Blaine,' he said at last, 'would it help explain my hatred for Reinhard Heydrich if I told you that he killed my father?'

Rick's head snapped up. 'What?'

'My father grew up in Vienna in the last days of the Dual Monarchy, and even after we moved to Prague, his work took him there often. He was a socialist and an architect. When, after Heydrich is destroyed and then Himmler is smashed and finally Hitler himself is annihilated, we ride in triumph through the streets of Vienna together, I will be proud to point out to you the buildings he designed.

'But after February 1934, when Dollfuss crushed the socialists, there was no more room in Austria for a man of my father's political persuasion. There was no more room for socialists in Vienna, period.' Laszlo lowered his head. 'With regret, he confined his practice to Prague. You know what happened: four years later came the Munich Pact, only this time instead of Dollfuss and his Fatherland Front there was Hitler and the Nazis. I was lucky: I got out of Prague alive. My father did not. Despite his experiences, he was one of those people who never sees the light, even when it is shining right in their eyes. Can you imagine?'

'Yes,' said Rick under his breath.

Laszlo's voice was rising now. 'Now I have this fiend Heydrich, another kind of architect, in my grasp. The man who more than any other except for Hitler himself has brought me misery. He must and will be stopped. Therefore I ask you once again, for the last time: Are you with us or are you against us? I ask you this time not in my name, but in the name of the woman we both love. In Ilsa's.'

Some choice. Rick looked at Victor. 'You talked me into it.'

CHAPTER TWENTY-SIX

The plan was for Rick to make immediate contact with Ilsa in Prague, with Renault following him into town a few hours later, by another route. Laszlo was to stay hidden at the house in Lidice, where he would be safe and where, more important, the operation would remain secure. His face was too well known in Prague for him to be able to walk the streets with impunity. All it would take was one phone call from one informer, and that would be the end.

Richard Blaine, however, was known to no man. The last place the Nazis would be looking for the murderer of Major Heinrich Strasser was right under the nose of the most powerful and feared secret policeman of the Reich. Armed with false papers proclaiming him to be a citizen of the neutral country of Sweden, Rick would be able to move about the city with relative freedom. The fact that he didn't look very Swedish didn't mean much, because a lot of Swedes didn't look very Swedish, either.

He made his way into the city that morning and registered

at the U Tří Pštrosů, right beside the Charles Bridge. It was one of the few decent hotels that hadn't been entirely commandeered by the Nazis. His room was small but pleasant, with a prospect of the Charles Bridge. He had insisted on a view, even though registration had assured him that the rooms on the other side were bigger and quieter.

He had Ilsa's address: Number 12 Skořepka, a short little street located about halfway between Bethlehem Chapel and St. Wenceslas Square. Before he went up to his room he slipped a bellhop some dough. 'I want flowers sent to this address, right away,' he said. 'No card. She'll know who they're from.' He ruffled the kid's hair. The kid happily accepted both Rick's money and his bad German and ran off to do his bidding.

He washed up, soaking his head under the hot shower and reflecting on how smoothly everything had gone thus far. Aside from his inelegant introduction to the country by the Royal Air Force, the safe house appeared to be really safe, his papers were very much in order, and – so far, at least – his presence in Prague had not attracted any undue attention. The next test, he knew, would come tomorrow, when the registry records of every hotel in the city would be examined by police, as required by law.

Maybe the Nazis weren't so tough. Or maybe that's just what they wanted you to think.

He had never met a German gangster before. Back home there weren't any. Why was something of a mystery. There were plenty of Germans in New York, and when they first got there they got dumped on like everybody else. They were people who liked their beer cold and their houses neat. They washed the windows twice a year, whether they needed it or not, and had flowers planted in the windowboxes outside their tenements on April 1. They spent their Sundays strolling in Central Park. They took their leisure *en masse*, hiring steamers to take their church congregations up and down the East River. They worked hard and stayed away from crime. They became bankers and businessmen and doctors and lawyers and sometimes even politicians. There were plenty of opportunities for chiseling, but they didn't seem to take them. You could cheat the children out of their lunch money and not have the father come looking for you with a rod in his hand. They seemed too square to be for real. Still, Rick knew it would be folly to underestimate them. When World War I finally sucked America in, the German New Yorkers volunteered in droves and went happily to France to shoot their relatives.

Rick dressed unobtrusively, in a dark blue double-breasted suit and a matching blue fedora. He felt naked without a heater in his waistband, but for safety's sake he'd had to leave his favorite .45 behind in the farmhouse.

He tapped his breast pocket once, to make sure he had his papers with him; he was not about to let some snoops get the drop on him again, as they had in London. Once more, he recited his new name to himself: Ekhard Lindquist, specialist in the oil importation business. British Intelligence had arranged for someone to answer the telephone at a Goteborg number just in case anyone called to check his bona fides. He took the stairs instead of the lift, the better to get an idea of the layout of the hotel. If the hit were going to come practically outside his window, it would behoove him to know the joint from top to bottom.

He was walking on the Charles Bridge, scoping the killing zone, when he felt a tap on his shoulder.

'But surely this is Mr. Rick Blaine?' said a vaguely familiar voice in German-accented English. 'Of the Café Americain in Casablanca? The walk is unmistakable.'

He wheeled around. There stood Hermann Heinze, the former German consul in French Morocco. Heinze was smiling, but he didn't appear glad to see him.

'There must be some mistake,' said Rick. Unfortunately there was no mistaking the identity of the man who stood before him.

Like many gangsters, and most of the Nazi top brass, Hermann Heinze was a short man. Rick himself was not very big: about five feet nine inches tall and weighing about 155 pounds. Heinze stood nearly a head shorter than he and probably outweighed him by 20 pounds or so. He had a pale round, moon face, a balding head, and rheumy little pig eyes, over which he wore a pair of Coke-bottle spectacles. In civilian life, Rick reflected as he looked at him, he would have been lucky to be the third guy in a two-man office. Under Hitler, though, his ignorance, his arrogance, his congenitally nasty disposition, and his bullying temperament had allowed him to rise quickly in the consular service. He was, in short, a born Nazi diplomat.

'I think not,' his interlocutor assured him. 'Would you be so kind as to come with me?' Heinze gestured in the direction of a BMW coupe parked near the curb. 'I have always believed that unpleasantness should be avoided in public places except when one is trying to make a point. Would you step into the car, please?'

Of all the rotten luck. What were the odds of his running into anyone he knew from Casablanca – or, worse, anyone who knew him? He would have put them at several million to one. Yet his number had come up. Well, that sometimes happened, even when the roulette wheel wasn't fixed.

Rick got in the car, for he didn't see any point in arguing or causing a scene that might blow everything. Whatever had to be done would have to be done elsewhere.

He did catch one break: no one else was in the car, no one hiding, waiting to take him for a ride. If this were New York, Rick knew he would be as good as dead already, with only the gunshot to the back of the head and the dump job somewhere in the Jersey flats remaining as a kind of formality.

'What's on your mind, Heinze?' he asked as idly as he could, lighting a cigarette and tossing the match out the window as the car started up.

'There are many unanswered questions surrounding your rather sudden departure from Casablanca,' said Heinze, 'but even more – in my mind, at least – concerning your appearance here in Prague. Of course you know our countries are now at war?'

'I've heard the rumors,' replied Rick.

'Oh, they are more than rumors, I can assure you,' Heinze observed as they crossed one of the bridges. 'They are very much the facts.'

'Do tell.'

'Yes,' said Heinze. 'And as an official of the Reich, it is my duty to take you into custody at once.' He made a little grimace. 'For your own protection. I'm sure you understand.'

'I'm sure I do,' replied Rick.

'This is no time for the joking!' Heinze shouted. 'You are wanted the length and breadth of Europe. You cannot escape. I don't know why you have chosen to come to Prague, or under whose auspices, but believe me, Mr. Blaine, you will not be leaving any time soon. Your papers, please!'

Rick made a pretense of fishing around in his jacket. He was not about to hand over his fake Swedish documents. 'I must have left them in my sock drawer.' He shrugged. 'In my country, a man doesn't have to carry a piece of paper to tell him who he is.'

They had crossed over an island in the Vltava and were now headed up a steep hill. Rick lit a cigarette. 'Where are we going?'

'Somewhere we can talk privately,' replied Heinze. 'I thought it might amuse you to see the best view of Prague from the top of Petřín Hill. I advise you to enjoy it, since it might well be your last view of anything for some time.'

'I get it,' said Rick. 'Somewhere that you and I might be able to do a little business, cut a deal, eh, Heinze?' Heinze's sideways glance told him he'd struck home. 'After all, I am a businessman.'

The car reached the top of the hill. Heinze killed the engine, and they both got out. Nearby stood an old monastery. Under Hitler, there probably wasn't much call for its services these days, although Rick suspected they were needed more than ever. It was very peaceful up there. Although the weather was fine, very few people were about. Those who were studiously avoided looking at them: two men in an official German car could only be trouble.

This, Rick reflected, was what life would be like if the Nazis won. Like Hitler's watercolors: all buildings and no people.

'It will go easier with you if you talk to me first, before I take you to Prague Castle and let the Gestapo have its way with you,' said Heinze, lighting a cigarette. 'I know you think you are – how do you Americans say – a tough guy, but believe me when I tell you that you have not yet met a real tough guy. Before Herr Heydrich's men are through with you, you will be singing the immolation song from *Götterdämmerung* – in the original soprano.'

'You can forget about that,' said Rick. 'I gave up vaudeville when I was thirteen.' He started to walk around a bit, planning his next move. Heinze had made a fatal mistake bringing him here, and he was about to find out why.

'Let us stop playing about the bush, Mr. Blaine,' said Heinze. 'Unfortunately for you, Major Strasser lived long enough to gasp out the name of his murderer. Your name was on his lips when he died.'

'I didn't know he cared,' said Rick.

'Then you admit you killed an officer of the Third Reich?' Heinze shouted.

'So what if I did?' Rick retorted. 'You'd do the same thing. It was him or me. He drew on me first. The last time I looked, self-defense was legal, even in Casablanca.' He lit a cigarette. 'Anyway, what was I supposed to do, take a bullet for Victor Laszlo? What did he ever do for me?'

'You let Laszlo get away,' accused Heinze. 'You drew your pistol on the Prefect of Police and prevented him from doing his duty. And you received the stolen letters of transit from the criminal Ugarte and hid them until you could sell them to Victor Laszlo. How do you explain that?'

'Like I said, I'm a businessman,' replied Rick. 'It wasn't any of my concern where those letters came from, or who I sold them to. I'm also a sporting man, and I bet Captain Renault ten thousand francs that Victor Laszlo would escape Casablanca, and I intended to win that bet, since the only kind of bet I like to make is a sure thing. Besides,' said Rick, 'America wasn't involved in the war then. Whether Victor Laszlo escaped or was arrested right there in my club like Ugarte made no difference whatsoever to me.' He looked at Heinze, waiting to see if his bluff had gone over.

Heinze's beady eyes were glistening. 'Through our spies in London,' he said, 'we have been picking up a great deal of activity between London and the Prague underground. The quality of their intelligence about our plans has improved enormously lately.' He eyed Rick with suspicion. 'You wouldn't know anything about that, would you?' he asked.

'Not a thing,' said Rick. Inside his head, though, alarm bells were ringing. Heinze must have seen Ilsa and Laszlo in the café, and Ilsa Lund was not a woman a miserable loser like Heinze would ever forget. She was the kind of woman a man like him could never have and therefore would always hate. If Heinze spotted her here, there would be hell to pay.

'It is of course unthinkable and impossible for the Czech rabble that calls itself an "Underground" to have placed an agent within Gestapo headquarters, but in any case a major operation appears to be under way.'

'It's called a counterattack,' Rick told him. 'You can't expect to keep punching a guy and not have him punch back.'

Heinze looked as if the thought had never occurred to him. Maybe it hadn't. 'Unfortunately we don't know what this operation might be,' he continued. 'Now here you are, which leads me to suspect that Victor Laszlo might not be far away, although I cannot believe he would have the effrontery to return to his former homeland. Which in turn leads me to suspect that whatever is being planned, it is going to happen here.'

'You know, Hermann,' said Rick, inhaling the tobacco smoke, 'you're a lot smarter than you look. You're going places, you know that?'

'I know,' gloated Heinze. It was about time. He had been rebuffed in his attempts to obtain a position at RSHA headquarters, been shunted off instead with minor diplomatic work involving Slovakia and the integration of Ruthenia into Hungary. Now a ticket to the castle had just been handed to him. He couldn't believe his good fortune. In his excitement, he began to pace, taking mincing little steps.

'Of course, it is impossible that the Czechs could harm us in any way,' he said. 'But there are always agitators, men like this Victor Laszlo, who claims to speak for the Czech people when all he represents are a few Communist malcontents who seek to enslave their own people by mouthing slogans about peace and freedom. Bah! How easily we Germans see through them!'

'I'll bet you do,' agreed Rick. He had yet to meet a German who didn't act like a hanging judge even when he was just buying a loaf of bread.

Heinze missed the sarcasm in Rick's voice. He threw away his cigarette. 'What can you offer me in exchange for your life?' he said.

Rick didn't move. Below him, the city was spread out like a child's toy model. It was not the beauty of Prague that had captivated him; rather, it was, of all things, a reduced-scale version of the Eiffel Tower. 'What's that?' he asked.

Heinze turned back. 'The Petřín Tower,' he said. 'Built in 1891. One-fifth the scale of the Eiffel Tower in Paris. Two hundred and ninety-nine steps from top to bottom. It was constructed out of old railroad ties in thirty-one days for the Jubilee Exposition. Ugly, isn't it?'

'Only to a Nazi,' muttered Rick. In his mind's eye he could see her again – her in the car as they tooled down the Champs-Élysées. Her as they dined together that first evening at the Tour d'Argent and cruised along the Seine in one of the *bateaux mouches*. Her as they walked together, hand in hand, in the Luxembourg Gardens and across the Pont des Arts. Her, always her.

Heinze hadn't heard him. 'The Führer has ordered it torn down. Why look at a model when you already own the real thing?' The consul threw back his head and laughed. 'Perhaps we'll even tear the real Eiffel Tower down someday as well and replace it with a proper monument to German glory!'

Rick waited for him to stop chortling. 'Well, enough sight-seeing,' he said. 'It's time to get down to brass tacks.' Rick nodded in the direction of the car. 'In there.'

They got back into the car. It was time to make his move, play his hand, spin the roulette wheel, throw the dice. He'd gambled before with lives and lost, lost big; now it was lucky number 22's turn to come up again.

Heinze was so dumb, he hadn't even pulled his pistol.

That was all the break Rick needed. With his right hand he tossed his cigarette out the window. With his left he swung hard and caught Heinze right in the throat with the edge of his hand. As Heinze's head came down, Rick drove his right fist onto the point of the man's jaw. Heinze didn't make a sound as the lights went out.

Just like old times.

He started the engine and left it in neutral. Nobody had seen or heard a thing. To all intents and appearances, they were two men sitting in the front seat of an expensive BMW, talking and looking out over the city.

Slowly Rick released the hand brake. The car was now in perfect equipoise at the top of Petřín Hill; the slightest push would set it moving.

He got out the passenger's side, went around the front of the car, leaned in the open window on the driver's side, and pretended to say good-bye to the man at the wheel. With his head in the window and his shoulder against the doorjamb, he leaned hard against the vehicle and gave it a shove. As it began to roll down the hill, he steered lightly with his right hand, aiming rather than driving. He could hear Heinze starting to come around.

A sharp curve lay just ahead as the car picked up speed.

'*Heil Hitler*,' said Rick.

The car missed the curve and went over the edge. He thought he could hear Heinze screaming as it went down, but that could have been his imagination.

The wreck brought people running. He walked the other way, back up toward the monastery, not hurriedly but briskly. From the top of the hill he looked back. This time, with Heinze's flaming BMW in the middle foreground, the view was better than ever.

His mind raced, trying to sort out all the information, all the suspicion. Unless Heinze had been lying to him, Ilsa was in mortal danger. They might not be able to pin anything on her right away, but even the Germans could eventually put two and two together and come up with her arrival and the beginning of the leaks. He had to get her out of there, no matter what.

Maybe the operation was already blown. Maybe, like Heinze's car, all it needed was a little push.

CHAPTER TWENTY-SEVEN

He was meeting her at a small restaurant called U Maltézských Rytířů, an ancient barrel-shaped cellar just across the river from his hotel in the Mala Strana that had once been, or so legend had it, a hospice of the Knights of Malta. Rick didn't know much about Malta except what he had read in *The Maltese Falcon* by Hammett, more than a decade ago, when he still had time to read. Despite himself, he was letting his mind drift back over the past when he spotted Ilsa walking down the stairs and into the dining room. Right away, he was back in the present.

How beautiful she looked! It hardly seemed possible, but she gained in beauty each time he saw her. In Paris she had merely been exquisite; in Casablanca, ravishing; in London, magnificent. Here in Prague, she was overwhelming. She put to flight the memory of every other woman he had ever known, save one, and even that one was finally beginning to fade.

He rose and stood stock-still as she approached. A

restaurant was no place for a display of public affection. There wasn't a man in the room who did not notice Ilsa as she strolled by, so different, so fresh in her beauty compared with the heavyset German matrons and the rawboned Czech girls. Let Rick stick his neck out by embracing her in the middle of the room, as he longed to do, and the show might close before it even opened.

'Mr. Lindquist?' she said pleasantly in Russian-accented English.

'At your service,' he replied.

They sat down, the waiter hovering as if he had just seen a miraculous apparition of the Madonna, and Ilsa spoke to him in rapid-fire Czech. Her command of languages amazed Rick, especially set next to his. The waiter's head bobbled on his shoulders like a funhouse doll's, and then he scuttled away to fetch their drinks.

'What did you order?' Rick asked her quietly.

'Some mineral water for both of us,' she said, smiling. He wished she wouldn't smile that smile. It reminded him too much of Paris. But there was nothing he could do about it, even had he wanted to.

'I've also ordered some roast duck.' She forced a light laugh. 'In Prague you can have anything you want as long as it's roasted. It's all they know how to do very well.'

'Is everything in order?' he asked, dispassionately.

She kept the smile plastered to her face, but answered in the negative. 'I'm very much afraid there has been some difficulty with the business that you and Herr Sieger' – their code name for Victor – 'have been discussing. It seems that he might no longer be able to arrange delivery of the shipment. I'm very sorry.'

'So am I,' said Rick, taking a sip of the water to conceal his surprise; today was full of surprises, all of them bad. 'This is rather sudden, isn't it?'

'Very much so, I regret to say.' Although hardly a muscle in her face had moved, to his practiced eye her whole demeanor was now different. 'Apparently something has come up, something very urgent. Frankly, we were hoping you might be able to explain it.'

'I'm afraid I can't,' said Rick.

When the waiter produced the duck, she dug into it, tearing it apart, and Rick noticed that her hands were shaking as she wielded her knife. They said very little else for the rest of the meal. Rick decided he hated roast duck. 'I hope we may discuss this matter further,' he said as he paid the bill.

'We would welcome that possibility,' she told him. 'Perhaps, if you have time, you could accompany me back to the office?'

'It would be my pleasure,' said Rick, putting on his hat.

They walked out into the bright sunlight. Ilsa reached into her handbag and pulled out a pair of sunglasses. She was wearing a broad-brimmed hat as well. Rick pulled his fedora down tight over his brow. Unless someone scrutinized them closely, their faces were well hidden.

They crossed over the Charles Bridge and headed toward the broad mall of Václavské Náměstí. On such a fine day, many folks were out for a stroll. The casual observer would be hard-pressed to tell there was a war on.

'What the hell is happening?' whispered Rick as they walked.

'I don't know,' she said, trying not to let her fear show. 'The Underground is pleading with London to call off the operation. They seem terribly frightened of what might happen if we succeed.'

'Maybe they have good reason to be.' He lit a cigarette, thinking about everything Louis had been telling him, about all the doubts the little Frenchman had been harboring since the beginning.

'Perhaps they suspect something.'

That was just what he had not wanted to hear her say. 'Maybe they suspect you.'

She took his arm as if for support, but beneath the sleeve of his jacket he could feel her fingers digging into him, hard. 'Do you think so?' she whispered. Frau Hentgen; it had to be. Frantically Ilsa raced back over her actions of the past month as Rick spoke again.

'I've just had a chance meeting with Heinze,' he said. 'You remember him – he was in the café with Strasser. Anyway, it was just my luck to run into him.' He patted her arm. 'Don't worry,' he said. 'Heinze won't be around to trouble us anymore. However, we've got to figure out what we're going to do, and we've got to do it fast.'

Ilsa didn't bother to ask why Heinze would no longer trouble them. 'No matter what,' she began, 'we have to go through with it. You don't know this Heydrich as I do. He is a monster – the worst kind of monster, because he is so seductive. Through terror and generosity he has corrupted a nation – my husband's homeland – and by denouncing people they hate, he has made himself popular with the masses.'

'Such as the Jews,' said Rick. It was the same old story.

'Yes, especially the Jews,' said Ilsa. 'Things are only going to get worse. Heydrich told me himself that at Wannsee they have planned nothing less than the total extermination of the Jewish people. Already they are building more camps, this time in the east, in Poland. And Heydrich is in charge! He boasts, as if it were the crowning accomplishment of his life! He says the fools in the West have not realized their intentions yet, and even if the word gets out, they will not believe it. It's too fantastic to be plausible; that's what he's counting on.'

That's what people like Heydrich always counted on, thought Rick: the ability of good men to see nothing, hear nothing, do nothing, and believe nothing they didn't want to.

'I can't ask Victor to stop now,' she went on. 'He has been dreaming of this revenge since he escaped from Mauthausen. And this is not just Victor's fight: to kill Reinhard Heydrich would be to save thousands, maybe millions, of people. What the Underground fears about reprisals – well, it's only speculation, isn't it? I mean, we don't really know what will happen, do we?'

'After Guernica, I think we can make a pretty educated guess,' said Rick. They had stopped walking.

'Perhaps you're right,' she said, wondering how to broach a more immediate, personal subject. 'There's something else you should know.' She looked at him through red-rimmed eyes over lowered sunglasses. 'Heydrich wants to make love to me. He tried last night. I didn't let him, but I don't know how long I can refuse him.' She lowered her eyes. 'He's not the sort of man one can put off for very long.'

He felt a rage boiling up inside him, the kind of rage he had not felt for years. He had not felt it as he rained mortar fire down on the Italian positions in East Africa. He had not felt it in Spain, not after Guernica, and not even at the Ebro River.

He had not felt it when the Germans marched into Paris, and he had not felt it when, at the train station, he read her letter. He had felt this kind of rage only once before, on October 23, 1935, the day before he fled America forever. The day Solomon and Lois Horowitz had died. It was time for him to face the truth: he was consumed with love for Ilsa Lund.

'Then we really do have to hurry,' Rick said flatly, moving again. Ilsa's refusal of Heydrich, he knew, would first arouse and then infuriate him; Nazis weren't used to taking no for an answer.

'Yes,' she agreed. 'But not just for me. For Victor and for my father and for all the people of Europe. What are we going to do?'

'Let me think for a minute,' he said.

If Heinze had heard something about a plot, and if the Underground was begging London to call a halt, the situation must be fraught indeed. The locals were getting cold feet, and for a very good reason: they wanted to live to fight another day. Far worse, from his perspective, was the danger Ilsa might now be in. He had already seen one woman he loved die because he couldn't protect her. He would be damned before he would let that happen again.

Mentally he ran over the situation, trying to figure out what to do. Victor Laszlo would never be dissuaded from attempting his mission, no matter what. Too much was at stake to let a little thing like his wife's safety stop him. There had to be a way to make it all come out right: there *had* to be.

The Nazis could bluster and threaten to murder the Jews of Europe, but could they really do it? Could they get away with it? He had to weigh the possibility of what Heydrich *might* do if he lived against the probability – no, the certainty – of what the Germans *would* do if he died. Maybe the best thing was for Reinhard Heydrich *not* to die, that others might live. Maybe the Underground was right: maybe they should call the whole thing off.

What had he learned in *shul* a thousand years ago? That even in a case where his life is in danger, a Jew is forbidden to save himself by spilling the blood of an innocent man, forbidden to save one man or even many by turning an innocent man over to a murderer, forbidden to hand over even 'one soul from Israel' to murderers. Nothing in there to address his current dilemma: that to save the lives of countless innocent persons, a murderer himself must be spared.

Which was the higher good? Was it better to let Heydrich go on killing people, many of them Jews, in order to save the lives of some Czechs, most of whom might be anti-Semites anyway? Or would the Hangman's death spare thousands, maybe millions, of people a hideous fate, at the expense of a couple of hundred innocents?

How do you save somebody who doesn't want to be saved? How do you rescue a nation that doesn't want to be rescued? He had never felt much like a Jew, at least not a religious one, but now seemed like a good time to start.

Where were the rabbis of his youth when he needed them?

Then Rick remembered where he was at that moment and why there were no rabbis for him to turn to.

In a flash, he saw his play. It was so simple, so beautiful, the way all the best plays were. It might even work. With any luck, it would shield Ilsa and spare Heydrich, with no one the wiser. 'We'll let him know he's going to be assassinated,' he said. 'He'll never see it coming.'

'What!' exclaimed Ilsa, as softly as she could.

'We've got to protect you, cover for you,' he said.

'What about the operation?' she protested. 'Victor will never agree to this!'

Oh yes: Victor. He had to put a plausible face on it, at least as far as she was concerned. As for Victor, he need never know.

'Don't worry,' he said. 'We're still going through with it.' Before she could start to complain, he went on. 'Don't you see?' he said, excited now, seeing a way out, seeing the way clear. 'It's the oldest trick in the book. You set a guy up by telling him exactly what's going to happen to him – and then you do it!' He pounded his hand into his fist. 'You've taken him into your confidence and lulled him to sleep: he thinks he's got you covered, and never sees it coming. Works every time.'

The look in her eyes plainly proclaimed her doubt. 'But he'll send his men looking for us,' she objected.

'If what you say is true, Heydrich's men are already looking for us. Don't you see, Ilsa, it's our only chance.'

How he hated lying to her! But they had to get the message to Heydrich. Not just to protect Ilsa, although she alone would have been reason enough, but because Renault was right: no one could doubt that the price the Czech people would pay for getting rid of Heydrich would be terrible. Laszlo was willing to pay that price, but he would have to pay it only once. The Czechs would go on paying for the rest of the war.

Once they had warned Heydrich he would have to change his route. Nobody was that stupid, not even a Nazi.

'Are you sure?' she asked.

'Trust me,' he said. 'Tough guys like him never believe it can happen to them.'

'How do you know?' she asked him.

'I know,' he said quietly, 'because it happened to me once.'

He reached for her hand, but he dared not grasp it. This was strictly business now. 'The most important thing is to protect you,' he said. 'Somehow, we'll get word to him. I'll think of a way, we'll . . .'

He was nearly babbling, his words pouring forth, when Ilsa calmly laid a hand on his arm. 'Richard,' she said, 'I know just what to do.'

He stopped and looked at her. She was no longer the shy, vulnerable girl he had known in Paris, but a more confident, more assured, more deadly woman. 'You do?' he said.

She did. She had been worrying all afternoon about how to bring up the subject of the Čechův Most, about how she was going to maneuver Heydrich back to the original site. Now she didn't have to. She didn't have to confuse the issue, didn't have to alarm Victor and Rick, didn't have to tell them anything. On her information, Heydrich would be looking for assassins on the Čechův Most; his security forces would be watching for trouble there. He, meanwhile, would be motoring blithely toward the Charles Bridge, and death. How fitting: the man for whom death was the solution for everything would find it the solution for him, too.

Her heart leaped as she replied, 'Yes. I'll tell him myself. Tomorrow night. At the castle. He's giving a party, and I'm to be the hostess.'

'You can't! It's crazy.' Now it was Rick's turn to grab, to dig. The hell with propriety: he took her arm and held it tightly.

Ilsa shook him off. 'I'm going to tell him everything. Tell him I've learned of a plot to bomb his car when he rides to work the next day. Beg him to be careful. Plead with him to take another route. That's what we need to do, isn't it? To get him where we want him?'

'Yes,' Rick said. 'That's exactly what we need to do. But why do you have to do it?'

'Because I am the one closest to him,' she explained. 'Isn't that why you and Victor sent me here in the first place? To get close to him, any way I could? Heydrich trusts me.'

'You can't do it,' he muttered. 'It's too dangerous.'

'If what you've just told me is true, it may be our only chance, the only way I can deflect suspicion from myself and make sure our plan succeeds.'

Rick was worried. He knew they were improvising now, which was bad. Improvisation made things messy. Improvisation made things dangerous. Improvisation made things go wrong, and when things went wrong, they went wrong for everybody. What choice did he have, though?

Ilsa was ecstatic. What had moments ago seemed a tangled and perilous path had now been made smooth. She would tell Heydrich that for his own safety he must cross the Charles, not the Čechův, and he would drive right into the trap. Rick was right: he would never see it coming; she would make sure of that. She hated keeping information from Rick and her husband. What choice did she have, though?

They were standing in front of her apartment building on Skořepka, facing each other as if they were practically strangers. 'Back in Casablanca,' she said, 'I asked you to do the thinking for both of us. I was a different person then. I didn't know what I wanted; I didn't know my own mind. I do now. When we parted the last time, it was on your terms, Richard. Now, we part on mine.'

They said good-bye with a formal handshake and a stiff bow. Then she was past the front door and inside, gone.

Rick walked down the cobblestone streets, thinking of Paris. Ilsa thought only of Prague.

CHAPTER TWENTY-EIGHT

New York, August 1935

As suddenly as she had left it, Lois Meredith came back into his life. Three years was a long time to carry a torch, but he had been managing nicely.

Business was good. The newly legal Tootsie-Wootsie Club had surpassed every other former New York speakeasy in total volume and turnover. It had the best booze and the best music, and everybody knew it. Rick Baline's place was the talk of the town. Even Damon Runyon was keeping a regular table there, having moved over from the Boll Weevil, which had closed. Privately Rick thought Runyon was a lush and a jerk, but he cultivated him just the same, for a mention in Runyon's column for any of his ventures meant a doubling of business almost overnight.

On this particular evening, Rick was looking out over the dance floor and counting the house. Life was about as good as it could possibly be. He had moved to an apartment in the San Remo on Central Park West. To ease his conscience about never seeing her, he had ensconced his mother in an elegant apartment building on 68th Street between Madison and Park. He had made peace with Salucci and Weinberg, although the Italian was still trying, from time to time, to lean a little on their policy rackets. Why anybody would care about the policy rackets was beyond Rick. The nickels and dimes collected from the people of Harlem, which was almost entirely black now, were negligible when set aside the money to be made in the legitimate nightclub business. Practically alone among the darktown clubs, the Tootsie-Wootsie had survived the end of Prohibition and flourished. The only problem now was to keep the white people coming north of 125th Street.

As for Solly, he had pretty much retired. He still lived above Mr. Grunwald's violin shop, although Mr. Grunwald had died several years back and the violin shop was now a colored grocery store. Rick had often asked him why he didn't leave the neighborhood, but Solomon always waved away the question.

'I should maybe move to Grand Concourse?' he would ask. 'As well you should ask me to move to the Champs-Élysées, which isn't as nice and is almost as far away. It's okay for Mrs. Horowitz, but me – I'm too damn old to change now.'

Rick didn't know Irma had moved to the Bronx.

'*Pfui*,' said Solly. 'Long time since. She loves baseball, she can walk to Yankee games. But me, not on your life. You should only shoot me first, I start talking about the Grand Concourse. Day Solomon Horowitz leaves Manhattan is day he grows tail and sticks it between legs!'

That put an end to that discussion.

Still, all the talk about Mrs. Horowitz got Rick to thinking about Lois, something he had trained himself not to do. He had also trained himself to stop reading the *Times*, except for the entertainment reviews, and all the other New York papers. Even Winchell's column was censored for him; any references to Robert Meredith or his wife were carefully blackened out by Abie Cohen's kid Ernie, whom Rick was training as a restaurateur. Ernie was dark haired and bright eyed, the way he used to be, and he seemed to think the world was his oyster, the way he used to. Well, let the kid think that; he would learn otherwise soon enough.

From time to time, Ernie goofed and Rick got to read about the rise and rise of Robert Meredith. From lawyer to state senator to (it was widely speculated) the next Republican candidate for governor of New York, Meredith had soared. His wife, Lois, had ascended along with him, her wardrobe ever more spectacular, the accounts of her charitable work ever more fulsome. If the press had any idea she was really the daughter of a gangster, it never let on, just as it never let on about the backgrounds of other prominent wives, such as the one married to the senator from Louisiana, who had been a high-class call girl, or the wife of the governor of Ohio, who was addicted to cocaine, or the . . .

Then he saw her. Even from a distance, the minute she walked in, he knew. He knew it by the way she moved, by the cut of her clothes, by the supreme self-confidence of her manner, well before he could see her face. The face that was more beautiful now than even he had remembered it.

She moved through the crowd, laughing the way he had remembered her, easily, as though she were dancing with Fred Astaire. Her hair was pulled back tight into a bun, and at her gorgeous throat she wore a dazzling diamond brooch that was not quite as big as the Ritz, but close enough. Otherwise she was the same: his Lois, before Meredith and O'Hanlon had taken her away from him.

She was alone. No photographer's flash popped. A few people gawked at the famous Lois Meredith, the future governor's wife, but in Rick's place they had long since learned to keep their heads down and their mouths shut. Preferred customers were always the quietest customers, and if you wanted to get a ringside seat for Lunceford's band or Elena Hornblower's dancers or, best of all, Sam Waters's piano, you'd best observe the rules.

'Karl, table four,' he commanded his *maître d'*.

'Right away, Rick,' replied Karl. Karl was a recent arrival in New York, having several months earlier fled his home in Bad Ischl in Austria, where he had been the *Oberkellner* of the famous White Horse Tavern. At table four, a couple of aides to Mayor LaGuardia and their girlfriends (Rick knew both their wives) were mollified by a bottle of free champagne and switched to table eight, which wasn't Siberia.

'Good evening, Mrs. Meredith,' he said.

'Hello, Rick,' she breathed. Her breath was like the finest perfume. He could have inhaled it all night.

'Champagne for two,' she told Karl.

'Are you expecting someone?' Rick asked her.

'You wouldn't let a girl drink alone, would you?'

'Not if I know what's good for me,' he said, sitting down.

'Maybe I'm what's good for you,' she said.

'I used to think so,' he said as Sam came on.

The lights dimmed, and then the spotlight hit the piano. The club could have afforded the best Astoria Steinway, but for some reason Sam preferred his old beat-up upright. 'She's my baby, boss,' he would explain whenever Rick would offer to buy him a new one, which was practically weekly. 'I ain't going to leave her and run off with some other gal.' Rick didn't see why not, but he kept his mouth shut. Sam's love life was his own business.

Sam started to play his signature tune, and the crowd applauded. The tinkling of the ivories was the only sound in the joint. Nobody was allowed to talk when Sam Waters played. Especially when he played 'As Time Goes By.'

'Isn't it beautiful?' asked Lois when Sam had finished. Rick agreed that it was. 'It reminds me of the old days. Just after my father put you in charge of the club. How I miss those days. We were so young then.' She squeezed his hand under the table. 'Have some more champagne. I feel like celebrating!'

Sam was playing a Gershwin tune, 'The Man I Love.'

'Rick, he's a monster,' she said after they had toasted something or other.

'No, he's a politician,' corrected Rick; he didn't have to ask who 'he' was. 'At least, that's what I read in the papers.' He sipped his champagne. 'Is he cheating on you?'

She nodded her head slowly.

'Why should you be any different? He cheats on all his constituents.'

In just a couple of years the last vestiges of his youth had been sloughed off, and Rick Baline looked at the world purely as an angle to be played and a profit to be made. In this he was a true son of Solomon Horowitz, who had taught him everything; but he was taking his mentor's cynicism to a higher level. Did Solly care about widows and orphans? Rick didn't. Did Solomon sometimes distribute money to the neighborhood children, who laughed and called him 'Mr.

Solly'? Rick didn't. Did Solomon keep his home in Harlem, even now that Harlem had changed? Rick didn't. It was nothing personal. It was just his way. In fact, he was thinking about moving the Tootsie-Wootsie downtown, closer to café society, like the rest of the surviving clubs.

He had many acquaintances, some of them female, but only one friend: Sam Waters. Having a black friend wasn't easy, but it wasn't easy for Sam, either.

Sam was the best fisherman Rick had ever met. A New York City kid didn't meet many great fishermen, but Sam had grown up not far from the Ozarks, and if there was one thing everybody did in the Missouri Ozarks, it was catch and eat catfish. Sam could smell a catfish resting at the bottom of the lake, and he had the patience of a saint. 'Ol' Mister Cat gonna get hungry real soon, boss,' he would say to Rick from the back of a rowboat, his hat pulled down over his eyes to keep out the sun. 'And when he do, we be right here waitin' for him.' A few minutes later the catfish would be reeled in, scaled, filleted, and put into the salt, there to rest until that evening's dinner. Sam knew at least fifty ways to cook a catfish, all of them delicious.

Fishing with Sam was one of Rick's few luxuries. The rest of his life was devoted to work. Officially the club opened at four P.M. and closed at four A.M., but that was a fiction. Rick was the first in the door at ten o'clock in the morning, to make sure everything had been properly cleaned up overnight, to work on the books, and to start planning the evening's menu with the chef. He was also the last one out at night, sometimes not getting back to his place until the sun was coming up. He didn't need much sleep, and when he felt the urge he could stop by Polly Adler's bordello and visit with one or two of his favorite girls. Polly and he had a reciprocal relationship. She and the best looking of her girls were always welcome in his place, and everything was always on the house. It was good for business to have some of the prettiest women in New York sitting unescorted at several prominent tables. Even the homeliest chump could hope to get lucky, for a price. In return, Rick was welcome at Polly's any time; except for his drinks, he paid as he went. He preferred it that way. So it was not unusual to see a beautiful woman walk through the door of his gin joint. Usually he was glad to see them. About this one, though, he was not so sure.

'Rick, I don't love him anymore,' Lois was saying.

'When did you ever?' he asked. He was trying to keep one eye on the house, the way he always did, but wasn't having much luck.

'Rick, darling, what shall I do?'

'Oh, so now it's "Rick darling," huh?' he said. Karl swooped by to pour some more champagne. Karl was professionally deaf. 'You should have thought of that when you ran off with him.'

'I didn't run off with him – he ran off with me!' she said. 'He swept me off my feet. You know that.'

'I sure do,' said Rick, 'I was there. In fact, I was trying to do the same thing and not making a very good job of it.' He lit her cigarette for her and popped one of his own in his mouth.

She inhaled deeply, as if the cigarette might save her life. 'Daddy wanted it to happen, you know that. He wanted his little girl to be somebody, and look at me now!'

'Yeah,' Rick agreed. 'Look at you. You're not somebody, Lois – you're married to somebody. Can't you see that?'

'Now he's thinking about running for governor.'

'He'll never beat Lehman,' said Rick.

'He thinks he can,' said Lois.

'I think I can fish, but I can't.'

'Oh, Rick,' she said, and began to cry.

Crying women were not unheard of at Rick's place, but he didn't like them crying at his table. He helped her to her feet. 'Come on,' he said, 'let's go back to my office.'

Karl saw Rick make a brusque downward motion of the chin that signaled to him to take over.

They went into Rick's private office and shut the door. Lois promptly collapsed on the couch that Rick used from time to time as a daybed.

'What am I going to do?' she sobbed. 'I can't leave him – it would ruin his career. It would break Daddy's heart.'

'You should have thought about that before you married him,' said Rick. 'You're a big girl now.'

She smoothed back her hair, which had fallen from its pinnings and now spilled across her shoulders.

'Can't you help me?' She unfastened the diamond brooch and placed it on a table. 'I hate this thing,' she said.

'So do I,' he said.

He wanted to stop himself, but he couldn't. She didn't want to stop herself, and she didn't. Lois was always stronger than he was, Rick remembered as he fell into her arms.

CHAPTER TWENTY-NINE

New York, October 1935

The affair was two months old when Robert Meredith found out about it. Rick knew this day had to come. He and Lois had been as discreet as possible, but this was New York City, the worst place in the world to have an affair. Some unwritten law stipulated that no matter what you were doing, someone who knew you would hear about it. Maybe it was because the city was so big: a town of eight million blabbermouths, each one living on top of his neighbor.

He had told himself their affair was wrong: not only morally – although that, he felt, was questionable – but professionally. Even with Repeal, Meredith could still make a great deal of trouble for him with the state liquor authority should he so wish, and how Solomon Horowitz would react to adultery between Rick and his daughter could only be guessed. As Rick was well aware, the union between Lois and Meredith was not only a marriage but a peace treaty, any disruption of which could mean a resumption of hostilities on a scale larger than before.

That was a war both he and Horowitz would lose, for Solly no longer had any taste for the hard end of the business. That was pretty much Tick-Tock Schapiro's private preserve these days. A couple of rival black numbers gangs had sprung up recently in open defiance of his covenant with Lilly DeLaurentien; the way Rick heard it, the Voodoo Queen herself was behind at least one of them. The Mad Russian, however, didn't seem to care, or at least he didn't make it a point of pride to punish the miscreants personally, the way he would have in the old days. 'It's their neighborhood now, Ricky,' he said when Rick broached the subject one afternoon. 'Let them have their turn.'

If Solly was slipping, Salucci remained lean and hungry. Weinberg, sitting at his adding machine and toting up the profits, was making him ever greedier with thoughts of city-wide domination. Unlike Horowitz, the ferret-faced Sicilian would have no compunction about restoring white rule to Harlem as brutally as possible, at least as far as vice went. Where O'Hanlon fit into this picture Rick was not sure, but Dion was far too smart to step in front of a Horowitz-Salucci feud. If anybody knew how to play the angles, it was O'Hanlon; there wasn't a card that was played, a roulette wheel that was spun, or a pair of dice that was rolled in a crap game he didn't already know the outcome of.

Of course, it was O'Hanlon who told Meredith about the affair.

The date was October 22, 1935. When the phone buzzed softly in his office that morning, Rick picked it up on the first ring. Very few people had his private number; still, he was not surprised to hear the Irishman's lilting voice at the other end of the wire.

'Mr. Baline?' said the voice. O'Hanlon never called him 'Rick.'

'Who wants to know?' said Rick.

'A word of friendly warning to you, my boy,' said O'Hanlon. 'I very much fear that Senator Meredith is on his way down from Albany to pay you what I expect will be a most unpleasant visit.'

Rick didn't have to ask what the visit was about. 'What's it to you?' he asked.

'Oh, nothing at all,' said the Irish gangster. 'It's just that I hate to see a young fellow like you come to grief over a woman, even one as attractive as Mrs. Meredith. Women are such a waste of time, don't you think? Especially when there's business to be conducted.'

Rick didn't think, but he let O'Hanlon go on.

'They practically grow on trees, and yet each one of them can make us feel that she's the only one in the world: the most precious, valuable commodity on earth. They want us to think that someday they're going to be scarce, like liquor under the Volstead Act. When, in fact, they're a glut on the market, if only a man chooses to see them in the proper light.'

'How much do you know?' snapped Rick.

'All that I need to.'

He might be bluffing. 'What makes you so sure that Meredith is gunning for me?' Rick asked.

'I thought a bright lad like you would have figured it out by now,' said Dion. 'For sure, didn't I tell him my own good self?'

Rick's blood ran cold. 'What did you do that for?'

O'Hanlon let out a low laugh. 'Let's just say that an unsatisfactory status quo is makin' me a bit bored and uncomfortable, and I thought it was high time someone stirred the pot a bit.'

'Let's talk.'

'Dion O'Hanlon, at your service. This is, after all, a business matter for both of us.'

'How soon can you get here?'

'Not the club. Your place. I'm already there. You'd better hurry if you know what's good for you.'

Rick didn't have to be told twice. The thought crossed his mind that O'Hanlon's request for a meeting could be a setup, a hit – but why would either O'Hanlon or Salucci want him dead? Killing him wouldn't get them any closer to taking over Solly's other Harlem rackets and would only ignite the very gang war they were all trying to avoid. Solomon Horowitz might be getting older, but he wasn't getting any nicer. He still could do some serious damage to both Salucci and O'Hanlon should they take him on, even if they eventually took him out.

Thoughts racing, Rick drove downtown. He was alone. Abie Cohen wanted to come, as he was under standing orders from Solly to do, but Rick had waved him off. 'It's my mother,' he shouted as he drove off. Abie shrugged and, for the tenth day running, tried to do the crossword puzzle. Even though he was cheating (the puzzle was yesterday's, and he had the answers in front of him), the going was still tough.

Rick pulled up in front of the San Remo in ten minutes flat. He left the car parked in front of the building for Mike the doorman to keep an eye on. The elevator operator greeted him as he entered. 'You have a visitor, Mr. Baline,' he told him.

O'Hanlon was standing politely in front of his door, clutching the brim of his hat in one hand and reading the sports pages of the *Daily News* with the other. 'Mr. Baline,' he said. 'How splendid of you to offer the hospitality of your home to a friend in the middle of a busy day like this.'

'Whaddaya want?' Rick asked brusquely, unlocking the door. He didn't feel like standing on ceremony and sure as hell didn't feel like offering O'Hanlon a drink, although that didn't stop him from pouring one for himself. 'What do you mean, you told Meredith about Lois and me? What the hell for?'

O'Hanlon was perched in one of Rick's easy chairs, his bird face shiny and scrubbed, his legs crossed at the ankles, his double-breasted suit cut so well that even when he sat the buttoned jacket didn't bunch up. If Rick's rudeness bothered him, he didn't show it.

'Mr. Baline,' he began, 'I have a confession to make.' Rick looked surprised. O'Hanlon forged ahead. 'You should feel flattered. Not even Padre Flynn down at Saint Mike's has heard Dion O'Hanlon's confession for more than a full month of Sundays.

'My confession is this: I have a terrible character flaw. For don't I always tell the truth to my friends, even when it hurts other of my friends? As it appears I have in this instance. But Senator Meredith asked me point-blank last evening whether the rumors he was hearing in Albany were true, and I had to admit that, insofar as I myself was privy to any trustworthy information at all, they were – distressing though such knowledge might be to all and sundry.'

'Now he's on his way here,' said Rick. 'What's he going to do? Shoot me?'

'Surely you don't expect an esteemed public official such as Senator Meredith to kill a man in cold blood?' O'Hanlon shook his head in disbelief. 'I believe he has people for that sort of thing. Lorenzo Salucci, for instance. He and Salucci have been doing business together for some time. I introduced them, of course, and have profited handsomely from the arrangement. A friend in the state legislature is almost as good as having the mayor of New York on the payroll. Who, of course, I also have.'

'Of course,' said Rick. Nobody could work both sides of the street like Dion O'Hanlon.

O'Hanlon dropped his voice to a deadly whisper. 'Now listen, and listen carefully, to what I'm about to say, boy. Your boss is finished. And do you know why?' He leaned forward as if to impart some great secret, which forced Rick to draw a little nearer to him.

'He's finished because he *doesn't listen*,' hissed the gangster. 'He doesn't heed warnings, either from his friends or, worse, from his enemies. No, he simply goes his own way, the same way he has gone before, secure in what he supposes is his puissance but is in reality merely his arrogance and his ignorance.'

O'Hanlon straightened up. 'Salucci is too strong now,' he said evenly. 'Believe me when I tell you that Weinberg has already organized a hit team from Murder Incorporated – one of whom, I regret to inform you, is a member of what you suppose is your own gang – to finish the job begun by those poor boys from Sicily so long ago. If Solomon is finished, then you're finished, too, because your rabbi has been sadly neglecting his flock, and he just can't muster a minyan anymore.'

O'Hanlon examined his fingernails, which were perfect. 'In twenty-four hours,' he said, 'the Mad Russian will be history.'

'What about me?' asked Rick.

'Oh, I would be more than happy to find a place for a man of your indisputable talents in my own organization,' O'Hanlon replied, 'but alas, I'm giving it up.'

That was a surprise.

'I'm quitting. Retiring. I've got enough money stashed away to take care of my family unto the generations. America's a great country, boy, and how thankful I am to it for taking a poor immigrant lad like myself and transforming him into a millionaire many times over. It's time for me to take my winnings, cash out of the casino, and head for home. Therefore, in the grand tradition of the magnificently corrupt Richard Croker of Tammany Hall, I have purchased myself a wee estate in County Mayo, there to enjoy the fruits of my old age in peace and plentitude.'

'That doesn't explain why you've ratted me out,' objected Rick.

'Oh, but it does, lad,' O'Hanlon said. 'I like things nice and neat, and I cannot abide the thought that after I'm gone a messy turf war for control of the rackets will break out in my beloved adopted city of New York. Your boss is a hothead, and New York is no longer any place for hotheads. We're businessmen now, Mr. Baline, and we've got businesses to run. We're not just gangsters anymore, we're public servants, and we've got to start acting like it.'

Rick looked at his unwelcome guest. 'So why tell me this? Why not let Meredith's men finish us off and let Salucci run the whole show?'

'Why not is because I like you,' replied O'Hanlon. 'I admire your moxie, boy. Why not is that you run the best saloon in town, so good it put my own darlin' Boll Weevil out of business – you and the regrettable end of the Noble Experiment, which brought such good fortune to us all. Why not is that you're cool under pressure. In fact, Mr. Baline, you remind me very much of me, which is the highest compliment I can pay you.

'You know that I am something of a connoisseur of the fight game,' continued O'Hanlon, 'and I'd like to see you have a fighting chance in this little contest.' He reached for his hat, which was never farther away than his outstretched arm could reach. O'Hanlon was vain about his hats. 'Well. I've said what I've come to say, and now I feel as shriven as if I'd made a clean breast of everything to Father Flynn. Full disclosure is a grand thing – except, of course, in a court of law.'

He patted Rick on the arm. 'As you know, we have freedom of the press in this country: every man is free to own a press and print what he likes. If he's not inclined to buy the whole newspaper, why, then he can always buy a writer or two. Call my friend Winchell,' he advised. 'Give him this, with my compliments.'

He handed Rick a dossier, produced from between the pages of the newspaper. Rick flicked through it and saw it was about Meredith and Salucci. There were letters, papers, photographs, documenting the extent of the mutually beneficial corruption. If this got into the papers, it would be the end of both the senator and the criminal. A play was starting to present itself – the only play that might keep both him and Solly alive.

'Why are you doing this for me?' asked Rick.

O'Hanlon responded to the question with an enigmatic smile. 'Although you're perforce not a churchgoing man,' he said, 'I nevertheless hope you've learned something from my little sermon today. The moral of which is: Always give your opponent just enough information with which to hang himself. Full disclosure, excepting those bits you don't choose to disclose, and of which no one will be the wiser until it's too late.'

O'Hanlon put on his hat and pulled it down low over his left eye, the way he always did. It was a beautiful piece of fur felt, just the right mixture of beaver and rabbit, dyed light but not quite baby blue. He wore it only on special occasions.

'Walter owes me more than he can ever repay,' said O'Hanlon. 'He'll take care of you. The rest you'll have to take care of yourself. If you're as smart as I think you are, you'll know what to do.' He gave Rick a long look. 'And if perchance, you're not, then rest assured that these documents will still get to Winchell. For I hate loose ends, boy; to me, they're a mortal sin. And don't I share with Mr. Darwin a belief in the survival of the fittest, no matter what Holy Mother Church may think of his theories?'

O'Hanlon turned the doorknob and stepped soundlessly into the hall. 'So long, Mr. Baline, good luck to you and may the best man win,' he said as he disappeared into the shadows of the stairwell. 'I'll be reading the papers, and not just the funnies, either.'

Two minutes later Rick was out the door himself, grabbing the elevator to the ground floor and jumping into his car, which was still parked in front of the building. Within fifteen minutes he was pulling up in front of the 45th Street offices of the *New York Mirror* and dashing into the lobby like a madman.

'Where's Winchell?' he shouted at a guard.

'Second floor,' said the guard. He'd seen plenty of nut-cases charge into the building before, and they all wanted to see Winchell.

CHAPTER THIRTY

Louis Renault had checked into the U Tří Pštrosů around noon under the name of Louis Boucher. He rang Rick's room but was told 'Mr. Lindquist' was at lunch. He strolled outside and took the air, among other things.

Plopping himself in an easy chair upon his return, he looked out the window at the Charles Bridge and the Vltava and assessed the situation. He was not sanguine, but it wasn't his job to be. He was a little woozy and more than a little sated, which was the way he wanted to be.

More than ever, he felt the plan had no chance. Throwing a bomb into a moving vehicle had been tried before, at Sarajevo, but Archduke Franz Ferdinand had saved his own life by knocking it away, into the path of another vehicle – only to be shot a few hours later by Gavrilo Princip on his way to the hospital to visit those wounded in the original bomb attack. Whoever had thought up the idea of a bomb attack, reflected Renault, was no student of history.

As in Bosnia and Herzegovina, the plotters had backup

shooters ready to finish the job. Renault doubted that Reinhard Heydrich would be as cooperative as Archduke Ferdinand, though. 'Hello, my good fellow, yes, please do climb aboard and shoot me right in the heart of my imperial tunic, there's a good lad!'

He hated this assignment. He hated having to lie to Rick about why he wanted to be here. He hated the double life he was being forced to live. He was even starting to hate himself, distressing evidence of moral scruples he thought he had long since put behind him.

He found himself thinking about Isabel de Bononcière. He had known her for such a short while, yet she had haunted him for a lifetime. Since the night he had stood by and watched her die because he was too cowardly to defend her, he had relied on his slick charm, his carefully cultivated sense of fashionable ennui, his penchant for the apposite bon mot, the cut of his clothes, and the tilt of his cap. Most of all, he depended on the power vested in him by the state, which was not his power at all.

True, he was taking part in the operation at the behest of the Resistance. But Louis Renault looked upon these circumstances as similar to the unfortunate turn of events that had led Mlle. de Bononcière to his doorstep on Montmartre. Fate had dealt him the cards, as fixed as any card game he had ever played in, but fixed this time by a higher power. His choice of the name Boucher, therefore, was fitting: if he had to die, let the ghost of Isabel die with him.

The other woman who was very much in his thoughts at this moment was Annina Brandel, the dark-haired Bulgarian beauty who had been willing to sacrifice herself to him in order that she and Jan might escape. He knew why she had affected him so: there was a purity about her he had never seen before. Most of the women who entered his back room resented their participation in the sordid act necessary for them to get what they wanted. They were aware that he used their bodies, and they were ashamed of it. But Annina, he knew, would have given herself to him and emerged uncorrupted. To be able to sup with the devil and yet still go with God: how wonderful that must be! Would he ever get the chance?

Rick's rigged roulette wheel, which had provided Renault so many hours of pleasant, effortless profit, had robbed him of Annina Brandel. She had been the end for Louis Renault in Casablanca, the woman who finally made him look in the mirror and behold the soulless creature he had become. What had become of her? He hoped she had arrived safely in America, pregnant and happy. Somehow, though, he doubted it.

His reverie was interrupted by a soft knock on the door. It was Rick.

'My dear . . .,' he began to say, but Rick held a finger to his lips.

'Save it, Louie,' he said softly.

Renault closed the door.

'We haven't got much time,' said Rick. 'We have to move fast, and we have to move smart.'

He went to the window to make sure no one was even remotely close to them. Although the afternoon was warm, he shut the window tight and stuffed towels under the room's front door. Renault cocked an eyebrow, bemused. All this reflection was getting him down. At least now he wouldn't be bored. When Rick was around, things were never boring.

'Here's the situation,' said Rick, practically chewing on an unlit cigarette. They were sitting in the center of the room. The radio was on, loud, just in case the room was bugged. They didn't have time to hunt for listening devices.

'Something's terribly wrong. Prague wants the operation called off, but it's too late. Laszlo is out at a safe house in Lidice with his assassination team. Ilsa's in trouble; I think they might be on to her.'

'What are we going to do?' Renault asked.

'We're going to do what you've wanted to do all along,' Rick said. 'We're going to blow the operation ourselves.' He took a long drag on his cigarette. 'Ilsa's going to tell Heydrich the whole story. Tomorrow night. To his face. She'll tell him he's going to be blasted sky high when he rides over the Charles Bridge on his way to work.'

Renault whistled softly. 'Ricky, I've taken you for many things,' he said. 'A crook. A liar. A thief. Even a murderer. But never, before this moment, a traitor. I congratulate you.' He was not entirely surprised. He had always wondered about the depth of Rick's Casablanca conversion. Wasn't this just a way to get rid of Laszlo and have Ilsa all to himself? He suspected it might be, as uncharitable as that interpretation was. Miss Lund lent herself very persuasively to all sorts of uncharitable interpretations.

'Get off it, Louie,' snapped Rick. 'You know what I'm doing; hell, you raised the issue first yourself.' He struck a match furiously. 'Something's been fishy about this whole show from the start. I've smelled lake trout that didn't stink this bad a week after Sam'd caught them and forgot to clean them because he was learning a new song.'

He inhaled so hard that Renault thought he must have

seared his lungs. 'You were right, Louie: Why did Laszlo escape from Mauthausen so easily? Why have the British outfitted him and his raggle-taggle team with the worst kind of assassination weapon, a bomb?'

'You tell me,' replied Renault.

'There's only one answer, and the Czechs have finally twigged to it. This operation isn't about Heydrich at all. It's about the war – the larger war. The Brits don't give a damn what happens to the Czech people. They got Laszlo out of Mauthausen because they needed him. Because they figure that by blowing Heydrich to hell and gone they can provoke the Germans into doing something really terrible and then the world will be on their side. God damn it, Louie, they're prepared to see hundreds, maybe thousands, of innocents die, *just for the sake of having them die*, so that the world will get a fresh taste of the Hun's inhumanity to keep its mind focused on the job at hand. The Czechs are on a sacrificial altar, my friend – and so are we!' He stopped talking, exhausted.

'What do we do now?' Renault asked.

'We go through with it,' replied Rick. 'I've already signaled Laszlo that we strike the day after tomorrow. We come to the bridge armed for bear. We have our bomb and our guns ready, because we may have to defend ourselves when Heydrich's goon squad shows up, looking for trouble.'

'That's just the problem,' Renault objected. 'They'll shoot us on sight.'

'No, they won't,' replied Rick. 'First of all, they won't know who they're looking for. Second, we'll be expecting them, which means the minute we spot them we can abort and look like heroes. We fall back to the Church of St.

Charles Borromeo, get word to Miles, request extraction, and live to fight another day. Once back in London, you can file your report to the Resistance – don't try to kid me, I can guess what you're up to – and tell them the British are the treacherous swine the French know they are. As for me, Sam and I'll open a new nightclub. London could use some decent nightlife.'

Renault smiled. The jaunty little police captain of Casablanca had banished the gloomy visage of M. Boucher. 'Ricky, you've outdone yourself,' he said delightedly. He laughed at himself for his earlier melancholy. 'One of the things I've always admired about you is your foresight. You've thought of everything.'

'Except one,' said Rick.

'Ilsa Lund.'

'Right.'

Renault was not about to let his friend dwell on that: some things God would simply have to sort out. 'One question: Do we inform Laszlo and the team that Heydrich is not going to keep his little date with us?'

'Obviously not,' said Rick.

'It's just the two of us, then? Our little secret, as it were?'

Rick nodded brusquely in reply.

'Very well,' said Renault smartly. 'It won't be the first one. You understand, though, that it is entirely possible that neither of us will win this game? That we both can lose?'

'Why else would I be playing?' said Rick. 'I'm sick of winning fixed crap games.'

'If Laszlo finds out you knew Heydrich was taking another route, then neither your life, nor, I regret to say, mine will be worth—'

'A plugged nickel,' finished Rick.

'Precisely,' Renault agreed. 'Whatever that is.' He fidgeted in his seat. 'Let me present you with a series of alternatives for your inspection. The first is that Heydrich heeds the warning, the plot goes for naught, we all escape successfully and live happily ever after in London. It's an attractive proposition, but unlikely.'

'Why?'

'Because the British will smell a rat the minute we return,' he said. 'Perfidious Albion suspects all the world's countries of being as duplicitous as she is. We will be lucky if we're not shot within twenty-four hours of landing in London.'

'You may be right about that.'

'I *am* right,' said Renault. 'Now, to point number two.' He fumbled with his cigarette case for a moment, then managed to open it. 'Let us say that Heydrich, despite your warnings, does indeed appear for his rendezvous with death, accompanied by overwhelming force. What then?'

'We run like hell,' replied Rick.

'And we're shot, either by the Germans or by the Czechs or by the British. It doesn't matter: the result is the same,' said Renault.

'Why the British?' asked Rick.

'Can a story of a failed Allied attempt on the life of a top Nazi be allowed to get out? I think not.' He made the sound of a machine gun, barking in a courtyard. 'Possibility number three is that Heydrich comes over the Charles Bridge and we are ready for him and against all odds Laszlo manages to throw his bomb into Heydrich's car and against even greater odds it goes off and against whatever odds you care to give it actually kills him. Then what?'

'I've been wondering about that myself ever since South Kensington,' answered Rick. 'After what you've just told me, I can't see why the British would want us back.'

'Nor can I,' Renault agreed. 'The rescue plane never arrives, we are all captured and shot, and the British are able to disavow any knowledge of our activities. You and Laszlo are forced to watch Ilsa's fate before being consigned to your own. Then the Germans really get mad, and raze whole villages, perhaps even small countries, thanks to our rash action. Is that what we really want?'

'It's not what I want,' said Rick, 'but nobody asked me.'

Renault observed his friend with wry detachment. Here they were, playing the most dangerous game of their lives, and the two of them were sitting around discussing their prospects as if they were talking about an upcoming football match in which they both had a vague rooting interest.

Well, maybe it didn't really matter. How they were going to get out of Prague had always seemed to Renault a bit of a polite fiction. Whether they succeeded or failed, no one on either side of this conflict would want to welcome them home, or even admit knowing them. No matter what happened – whether Heydrich died or, far more likely, they were either killed on the spot or rounded up and shot later – it would all be over soon.

'Ricky,' he said at last, 'what do you want to have happen? I mean, if you could make everything turn out exactly to your liking, what would it be?'

Rick lit a cigarette to help him think. 'I don't know,' he said. 'I guess I would say that Heydrich dies, nobody else gets hurt, and we all get away safe and live happily ever after.'

Renault smiled. 'Except for Victor Laszlo, you mean.'

'Maybe.'

'No "maybe" about it. Why, if I didn't know you better, I would say that you've set this whole game up to get Victor Laszlo killed, not Reinhard Heydrich.'

Rick rose and paced the floor. 'But Heydrich deserves to die because he's a Nazi and a murderer and a thug and a gangster! Because if he doesn't, millions of people are going to suffer. And yet . . .'

Renault offered no reply to Rick's dilemma. Instead he said, 'Victor Laszlo told Major Strasser something back in Casablanca – in your own café – that's been haunting me: that, if anything happened to him, hundreds of men like him would rise up from every corner of Europe to take his place. Isn't the same true of Heydrich? Maybe we can kill him. Others just like him, even worse, are only too willing – eager! – to take his place. I'd like to think the supply of good men in the world outweighs the number of bad, but right now that's a bet I'm not quite willing to lay.'

'So you're saying . . .?' asked Rick.

'So I'm saying that, whatever we decide and whatever we do, the larger issue is not going to be determined by our actions. We can't win this war all by ourselves, Ricky, and if we're smart, we won't even try. All we can do is hope to get out alive.'

'Maybe you're right,' said Rick. 'The Germans are sitting pretty in Europe, and there's no way the Allies can strike at them. The Russians are getting their teeth kicked in on the eastern front; they've already been pushed all the way back to Stalingrad, and it doesn't look like they'll be able to hold out much longer. When the Nazis are through with them, they can turn the full force of their armies on the West – on us.

The British are trapped on their little island, the French have quit – no offense, Louie – and the Americans are busy with the Japs in the Pacific.' As he finished his cigarette he immediately lit another.

'Don't underestimate the Russians, my friend. They'll probably blunder into Berlin before this is through.'

'On the other hand, what can the Germans do?' Rick went on. 'They can't even get across the English Channel, much less knock out the British. Hell, the English are still having dinner parties in London. And if the Nazis can't get across the Channel, they sure as hell aren't going to be able to get across the North Atlantic.' He breathed deeply. 'So America, at least, is safe.'

'But not, I remind you, central Europe,' said Renault. 'Where we find ourselves now.'

'We do indeed,' said Rick.

Renault's mind was racing. As far as the Resistance leaders back in London were concerned, the plan must fail. The British must not be allowed to pull off a coup like assassinating Heydrich. While his orders were to monitor the operation rather than explicitly to sabotage it, he was rapidly coming to the conclusion that Victor Laszlo's plan must go no further. That was fine with him; for the first time, he and Rick Blaine could be allies in good conscience.

The larger question, though, weighed on his mind. Which outcome was in the best interests of France – not occupied France, or Vichy France, but *la belle France*? His brave words of greeting to Major Strasser – 'Unoccupied France welcomes you to Casablanca' – he knew to be so much bravado. He was nothing more than a collaborationist, a weak man, a camp follower. A whore.

A whore. The kind of woman he had spent his life despising. The kind of woman he had so diligently sought to turn all of womankind into, just to assuage his conscience. He had made them sleep with him, the enemy, because he could. He had been sleeping with the enemy because he wanted to. Because he *was* the enemy. Not anymore.

He slept soundly that night, for the first time in centuries.

CHAPTER THIRTY-ONE

SENATOR, GANGSTER IN RACKETS PROBE!

read the headlines in the October 23, 1935, edition of the *New York Mirror*. The byline was Walter Winchell's. Winchell didn't often stoop to news stories, but this one was different. This one was *news*.

> What does the face of evil look like? If you are a regular moviegoer, you may think you already know: a hard guy with a fedora and a heater. But what if it was the face of the man next door? Your best friend, or his best friend – or worse yet, the fellow you voted for in the last election?
>
> Flash! This column has learned that Senator Robert Haas Meredith, widely mentioned as a contender for the Republican gubernatorial nomination in the next election, may be the target of an investigation into his ties to a notorious gangland boss.

That would be none other than Lorenzo Salucci, the favorite tenant of the Waldorf-Astoria. There's hardly a working girl in this town who doesn't owe her livelihood in one way or another to the sinister, olive-skinned Sicilian – who's not even an American citizen!

According to documents received by this office, Senator Meredith and Lorenzo Salucci – assisted by his aide-de-camp Irving Weinberg – have been in cahoots for several years. Salucci, it is said, helped rig the election that saw the victory of the Republican Meredith over the Democratic incumbent in heavily Democratic New York State.

Maybe now we know why.

The documents clearly show a pattern of corruption extending back years. With his partners, Meredith has been involved in prostitution, loan-sharking, and, before the blessed end of Prohibition, bootlegging.

Hold on to your hats:

Meredith's lovely wife, the former Lois Harrow, is not the former Lois Harrow at all. On the contrary, she is the former Lois Horowitz, the only daughter of Mr. and Mrs. Solomon Horowitz of W. 127th Street in Manhattan and the Grand Boulevard and Concourse in the Bronx. Mr. Horowitz, the uptown rackets king, is the proud possessor of a rap sheet as long as my leg. And that's pretty long!

What's more, we're told, the former Miss Horowitz has been keeping company on the QT with the suave, handsome Rick Baline, proprietor of the Tootsie-Wootsie Club, the former uptown speakeasy that some say is really owned by Solomon the Wise himself.

This column tried to reach the Senator last night at his home in Albany. But we were told that Meredith was 'away on business' and had no comment. Business, yes – but what kind?

Mr. and Mrs. America and all the ships at sea: Stand by for further developments!

Rick read the *Mirror* with almost no emotion. The bit about Solly and Lois was a typical O'Hanlon touch, just to keep him honest.

He sat in his office, waiting. A cup of coffee lay on his desk, untouched. He was thinking about touching it when the buzzer alerted him to the imminent presence of a visitor. His loaded .45 lay right next to the coffee. He didn't have to think twice about touching that. He picked it up and slipped it in his pocket.

The door opened without a knock. It was Meredith.

'Come on in, Senator,' Rick said as affably as he could. 'I've been waiting for you.' He wasn't worried. He'd confronted a lot tougher characters than Robert Haas Meredith. Even so, he wasn't sure what to expect. An irate husband, a ruined politician, a homicidal maniac.

He got all three.

The senator tossed his copy of the *Mirror* on Rick's desk. Rick waited for him to say something. He did. 'What is the meaning of this?' sputtered Meredith. His face was red, his tie was askew, and he hadn't shaved that day.

'Why don't you ask Winchell?' said Rick. 'It's his byline. You'll find him down at the *Mirror*.'

'I don't want to talk to some cheap newspaperman,' Meredith hissed. 'I want to talk to you.'

'Be my guest, but make it snappy. I'm a busy man, Mr. Meredith. I've got a nightclub to run.'

'Don't get smart with me.'

'Why don't you cut the small talk and tell me the real reason you've come here? Better yet, I'll tell you. You've come here to find out what I know beyond what was in Winchell today,' Rick said. 'The answer is, I know plenty. I know all about you and Salucci, about how he supplies you with girls when you come home to visit your "constituents" in New York.' He blew a smoke ring in the senator's direction. 'I also know how Weinberg cooks the books for you so you can cheat the revenue service of what's coming to it. I also know . . . but why go on? I know everything, and what I don't know O'Hanlon surely does. About the only thing I don't know is why you must have double-crossed Dion, because, friend, that is like welshing on a bet with the devil.'

Meredith sat there in the visitor's chair across from him, with only the gleaming leather surface of Rick's desk between them. 'You think you're a pretty smart guy,' he said.

'I am,' answered Rick. 'You're not. You're through, Meredith, and so is Salucci and so is Weinberg.'

Meredith snorted. 'We'll see about that. If I were you, I'd be worrying about Horowitz right about now.'

'Tick-Tock and Solly can handle anything your boys can throw at them,' said Rick.

'I wouldn't be too sure about Schapiro's loyalties.' Suddenly the senator's head snapped up. 'Where's my wife?' he demanded.

'She was my girl before she was your wife,' said Rick. 'I can't help it if she's decided that she prefers it that way again.'

He looked into the back room. 'Why don't we let the lady decide for herself. Lois?'

'I'm right here, Rick.'

She looked glorious. Her ebony hair was swept up, and her face was flushed with color. She was still the most beautiful woman either man had ever seen, and Meredith realized at last he had been a fool to cheat on her, a fool to risk the wrath of her father, a fool to risk the ire of O'Hanlon, a fool to mingle with gangland because it gave him a thrill, a fool to have carried hypocrisy as far as he had when he wasn't cut out for it, a fool to have trusted these people, who didn't even trust themselves.

She walked toward both men, as alluring as Eve. She smiled at Meredith and then threw her arms around Rick Baline and kissed him as lustfully as she had ever kissed a man.

'Do you want to go back with him?' Rick asked her. 'Although why bother? Hubby here'll be doing a long stretch in the jug, you'll still have the house in Westchester, and I can start visiting in the daytime instead of the middle of the night when he's down at one of Salucci's whorehouses. What do you say?'

He knew he shouldn't taunt Meredith, but he couldn't help himself. Robert Haas Meredith stood for everything in New York that he despised, because it despised him.

In reply, Lois put her arms around Rick's neck and hugged him again. 'Please, Rick, take me away. Let's run, while we still can – let's run far, far away, where no one will ever find us.'

'I guess that's your answer, Senator,' he said.

He looked at Meredith and mentally replaced his patrician

features with Solomon Horowitz's. Solly, who had so diligently chased respectability, and at what price. Solly, who had been willing to sacrifice for it his only daughter, his only child, the only person in the world he loved, really loved, without reservation, and whom he had therefore condemned to a life without love. How could he have gotten it so terribly wrong?

Lois removed her head from Rick's chest and looked at her husband.

'I hate you, Robert,' she said. 'I thought I loved you. I tried to love you, not for your sake or even for mine, but for my father's. He wanted a better life for me. So I let myself believe that I was happy with you, and for a while I was, because I wanted out and you were my ticket. You sure had me fooled.'

She stood up straight and proud. 'I learned soon enough that you were a fraud. Sure, you lived in a better part of town and you wore fancier clothes and you hung around with people who didn't drop their g's and knew which fork to use and vacationed in the South of France. But deep down you and the rest of your crowd weren't any different from the men I had watched come in and out of our house since I was a little girl. You cheated the government and you paid off the cops and you looked down your noses at people like my father even while you were doing business with them. Sometimes you even put them in jail, just to show them who's boss.

'When I found out, did I leave you? I should have, but I didn't. I put up with your hypocrisy, and I turned a blind eye to your whoring and your cheating and your chiseling. Not for your sake, but for my father's. No more. Look at you!'

she spat with as much contempt as she could muster. 'You're not a man! You're nothing!'

Meredith stood up. In his right hand he held a pistol. 'I'll show you who's nothing,' he said.

Rick had one arm around Lois. He had his right arm free, but not free enough. 'Put that thing away before you hurt somebody, Senator,' he said, reaching for the .45 in his pocket.

'You don't have the guts, you cheap hood,' said Lois.

Meredith aimed and fired. He hit Lois square in the chest. She was dead before she collapsed across the desk.

Rick's answering bullet found its mark surely and swiftly, knocking Meredith out of his chair, onto the floor, and into eternity.

Suddenly alone, he cradled Lois in his arms, just as he had done on that day so long ago, on the elevated running down Second Avenue, on his way to buy his mother a knish. Only this time he was powerless to revive her.

He was kissing her when Abie Cohen crashed through the door, his gun drawn. He saw Robert Meredith dead on the carpet and Lois Horowitz Meredith dead in Rick's arms. 'Jesus, boss,' said Abie.

'Make sure Solly's okay,' said Rick. 'Now.'

'He's up in the Bronx,' Abie told him. 'As soon as he seen the papers this morning he cleared out.'

'Tick-Tock's with him?'

'I don't know. I ain't seen Tick-Tock all day.'

Something wasn't right. How long did it take to get up to the Concourse, anyway? From Harlem it couldn't take longer than twenty minutes or so even at this time of day; all you had to do was shoot across 125th Street to Third Avenue, over the bridge to the Bronx, and there you were, on the Grand Concourse in the New Jerusalem. Guns drawn and blazing, if need be.

He got to his feet, Lois's body slipping out of his arms for the last time. This was where laziness got you, this was where carelessness landed you, this was where inattention washed you up – all for committing the sin of thinking yourself respectable in the eyes of polite society. Polite society was still Mrs. Astor's ballroom, no matter how much that ballroom liked to drink. Polite society married its daughters off and didn't have their husbands come back to haunt them with ghouls like Salucci and Weinberg in tow.

Salucci and Weinberg. Payback time. The clock was ticking on all of them.

Cohen and Lowenstein and Tannenbaum, squad leaders, Abie downtown to Mott Street, Laz and Pinky to the West Side, on the double, with four or five of their best gunsels. Hit Salucci and hit Weinberg and hit them hard and hit them dead. Get them in their cribs now, on Mott Street, around the old Points, on the Bowery, in the penthouse at the Waldorf if need be, but get them and kill them and worry about the aftermath afterward.

His last act was to clean out the safe. He had never counted the money in it, because, up to this moment, the amount was none of his business. Now it was. He was going to need cash, and lots of it.

He rifled through the carefully arranged stacks of hundred-dollar bills and whistled to himself. The safe was stuffed with half a million dollars, maybe more. Solly had been saving it for Lois. Now Rick was stealing it. He stuffed it in a suitcase and ran.

His last view of the club was the awning, and the poster in front, the poster he had had printed up just the other day, which advertised 'Tonight in person. Lunceford and Hupfield, together again. Performing your favorite songs, including the hit, "As Time Goes By"! With Sam Waters at the piano.'

He made the Broadway bridge six minutes later, a new Manhattan speed record, but luckily the cops were not around to record it. He didn't want to have to explain why he was driving so fast, or what he was doing with a suitcase filled with half a million dollars in the trunk of his car. At this point, he preferred to let his .45 do the talking. If it wasn't too late.

CHAPTER THIRTY-TWO

Renault had wasted no time in finding suitable female companionship among the locals. Failing to find Rick shortly after his arrival, he was strolling up on Petřín Hill – the faux Eiffel Tower he found irresistible – and had promptly made the acquaintance of a young lady named Ludmilla Maleeva. He had succeeded in getting her to make love to him after tempting her with some small luxuries, as well as with his tales of how the real Eiffel Tower looked and how beautiful Paris was in the summer. She slept with him that afternoon with enthusiasm, if not ardor, for M. Boucher was as close as she was going to get to Paris at this point in her life.

Her passion, however, she was reserving for Karel Gabčík, a Czech boy from the countryside who had come to the city to study at the university. Ludmilla had great hopes for Karel – until the Nazis closed the universities. After the big student demonstrations in September 1941, the Germans had shot nine students and sent 1,200 more to concentration camps. Luckily Karel was not in either group; like his older brother, Josef, who had escaped to England to continue the fight, he remained adamant in his hatred of the Germans.

Ludmilla could not quite understand what the Gabčíks had against the German occupation. She was not old enough to care whether the place she lived in was called Czechoslovakia or Bohemia or the Greater German Reich, as long as she was happy. Though the rest of Europe might be at war, Bohemia was at peace. Her beautiful hometown of Prague had not been bombed or disfigured by fighting in any way. There had been rationing, of course, but food was plentiful, even meat, and the beer still flowed freely. How much worse it could be!

Still, she had already figured out that information was the coin of the realm. So when Renault, after downing most of a bottle of the Czech liqueur called Becherovka, hinted at an important event that would soon occur, she listened very carefully. This information would delight Karel, she was sure, as well as raise her in his estimation. She wanted Karel to love her as much as he loved his country. The way she saw it, if she could pass on a tip, then Karel could pass it on through his brother's network, and perhaps they would eventually throw the Germans out and live happily ever after, the way couples did in fairy stories. She had to admit that last part of the fantasy was a long shot, but long shots won every now and then, even in central Europe.

She was only seventeen, but she knew enough to know that what she knew was worth knowing.

The next evening she met Karel in a country tavern in a little town outside Prague named Bubenec. She didn't mind traveling to meet her lover, because she was wearing a new dress that the nice M. Boucher had purchased for her, as well as a pair of French silk stockings that he had produced from God knew where. She liked the way the men admired her as she walked down the street, the way they seemed to savor her very existence as a woman. Her voluptuousness would not last forever, that much she knew; she was determined to make it last as long as she could, and for it to pay off.

Sitting at a table with some of his friends, Karel looked up as she made her entrance. He noticed her new dress. Good, she thought. Let him wonder where I got this dress. Let him wonder where I got these beautiful stockings. Let him start paying me more attention than resistance and revolution.

Karel kissed her as she sat. She loved the way he tasted, of fresh Czech beer and strong cigarettes. So much better than the little Frenchman, who could not handle even a single bottle of Becherovka, which any self-respecting Czech could down before dinner, before the serious drinking began.

Ludmilla wasted no time in getting to the point.

'Karel,' she said, 'something is going to happen.'

Karel was careful to evince no reaction. 'What kind of something?' he asked.

'I don't know,' she replied. 'Something very big.' She dropped her voice. 'A bomb!'

The part about the bomb she made up, but it sounded good. In fact, M. Boucher had not said anything at all about a bomb but only had muttered something about an event that would shock the world, something involving weapons and death, until he'd finally fallen asleep and she'd had to squirm out from underneath him, the pig. The French were supposed to be such great lovers.

'Hush!' Karel drew her mouth toward his and pretended to kiss her. 'Who told you this?' he muttered under his breath.

She could see the alarm in his eyes as he held her face close to hers. 'A Frenchman I met yesterday,' she confessed.

'Did you sleep with him?' demanded Karel, sounding more distressed than jealous. 'Is that where he told you? In bed?'

'Yes,' she confessed glumly.

Karel Gabčík was willing to forget about Ludmilla's infidelity for the moment. Far more important was his brother's operation. Could she be referring to Operation Hangman? What else?

After a brief interrogation, he made some small excuse, got up from the table, and ran out the door to grab his bicycle. The other men in the tavern saw Ludmilla alone, and Ludmilla saw them. A brief, decent interval, and then she was no longer alone.

After an hour of furious pedaling, Karel reached the farmhouse in Lidice. The first person he saw was Victor Laszlo, staring at the sky and smoking contemplatively.

'Mr. Laszlo!' exclaimed Karel. He could not bring himself to call the famous Resistance leader 'Victor.'

Lost in thought, Laszlo finally deigned to take notice of him. 'What is it, boy?' he asked.

If Laszlo was nervous, thought Karel, he did not show it. Karel hoped that when his time came to strike a great blow against the oppressor, he would be as brave as Victor Laszlo.

Breathlessly Karel told him what Ludmilla had said. So great was his respect for Victor Laszlo that he suppressed none of the details about Ludmilla's dalliance with the Frenchman, even though it shamed him. Victor calmly thanked Karel for his wit and loyalty in coming to him so fast, although his insides were roiling. 'Speak of this to no one, do you understand?' he said. 'No one. Make sure your Ludmilla does not, either.'

Panicked, the boy jumped on his bicycle and disappeared back in the direction of the city.

It was Renault; it had to be. The vain, strutting, pompous little fool. Could he not forgo the pleasures of a woman's body for even one day? For one hour? Damn him to hell.

He thought furiously. The operation must go ahead; that much was certain. He had received Blaine's signal via the Underground, and his team was ready to move in the early morning. They had come too far to give up now. They had planned too carefully to let one careless slip stop them. Already they had risked too much to let one foolish little Frenchman interfere with the most glorious deed in Czech history. Tomorrow morning Reinhard Heydrich would die, just as surely as the sun would come up to witness his death.

CHAPTER THIRTY-THREE

New York, October 23, 1935

He made it to the intersection of Grand Concourse and McClellan Street, a few blocks north of the Bronx County Courthouse and Yankee Stadium, in no time flat. The building was a large, imposing, prosperous-looking structure that commanded the west side of the broad boulevard with pride; an immigrant's slice of American heaven. He parked his car right in front, ignoring whatever danger might be lurking.

The door to the Horowitzes' apartment was ajar. Rick drew his pistol and stepped inside.

Irma Horowitz was sitting on the couch. The couch was the only place left to sit. The rest of the room – indeed, the rest of the flat – looked as if a hurricane had hit it. Furniture was toppled over, pictures had been knocked from the walls, drawers emptied and plates smashed. Smack in the middle of the floor lay a dead man, a bullet wound in the back of his head. He lay on the floor, spread-eagle, as if he had suddenly attempted a half-gainer on dry land. His gun lay a foot away from his outstretched right hand.

In the eye of the storm, Irma was sitting quietly, talking to herself.

'Mrs. Horowitz,' Rick said with urgency. He had never called her Irma. He was not about to start now. Besides, he wasn't even sure if she recognized him. Her eyes were open, but they were staring, unfocused, straight ahead.

He bent close to the stricken woman. 'Where's Solly?' he asked. Then he remembered she didn't speak English, not that well. '*Wo ist Solly?*'

'*Weg*,' she murmured: gone.

'*Wo?*' he asked again.

She didn't answer. Maybe she didn't know. Maybe that was what had saved her life.

Rick's practiced eye could tell at a glance what had happened. Hunting for Solly, a Salucci hit team had paid the Bronx apartment a visit. Even Salucci's boys, though, were not about to shoot an old woman in her own living room, so they had to content themselves with tossing the place and terrorizing her until they got bored and went away, leaving one of their number to stand guard. Solly must have concealed himself, or maybe had arrived just after the hit team, because clearly he had waited until the odds were more in his favor and then had shot the guard from behind and taken off to plot his revenge.

He had a pretty good idea of where Solly was. Not cowering in fear in some crib even Rick didn't know about. Not holed up in a third-floor walk-up on the West Side with only a collection of weapons and a mattress for comfort. No, if he knew Solly, he was in the old blind tiger near City College, where he felt safe.

Tick-Tock was probably with him, awaiting the arrival of Salucci. He had to get there before it was too late.

There was not much he could do for Irma now. She was well taken care of financially – but what if something happened to Solly? What if something had already happened? He had a couple of grand in his pockets, which he pressed into Irma's unresponsive hands; it wasn't much, but it would have to do. Then he picked up the telephone and called the police, which was the first time he had ever done that. You never knew when Salucci's boys might come back.

He kissed her lightly on the cheek. She paid him no notice at all. As he left he realized with a shiver that she was reciting the Kaddish, the Jewish prayer for the dead.

He raced back over the river to Harlem.

The front door of the hangout was open as he cruised by. Rick didn't see any cops outside, which meant if there had been trouble, it was extremely recent.

Wait a minute. There was something. That oncoming car. The one with four occupants, all men.

Rick nipped around the block and pulled off the road and into the park, where his car would not be seen, especially by downtown hoods who didn't know the neighborhood. He jumped from the car.

The car, a big Chrysler CA brougham, parked right outside, its motor running. The wheelman was looking intently at the doorway. He never saw Rick come up to his window, which was open.

Rick jammed the muzzle of his gun against the man's head and fired. He sprinted through the door right behind Salucci's men. This was what he saw:

Solly at the back table, reaching for his gun.

No Tick-Tock.

The three gunmen drawing theirs as they charged.
Solly shooting the first man in the face as he rushed forward.
The second man firing as he advanced.
His first shot catching Solly in the neck.
Tick-Tock emerging from the back room.
Solly, bleeding, continuing to fire.
The second man falling, hit in the thigh by a low shot.
Rick firing at the second man, but missing, because he was already down.
Tick-Tock coming up with his piece and pointing it not at the gunmen, but at Solly.
The third man firing, hitting Solly in the left arm, and starting to turn toward Rick.
Rick firing in response, blowing the man off his feet.
Tick-Tock firing at Solly, hitting him.
Solly slumping in his chair.
Tick-Tock firing again.
Solly jerking as the last bullet hit him.
Rick firing at Tick-Tock.
Tick-Tock, with his brains decorating the wall behind his head.
Horowitz lying with his head on the table. He was still alive, but not for long.

'. . . bitches bastards,' snarled Solly through his bloodstained lips as Rick reached him. He was blowing blood bubbles, which meant a hole in his lungs, which meant the end.

Horowitz's eyes struggled to focus on Rick's face.

'Lois,' he said faintly, and his eyes formed the question. Rick didn't have the heart to answer it.

'I'll take care of her, Sol,' he promised. 'I'll take real good care of her from now on.'

Solomon Horowitz shuddered once and died in Yitzik Baline's arms.

Rick hugged his dead boss fiercely. He was dimly aware of shouts in the street beyond, of commotion.

At the other end of the long room, faces peered in the window, black faces with curiosity and fear wrestling for control of their features. He looked at them blankly.

A groan came from somewhere in the room. It was the second man, who was scrabbling for his gun, trying to get to his feet, but his feet wouldn't obey him. Rick looked at him and didn't recognize him. He didn't expect to.

He put Solly gently to rest. He stood and, as he walked over to the wounded man, reloaded his pistol.

'Where's Salucci?' he barked. The black children who had been gawking through the open doorway pulled their heads back.

The gunman had almost reached his gat when Rick kicked it away and stomped the heel of his shoe onto the man's fingers. At least one snapped.

'Where's your boss?' he asked, pulling back the hammer and pointing it at the man's head.

The dying gunman tried to force some spittle to his lips but failed.

'I'm asking you for the last time,' said Rick.

He spat. Rick fired.

'Suit yourself,' he told the corpse.

He went out the back way and was headed for his car when he heard a familiar voice. 'Mr. Richard,' it said, 'over here.'

It was Sam, sitting in the Buick Series 50 two-door coupe that Rick had given him for Christmas. Little Ernie Cohen was in the backseat, excited and scared.

'They ain't goin' to be lookin' for a colored boy, boss,' said Sam. 'Get in and get down.'

Rick did as he was told. Sam gunned the engine and the car flew away. 'Where to?'

'As far away as possible, Sam,' said Rick, slumped deep into the seat.

'Good,' said Sam. 'I always wanted to go there.'

'Let's start with Mott Street.'

Trying to nail O'Hanlon in his penthouse on West 34th Street would be pointless. O'Hanlon was far too smart to hang around, waiting for anyone to come after him. Having stirred the pot, he was no doubt enjoying the turmoil from a safe vantage point somewhere. Hell, Rick wouldn't put it past O'Hanlon to be sitting in the police commissioner's office on Centre Street, smoking a cigar with the chief and commiserating about the difficulty of keeping law and order these days.

Salucci, however, was not that smart and not that good. At least, Rick hoped he wasn't.

Rick was wrong. A block away from Mott Street, he spotted Abie Cohen's car. Then he saw Abie in it. Abie was missing one eye and most of his nose, and almost all of his blood, which had escaped out the slash in his throat. He would get no help from Abie or, he realized with a sudden stab of insight, from any of his other boys. The Horowitz gang was through.

Rick didn't want Ernie to see his dad this way, but it was too late. Ernie bit his lower lip hard, but he didn't cry. He was a tough kid; it was just too bad he had to do all his growing up in the space of two minutes.

Rick put his hand on the door handle and started to get out, but Sam grabbed him. 'You can't go in there, boss,' he said. 'It's suicide.'

'I'm in the mood for it, Sam,' said Rick.

In front of Salucci's headquarters were a couple of his boys, watching out for trouble. Rick knew more would be inside. Maybe he could take the jokers at the door, but how was he going to get anywhere near Salucci before they blew him to bits? He'd seen Cagney try it in *The Public Enemy*, take on a whole gang, and look what had happened to him: ventilated. He gazed up at the building, knowing that Salucci was in there somewhere, probably with Weinberg, laughing their heads off and already starting to carve up the Mad Russian's empire.

Sam kept one hand around Rick's wrist, his pianist's grip strong. 'Boss,' he said, 'no matter what kind a mood you in, I ain't lettin' you go. You try, you gonna have to shoot me first. That's the way it is.'

Rick turned to look at him. 'What's it to you?' he asked.

'It's a good job, is what,' replied Sam. 'Good jobs is hard to come by these days, in case you ain't noticed.'

Slowly Rick released his hold on the door handle. 'I don't have a club anymore, Sam. Which means you don't have a job anymore. So I guess you're fired.'

Sam shook his head again. 'Heck, boss, that don't make a bit of difference. You'll get another club someday. It just don't have to be here, that's all.' He hit the gas pedal. 'I ain't fired, neither. As long as you alive, I got me a job, even if it's just teachin' you how to fish.'

They had driven around the corner and had turned onto Delancey Street, heading east.

'Maybe you're right, Sam,' Rick admitted as the car approached the Williamsburg Bridge. He twisted in his seat, looking back at Manhattan. He wondered if he would ever see it again.

'Sometimes the good guys don't win, boss,' said Sam. 'This ain't the movies.'

Just before they crossed over to Brooklyn, Rick told Sam to stop the car. He jumped out, opened the trunk, and stuffed his pockets with as much cash as he could carry. He snapped the suitcase shut. 'Get out, kid,' he said.

'Ain't I coming with you?' asked Ernie.

'No. You're the boss now. You gotta take care of things. Mostly, you got to take care of yourself. Here, take this.'

Rick handed Ernie the suitcase. Whatever else Salucci might be looking for, he wouldn't be hunting for a kid with a suitcase. 'Bring this to my mother,' he said. 'Don't look inside, just take it and go. You remember where she lives, don't you?'

Ernie nodded. 'East Sixty-eighth.'

'Right,' said Rick. 'And this is for you.' He handed Ernie a thousand dollars, which would go a long way in the Depression. 'Don't blow it on the ponies. Save it. Help out your ma. Go straight. You'll be glad you did.'

'I will, Rick,' said Ernie, trying hard not to crack. The kid was all right. Rick patted him on the head, then shoved him toward the Third Avenue streetcar line.

'One more thing,' he shouted. 'Buy my mom a knish, will ya?'

They drove all day, reaching Boston in the late evening.

The next morning, on his way to the steamship company to buy two passages to Le Havre, Rick grabbed a copy of the *Boston American*, a Hearst paper that would carry Winchell.

EIGHT DEAD IN GANGLAND SHOOTOUT
Senator Meredith, 7 Others, Perish in Mob Mayhem

In an outbreak of gangland ferocity unequaled in the city's history, fast-rising State Senator Robert Haas Meredith, his wife, and six hoodlums died yesterday in a hail of gunfire.

The shootings took place at two Harlem locations: the Tootsie-Wootsie Club and a social club near the City College of New York.

In addition to Senator Meredith, the dead included his wife, Lois, and Solomon Horowitz, gang chief of upper Manhattan and the Bronx. The other victims are still being identified by police.

Yesterday's column reported allegations that the Senator was linked to mobster Lorenzo Salucci in a host of shady business dealings over the past several years.

But we are pleased to report today that according to highly placed sources in New York and Albany, the documents were fakes, circulated by Yitzik 'Rick' Baline, the disgruntled manager of the Tootsie-Wootsie Club, in a failed attempt to blackmail the Senator, steal his wife, and move in on Horowitz's crime empire.

Police have named Baline the prime suspect in the shooting of Mr. and Mrs. Meredith, whose bullet-riddled bodies were found in Baline's office at the Tootsie-Wootsie Club. Police theorize that the Merediths went there to confront Baline personally and were murdered in cold blood.

Baline is also the leading suspect in the death of Horowitz. Additionally, he is alleged to have stolen a considerable sum of money from the club's coffers to finance his getaway.

'We'll get him,' said Police Commissioner Thomas J. O'Donaghue. 'We'll hunt him down like a dog. There's no place in this great land of ours that's safe for him to hide.'

Typical Winchell, thought Rick: he left out Abie Cohen and the yegg in the Bronx. He threw the paper away. He didn't need to read any further.

'In what name are these passages being booked?' asked the steamship line clerk.

Rick thought for a moment. If Isidore Baline the songwriter could reinvent himself as Irving Berlin, why couldn't he? The first name on his passport was Rick, and it would be a simple matter to reverse two of the letters of his surname.

'The first one is for Mr. Samuel Waters,' he said. 'The other's for Mr. Richard Blaine. And yes, that'll be cash.'

CHAPTER THIRTY-FOUR

On the evening of May 26, a glittering promenade was taking place in the Protector's residence in the castle. The ball was in celebration of the Wehrmacht's advances in the Soviet Union. In little more than a year the German armies had rolled back the Russians along a front a thousand miles wide, had driven to the gates of Moscow and Leningrad, and were poised to smash the Red Army once and for all. The war would be over very soon, and then, their *Lebensraum* secured, the Germans could turn their attention toward the real enemy: the Western democracies.

Ilsa looked ravishing. Her shoulder-length hair brushed her bare shoulders, and around her throat she wore a spectacular diamond pendant, which Heydrich had given her for the occasion. Her dress, which plunged daringly in the back and came down to her ankles, was a deep russet.

'But surely blue is your color, my dear,' said Heydrich as he greeted her.

'No, not blue,' she protested. 'Never blue.'

Heydrich laughed. 'Why not? Blue is the color of your eyes, the color of the Bavarian sky, the color of the North, the color of the Aryan. Besides,' he added, 'blue is the color of my eyes as well.' He was standing very close to her, and she could feel his breath on her shoulder.

Heydrich mistook her quiver for desire. 'Yes, my dear,' he said, 'I feel it, too.' He ran his hands over the bare skin of her back. Such delicious skin, which had so utterly beguiled him, and in such a short time. That flesh, which he had not yet sampled – but which he intended to, very soon.

'Please, Reinhard,' she said, squirming gracefully away from him. 'You want me to look my best, don't you?'

'Of course I do,' he said, stepping back in his military way to admire her. What a magnificent woman she was! It was true that German doctrine held the Slavs to be *Untermenschen*, but there were exceptions to every rule, and Tamara Toumanova was certainly one of them. Besides, with a name like that, she wasn't really a Slav, but a noblewoman. Why, she could easily be related to Kaiser Wilhelm II himself. As he looked more closely at her, he was convinced he was right. Reinhard Heydrich prided himself on his ability to detect members of the Master Race, no matter where they were from.

She was not like other women. He had no pleasure in taking them, and no challenge, because they could not resist. They were afraid of him, because they feared the worst should they deny him. He had imagined that an unending supply of willing women would be the highest form of pleasure, but how quickly it had turned to ashes in his mouth. It was like battling an opponent who wouldn't fight back, who surrendered so quickly that there was no time to enjoy his discomfiture, who sought to kiss your hand even as it was poised to strike him. Who deprived you of the pleasure of beating him. For such people, whether men or women, the Protector of Bohemia and Moravia had only the bitterest contempt. They were not human beings. They were animals and deserved to be treated as such.

Tamara, however, had resisted. She did not seem to be afraid of him. Most women would sleep with him because of what he represented, not because of who he was. This one, he thought, might be different.

Before he got too carried away by Miss Toumanova's beauty, he reminded himself that there was a war on against the Russians, and when victory came she might have to suffer along with the rest of her countrymen. A pity, but it could not be helped. Besides, the Germans had been told to expunge the word 'pity' from their vocabulary. It was weak, it was Western, it was Jewish. Mercilessness must be the hallmark of the New World Order, lest the world think less of its conqueror.

'Do you see that tower, there?' he asked her, pointing out the window and into the courtyard of the castle. 'It used to be a prison; perhaps it will be necessary to make it so again someday. It is called Dalibor Tower after its most famous inmate, who had been condemned to death and was incarcerated there for many months while his fate was being sealed. To console himself, Dalibor spent hours each day playing his violin, with such surpassing beauty – or so the story goes; these Slavs are such sentimentalists – that people would come from all over the city to hear him play. On the day of his execution, thousands turned out to see him die, weeping copiously.'

'Surely,' Ilsa said softly, 'he could not have played more beautifully than you.'

'But,' said Heydrich, 'on the day of my death, will so many weep?'

No, thought Ilsa, but her lips spoke otherwise. 'Let us not have these morbid thoughts on such an auspicious occasion,' she said. 'Shall we greet our guests?'

That was why he preferred Tamara to the hundreds of other women available to him. Because she could appreciate his genius – yes, his artistic genius – when few others could. They said – those *Jews* in Halle – he would never be good enough. Look at him now: ruler of all he surveyed and accompanied by the most beautiful woman in Europe.

How glad he was that she was with him on this important evening. Several of the military leaders and party officials would be present, including General Keitel, Admiral Dönitz, and Himmler, as well as that Austrian pig Kaltenbrunner, who probably plotted against him in his sleep. The real generals, Heydrich thought as he examined the brass buttons on his tunic for signs of smudged polish, unfortunately would not be there. They would be fighting on the Russian front: men like Guderian, the Panzer commander, and von Paulus, who was even now driving on Stalingrad – men who were actually carrying the fight to the enemy, instead of strutting in Berlin.

He studied his reflection in his shoes.

That evening, the lights of the castle blazed as never before. As the guests departed, they all proclaimed that never had they seen such an elegant gathering. The Protector came in for the most extravagant praise, for the quality of the guest list (and with a war on!), for the distinction of the food (and with a war on!), for the elegance of the ladies (and with a war on!), and most of all, for the loveliness of his companion, the enigmatic Tamara Toumanova, descendent of the Czar of all the Russias, whose comeliness was surely unsurpassed in Prague, Bohemia, or even, according to some (who perhaps had imbibed too frequently of the French champagne), in all of Germany itself.

How lovely she looked tonight in her scarlet dress! they all told him.

As for his own clothes, he preferred gray.

Across the river, Rick Blaine saw the lights of the castle. 'Live it up, you Nazi bastards,' he said.

'Now, Ricky, let's not be jealous,' said Renault, puffing on a Gauloises. He loved the name – 'Gallic girls.' It reminded him of his favorite subject. 'There are very probably some extremely beautiful women up there. In a happier time, our task would be to lure them down here.' He laughed bitterly, more at his former self than anything. 'The thought of those German hands on such lovely creatures . . . It's a crime against nature, is what it is.'

Renault saw his friend wasn't paying attention. 'Well, good night. Be sure to get plenty of rest tonight. Somehow I suspect tomorrow's going to be a very busy day.'

Rick said nothing as Renault departed, but continued staring at the castle until the last light had gone out and everybody had gone home to bed.

Ilsa Lund returned with Reinhard Heydrich to his villa that night. She had no choice.

'*Etwas trinken?*' he asked, not waiting for an answer. One

of his stewards had already poured them each a glass of champagne.

Ilsa didn't want any, but she thought it best not to refuse. She had managed to get by at the party by sipping a little of her drinks and then discreetly pouring most of them into some houseplants. She needed all her wits about her now.

They toasted each other. She let him lead. 'To the most magnificent hostess in the Reich,' said Heydrich.

'To a wonderful party,' she said as they clinked glasses.

They drank in silence.

'Another?' asked Heydrich, beckoning to the servant.

'No, please,' she said gaily. 'It's going right to my head, and I've had so much already.' She threw her champagne flute into the fireplace and listened with satisfaction as it shattered.

Heydrich followed suit, flinging his glass into the hearth. 'The finest blown glass, from Rattenberg in the Ostmark.' He laughed, using the Nazis' new name for Austria. 'How easily we consign it to dust!'

He collapsed into an armchair and sat appraising her. He was largely drunk, and very dangerous. She was mostly sober, and even deadlier.

'Stand by the window, that I may savor your beauty in the moonlight,' he commanded her, and turned to the butler. 'That will be all, Ottokar,' he said. 'Tell the staff they may retire for the night. All of them.' The manservant gave the Nazi salute and bowed gravely as he backed out of the room.

They were alone now and facing each other across the room like hunter and prey. 'See how *das deutsche Reich* greets its future Führer.'

'*Führer?*' she asked playfully. 'But surely—'

'No.' Heydrich laughed. 'There is nothing wrong with Adolf Hitler. May he live a hundred years! But our Führer is a wise man, and he realizes that every leader, no matter how great, needs a *Nachfolger*, a successor. I am proud to say that he has given me reason to believe that, in his eyes and in his heart, I am that man. I intend to prove myself worthy of that great honor. Imagine: the opportunity to complete the glorious work begun by the Greatest Field Marshall of All Time, Adolf Hitler!'

She glimpsed a condescending little smile, and in a flash she knew that, even were she the real Tamara Toumanova, even were she a member of the noblest family in Russia, she would still be in his eyes only a Slav, a slave, and there would never be any place for her in his world, or in the New World Order the Nazis had planned.

The window was open, and the night was chilly. She shivered, unprotected in her evening dress. Heydrich rose and snaked one long arm around her quivering form. 'What is it, my little treasure?' he asked. 'There is nothing to fear. Not with me to protect you.'

With terrible clarity, she knew exactly what to say. 'Oh, but there is!' she cried. 'There is everything to fear.'

Heydrich laughed at her as if she were a child, afraid of the dark. 'There now,' he began, and got no farther.

'They are going to kill you!' she exclaimed.

'Who?' asked Heydrich. He laughed dismissively.

'The partisans,' she told him. 'They are going to bomb your car on the way to the castle tomorrow. On the Čechův Most.'

'The Čechův Most, you say?' he asked warily. 'How would they know I have been planning to change my route?'

The moment of maximum danger was here. How many other people had he told about his intention? If she was the only one, then she was as good as dead. Please, she prayed, let there be someone else.

In a flash, he had spun her around. His grip was not so tender anymore, and the contemptuous smile was gone from his thin lips. 'How do you know this?' he demanded.

'There's a traitor in your office,' she said. 'Someone close to you. Someone very close.'

He had to believe it. He *had* to.

She took a deep breath. 'Someone who has decided to betray you: Frau Hentgen.' All her chips were on one number, and she hoped it was lucky.

'That is impossible,' said Heydrich. 'Frau Hentgen has been with me since my arrival in Prague. She is a valuable servant of the Reich. Why would she betray me?'

He spoke confidently, but Ilsa could see a tiny flame of mistrust in his eyes. All she had to do was fan it. 'She is jealous of you. She is jealous of me. She is jealous of *us*.'

'Bah!' snorted Heydrich. 'Frau Hentgen is beyond such petty emotions as jealousy. Those are for other, lesser women.'

Ilsa saw her opening and made a silent prayer of thanks. 'She is still a woman, though,' she reminded him. 'And you are a man. The most glorious man in the Third Reich.'

Heydrich looked at her warily, trying to decide what to believe. Ilsa could sense him teetering. All he needed was a little push.

She pushed. 'Oh, Reinhard,' she said. 'Until tonight, I didn't know how to tell you of my suspicions. I was afraid you wouldn't believe me. I needed proof. This afternoon, I got it.'

She unfolded the piece of paper Helena had given her. 'I found this on her desk. In her haste she must have forgotten it.'

The blue parrot. Operation Hangman. Tell London. Danger.

'I checked immediately with our network of informers, of course,' she went on. 'The details are still sketchy, but what is clear is that "Operation Hangman" is an assassination plot, directed from London, and spearheaded in Prague by—'

Heydrich slammed his fist against the wall so hard, it nearly made her jump. '*Die verdammte Sau!*' he roared. 'I have suspected something like this for some time. There have been unexplained leaks, unaccountable security lapses.' His eyes grew very small. 'That business in the Böhmenwald, for example. How did they know we were coming?'

She took her cue. 'Frau Hentgen,' she said.

'No.' He shook his head. 'Frau Hentgen is only a functionary. This conspiracy goes much higher.'

He began to pace furiously around the room. 'Kaltenbrunner,' he said at last, trying to shake the muzziness from his head. 'I might have known better than to trust any Austrians. They are innately treacherous. To think he came here tonight, to enjoy my hospitality, to sit at my table, to drink my wine!'

Ernst Kaltenbrunner: the tall, ugly, pockmarked killer whose appearance filled everyone with loathing. A sadist who was known to torture his victims personally. The deputy who wanted his boss's job. The man who would be Heydrich.

'Yes, that must be it,' she said conspiratorially. 'Kaltenbrunner. She is working with him against you. He hates you and he wants your job, but he is too much the jackal to try to take it from you. That is why he is working with the British. So no one will suspect him.'

He stormed over to the telephone, a direct line to the castle. He spoke quietly, but rapidly and angrily.

'I have just ordered the arrest of Frau Hentgen,' he told Ilsa after he had hung up. 'She will be interrogated in the morning. Thoroughly.' An evil smile played across his mouth. 'Perhaps there will soon be a senior position available in my office.'

'What about Kaltenbrunner?' she breathed. She didn't have to fake her eagerness for his blood, too.

'That I cannot do,' Heydrich replied. 'Not just yet. But soon.'

He went to a cabinet, rummaged around, and came up with two more champagne glasses. Unsteadily he poured them full and handed one to Ilsa.

'We must drink,' he said. 'To the late Frau Hentgen!' He downed his at once, tossing his head back to drain the glass, which gave Ilsa time to empty hers out the window, unnoticed.

She rushed to embrace him. 'Magnificent,' she said.

To her surprise, he put up his hands to hold her off. 'Perhaps I should order your arrest, too,' he said.

'What?' gasped Ilsa. In his eyes she could see mistrust mixed with desire.

'I did not become chief of the Reich security service by being careless. One should always interrogate all witnesses. A night spent in my custody would be good for both of us,' he said, trying not to slur his words.

He grabbed her. He tore at her dress, he kissed her violently, he ran his hands up and down her body.

For a brief moment she was tempted to give in. Why not? He was in the trap now and had to be drawn in even more tightly, until he suffocated in it. Then she thought of Victor. Then she thought of Rick.

She slapped his face, hard. 'Stop!' she cried. 'Do you think I am one of your whores?'

He loosened his grasp. 'Aren't all women?' he sneered.

'If I were,' she said gently, 'if I were only a whore, would Frau Hentgen hate me so?'

He said nothing.

'If I were only a whore, would you want me so?'

Heydrich released her and sat down heavily on the floor. 'You are a witch,' he sighed, 'who has enchanted me.' He laughed bitterly. 'See how the Protector cowers before you.'

She tried to control her revulsion as she stroked his hair.

'Do you love me?' he asked.

'Why else would I be trying to save your life?' she replied.

Now she could see him for what he was. The mask of the beast had fallen away. She no longer felt guilty about what was going to happen to him. It would be a mercy killing.

She bent down and raised his face to hers. His unreasoning desire was his Achilles' heel, and now, like Paris of Troy, she was going to shoot her arrow into it and kill him.

She took aim and fired. 'A man called Victor Laszlo is behind it,' she whispered.

Her words had the effect she desired. The Protector's eyes were on fire once more. 'Laszlo!' he spat. 'That pathetic weakling! The *Feigling* who runs from the very sound of my name! Who prints the foulest lies about me and the Reich and thinks himself a hero! I will kill him with my bare hands!'

Now, at last, she knew why Victor had been protecting her all this time. She felt a sudden, urgent stab of love for her husband.

Unsteadily Heydrich rose to his feet. She could feel his breath on her face, smell his cologne, see his hatred, and taste his fear as he grasped her for support.

'This Laszlo is a dangerous man,' said Ilsa. 'Send your best men to the Čechův Most. Station them there to watch for him. You and I, however, will be at the Charles Bridge tomorrow.'

Heydrich flailed the air with his fists. 'I will not run! I will not let Laszlo think that I am afraid of him. The true Aryan flees from no man!'

'You are not fleeing,' she assured him. 'You are sparing the people who love you from unpleasantness. What does it matter if you cross the Čechův Most the next day, or the next week? In the Thousand-Year Reich, that is but the blink of an eye. You have all the time in the world. Victor Laszlo will sleep for eternity.'

He looked at her in defeat. 'Make love with me,' he begged.

'No,' she said. 'This is not a time for love. This is a time for hatred.'

He drew himself up, struggling for his dignity. 'You are right,' he said. 'A German must put aside weak emotions like lust in favor of the grander passions. I shall order my men to the Čechův Most. You shall stay here tonight, and ride with me over the Charles Bridge in the morning, that all Prague might see the Protector and his consort together!'

Stiffly he bade her good night. 'Hear this, however: If my men find nothing on the Čechův Most, you will die. If anything untoward happens on the Charles Bridge, I shall kill you myself.'

He offered her a formal bow. 'Sleep well, Fräulein Toumanova.'

CHAPTER THIRTY-FIVE

In the early dawn light of May 27, 1942, Hradčany Castle looked like something out of one of Franz Kafka's dreams. Then Rick remembered that it wasn't Kafka's dream at all, but Kafka's nightmare. Rick hoped his experience would have a happier ending, but he wasn't optimistic.

Even in late May, a chill was in the air. Nobody was up or about. There were no cars in the streets, no subways rumbling underfoot, no newsboys hawking bulldog editions, no colored cleaning ladies trudging home to their families, no Italian greengrocers washing down the produce for the opening of business, no Irish train conductors in freshly pressed uniforms heading over to Pennsylvania Station for the first run down to Baltimore, not even any cops, idly chatting up the late-shift drabs in Times Square and hungrily awaiting the opening of the bakeries in an hour.

This is not the way it would be in New York, thought Rick. He was suddenly terribly homesick.

As he stood there, looking up at the castle, his mind raced

back to a legend his mother had taught him when he was small. It was the story of the Golem of Prague, Rabbi Loew's mythical creation who righted the many wrongs committed against the Jews of medieval Prague. In Yiddish, a golem was also an unlettered, half-formed creature, a robot, a fool. How well all those adjectives described him. Fine: from this moment on, he would be the Golem of Prague come to life once more.

At last he had found a cause worth dying for. Only this time he had no intention of doing so.

Ilsa was awakened by one of Heydrich's maids. 'The master is impatient,' she said. 'The master is always impatient.'

The clock on the dresser read precisely 7:00 A.M. She would have to move quickly to be ready when the car left at 7:25. The Protector was never late, even for his own demise. She dressed quickly.

She had to wear the same dress she had worn last night. If she had to die, she wished she could do so in something fresh, something pure, but she had not been planning to sleep at the villa. Perhaps this way was better, though: that she should perish not in blue, but in scarlet. She only hoped that Victor would forgive her as he threw the bomb. That he would have the courage to do so, she had no doubt.

Downstairs, Reinhard Heydrich was pacing the floor. In the morning light his skin looked paler than ever, more like a cadaver's than a living man's, and his eyes did not shine as bright as they had the night before. Still, his uniform was freshly laundered and pressed, his jackboots shined by his batman to an unearthly finish. He looked every inch the Nazi officer.

'You Slavs are like children.' He sighed. 'You have no sense of time, no sense of urgency. Always late!'

'I want to look my best, Reinhard,' she said.

He slapped his swagger stick against his thigh. 'I hope you are ready for what should prove to be a most interesting day,' he said. 'Shall we go?'

It was 7:31 A.M. Because of her, they were six minutes behind schedule.

The limousine's motor was purring softly in the courtyard. There appeared to be no chance of rain, which meant the convertible's top would stay down. The uniformed driver had his gloved hands on the steering wheel. Ilsa got into the backseat of the car, behind the driver. Heydrich took the seat behind the bodyguard.

Her heart nearly stopped when she heard the Protector give instructions to his driver. 'The Kirchmayer Boulevard,' he said, 'and the Čechův Most.'

The Čechův Most? It couldn't be! Victor and the others would be waiting at the Charles Bridge. She had to get him to change his route, now. But how?

'I thought it might amuse you to see how the Reich deals with traitors,' he said as the car started forward.

'Well, Ricky, how are we this fine morning?' said the voice at his side as Rick stepped into the street. It was Renault, dressed as elegantly as ever. 'Ready for a funeral or two?'

'As ready as I'm going to be,' replied Rick. He patted his pockets idly for a pack of cigarettes, then remembered he had run out, smoking the last of his precious Chesterfields in the middle of the night while he replayed an old Alekhine game in which the problem had been to force mate in six moves from a position that was superficially hopeless. That was the game that had won the Russian the championship in 1927, when he beat Capablanca. When he finished Capablanca.

He bummed three smokes off Louis. That's all he would need. After that, things would be too exciting for him to worry about smoking.

Renault inspected the knot of his tie and made sure the cravat was straight and true. Around them, life was beginning to stir as men and women trudged, rode, strode, staggered, stumbled, and ambled to their jobs. The weather was breaking clear and cloudless, the way it did in New York at this time of year. A good omen, thought Rick.

Around the corner came the car bearing Kubiš and Gabčík. They were dressed as common laborers; Kubiš was disguised as a city street sweeper, while Gabčík was outfitted as a telephone line worker. When the time came, Josef would be up and off the ground, his work belt concealing a Sten gun, with which he was to open fire on the convertible. Jan's assignment was to stand by the bridge approach and, after the car had passed, rake it with gunfire from behind.

Rick nodded imperceptibly to the two Czech patriots as they took up their stations. He hoped they wouldn't be too disappointed when Heydrich didn't show up for his own assassination. He hoped they'd get out alive. He hoped they would never find out that he and Ilsa had tipped off the Protector.

Where was Laszlo? Rick tried hard not to search for him too conspicuously, but Victor was nowhere to be seen. That was partly to be expected, because Laszlo could not show his face until the last minute. Still, he should be at his station by now, which was just beside the Clementinum, the huge, ancient, fortresslike complex of buildings and churches that dominated the Old Town side of the bridge. A good place for him, Rick thought: in the thirteenth century, the Clementinum had been the headquarters of the Inquisition, and even after the Jesuits replaced the Dominicans as the inquisitors-in-chief, they'd continued their forebears' practice of the forcible conversion of as many of Prague's Jews as they could lay their hands on.

What if something had gone wrong? Rick tried to control his imagination, but it was running away with him. What if Laszlo had been captured on the way in from Lidice? What if something had happened to Ilsa? What if Heydrich hadn't fallen for their ploy and had instead suspected the messenger instead of the message? Split-second timing was everything: the minute Heydrich's troops showed up, the hit team had to be ready to run. The problem was, only Rick would be expecting them. Only Rick *could* expect them.

Only one outcome was worse: What if, despite their warning, Heydrich *did* show up? That would be just like a Nazi. Well, he'd done his best to make it not happen. Now it was up to God.

'So long, Louis,' he said. 'See you back at the ranch.'

'I shall look forward to it,' replied Renault, 'wherever the ranch might be.'

Rick took up his post halfway across the bridge. He would not stand out here. The Charles Bridge was always crowded with sightseers come to admire the famous statuary – and, of course, to cheer on the Protector as he made his stately way across the river and over to the castle. He had concealed the smoke bomb in a small basket, the kind of thing one carried groceries in. To make it look good, he had bought a couple of loaves of fresh bread that morning and stuck them on top.

The smell of the bread reminded him he had forgotten breakfast. No time to worry about that now.

From his vantage point, ostensibly admiring the weather-beaten countenance of some nameless Christian martyr, he could see the two Czechs and, in the distance, Louis Renault.

Then he spotted Victor Laszlo, who had appeared in front of the Clementinum. Even from this distance, Rick could descry Laszlo's height and form, could see him conversing with Renault.

Rick looked down at his watch. It was 7:39 A.M. Fifteen minutes from now it would all be over, one way or another.

When he looked up again, Laszlo and Renault had disappeared.

That wasn't part of the plan.

'Good morning, Victor,' Renault said jauntily as Laszlo stepped out of the car in which he'd been riding.

'Good morning, Captain Renault,' replied Laszlo.

Laszlo's tone caught Renault's ear. 'Anything wrong?' he asked.

'What could be wrong?' asked Laszlo. Wrapped in a long cloak against discovery, he had his hat pulled down low over his forehead, and his hands were jammed in both his pockets. 'Today, I shall realize an ambition that has burned inside my breast for a long time. Today I shall kill the man who is destroying my country and those in it I love. What more could one ask? Were it raining and storming, I should think this the most beautiful day of my life.'

Renault nodded. 'I think I know how you feel,' he said. He checked his watch. It was 7:42 A.M. Time for them all to be getting into position; almost past time.

Laszlo spoke in the same controlled monotone. 'How can you presume to know how I feel? You, who until just a few months ago were in the paid employ of my enemy.'

'I don't think we need to go back over all that right now,' Renault said stiffly. 'We have a job to do. With luck, we shall succeed. With the help of God, we shall escape. We will have plenty of time to discuss all this back in Lidice or, better yet, London.'

'I hope so,' said Laszlo.

Ilsa tried to control the fear in her voice. 'The Čechův Most?' she said softly, trying not to be overheard by anyone else. 'Last night you said—'

Heydrich cut her off. 'Last night I said a good many things, most of which I prefer not to remember. Today, however, is a new day – a day of terrible vengeance and great joy!'

He consulted his timepiece. 'Even now my men are taking up their positions in Josefov. Surely you would not deny me the satisfaction of witnessing the capture and execution of Victor Laszlo? Really, my dear, I am surprised that you think so little of me.' He rubbed his hands briskly together and looked heavenward. 'A superb day, don't you agree, Miss Toumanova?' he observed.

'Yes, Herr Heydrich, it is,' she agreed. They were no longer in his house; first names no longer applied. From now on, everything would be strictly business. That would have to change, too.

Rick stood on the Charles Bridge, smoking the first of his borrowed cigarettes and waiting. He hoped he was waiting for nothing. He hoped he would stand there, waiting, until Heydrich was five minutes late, run for it, get word back to London that the plot had failed, and request immediate extraction. Boredom: that was the best case scenario. He didn't want to think about the worst case.

7:45 A.M. Traffic moved slowly back and forth across the bridge. On one side of the river, the Old City, all spires and turrets. On the other, the imposing majesty of the castle. He looked up and down but could see nothing out of the ordinary. No big black Mercedes-Benz, swastika pennants flapping briskly. Just workaday Prague, going about its business.

Heydrich was always on time, they had said. Point of pride. Measure of Aryan superiority over the lesser breeds. Indicator of supreme self-confidence. Here, the trains ran on schedule, and so did the officials.

7:46 A.M.

Set a good example.

7:46:30.

Always on time.

7:47.

Ha!

Rick lit his second cigarette. He couldn't let them know that he had tipped off Heydrich in order to save Ilsa and spare the lives of innocents across Europe. He couldn't say a damn thing. He just wanted to go home.

7:47:30.

Inhale.

7:47:32.

Exhale.

7:48:30.

Time to start the cycle over. Light another cigarette, the last one. Almost time to go home. Inhale.

The bodyguard was armed with both a pistol and an automatic rifle, and two more rifles were stashed away beneath the dash. Heydrich himself wore a pair of sidearms, one on each hip; Ilsa knew as well that he also carried a large killing knife in the calf of his right polished boot. Finally, there was a brace of shotguns across the back of the front seats, within easy reach. Ordinarily the Protector did not expect trouble from his Czech subjects, but he was ready for it just in case.

The car moved away from the villa, picking up speed as it hit the open road that led in to the Old City. Abruptly he removed one of his twin Lugers from its holster and checked the clip. 'My men are looking for Laszlo right now,' he said. 'As soon as they spot him, they will arrest and hold him until we arrive. Then I shall shoot him.'

He sighted down the barrel of his Luger at a road sign. The sign read PRAHA.

'Like this.' He squeezed the trigger. There was a bullet hole directly through the center of the middle 'A.'

7:49.

Rick surveyed the scene once more. On one side of the bridge Jan Kubiš was bent over his street-sweeping duties, methodically working back and forth across the roadway. This part of the bridge had probably never been so clean, thought Rick, and never would be again. Meanwhile, up on a window ledge, Gabčík was perched on the side of a building, pretending to inspect the telephone lines. As Rick watched, he saw Josef slide into position along a wide window ledge: the perfect vantage point from which to rain lead into the car.

Rick looked back down the bridge. No sign of Renault. Odd: Louis should be ready to go by now, ready to step out into the street just as Heydrich's car was turning. Of course, Heydrich's car wouldn't be turning, but nobody besides him and Louis knew that.

Where the hell was he?

He glanced at his watch. Ten seconds before 7:50 A.M. No sign of Heydrich. His watch was right. He knew it was right. It had to be right.

He started to breathe easier.

There was Renault!

He could see the little man's elegant form standing on the sidewalk near the Clementinum. Right behind him was Victor Laszlo. Although half-hidden in the shadows, he was unmistakable. Laszlo appeared to be whispering something in Louis's ear. Louis was shaking his head, violently disagreeing. What were they saying?

7:51 A.M. No Heydrich.

7:52 A.M. No Heydrich.

Rick let out a deep breath.

7:53 A.M. No Heydrich.

7:54 A.M. No Heydrich. Another minute and that would be that.

He was patting his pocket for another cigarette, and coming up empty, when the sound of martial music wafted across the river and into his ears.

'Where is he?' said Laszlo, his voice growing tense. 'He's not coming. *Why?*'

'Really,' said Renault over his shoulder, with as much savoir faire as he could muster, 'I don't have the slightest idea.'

Louis was standing on the sidewalk of Karlova Street, ready at Kubiš's signal to step into Křižovnická Street and into the path of Heydrich's vehicle as he made the turn. Heydrich was four minutes late; no German had ever been four minutes late for anything. That meant Rick's warning had been successful, that Heydrich had taken the other bridge after all, that the operation was a failure – all the things he had been hoping for, with one more to go: to get out of Prague alive.

As he looked at it, Renault's watch ticked over to 7:55 A.M. Time to stand down. 'It appears that our little rendezvous with destiny has been canceled,' he remarked. 'What a pity.'

Louis could feel Laszlo behind him, pacing back and forth. 'It can't be,' Victor was growling. 'Not now.'

'I believe it was agreed that if our friend was one second past five minutes late the operation would be aborted,' Renault reminded Laszlo, pointing to his watch.

'No,' said Laszlo. 'He's coming. I know he is.'

'I am confident he is not,' replied Louis. It was time to end the charade. He just wanted to get out and get away before they were all arrested and shot.

He started to leave but was jerked back roughly into the darkness of the Clementinum. 'You are very anxious to leave, aren't you, M. Renault?' said Laszlo. 'I wonder how you can be so certain that the target is not coming. Perhaps you know something I do not.'

Laszlo tightened his grip on Renault's arm. 'I have heard all about your babbling to that stupid girl. At first I took it as simple irresponsibility. Now I think otherwise.'

Laszlo spun Louis around. They faced each other in the damp gloom of the ancient building. 'That's why Heydrich isn't coming, isn't it? Because you tipped him off. I have always suspected you, and now I know the truth: you are a traitor.'

Louis was about to raise a word of objection in defense of his honor when Victor Laszlo pressed the muzzle of his revolver against his chest. 'This is how we deal with traitors,' he said, and fired a single, muffled shot.

7:56 A.M. As Louis lay bleeding, he heard the music. He had heard it many times before in Casablanca, whenever a Nazi dignitary had come to visit: the *Hohenfriedberger March*, a symbol of imperial Germany, composed by Frederick the Great. There could be little doubt whom it was meant to be serenading.

'*Mon Dieu!*' gasped Renault. He had not prayed to God for a long time, and was trying very hard to remember what was supposed to come next, when he died.

CHAPTER THIRTY-SIX

As they approached the center of the Old Town, Ilsa could hear the faint sounds of music. How incongruous they seemed. Her heart was hammering as she turned to Heydrich with feigned enjoyment. 'It's marvelous!' she cried. 'What is it?'

Heydrich glanced down at her. 'That is my private military band, sent down from the castle on my orders to serenade you,' he replied. 'They could not know I would change my mind this morning.'

He was standing up in the car now, for they were nearing the Staroměstské Náměstí, the central square. A large crowd had gathered in the byways, to view the Protector in the flesh. He stood ramrod straight, his right arm outstretched. As they passed by, the pedestrians stopped to gape in awe at the great man, and she could hear shouts of '*Heil Hitler!*' from the crowd.

'See how my people love me!' he exulted.

'No more than I!' she cried desperately, and reached for

his free hand. 'If perchance you love me, too, spare me the sight of the death of this Victor Laszlo. I am only a poor girl, unaccustomed to blood and pain, and I would not wish to disgrace my Protector at the Čechův Most by any sign of weakness.' Her voice filled with alarm. 'And should anything happen to you there, I could not bear it! Please! I beg you!'

7:56 A.M. The car was passing through the square. From here, they could either turn into Pařižská Street, drive through Josefov and then over the Čechův Most, or continue straight on Platnéršká to the river, left at the Clementinum, right onto the Charles Bridge, and straight to the end.

'Please, Reinhard,' she said. 'Take me over the Charles Bridge. Let me hear the music and bask in your glory. I was a fool last night to turn down the love of a man like you. I know that now. Tonight will be different, I promise. Kill them all, but not in front of me. I beg you!'

Still clasping his hand, Ilsa looked up at the Protector. He was staring straight ahead.

The music grew louder.

Ilsa managed to catch a glimpse of her watch. They were six minutes late.

Heydrich's hand squeezed hers gently as he barked an order to the driver. 'To refuse to subject a beautiful woman to the sight of death is the mark of the true German gentleman,' he said.

The car went straight ahead.

'Thank you, Reinhard,' she said, finally exhaling. She started to laugh, giddily, hysterically, all the pent-up emotion and terror flooding out of her at once.

They turned left onto Křižovnická Street.

She was about to say something more when she heard a faint, barely perceptible pop.

Instinctively Heydrich sniffed the air for the smell of cordite with his long, wolfhound nose. He knew that sound, he knew that smell, and he knew what they meant.

Roughly he tried to yank his hand from hers. In the same motion he brought his right hand down and began to unholster his sidearm.

'What is it?' she asked. She gripped his left hand to keep him off balance. If it was time to die, she was ready. All she asked was that it be quick.

'Gunfire,' he replied.

Even before he heard the shot, Rick saw Renault collapse on the sidewalk. He knew immediately his friend was dead. There was no time to mourn him. There would be plenty of time for that later. Or not, as the case may be.

He started to run, run as fast he could along the bridge, toward the Clementinum.

He could see the big car now, turning left. He knew it was Heydrich's car. Damn the man to hell! Couldn't he listen to a warning?

Faster, faster. He was getting closer to the intersection. He was almost there. He was there. Not too late this time, please God. Not too late.

He saw Louis's body, puddling blood in the gutter.

He saw Heydrich standing in the backseat, his right hand groping for his sidearm, his nostrils flared like a wild animal's, his eyes wide and sweeping the streets for danger.

He saw Jan Kubiš, throwing down his street sweeper's tools and coming up with a pistol.

He saw Josef Gabčík on the ledge, a Sten gun in his hand.

He saw Victor Laszlo throwing off his cloak and stepping out in the street, approaching the left side of the car. The bomb was in his hand.

Rick was at the intersection now. The Mercedes was just starting to turn onto the bridge. Victor Laszlo was right behind it. Rick was right in front of it.

Then he saw something else, something he wasn't looking for. In the backseat, seated behind the driver. Another passenger. A woman.

Ilsa Lund.

She was sitting beside the Protector, clad in a rich red dress and clutching his left arm.

Rick hesitated. After Heydrich, she was the last person he expected to see.

Laszlo kept going. If he felt any surprise, any emotion at her presence in the car, his face did not register it.

The limousine slowed nearly to a complete stop as it turned right onto the bridge. Laszlo was two steps away.

'No!' cried Rick, sprinting toward him.

'Victor!' shouted Ilsa. 'Hurry!' She pulled Heydrich hard, nearly toppling him.

Heydrich had his pistol out. Rick thought at first he was going to shoot Laszlo. Instead the Nazi pointed it at Ilsa.

Before the driver or the bodyguard could react, Rick dove into the car.

Rick hit Heydrich just as he fired at Ilsa. The shot went wild.

In the same instant, Laszlo jumped onto the running board and flung the bomb into the backseat.

Ten . . .

Rick lunged for the bomb, which was rolling around on the floor. Victor saw him and understood his purpose immediately. 'Get away!' he shouted, clambering aboard. Heydrich hesitated, confused, uncertain whether Rick or Laszlo posed the more imminent threat.

Nine . . .

Ilsa was aghast. Why was Rick trying to stop her husband from killing Heydrich? Trying to stop *her*? 'Rick, no!' she cried.

Eight . . .

Rick could hear the sound of gunfire as Kubiš and Gabčík opened up on the front seat's occupants, and he could hear the groan of the bodyguard as their shots slammed into him. Glass shattered, wood splintered, and leather split. Blood flew.

Seven . . .

Heydrich wheeled and smashed his gun butt on Rick's head. Rick went down. Heydrich was about to hit him again when Laszlo grabbed him from the other side.

Six . . .

Rick's hands shot out again, frantically seeking the bomb on the floor. He knew there wasn't much time left. His hand found Ilsa instead of the bomb.

Five . . .

Shot by Gabčík, the driver's head exploded. Incongruously, his chauffeur's cap blew off his head and flew, spinning over the abutment and into the river, like a child's paper airplane.

Four . . .

'Come on!' Rick shouted, hauling Ilsa to her feet.

Three . . .

Laszlo had one hand around Heydrich's throat and jammed a gun into his midsection with the other. Heydrich flashed a knife.

Two . . .

'Victor!' cried Ilsa.

'Jump!' Rick screamed.

Victor shot Heydrich in the abdomen. Heydrich stabbed Victor through the heart.

One . . .

Rick and Ilsa were out of the car, his arms around her, rolling and tumbling together as fast and as far as they could.

Zero.

The explosion lifted the Mercedes off its wheels and into the air, as if it were a child's jack-in-the-box. Rick's head hit the pavement, and he brought his hands up to shield his face. He caught a glimpse of Ilsa, lying limp against the stone wall.

Glass and metal rained down from the sky. The smell of burning rubber was followed quickly by the sickening stench of burning flesh.

Fire, now, and then another report as the gasoline tank ignited. Rick scrabbled as fast as he could away from the burning wreck, trying to get to his feet, trying to get to Ilsa.

Ejected from the wreckage, one of Heydrich's Lugers lay at his feet. Rick grabbed it like a drowning man clutching a life preserver. It felt good in his hand; it felt like old times.

Someone yanked him to his feet: Kubiš. With one arm around Rick, he was still spraying the wreckage with gunfire with the other.

'Ilsa,' Rick gasped.

'That Nazi whore!' spat Jan.

Rick stuck the bodyguard's gun in his ribs. 'Ilsa,' he commanded. 'Now.'

Commotion everywhere. Rick glanced back along the bridge. The band had dispersed to the sides of the span. Down the middle came a security detail, undermanned but on the double.

Bullets whizzed past their heads. Gabčík returned fire. Nazi soldiers dropped. The kid was a hell of a shot, thought Rick; we could have used him way back when and oh so long ago.

Three steps, and there was Ilsa alive and conscious. He lifted her to her feet.

'Victor!' she screamed, and tried to run toward the car. 'Where are you?'

He slapped her. 'He's dead,' he said. In the twisted debris he could just make out Victor's body, Heydrich's knife protruding from his chest, his eyes open, gazing toward the sky.

For the first time, he saw Victor Laszlo at peace.

Ilsa's eyes cleared. 'You tried to stop him! You tried to sabotage us! *Why?*'

Now it was her turn to slap his face. That hurt worse that anything he had ever suffered.

'You bastard! You killed my husband!' she said.

She was pounding on his chest now, raining blows down on his head. He could hear the whistles of the police and sirens and shouts. There was no time.

He socked her, hard. She fell unconscious into his arms. He slung her over his shoulders and ran as fast as he could, away from the bomb site, away from the bullets, away from the river, away from the bodies, toward the church. Of all things, the church.

A hundred yards ahead of him he could see Kubiš and Gabčík. They were fleeing to different places, but they were all going to sanctuary. He and Ilsa to the Church of St. Charles Borromeo, the patron saint of administrators and diplomats. The Czechs to the Church of Sts. Cyril and Methodius, the apostles to the Slavs.

The Protector of Bohemia and Moravia lay sprawled on the pavement. At a glance Rick couldn't tell whether he was alive or dead. Then he saw his right leg twitch and heard him calling for help, softly, in German. Heydrich's trigger finger was still firing, but his hands were empty. He thought about shooting him right there. But there was no time. Let God take care of him, if He cared to. If not, let him go straight to hell, where he belonged.

The Czech civilians were too stunned to do anything. No one tried to stop them. No one was quite sure exactly what had happened yet. It was like a hit in a Bronx restaurant. Everybody had seen it, yet nobody knew what he had seen.

They passed Louis Renault's body as they ran. The little man looked as dapper in death as he had in life. 'So long, Louis,' said Rick. 'It was a hell of a beautiful friendship. I just wish it could have lasted longer.'

The church was close by. Its doors were opened to receive them. They made it through. The doors slammed shut.

'This way,' said a priest.

Ilsa woke up. 'Can you walk?' Rick asked her.

The fight had gone out of her. 'I think so,' she replied in the voice of a woman who couldn't believe she was still alive. She was missing a shoe. She kicked off the other one and walked barefoot. Her brilliant red dress was soaked with blood. Heydrich's, of course, and Victor's.

From a distance, he could hear sirens. In the distance, he thought he could hear screams. In his head, he could hear the voices of the dead. Victor Laszlo had just joined the chorus.

The priest led them through the sacristy, down some stairs, and into the crypt: the bones of the saints and martyrs and those who were just plain unlucky, who had died for their beliefs or were killed for their faith or who were just in the wrong place at the wrong time. The crypt led into a tunnel, which led into another tunnel, which led under the street. How far under the street, Rick was not exactly sure. He supposed this was what Pell Street in New York must be like, minus the saints and martyrs and plus the Chinese food. He had never been to Pell Street, but then he had never expected to be down here, among the honored Christian dead, either. He had never expected to find Chinatown in Czechoslovakia.

Some stairs rose up to the street.

'Are you all right?' Rick asked Ilsa. She said nothing. She just stared at him with the most profound sense of disbelief he had ever seen in the eyes of another human being.

'Why did you do it?' she said bitterly.

'Later,' he wheezed.

'I hate you,' she said.

Then they were up the stairs and into the street. They piled into the back of a waiting produce truck. 'Get down,' advised the padre, 'and stay down.' A couple of workmen dumped a pile of rotting, discarded lettuce over them, and then the truck started to move away, slowly, toward Lidice.

Huddled together under the cargo, they were locked in each other's arms as intimately as lovers. Never had they felt so far apart.

CHAPTER THIRTY-SEVEN

Rick and Ilsa were fortunate. Jan Kubiš and Josef Gabčík never made it back to Lidice. The Nazis caught up with them in the crypt of the Church of Sts. Cyril and Methodius. An Underground meeting was going on in the church at that time, where 120 members of the Czech resistance were awaiting word of the assassination.

The Czech patriots gave a good account of themselves, but they were outnumbered and outgunned. They shot the Germans coming down the stairs, shot them crashing through holes they had blown through the church floor, shot them until they were out of ammunition, and then continued fighting with rocks and stones and knives and their bare hands until the German troops poured down the stairs and into the crypt in such numbers that there were no longer enough Czechs to withstand them. The last two left alive, down to their last two bullets, shook hands, kissed each other, shot themselves, and fell dead on the floor alongside the saints and the martyrs.

The Nazi intelligence apparatus finally was able to separate Jan and Josef from the rest. The priests tried to sprinkle holy water on their bodies, but the Germans would have none of that. They cut off Jan's head and they cut off Josef's head, and then they stuck both heads on the points of bayonets. The Germans brought the bayonets above ground, onto the streets and into the city and back down to the Charles Bridge. There they fixed the bayonets with the heads still on them into the arms of two of the statues of the saints, into the arms of St. John of Nepomuk and St. Luitgard, and left them there until the birds of the air so beloved of St. Francis had pecked away the eyes and taken off their noses; left them there until they had rotted away to just a pair of skulls. Then the Nazis smashed the skulls to bits with rifle butts and threw the shards into the river for the fish to eat.

The bodies they hacked to pieces with cleavers and axes. They dug a hole in unconsecrated ground in a farmer's field in the dead of night and threw the pieces in. They covered them with lime and then they covered them with dirt and then they spat on the dirt and pissed on it. The other bodies they burned in the concentration camp at nearby Theresienstadt, the model camp, which was the only one the Red Cross was allowed to visit.

From the identity papers found on Josef Gabčík, they learned he was a resident of the village of Lidice.

Victor Laszlo's body was never seen again.

Reinhard Tristan Eugen Heydrich, the Protector of Bohemia and Moravia, the host of the Wannsee Conference, the architect of the Final Solution, lingered for eight agonizing days. His back had been broken by the blast. Much of his handsome face was gone, including his aquiline nose, of which he had been so vain. His body had been penetrated by shrapnel from the explosion and by the horsehair from the stuffing in the seats; the wounds became infected and suppurating. The gunshot wound to his abdomen, which Victor Laszlo had inflicted with his last dying effort, finally killed him. The best doctors in the Reich could not stanch the bleeding or ameliorate the agony. On June 4, 1942, Reinhard Heydrich died. He was thirty-eight years old, the same age as Rick Blaine.

In Berlin, Adolf Hitler proclaimed a month of national mourning. In Prague, fifty thousand sympathetic Czechs took to the streets to protest an act of Allied terrorism.

Heinrich Himmler vowed that the SS and the Gestapo would not rest until everyone responsible had been brought to justice. From behind thick glasses and a weak mustache, he read the speech that Goebbels had written for him. 'German justice,' he proclaimed, 'will be both swift and terrible.'

Ernst Kaltenbrunner moved a notch up the ladder. The night Heydrich died, he removed his former chief's Gestapo file from his private safe and burned it. He had no further use for it.

In Prague Castle, SS men went over Heydrich's office carefully, confiscating any sensitive *Akten*, or files, that could have proved damaging to any of the surviving members of the Third Reich hierarchy. One of them took Heydrich's priceless violin and stomped it to pieces with his boots, which had been polished to perfection just that morning. Then he threw the shards out the window, in the direction of Dalibor Tower.

The first to suffer were the Jews. A few hours after the attack, 3,000 Jews from Theresienstadt, not far from Prague, were ordered shipped to Auschwitz immediately. Nobody ever returned to Theresienstadt from Auschwitz.

In the aftermath of the bombing, Goebbels ordered 500 of the remaining Jews in Berlin arrested. The day of Heydrich's death, 152 of them were executed in reprisal. No one informed them why they were being killed.

Neither Rick nor Ilsa knew anything of these developments. They were at the farmhouse in Lidice, recuperating from their injuries and waiting for the British plane that had been promised them. They did not know when it would come. They did not know if it would come. They could only hope the British would keep their promise.

On the third day, Karel Gabčík came to see Rick. Containing his emotions, Karel told Rick what had happened in Prague. 'Heydrich lives,' said the boy, and then he broke down and started to cry. 'He is severely wounded – they say his spine is shattered. But he is still . . . alive. . . .'

'At least I hope he's suffering badly,' said Rick. 'Nobody deserves it more.'

'What if he doesn't die?'

'What difference does it make? We're in just as much trouble if he does. What do you hear from the Underground?'

'Nothing.'

Nothing: that was all they'd heard so far. Where was that plane? The agreement was that it would be dispatched shortly after news of the attack was relayed to London. Surely Major Miles would have received word by now. One possible explanation was that the weather had remained sunny. Sunshine was good for normal flying, but bad for covert operations: they needed a cloudy day for the light-wing aircraft to slip in under cover and, more important, get out the same way.

Rick had not seen Ilsa since they had arrived. She had been taken to a back room on the second floor of the farmhouse, and when he had inquired about her, he had been told that she was all right – bruised and still a little stunned from the events on the bridge, but otherwise unharmed. She did not wish to see him.

For the first few days he respected her wishes. Today he didn't care. He knocked at the door of her room. 'It's me,' he said quietly. 'We have to talk. You've got to let me explain.'

On the other side of the heavy oak door there was only silence.

'Ilsa?'

Rick put his ear to the keyhole. Very faintly he could hear her breathing.

He walked away, feeling more dead than alive.

On the eighth day, word came that Heydrich had died of his wounds. Karel Gabčík told him the news as they took their evening meal.

'The Protector is dead,' Karel announced without preamble. 'Our names will echo down through history.'

Rick took no pleasure from Karel's triumph. 'Don't be too sure of that,' he warned the youth. 'History has a way of forgetting about a lot of things. It always finds something else to remember.'

They ate in silence. The fare of bread, farmer's cheese, and slices of roast pork was simple. Rick's emotions were not.

'I'd get ready for trouble, if I were you,' he told Karel Gabčík. 'In the meantime, is there any word about us? About the plane?' He meant about him and Ilsa. He meant about the promised extraction. He meant about getting out of there.

'No,' said Karel.

Where the hell was that plane? Or was this just one more double cross? The last one?

In her room, Ilsa was dining alone. Rick had still not laid eyes on her.

On the ninth day, Rick Blaine was still waiting for the airplane and still trying to speak with Ilsa. He was disappointed on both counts.

The tenth day was just like the ninth. He was beginning to give up hope.

He had lived with the artful double cross all his life. Each time he had been on the losing end. He had only half trusted Major Miles in the first place, the way he had always only half trusted the world. Hell, if he were the English, he wouldn't send a plane, either, not after what had happened. Laszlo, Renault, Kubiš, and Josef Gabčík were all dead. Rick Blaine and Ilsa Lund might still be alive somewhere, but they were foreigners, little people, expendable.

Late that night he knocked on Ilsa's door. He had nowhere else to go and no one else to turn to.

To his surprise, the door opened. 'What do you want?' she asked bitterly.

He couldn't see her face, only one red eye and a strand of hair that fell across it to cover her tears. 'To explain,' he said.

'Nothing you can tell me, no explanation you can give me, will I either believe or accept,' she said coldly.

'That's where you're wrong. Someday, I hope you'll let me try.' He had to keep talking, to keep her listening.

'Besides, why were you in that car? That was never part of the plan. What did you expect me to do when I saw you? Let Victor kill you? I was prepared to do a lot of things, Ilsa, but seeing you die wasn't one of them.'

Slowly, she opened the door a little wider. Rick wasn't sure if her gesture was an invitation to enter or an invitation to speak. He kept talking.

'For a long time, I thought we'd go through with it,' he began. 'I told Victor I'd help him, and I meant it. Part of me *wanted* to go through with it. For you, if nobody else.'

Ilsa remained silent.

'When you told me about how the Underground was begging London to call it off, that got me thinking about something Louie had been saying, that he had never trusted the British all along, that they had duped Victor into taking on this mission: not because they wanted to kill Heydrich, but because they want to provoke the Germans and get the Czechs fighting again. In fact, they pretty much admitted it to me themselves.'

'Why would they do that?' she said.

'Politics,' replied Rick. 'Good old-fashioned power politics. That's what this whole thing is about. That's what it has always been about. We may think we're kings and queens in our own little worlds, but to them we're just pawns in the game, ready for sacrifice without a second thought.' He thought about the absent rescue plane. He'd just about given up hope but decided not to let on.

The door opened all the way, and Rick could see Ilsa nodding. 'Reprisals,' she said. 'That's what Heydrich said to me the last night.' Her voice caught. 'That if anything happened to him, their vengeance would be terrible.'

'I'm afraid he wasn't kidding,' said Rick. He realized he

was standing in the hallway, which was no place for the conversation they needed to have. 'Do you mind if I come in? There's a lot of things you ought to know.'

She let him in and closed the door. Seated on a chair, he told her what had happened to Jan and Josef and the others in the church. He fumbled for a cigarette, then remembered he had smoked his last one. It had been a gift from Renault, just before everything. The hell with cigarettes. There were enough nails in his coffin as it was.

'It looks like Louie was right, that it was all a setup, from the start,' he said. 'The British care only about themselves, about whether they're going to come out of this war in one piece and with Hitler defeated by any means necessary. And why shouldn't they? They're only human.' He let out his breath. 'Just like the rest of us.'

'But what about the cause?' asked Ilsa, her eyes softening. 'The cause we all believed in?'

'*They're* the only cause they believe in,' he told her. 'Just like we're the only cause I'm interested in.'

'Victor died for what he believed in,' said Ilsa, her voice ardent once more.

'He was willing for you to die, too. I wasn't. I guess that's the difference between him and me.'

'I was ready if I had to.'

Impulsively Rick swept Ilsa into his arms. 'I couldn't let you. For a long time I thought I wanted to die, because of something I did years ago. Then I met you. You gave me back my life, Ilsa. I thought I'd lost it, but I got it back, thanks to you. My life came with a price, though: yours.'

Now, at last, he could put the ghost of Lois Meredith to rest, once and for all.

'I can't live without you, Ilsa. I thought I could. God knows I tried. But I couldn't. Not after Paris. Not after Casablanca. Not now. Not ever.'

'Oh, Richard,' she murmured as he held her tight. 'Do you know how much I love you?'

They clutched each other as if they were the last two people on earth. 'I thought you hated me,' he whispered.

'No,' she breathed. 'The time for hating is over.'

'You're right,' he said as he roughly drew her mouth to his.

That night they got word from Karel that a small plane would land in a farmer's hops field six kilometers outside Lidice at eight o'clock the next morning and that he and Ilsa were to be there and to be ready. The plane would land for exactly five minutes: if they were late, it would leave without them.

They awoke to the sounds of men yelling. Rick was instantly alert and on his feet.

'Get up, Ilsa,' he said. 'We've got to hurry.'

Ten truckloads of German security police were pouring into the village, firing at anything that moved.

Karel Gabčík burst into the room. 'This way,' he said.

'Take Miss Lund to the plane.' Rick turned to Ilsa and thrust his Colt .45 into her hand. 'This may come in handy. I'm staying.' He reached for a rifle.

'No, you're not,' replied Karel. 'It's our fight, not yours.'

Rick started to object, but young Gabčík already was hustling them out the door and into a waiting car. The minute Ilsa and Rick climbed in, it sped off.

'Tell the world,' Rick could hear Karel shouting. 'Tell the world what is happening here. Don't let them forget.'

His words disappeared in a burst of machine-gun fire.

The battle of Lidice was over almost before it had begun. Taken by surprise, the villagers had no choice but to surrender. One boy, aged twelve, ran away. He was shot trying to escape. An old peasant woman, seeing the soldiers, tried to flee. A German marksman dropped her in her tracks.

The Germans ordered every male over the age of sixteen to gather in the barn of a farmer named Horák, who was also the mayor. Then they were taken out in groups of ten and shot. Anyone still moving after the initial volley received a pistol shot to the head as a coup de grâce, but there was no grace or mercy in it, only malice. One hundred and seventy-two men of Lidice died this way, Karel Gabčík among them.

Seven of the women were taken back to Prague and shot in the courtyard of the castle, in the shadow of Dalibor Tower. Four of the women, who were pregnant, were taken to hospitals in Prague; when their babies were born, the infants were murdered on the spot. The new mothers, along with the rest of the village's 195 females, were shipped to the Ravensbrück camp in Germany, northwest of Berlin.

The children of Lidice were taken to Gneisenau, where they were examined by doctors, given new names, and placed with German families so that they might be brought up properly as Aryans.

When all the people were disposed of, the Germans burned the village to the ground and blew up the rubble with dynamite. They then brought in heavy earth-moving equipment and erased all traces of Lidice's existence.

The car carrying Rick and Ilsa sped toward the rendezvous. It was not alone.

A single German unit, an open jeeplike vehicle equipped with a mounted machine gun, had followed them out of the village. It was faster, it was gaining, and it was firing.

'Get down!' shouted Rick. He had only Heydrich's Luger in his hand, useless at this distance, but it was better than nothing. One of his shots hit a headlight, but the German car kept coming. Another shot pinged off the windscreen, inflicting about as much damage as a moth.

The Germans had found their range now, and their machine-gun fire was ticking up the trunk of their car.

Rick found himself wishing for his speedy Buick, for Sam at the wheel, and for Abie Cohen and all the good boys back home he had not been able to save.

The plane was just up ahead, its twin engines revving furiously. Figures of men were moving about in the hatchway. Rick hoped to God they were armed.

The car was headed straight for the aircraft. Another few seconds and they would crash right into it.

'When the car stops, run like hell,' he told Ilsa. 'Don't worry about me. The minute you get on board, tell them to take off. Do you understand?'

'I won't leave you,' she said.

'There's been enough dead heroes for one day,' he snapped. The car screeched to a halt. 'Run!'

Ilsa jumped out and ran. Rick jumped out and came up firing.

Out of the corner of his eye he saw Ilsa reach the safety of the plane. He fired back, hoping to draw the return fire.

He estimated the distance between him and plane: about ten yards, and increasing. The plane was starting to move.

'Get out of here,' he told the driver of his car. Their wheel man was only a boy. He couldn't have been more than fourteen years old, but he drove like a pro. He deserved to live.

The boy shook his head.

'Beat it,' barked Rick. He squeezed off his last two shots, hit somebody, and made for the plane.

The kid floored the car and vanished into the forest.

The yards disappeared under his stride, one at a time. Bullets kicked up the dirt all around him. This time there was an answer back from the plane: the nose of an automatic rifle poking through the interior darkness, spitting death back at the Germans.

He was almost there.

A slug caught him in the back of the left leg, above the knee. He stumbled and almost went down.

'Rick!' screamed Ilsa. He could see her in the doorway of the plane, and then she was jerked back by a pair of unseen hands as the plane continued to taxi.

He managed to stay on his feet, but he had lost some precious ground. The plane was starting to pick up speed, the bullets were zinging faster. Only two yards to go, goddammit!

A German bullet grazed the back of his right hand and he dropped the Luger. The hell with it: it was empty anyway.

One yard to go.

He sensed rather than saw the gunman standing in the car and preparing to fire off the killing shot.

Reach and pray. Reach for a pair of hands that were thrust out from the hatch. Fingertips . . . palms . . . touch . . . grasp . . . gasp . . .

A flash of light burned from the interior of the plane, accompanied by the unmistakable report of a handgun. As

Rick realized that someone had fired at the Germans behind him, another bullet hit him in the right shoulder, below the scapular. He felt the bone shatter. But the impact drove him forward, just a bit, just enough, into someone's arms. His feet left the ground, and for a moment he was flying through the air.

Rick wasn't around to accept delivery of the next bullet with his name on it. It clanged off the door as it slammed shut, which was just after he was yanked inside, which was just before the plane began to throttle back full, full, full, picking up velocity, speeding away from the armored car, increasing the distance until finally it soared up and into the air and away from Lidice, away from Czechoslovakia, away from the Greater German Reich, and back toward freedom.

He lay on the floor, trying to figure out which parts of his body still worked. He managed to raise his head high enough to look for Ilsa. Safe in the arms of a burly Scotsman, she was still holding Rick's smoking .45, which she had taken from the farmhouse – and with which she had just saved his life. She had deflected the Nazi's aim just in time.

He caught her eye. The look on her face – fear slowly turning to worry and now joy – spoke more eloquently than anything she could say. As soon as she saw him move, she flew to him, cradling him in her arms like a baby. He lay there with her, not wanting to die and, for the first time in years, fighting to live.

A man leaned over him. A man he recognized. A man he never expected to see again.

'Good morning, Mr. Blaine,' said Major Sir Harold Miles. 'Welcome aboard. It's good to have you both back on English soil.' The major beamed and lit up a cigar. 'Congratulations on a job well done.'

Rick just stared at him. 'Miles, you bastard,' he finally croaked.

'My dear fellow,' replied the major, 'someone has to be. There's a war on, don't you know.'

CHAPTER THIRTY-EIGHT

Seven months later Rick Blaine and Ilsa Lund boarded another airplane. This one was bound for Casablanca. The passenger manifest read 'Mr. and Mrs. Richard Blaine.' Sam Waters came along for the ride.

'Are you sure you want to?' Rick asked him.

'How many times you gonna ask me that, boss?' said Sam. 'What'm I supposed to do, stay here the rest of my life? Time for me to start learnin' some new songs and finally get that raise.'

'You can always go back to New York, you know. They aren't looking for you, if they ever were.'

'They never lookin' for a colored boy, Mr. Richard. I told you that a long time ago, and I don't suspect things is changed that much.' Sam clapped Rick on the shoulder with one powerful hand. 'Besides, I expect the Tootsie-Wootsie ain't what she used to be.'

'Neither are we, Sam,' said Rick. 'Neither are we.'

Rick was walking with the aid of crutches. His shoulder

had healed well enough for him to move his arm freely, but the slug that had taken up residence in his left leg had fractured his kneecap. The sawbones told him he'd walk again, with a limp, but his dancing days were over.

He and Ilsa had gotten married anyway. Sam was the best man. Major Miles gave the bride away.

On their wedding night, the fundamental things applied.

In November, the Allies had stormed ashore at North Africa, landing in three different places and sending the Afrika Korps reeling back across Algeria to Tunis. It was the beginning of the end for the Germans, and everybody knew it but them. Typical, thought Rick: the sucker was always the last to know.

The French had fought side by side with the Americans and the British as they drove Rommel the length and breadth of *une Algérie Française* and then kicked him right the hell out.

Casablanca was one of the Allied landing sites. Back in London, Mr. and Mrs. Blaine followed the progress of the invasion closely.

Three days after the city was secure, Rick had turned to Ilsa. 'Are you thinking what I'm thinking?' he asked her.

She was.

It was the least His Majesty's government could do. Rick, Ilsa, and Sam returned to Casablanca in time for Christmas 1942.

Aside from the war damage, it was the same place they had left a year ago. As they approached the airport, Ilsa gazed out the window in anticipation. 'Look, Richard, there it is! It's still there!'

He could see the sign, too. Ferrari had not taken it down:

RICK'S CAFÉ AMERICAIN. It looked better than ever, even with a few bullet holes in it.

Everybody came to Rick's. They still would.

Rick and Ilsa walked from the airport to the café. It wasn't far. It wasn't hard.

The place was closed, but the door was open.

Not too bad, thought Rick as he got a load of the joint. He'd cleaned up worse messes than this after a bar fight.

They found Carl inside, doing the books. 'How long can we afford to stay closed, Carl?' Rick asked him.

Carl looked at him as though he had never left. Carl looked as though he had never left. His jowls still shook when he talked, and his eyes still sparkled.

'Herr Rick,' he said, 'two weeks – maybe three.'

'Don't call me "Herr" anything, Carl,' he said.

'Yes, Mr. Rick,' said Carl. 'Welcome home. And you, Miss Lund.'

'That's Mrs. Blaine to you,' said Rick.

'Yes, Mr. Rick,' said Carl, beaming. If there was a question in his mind, it stayed there. 'Congratulations.'

'Where's Ferrari?'

'Gone off with the Americans.' Carl chuckled. 'You know how he likes sure things.'

'How about Sacha?'

'It's his day off. Or have you already forgotten?'

'Right,' said Rick. 'What about Emil and Abdul?'

Carl shrugged. 'Where would they go?'

'Is there any champagne on ice?'

'Are you joking?' said Carl, and bustled off to fetch it.

Sam's piano was shoved away in a corner. It was dusty, but otherwise unscathed.

'Some of the old songs, Sam,' said Ilsa.

'You know what she means,' said Rick.

She smiled that dazzling smile no man could ever resist. 'You still remember it, don't you? Then play it, Sam. Play "As Time Goes By."'

He played it.

Ilsa opened one of her suitcases. She reached inside and took something out. She held it up for Rick to see.

It was her blue dress, the one she had worn at La Belle Aurore.

'Do you want me to put it on?' she asked him.

'Not now,' he said. 'Wait until we march back into Paris. Maybe not next year, or the year after that. But soon. We've got time. We've got all the time in the world.'

Carl popped open the champagne and poured four glasses. Even Sam was having some this time.

Now, at last, it was a story with an ending.

'We'll always have Paris,' said Ilsa, throwing her arms around Rick's neck and kissing him until she couldn't breathe.

'Cheers,' Rick said, holding up his glass.

'Here's looking at you, kid,' said Ilsa Blaine.

FADE OUT

AFTERWORD

Everybody knows *Casablanca*. Everybody loves *Casablanca*. Therein lies both the challenge and the danger of writing a novel of *Casablanca*.

My solution has been to present the lives of the characters before and after the action of the movie (which lasts only three days and two nights), placing Rick Blaine, Ilsa Lund, Victor Laszlo, and the others in a larger historical context and without 'novelizing' any aspect of the original screenplay. Imagine the film elongated at either end to reveal the epic, wide-screen version, of which the events depicted in *Casablanca* are but the middle of the story.

The basis for the movie's screenplay was Murray Burnett and Joan Alison's 1940 play, *Everybody Comes to Rick's*, which was purchased by a sharp-eyed Warner Bros. reader, Irene Lee, in 1941 for the sum of $20,000. In Hollywood, the script was adapted, reconceived, developed, and adjusted by no less than seven screenwriters, principally the twin-brother writing team of Julius and Philip Epstein (who were responsible for most of the wisecracks); Howard Koch, who punched up the story's political significance; and Casey Robinson, who first suggested turning the character of Lois Meredith, the American divorcée of easy virtue, into the lustrous Norwegian heroine, Ilsa Lund.

Because *Casablanca* was composed, however unwittingly, by committee, it is famous among movie buffs for its loose ends and unanswered questions. Why can't Rick go back to America? (According to Julius Epstein, the brothers tried to think of a reason but failed.) Where is the Czech patriot Victor Laszlo really going when his plane takes off for Lisbon? Why should the Germans honor letters of transit apparently signed by De Gaulle? Why doesn't Strasser just shoot Laszlo on sight?

Some of these questions, it seemed to me, had obvious answers. Since a hallmark of Rick Blaine is his cynical honesty, I chose to take at face value his answer to Renault – 'It was a combination of all three' – when the police captain grills him about why he cannot return to New York and suggests embezzlement, a love affair, and murder. (The closest Major Strasser ever gets to the truth is 'The reasons are unclear.') Laszlo's real destination similarly admits of easy explanation, since the Czech resistance in December 1941 was headquartered in London. The problematic De Gaulle signatures, however, are better left unexplained – except to note that in both the play and the shooting script, the name attached to them is not De Gaulle's, but Weygand's. In general, however, all the action of *As Time Goes By*, both front and back story, derives from statements or clues in the screenplay that, when examined, are the only logical explanation for what happens in the movie, *Casablanca*.

Previous attempts to expand or rework the material of *Casablanca* have made the mistake of either trying to reprise the action in the same locale or changing the essential nature of the characters, or both. As early as 1943 Warner Bros. was planning a sequel called *Brazzaville*, written by Frederick Stephani. Stephani's scenario, which never got beyond the planning stage, supposed that Rick and Renault had been working for the Underground all along, thus negating both Renault's political conversion and Rick's personal sacrifice – two of the plot elements that have made *Casablanca* so enduring.

In his own 1988 attempt at a sequel, Howard Koch moved the action forward a generation, inventing an illegitimate son for Rick and Ilsa, who returns to Morocco to try to learn what happened to his father. The 1955–56 television series *Casablanca*, which lasted seven months, trapped Rick Blaine in his Café Americain forever 'as a North African Mr. Fix-it,' as Aljean Harmetz noted in her 1992 book *Round Up the Usual Suspects*. Another TV version, in 1983, starred David Soul as Rick; it lasted only three weeks.

Fortunately the shooting script provides plenty of clues not only about the nature of the characters, but also about the direction their lives are heading at the time we meet them in *Casablanca*. By hewing to the self-contained world of the original – which itself followed contemporary history more closely than the casual viewer might at first suspect – it seemed to me that a plausible, convincing story could be told about the fate of Rick, Ilsa, Laszlo, et al., that was at once fresh and interesting while maintaining a scrupulous respect for the source.

That the source is a movie cannot be gainsaid or avoided. No one reading this book can fail to envision Humphrey

Bogart as Rick, Ingrid Bergman as Ilsa, Paul Henreid as Laszlo, or Dooley Wilson as Sam. Accordingly, I have embraced the material's cinematic source, right down to incorporating selected dialogue from the script into the novel, partly in homage, partly from dramatic necessity, and partly to let the reader know that the author is in on the fun, too. Rick's bitter wisecracks, Laszlo's lofty pronouncements, Sam's wise empiricism, and Ilsa's passion and confusion all find their source in *Casablanca*.

Therefore, I have endeavored to

- Match the novel's characters to their screen counterparts, sometimes by description and other times by the simple matter of omission. There would have been no point, for example, in describing Rick Blaine as blond or Victor Laszlo as small or Sam as white: Bogart, Henreid, and Wilson tell us otherwise. Because the memory of *Casablanca* is fresh in most readers' minds, I have tried to give my characters dialogue that evokes the motion picture script, while at the same time keeping the physical description of the characters to a minimum.

  One bit of film business I have incorporated is the incessant smoking and drinking of nearly all the characters. In the movie, a cigarette or a drink appears in nearly every scene, just as in *As Time Goes By*. We may look askance at behavior we regard as antisocial and self-destructive (Bogart died of the effects of alcohol and tobacco at age fifty-seven), but the social attitudes of half a century ago were very different and have been faithfully reflected here. Besides, the two-pack-a-day and three-martini-lunch generation not only overcame the Depression, it won World War II.

- Match the novel's action to historical circumstances. The film itself is replete with references to contemporary history – indeed, it relies on then current events for the basis of its plot. In this book, it made sense to wed the new story to the time and place of the movie – that is to say, post-Pearl Harbor for the front story and New York City before 1935 for the back story. Thus, if Victor Laszlo is Czech, then London – not New York – must be his real destination. Furthermore, the assassination of Reinhard Heydrich, the only Nazi official murdered by the Allies during the war, must be what he is planning, since it was the only significant act of Czech resistance.

The most controversial application of this philosophy, however, is likely my contention that Rick Blaine was a Jewish gangster and former speakeasy owner from East Harlem named Yitzik Baline. But consider the evidence: The script tells us that Rick is thirty-seven years old in 1941, which places his young manhood in the years 1922–1935 – roughly the Prohibition era. He is a political leftist (as evidenced by Ethiopia and his fighting against Franco). His best friend is a black man. He is handy with a gun. He runs a saloon. He disappears from New York shortly after the October 23, 1935, assassination of Dutch Schultz (the model for Solomon Horowitz) 'the beer baron of the Bronx' and one of the last of the great fighting Jewish mobsters and nightclub owners. At one point early in the film, Ugarte remarks that Rick, who's just ejected a strutting German from the Café Americain's casino, looks like he's 'been doing this all [his] life.' Rick replies, 'What makes you think I haven't?'

The evidence, however, goes further. Murray Burnett,

the playwright, insisted to the end of his life that he saw himself as Rick Blaine and had written the character as a projection of his own desires and fantasies. 'Rick – tough, morose, the man who didn't need anybody – was the man Burnett wanted to be,' writes Harmetz in *Round Up the Usual Suspects*. Most of the screenwriters – indeed, most of the creative people – associated with *Casablanca* were Jewish, including the Epsteins, Koch, Jack Warner, Hal Wallis, Michael Curtiz, and composer Max Steiner. It also was long the custom in Hollywood to disguise Jewish characters as WASPS. Finally, until he became a leading man in *The Maltese Falcon*, Bogart played a succession of ethnic gangster types at Warner Bros., often as a rival to Jimmy Cagney, whose Irish ethnicity was obvious to all.

- Match up names, dates, places, and so on associated with *Casablanca* with the action of the novel. A few examples:

1. The character of Lois Meredith as Rick's first, lost love. 'Lois Meredith' was the original female protagonist in *Everybody Comes to Rick's*. She was a tramp and an adventuress, far less sympathetic than the virtuous Norwegian into whom she was transformed.
2. The use of the pseudonym 'Tamara Toumanova' as Ilsa's nom de guerre in Prague. This was the real name of the Russian ballerina who inspired screenwriter Robinson to create the character of Ilsa Lund. Toumanova, who later married Robinson, even tested for the role.
3. The name 'Baline' as Rick Blaine's real name. As noted in the novel, this was the real name of Israel (Isidore) Baline, better known as songwriter Irving Berlin,

whose music permeates and defines the period. The resemblance is too remarkable to be entirely accidental, and on some level, I believe Murray Burnett had the Baline/Blaine correspondence in the back of his mind when he wrote his play. Unfortunately, Burnett died in September 1997, so there is no way to know for sure.

4. The name 'Laszlo Lowenstein' for one of Solomon Horowitz's gang members. This was the real name of Peter Lorre (albeit spelled with an 'ö'), who played Ugarte.
5. The name 'Irma Horowitz' for Solomon's wife. Irma Solomon, in real life, was Jack Warner's first wife.
6. The interpolation of Herman Hupfield, the composer of 'As Time Goes By,' into the narrative as the house composer in Rick's Tootsie-Wootsie Club.
7. The movie *High Sierra*, starring Bogart, which Rick and Sam notice as they trudge through Leicester Square. This film, released the same year as *The Maltese Falcon*, also was produced by Hal Wallis and written by someone named Burnett: in this case, the novelist W. R. Burnett, who earlier had written *Little Caesar*, which starred Edward G. Robinson, whose real name was Emanuel Goldenberg and . . . well, you get the idea.
8. The use of many of the film's most famous lines either directly or in a modified form, casting new light on their meaning or origin. These will be obvious to the avid fan. I felt it mandatory, however, to save 'Here's looking at you, kid,' for the book's conclusion and to put the words in Ilsa's mouth, not Rick's.

Like Rick Blaine, some readers may wonder why the Allied governments did not go after Adolf Hitler instead of a lower echelon Nazi like Reinhard Heydrich: in fact, under The Hague Convention IV of 1907, it was international law that belligerents could not attempt the assassination of each other's heads of state or government (a principle the United States still observes today). With hindsight, it is easy to forget that in 1942 the ultimate horror of the Final Solution was still in the future, and Hitler was seen, for better or for worse, as merely the German Führer, not the monster we now know him to have been.

A few minor historical liberties, additions, and conflations occur in my treatment of the Heydrich assassination. In reality, the Protector of Bohemia and Moravia was killed on the Kirchmayer Boulevard, not the Charles Bridge. Otherwise, though, my account of his horrific and agonizing death is largely accurate, as is its terrible, bloody aftermath.

A final word: Although the action of the book takes place in the 1930s and 1940s, the novel is written in the late 1990s. Thus it was important to enlarge the scope of action for several of the characters, most notably Ilsa and Sam, while maintaining plausibility. Dramatically, Ilsa needs to be more than simply the object of desire and competition between Rick and Laszlo, but she cannot grab a tommy gun and start shooting Nazis. Similarly, the spirit of Sam's dialogue, which in the original script verges on dialect, must be maintained, but I saw no reason not to give him a far richer inner life than is apparent in *Casablanca* – not to mention a considerable, indeed crucial, role in Rick's activities in the New York back story.

With the double ending, I sought not only to evoke the

bittersweet mood of the film (Rick and Ilsa once more at cross-purposes), but to add a dash of cynicism (Major Miles congratulating them on a job well done), and, at last, to bring the lovers together in the only way possible.

Roll credits, and fade to black.

ACKNOWLEDGMENTS

As Time Goes By is based on the play *Everybody Comes to Rick's*, by Murray Burnett and Joan Alison, and the 1942 Warner Bros. motion picture *Casablanca*, screenplay by Julius J. and Philip G. Epstein and Howard Koch, produced by Hal B. Wallis, and directed by Michael Curtiz. Any thanks must perforce begin with them.

Thanks as well to the screenwriters whose contributions went uncredited, among them Casey Robinson, Aeneas McKenzie, and Wally Kline (who wrote the first draft), and Leonore Coffee; to Irene Lee Diamond, who bought the script; to Steven Karnot, the Warner's story analyst who saw and identified the cinematic possibilities inherent in the play; and to Jack Warner, president of Warner Bros., who knew how to green-light a good thing when he saw it – and proved it by running up on stage at the 1943 Academy Awards to snatch the Best Picture Oscar from Wallis.

Thanks as well to Humphrey Bogart, Ingrid Bergman, Paul Henreid, Claude Rains, Arthur 'Dooley' Wilson,

Leonid Kinsky (Sacha), and S. Z. Sakall (Carl), whose performances gave their characters lives, personalities, and voices for me to listen to.

Thanks to Maureen Egen, president of Warner Books, who suggested the project to me. 'What would you think about writing a novel of *Casablanca*?' she asked me one day over lunch, and the reader has just finished my reply.

Thanks to my wife, Kathleen, and our daughters, Alexandra and Clare, and to my colleagues and students at Boston University, and to my Hollywood rabbi, the producer Daniel Melnick, for his calm, professional support. Thanks also to the late Martha Duffy, my editor at *Time* magazine for more than a decade, whose formidable spirit was with me every step of the way.

Finally, many thanks to my editor, Susan Sandler, whose careful, analytical, and loving work on the manuscript honed and sharpened both plot and characterization; of all the editorial gin joints in the world, I'm glad I walked into hers.

– March 1998
Lakeville, Connecticut

THE THORN BIRDS

Colleen McCullough

THE THORN BIRDS
The ultimate epic bestseller

'The Australian answer to *Gone With The Wind*'
Guardian

'I simply could not put it down. If it hadn't been wrenched from me at mealtimes, I'd have starved'
Dail Mail

'Miss McCullough's novel is excellent'
The Times

'One of the biggest-selling, most widely read books in the history of fiction'
Observer

'*The Thorn Birds* ... is one of those books which will be read as long as women love, and men care'
Daily Mirror

Also by Colleen McCullough from Warner Books

AN INDECENT OBSESSION
A CREED FOR THE THIRD MILLENNIUM

84 CHARING CROSS ROAD

Helene Hanff

'An unmitigated delight from cover to cover'
Daily Telegraph

'One of the most charming books I have ever read'
Sunday Express

Documenting twenty years of correspondence between Helen Hanff of New York and Messrs Marks and Co of London, sellers of rare and secondhand books, *84 Charing Cross Road* is a unique testament to the bonding power of the written word.

Helene Hanff's enthusiasm and *joie de vivre* contrast delightfully with the professional reserve of Marks and Co's staff, but as the years go by, and the austerity of post-war London is continually brightened by the New Yorker's gifts and letters, formality slowly melts into genuine affection, even intimacy. Fascinating and heart-warming, this volume also includes the sequel, *The Duchess of Bloomsbury Street.*